THE EDWARD KING SERIES
BOOKS 4 - 5

RICK WOOD

Rick Wood
Publishing

ABOUT THE AUTHOR

Rick Wood is a British writer born in Cheltenham.

His love for writing came at an early age, as did his battle with mental health. After defeating his demons, he grew up and became a stand-up comedian, then a drama and English teacher, before giving it all up to become a full-time author.

He now lives in Loughborough, where he divides his time between watching horror, reading horror, and writing horror.

ALSO BY RICK WOOD

The Edward King Series:
Book One – I Have the Sight
Book Two – Descendant of Hell
Book Three – An Exorcist Possessed
Book Four – Blood of Hope
Book Five – The World Ends Tonight

The Sensitives:
Book One – The Sensitives
Book Two – My Exorcism Killed Me
Book Three – Close to Death
Book Four – Demon's Daughter
Book Five – Questions for the Devil
Book Six - Repent

Chronicles of the Infected
Book One – Finding Her
Book Two – Finding Hope
Book Three – Finding Home

Cia Rose:
Book One – After the Devil Has Won
Book Two – After the End Has Begun

Standalones:
When Liberty Dies

BOOK FOUR: BLOOD OF HOPE

RICK WOOD

THE EDWARD KING SERIES

BOOK FOUR

BLOOD OF
HOPE

CHAPTER ONE

uly 25, 2002

IT IS a rare sight to see an angel so angry.

Gabrielle's unfaltering anger could never detract from her inherent natural beauty – but the scorned fire in her eyes was clear.

These were bad times. Gabrielle and every other angel of heaven were on their knees, begging to a fallen angel's prince to stop their evil deeds. The balance that had been kept since life's inception had been compromised.

They met on what used to be mutual turf. It shattered her heart into a thousand pieces to see what beauty could so soon be destroyed.

Earth.

If hell had its way, then flames would consume this entire planet. Every human a slave, every lively flower and beautiful tree turned to flickering ash.

These negotiations were a last resort.

If this conversation did not work, then earth, heaven and hell's fate rested on an inexperienced sixteen-year-old boy.

Gabrielle tossed her long, elegant curls of hair to the side. As she saw him approach, her luscious black skin grew stained with a menacing frown.

A helpless man prompted the bell above the door to ring. This man was a puppet – a poor, helpless, manipulated conduit. He was tall, with bags under his eyes, and a chest so thin his ribs were visible through his ragged shirt.

But this was not that man. This man was here in body, yes – but what drove that body was something else. Something sickening. Something she detested with every ounce of her being.

Gabrielle glanced around the coffee shop. Happy lovers shared a cake. A new mother breastfed her child. A lonely old man ate a bacon roll.

These people were clueless. Completely unaware of the gravity of the conversation that was about to take place in the window of that coffee shop.

"Balam," Gabrielle spat, acknowledging the presence of the demon possessing the unkempt man.

Balam. A demon who had been once been vanquished from a young girl's body by Edward King on millennium night. One of the devil's most loyal princes.

"Gabrielle," Balam spoke through the helpless man's lips, spreading an infuriating grin across his acne-laden face. He strutted in and took the seat opposite her, retaining his cocky grin, sitting back with smug poise.

"You really are a bastard," Gabrielle declared, shaking her head.

Balam guffawed so loudly a few of the café's patrons momentarily turned their heads.

"What language, from an angel!" Balam mocked. "I would have expected far better from your lips."

"It's no less than you deserve. Than all of you deserve."

"Than all of us deserve? Your God is the one who cast the devil down from hell! A fallen angel, forced to live in the underworld forever more." He leant closer to Gabrielle, drooling over her half-empty latte. "Your loving, doting God did this to the devil. How can he not expect revenge?"

"The devil committed the vilest acts! He abused his position as an angel. He tortured, he burnt, even raped, innocent humans – he deserved what he got."

"*Innocent* – did you declare?" Balam's knowing smirk turned to a sinister glare. "No human is *innocent*. You've shared enough eternities with us to know that truth."

"So, that's it, huh? Eternities of keeping the balance, then this. Why? Why now? Why, after all this time, sharing this unbearable truce, has your devil chosen to break it?"

Balam smacked his conduit's cracked lips together, moistening a dry, bloody mouth with what little hydration the demon had spared the suffering man. Taking a moment to enjoy his rare dominion and power over of an angel, he leant subtly toward her.

"Edward King," he announced.

Gabrielle huffed and vigorously shook her head.

"Rubbish. You have had loads of humans, thousands of them, born over the years with the potential to be the devil's heir. What's so different about this one?"

"What's so different about him?" Balam chuckled. "You should taste him. I tasted his sister, and that was enough for me. His sister, who I believe is one of you now, is she not?"

"Answer the damn question."

Balam pulled a face of pretend-offense, raising its eyebrows, and pursing its lips. It took a glance around the coffee shop, surveying the potential victims.

"You know, I could release this man right now, jump out of this man's skin, reveal my true form and kill every one of these people. And you know why?" He turned his face slowly to meet Gabrielle's eyes. "Because of Edward King. Yes, we have had many born with his potential to become what he is becoming. And yes, we have attempted to trick heaven many times before, and failed. But this time – *finally* – we succeeded."

"You shouldn't have tricked us."

"We are evil!" He gestured wildly, gesticulating to indicate the ridiculous nature of her statement. "What did you expect? You know the arrangement. Hell conceived Edward King, so heaven conceived his sister to balance the equation. Just as a thousand times before, we agreed to mutually kill these two people, to remove our presence from the earth. Because, as the deal goes, neither heaven nor hell is allowed presence on earth, otherwise we mess with free will. Which, by the way – we totally have."

"Yet here we are," Gabrielle stated with a glum matter-of-fact snarl.

"Yes, my angel, here we bloody well are! We tricked you! We held Edward King in purgatory, while you shipped his sister off to hell, then brought him back, and you didn't even have a clue!"

Gabrielle grimaced, doing all she could to keep her angelic patience.

"Now you have no one left to balance the equation," Balam sang. "Now he is our access to earth. He is the devil's heir, and through him, demons will no longer need the people we possess – we will spill onto this earth and destroy God's creation, and take it for our own. Once the heir has risen to his full power, there will be nothing you could do to stop us."

"That is why we are here to negotiate."

"Yes, here we are. But to negotiate, you need to have something to bargain with. What could you possibly have that would be so valuable to us, that it would make us stop our ascension now?"

Gabrielle folded her arms, gazing out the window.

A child rode past on a bike, his friends following, laughing in joyous pleasure.

She loved that child, just as God did, just as heaven loved every living being on earth.

Balam did not care. Within a flick of its wrist, that child would go up in flames. No remorse from the demon, just laughter. What was Gabrielle supposed to do to stop that?

Through Edward King, the devil had found his route to earth.

Gabrielle had little she could fight him with.

"Unbeknownst to hell, we have balanced the equation once more," Gabrielle spoke, quietly, numbly.

"I beg your pardon?"

"There is a person, on this earth, with the powers needed to stop you. We conceived him. See, you aren't the only ones who can go behind your enemy's back."

"*You lie!*"

"I am an angel. I do not lie."

"Then the heir of hell will destroy every potential candidate there will be before we have our ascension! He will ensure no one that stands in his way!"

Gabrielle shook her head knowingly; this time it was her turn to give him a knowing chuckle.

"That is why we have hidden our piece of heaven in the most unlikely candidate. Hidden in a person you would least suspect. Edward King will not find him."

Balam's eyes grew with venomous rage. If she was not lying, then this could be devastating. It would undoubtedly delay their plans. Something the devil would be irrefutably devastated to do.

"You shut this person down *now!*"

"We will shut ours down, if you shut the heir of hell down."

Balam rose from the table, fists curled into tight balls, the table before it flying to the side, the chair it was perched upon soaring through the glass of the café, shattering it to pieces. Fire flickered slowly around its knuckles, its eyes turning to red.

Gabrielle smiled.

Balam calmed its anger. Dropped its hands. Ignored the dumbfounded open jaws that gaped at him.

"The heir of hell will destroy everything and everyone who could possibly stand in our way," Balam decided. "He *will* achieve his full power. Then you will bow down on your knees and call the devil your God."

Balam turned and marched away, forcing people aside, barging innocent bystanders out of its path.

Gabrielle looked around at the terrified looks of the people staring.

She shouldn't let them see this. But what difference would it make? They would all be dead soon anyway, if the heir and the devil had their way.

She bowed her head and, with a momentous, overwhelming, blinding light, disappeared, leaving the disbelieving onlookers stunned.

"Be sobre-minded; be watchful. Your adversary the devil prowls around like a roaring lion, seeking someone to devour."

1 Peter 5:8

CHAPTER TWO

anuary 1, 2003

THREE YEARS since millennium night

THE CHURCH OF NATIVITY, Israel

THE HARD BUMPS of the pavement grated against Martin's face, greeting him with an early morning prick. Lifting his head up, he rubbed the grogginess out of his eyes. As his vision hazily returned he adjusted to the sight of the city around him.

If he was going to fight hell, they could at least pay him.

Instead, here he was. Tired. Downtrodden. Sore. Sleeping on the streets, just hoping he didn't get pissed on at night.

Not that it would make any difference if he was back in

the United Kingdom. If you're skint in the midlands, you're still skint in Israel.

Martin hardly had a huge inheritance to rely on.

Not a seventeen-year-old orphan like him.

His ma's death had been tough to take, but it was inevitable. Cassy had told him about her life, and the purpose of her death, what it achieved in having to stop the ritual of the devil's three.

Not that it did any good.

The devil still rose, and his heir took its form. And through all of it, Martin couldn't help but feel like his ma had been used. An insignificant sacrifice for a greater cause.

He felt bad, but he tried not to think about it.

Dwelling on foul thoughts leads to a foul mind.

Another wise cliché from Derek, adding to the list of wise clichés Derek had imparted upon him as he left the country.

Derek could have left him some money. As useful as the clichés were, money would have been far more useful.

He propped against the stone wall and brushed the dust from his face. He hadn't expected the place to be this dusty. It was ridiculous. On every surface and every wall, dust seemed to gather like flies on shit. He could barely move without coughing.

The sun cast a palpable haze over the bright morning, and people were already bustling back and forth. Most looked like tourists on a pilgrimage, strolling toward the landmark Martin also aimed for – but for different reasons. The few tourist shops scattered along the path already had awkward sightseers bumbling around, with bum bags around their waist, polo shirts and jumpers slumped over their shoulders. Martin could even see the Israeli pick-pockets eying them up, deciding which idiot they would nick a wallet off and give a nightmare holiday to.

Martin didn't have time to help them. He had a mission.

The church bells were clanging, singing a tuneful melody that echoed down the narrow street.

It was time.

He climbed up, grabbed his bag, and threw it over his shoulder, surprised no one had targeted him in the night.

Then again, he shouldn't be surprised. No one could wound him as he slept.

He was under the protection of an angel.

Well, protection from mortals, anyway.

Forcing his tired legs up a set of stone stairs, he began the ascent toward the church. His legs waded upwards like lead weights through water. He sighed over his tired muscles – the hard work hadn't even started yet.

Once he reached the top he leant against the wall, gathering his breath before joining the queue.

It was already a long queue, consumed by visitors from all parts of the world. A family in front of him wore crosses around their necks, undoubtedly devout religious nut-jobs awaiting their turn to hail the birth of their messiah.

Martin scoffed.

Religious nut-jobs.

Funny how he still referred to them as that. He used to be such an adamant atheist, but that all changed.

Then again, witnessing an angel coming forth after your ma was possessed by a demon in a ritual to bring forth the king of hell – that kind of incident will shake your beliefs.

At least he knew what he was devoting his life to, and he knew the full extent of the greater forces. These people would never realise how little they knew about the God they praised and the devil they feared.

He still found their belief system weird, if he was honest with himself. Sure, it was easy for him; he had clear evidence. These people were basing so much on so little.

Behind him were a young couple, hand in hand, kissing

with uncomfortable frequency. Obvious honeymooners, getting eyeballed by the religious sector around him.

I wonder if I'll ever get to kiss a girl again.

Finally, his turn in the line came, and he approached the man behind the counter.

"Hi, I'm here to see Father Douglas."

"It is money to get in," replied the frowning man, with a thick Middle Eastern accent.

"You don't understand, he is expecting me."

"It is money to get in!" he repeated, growing increasingly irate.

"I was sent here."

"It – is – money!"

"It's okay," came a kind, gentle voice from behind the guy with appalling customer service. A small man with grey hair, grey beard, and kind eyes appeared out of a far shadow. "I've been expecting him."

"Cassy sent me."

"Then it is true. He has risen."

Martin said nothing. He hoped his silence was enough confirmation.

"You'd best hurry in. We have much to do."

CHAPTER THREE

*J*uly 15, 1984

EDDIE WAS SO grateful for his legs. Grateful for the amazing things they do: running, walking, kicking, stomping – hell, even dancing. Never had he acknowledged what wondrous things they were.

He was especially grateful because it was the first time he had used them to their full ability in months.Seventy-six days, to be exact.

Seventy-six days since the accident that had left him in a coma for over two weeks.

Seventy-six days since the accident that killed his little sister.

A month of being confined to a wheelchair, followed by a

month and a half on crutches, and now, finally, he was walking without them. A full recovery had been made.

At least, his body had made a full recovery.

His mind still had some way to go.

"Take it easy," Jenny assured him, putting her arm around his waist as he hobbled into the room. He smiled at her and her parents, who sat excitedly on the sofa, clapping their hands at his success.

Jenny's parents were there. Clapping their hands in sheer jubilation.

His parents were likely to be at home. Or in a bar. Or in a gutter. Somewhere where his dad would be completely wasted and his mum would be cowering beneath his eager fist.

"We are so proud of you!" Jenny's mother cried out. "You've done so well!"

He forced a fake smile in her direction.

"How about we go out for a walk, hey?" Jenny prompted, seeing a grimace of pain flash across Eddie's face. He firmly nodded.

As they walked away from her parent's house, over the field and toward the park Eddie and Cassy used to spend so much time at, they remained quiet. But he could feel her watching him.

Jenny abruptly stopped walking. Eddie stopped too, but looked to Jenny with confusion.

"Why have we stopped?"

"I'm sure they are proud, you know," she told him, wearing a serious expression.

"What? Yeah, they told me, remember?"

"Not my parents." She put her hand on his shoulder. "Yours. They may not be here, and they may not be in the best state right now, but they are. I know it."

Eddie looked to his feet. He neither wished to talk about

them or think about them. He had his memories of the doting parents he had before age eleven. Memories of a dad who would smile as he rode his bike for the first time, his mother who would lovingly hand him his packed lunch before he set off to school, two parents who would happily joke with each other and tease one another in front of them.

But that's all they are now, he acknowledged to himself. *Memories. Just like Cassy.*

He felt himself welling up so he forced the thoughts away, covering the back of his mind with cement, burying the anxiety into the corner of an unconscious he would never need to access.

That's where he would keep those memories. Safely locked away where no one could get to.

Jenny kept her arm around Eddie to keep him steady as they approached the swings. A few lads walked past, sniggering at him, and Eddie was sure one of them made a comment. But he ignored it, as did Jenny. He was in no state to fight anyone, and Jenny was far too mature to rise to it.

After she had made sure he was balanced safely on a swing she perched on the next one, gazing at him.

Despite everything that had happened in the last few months, his face was no stranger to her. She recognised it; every rumpled frown line, every melancholy fake smile, every twitch of the eye keeping him from crying.

She could read him so well. They had met at three years old. She had no memories of him not being in her life. Every day, the same welcome face, and more recently, the same pained expression.

"They just miss her too, you know," she assured him.

"Yeah, well, they have a funny way of showing it."

He didn't return her gaze. It was too hard. He just kept his eyes focussed on his feet, kept them away from Jenny, away from her sweet, soothing eyes.

He knew that just one look at her eyes would break him.

And he was a man. Eleven years old or not, he was a man. He would not cry.

He refused.

"But it's all just a big mask, isn't it?" she smiled, hoping that even though he wasn't looking at her, he would sense it. "They mask their hurt with beer and hate. Just like you mask your hurt with... refusing to look at me. Staring at your feet so your eyes don't break."

"Stop reading me, okay?"

"I can't help it. I've known you too long."

He sighed. Looked up to the sky. He would stop looking at his feet, but he wouldn't look at her yet. He would look up. That was half way between.

Surely that was good enough for now?

She reached out and stroked his arm.

"Do you think we'll still be friends like this when we're older?" he mused.

"Of course," she replied without a shred of doubt.

"No, I mean, when we're like, old. In twenty years' time. My mum and dad haven't kept up their friendships with people they knew as kids. Neither have yours. Or anyone else I know."

She dropped her hand from his arm and put it in his hand.

"Then we'll be the exception," she assertively declared.

Finally, he returned her gaze.

And as he did, he let the tiniest of tears trickle down his cheek, drop from his face, and land on the floor.

CHAPTER FOUR

*J*anuary 3, 2003

THREE YEARS since millennium night

JENNY LIFTED HER HOOD UP, but it did little to shelter herself from the rain. She stuffed her hands in her pockets and stared at the swing set before her.

They looked different from how she remembered.

The metal had rusted, the plastic seats had since been changed, and someone had graffitied obscene words on the floor.

And they looked far smaller than Jenny remembered. As a child, she would spend so much time going as high as she could off the ground, feeling like she could fly. She and Eddie laughing, exhilarated by the risk. But if she were to try it now, her feet would likely not leave the floor.

"What is it?" prompted Derek.

"It's…" She thought deeply about what to say. "It's nothing."

She turned and walked down the street with Derek.

Despite the rain, he still wore his smartest attire. No hoodies for Derek – it was waistcoat, tie, shirt, and jacket, though he had allowed himself an expensive-looking trench coat.

"Have you got the list?" Jenny asked, getting straight to business.

"I have, I have," Derek nodded. "I believe it has been posted. It should arrive in the next few days. And, what's more, I have heard that Martin made contact with Father Douglas in Israel."

"Good. That's good."

They shared a moment of contemplation, and a moment of comfortable silence. They both kept their heads down, deep in thought.

"And you think these people on the list," Jenny asked, "they will be able to help us?"

"Yes," he nodded. "They are incredibly powerful people. Some religious, some paranormal investigators, some exorcists, and everything in between."

He looked up and allowed a few drops of rain to settle on his head and drip from his neat goatee.

"They should be able to help us kill him," he continued.

Jenny froze, forcing Derek to halt, turning toward him with a perplexed expression.

Jenny's fists withdrew from her jacket and she leant toward Derek, raising her hand, and jabbing her finger toward him. Her teeth ground, her eyebrows narrowed, and anger erupted through her voice.

"Let's get one thing straight, or I will block this bloody list from ever getting to you," she snarled, louder than she realised. "We are not in the business of killing him. We – do not – kill Eddie. You understand?"

Derek sighed. "Jenny…"

"No!" she snapped. "No! You do not Jenny me. I am making this clear. We are not killing him. We are saving him. We are *saving* Eddie."

Derek ran his hand over his beard and lifted his head, giving himself time to be calm, to think, to respond in sound mind.

She did not move. Her finger remained rigidly pointed in his direction as she irately awaited his response.

"Jenny," Derek began, lifting his hand slowly and lucidly, using it to push her hand back to her side. "What we are dealing with is no longer Eddie. You must understand this."

"Eddie's in there."

"No one wants him back more than I. But you see, this thing he has become, it has removed every piece of Eddie, replaced by nothing but evil–"

"No!" Jenny snapped. "He is in there. And I'm getting him back."

Derek understood how she felt all too well. He wanted the exact same thing; he wanted the man he had trained back at his side. The man he had watched become such a powerful exorcist, such a brilliant force in the world of defeating demons.

But that's not who they were dealing with anymore.

Eddie was no longer his right-hand man.

He was Satan's.

"I grew up with him." Jenny vehemently shook her head, seeing Derek's hesitance protruding from his terrified eyes. "You've known him for a while, sure. But I was with him when we were three. I can't…"

She broke up. She couldn't. Where was Lacy when she needed her?

Lacy was always so good at being cool whilst Jenny was anxious.

Eddie had pointed it out within moments of meeting Lacy – what a calming influence she was.

"Jenny, I will do everything in my power to restore the old Eddie. But you need to understand, that may not be an avenue open to us."

"Then the world burns," Jenny growled. "Then the whole world burns by Eddie's hand, and us with it. Everything we know, everyone we meet, will be dead. I don't care. We do not kill Eddie."

Derek smiled sympathetically and put his arm on her shoulder.

"Come on," he spoke resolutely. "Let's gather our army before we decide on our strategy."

Jenny nodded and they carried on walking.

Just before they turned the corner, Jenny had one last glance over her shoulder at the swing set. She could swear she saw a young boy and a young girl sitting on them, sharing a fragile moment.

Dear Martin,

I hope this letter finds you well, and that you have successfully begun your training in Israel.

Things are looking bleak here. I am awaiting Stella Clutching's list with keen anticipation. As soon as I have this list of people, we can begin assembling our army and combining skillsets.

Fortunately, I won't have to explain too much to these people. They shouldn't be hard to recruit. When an event such as this occurs, it causes a ripple, and anyone in the know will have felt this ripple and be aware of what the omen means.

The only frustrating thing is that they won't perhaps fully realise how morbid a situation we have.

Edward King was one of the greatest exorcists, and one of the greatest men, we have ever known. What we must realise is that this man no longer exists. That piece of evil that was put in him since before birth has taken over now. What we are dealing with is the son of the devil, the bringer of the apocalypse, the most dangerous demon to be facing this earth.

Jenny is convinced this is just some demon inside him that we could exorcise, same way we exorcised all these other demons throughout our quests.

I only wish she was right.

And his quietness since this entity within him found its feet on the earth is most unsettling.

So work hard. Learn what you can. The world is on your shoul-

ders, and you may feel this pressure on you. And quite rightly, considering what is at stake.

Just remember to be prepared.

We never know when he will strike or how he will do it.

You will become a powerful sorcerer yet. Cassy will be there to support you, and Father Douglas will teach you.

Keep me updated, my friend.

Take care,

Derek Lansdale

CHAPTER FIVE

*J*anuary 5, 2003

MARTIN STUMBLED TO HIS KNEES, howling from the pain of his sore limbs and bloody skin.

"Get up!" demanded Father Douglas, frantically waving his hands. What little hair he had left around circular bald patch stuck in the air with an aerodynamic static. He was a short, podgy man, but could convey his hostility with utmost ease.

"We have been at this for hours," Martin begged through gritted teeth and tired tears. "I ain't no born hero. Gimme a break, would yuh?"

Douglas seized Martin at the collar with a firm hand and shoved him against the large stone bricks of the church – built so long ago, yet so rough and steady it submerged Martin's back into throbbing jolts.

"The devil will not wait for you to be ready," Douglas snarled. "Wake up and smell what you're facing!"

Martin pushed Douglas off him with everything he had. He had such little energy left, his grappling caused only a stumble from the old man. Martin dropped his head, feeling a tinge of humiliation.

In further retaliation, and to preserve some masculine integrity, Martin charged forward at Douglas. Embarrassingly, Douglas just swiped Martin's ankle from beneath him and sent him sailing onto his back.

Beaten up by a bloody priest, Martin thought, shaking his head to himself.

He stayed down, hoping this would mean Douglas would give him mercy and back off.

"Really?" Douglas stood over Martin, his hands sturdily poised on his hips. "This is what they send me? I ask them to give me a man who understands what's at stake, who could acquire the ability to become a great sorcerer and take on the worst evil the world has ever seen. And this is what I get?"

"Fuck you," Martin gasped, forcing a croak out through his rapid panting. "I'm sixteen. I'm a kid. My ma fucking died. I ain't shit."

Douglas nodded in agreement. Muttering further irritancy under his breath, he waddled away. Back inside to pray, or ruminate, or bitch on the phone to Derek, or whatever it was Martin predicted the arsehole was going to do.

Martin sat up, leaning his elbows on his knees and burying his head, staring at the gravel beneath him.

Travelling for weeks. Sleeping on the streets. Then, arriving at some church to get battered by a fat, celibate, Bible-loving knobhead was not how he had imagined his life going.

Sweet girls hanging off his arms, an overflowing cash

account in the bank, a sick pad where he could entertain and give the best house parties ever... That was his dream.

Not being trained like a bitch in the back garden of some crummy church by a relentless priest with no life.

"He's not that bad," came a soothing, feminine voice from behind him.

Martin felt a familiar hand gently pressing his shoulder, filling his body with hope, soothing his anger with instant clarity. A smile unknowingly presented itself on his face as he turned around and gazed at Cassy with eyes of adoration.

"Were you watching that?"

She sat down and crossed her legs, sitting beside Martin, leaning against the wall of the church, affectionately grazing her hand up and down his back. She glowed with luminous beauty, long, flowing hair, and a white dress far brighter than humanly possible.

She was the epitome of an angel: gliding, gracious wisdom with every soothing smile she gave.

"No," she smiled. "You think too loud."

"So, you're reading my thoughts now?"

"Reading them? No. But they are giving me a headache."

He stood in a moment of frustration, and the pain in his legs instantly reminded him why he had sat down. He knelt, grabbing his calves that burnt like rubbery coal.

She placed her hands either side of his face and lifted his eyes toward hers. As soon as her smooth skin touched his filthy cheeks the pain went, replaced by giddy pins and needles.

"You are waging a war," she reminded him. "And you are the soldier I have chosen."

"Why?" he scoffed. "Why me? A screw-up, a loser?"

"No. A champion. Someone who knows what it's like to be on the outside, looking in at the world."

He took hold of her arm and removed it from his cheeks. The pain was restored to his legs.

But he preferred the real pain, rather than the false illusions coming from the touch of an angel.

"You've got the wrong guy."

He turned away from her and limped back toward the church.

The church, with his small, square, stone room, without any air conditioning, and rats scuttling around his feet.

He thought about Ma. Thought about what she would say to him now.

What lecture she would give. What moans, bizarre anecdotes, and unsolicited advice.

But she was dead. Gone. No more.

As was his foreseeable purpose.

He couldn't do this.

He wasn't a hero.

CHAPTER SIX

*T*he moon glittered idly in the steady lake. It was the kind of evening that made one think deeply, consider philosophy, and gain a translucent clarity over their view on life.

Stella Clutchings lived for such nights. Such serenity in nature was crucial for reflecting with a quiet mind; something essential in her line of work. She always made sure that, at least once a month, she witnessed a sunset and a sunrise. It helped her realise that there was something out there, looking over her. It made her feel importantly small. That, despite the many lives that have lived and died, her insignificance could still create a ripple in the waves of time.

Unfortunately, her time to create such a ripple was limited. And she felt it. Something fluttered in her belly, lucidly firing through her bones.

That's why she wasn't stressed. Not allowing her anxiety to take hold of her. Not giving in to the feelings she had spent her whole life controlling.

If she had managed to control her mind for her whole

life, then why give in now? Why give in at her final moments?

She finished her letter, writing her final words and signing it.

REMEMBER, *this comes to us all eventually. I may as well face it with dignity.*

YOURS IN MIND AND SPIRIT.

STELLA CLUTCHINGS
Psychic Extraordinaire

SHE CHUCKLED to herself at her label of 'psychic extraordinaire.' Death was no time to be modest. She may as well go out with an amusing flourish.

It was her community, after all, that considered her the most established, prominent psychic in generations gone – not her.

If she was indoors, this would be a time for her to scour her bookshelf for new literature to devour. That is what she always imagined doing in her final moments. Sitting there, holding a book in her hands, her corpse harnessing a comforting smile to those who found it.

Maybe she'd even hold one of her own books for the irony of it. *Psychic Phenomena for the Modern Century* would look rather amusing in her hands, as they had to pry it out of her stiffened clutches, secured in her grasp like stone as rigor mortis set in.

Is this really what her final thoughts were going to be?

Silly things to think about, really. To most, it would be a morbid thought to consider yourself with stiffened rigor mortis. To Stella, it was a beautiful kind of irony. A last chuckle at the world that did nothing to defend her from what was to come.

Where was God now?

The one she had fought in the name of, doing nothing to intervene.

Thanks for nothing.

She knew the devil's heir was rising. Anyone who had any kind of power or experience in the field of paranormal could feel it.

Something was coming.

And it wasn't something good.

But she also felt the other side of the equation balancing itself out. Balancing itself as an act of deception to the devil in the form of a sixteen-year-old wayward boy.

Everything rested on that boy's shoulders.

Trust in that boy was the final thing she wrote on the final line of her final letter. She placed it into an envelope, sealed it, and placed it on the table next to her. The calm evening fluttered the envelope's edge in the cool evening breeze, so she finished off her wine and placed her glass on top of it, so as to keep it still.

She took in the moment once more. The darkness of the hours, the magnificent faded green of the fluttering leaves, the slight, shady ripple through the lake that had never brought her anything but happiness.

It was a beautiful world.

This was a good life.

She had lived it well.

A portal of fire engulfed the horizon before her.

Rising off the ground and growing from a small spark to

a thrashing, manic, spewing, intense circle of flames covering the skyline, it poised.

"Come on then you son of a bitch," she spat. "Do your worst."

With that, a demon sprang out of the portal. Her jaw dropped – this was no demon like she had ever seen before, in person or in picture. She felt its presence overwhelm her, unscrupulous power protruding from its pores.

It was hideous. Disgusting. Foul. Carnivorous. It terrified her, shook her, took hold of her. She could smell its heat, taste its flickering flames alighting its arms, hear its anger in its growl.

"And to think," whispered her final words, staring straight into the eyes of evil. "You were once a great man."

Its arm turned into a spike, sharp and pointed for at least six feet beyond it.

This spike rapidly grew bigger and bigger, faster than was visible to Stella's eyes and, in doing so, went straight through Stella's chest, through her chair, and dug into the ground behind her.

The monstrous creature allowed this spike to be free of its arm, leaving it wedged in the ground through Stella's heart.

Stella's body sank further down the spike. Blood gurgled down her chin. She coughed on it a few times, her chest doing all it could to catch breaths that didn't come.

She saw the smile on the awful visage of the fiend's features.

Her eyesight went next.

Then she felt the heat of the flames disappear from her skin.

She ceased hearing the growls and the flickers that had attacked her ears.

She could no longer smell the hatred that exuded from this creature.

But for a few final moments, she could still feel the edge of her fingers, quivering in the rabid heat. She stretched her hand out, trying to grab whatever it could. A helping hand, a loved one's reassurance, maybe even her own skin – anything that allowed her to feel something just one last time.

But she didn't feel anything.

Because her hand went limp.

CHAPTER SEVEN

*J*anuary 6, 2003

JENNY FIDDLED with the phone wire whilst vacantly glaring at the handset. She knew she should use it to call Lacy and tell her she was going to be late.

But it would only annoy Lacy. It would only cause further problems.

Jenny was fighting for the world.

That's what she'd told her the previous night. She could still hear Lacy's response echoing in her mind.

"Once, you were fighting for me."

It made Jenny's eyes well up. The two people in the world she loved the most, and one was evil, the other annoyed with her.

"What's the matter?" came Derek's irritatingly well-spoken voice, interrupting her trail of thought.

"Oh, nothing," she lied, shifting her position, lifting her

head from her resting arm. She sat forward, forcing herself to pay attention.

Derek's study was a tremendous but stuffy room. His bookcases were full of dusty literature, spewing vast amounts of information about demonology, paranormal, supernatural, cults – it had everything.

Well, almost everything. It didn't have a book on what to do when you need to prevent your best friend from bringing forth the apocalypse.

"It's arrived," Derek announced, sitting beside her with eager trepidation, clutching a sealed envelope.

"Well?" she prompted.

He directed her an anxiously lingering glance, then ripped it open. Inside were two letters. The first, a coherently written letter, the second, a list.

"What does it say?" Jenny asked.

Derek cleared his throat.

"Dear Mr Lansdale," he began. "I apologise I am unable to share this information with you in person, but unfortunately, we each much meet our fate. Enclosed with this letter is a list of names. On this list you will find all the most powerful people in the world in our field. Paranormal investigators, exorcists, psychics, priests, and mediums. Even telepaths, empaths, and those whose powers still remain undefined."

Jenny took the list in and mulled it over as Derek continued to read.

"I have arranged this list in order of importance, relative to power. Retrieve them. Train them. Under your guidance, you can build your army. They will all be ready, they will all know something has risen. This is our only chance.

"Remember, this comes to us all eventually. I may as well face it with dignity. Stella Clutchings, psychic extraordinaire."

"That it?"

"No. It finishes with a final sentence. *Trust that boy.*"

They shared a moment of contemplation, a silent understanding of the perplexity of what had been delivered.

"Why is she writing this with such sorrow?" Derek thought aloud. "As if she has…"

He trailed off.

"What was her name again?" Jenny asked with a sudden spark of thought.

"Stella Clutchings. She was an incredibly powerful psychic; we wrote to each other a few times."

Jenny paused, deep in thought, a vague memory inching its way across her mind. She abruptly stood and reached for her bag. She withdrew a newspaper and shoved it in Derek's direction.

He took this newspaper and, as he held it in his hands, found that the newspaper was trembling.

The headline read:

WOMAN STABBED *through heart with giant spike.*

THE FIRST FEW lines went on to say a psychic, by the name of Stella Clutchings, had been found dead, stabbed through the heart with –

That's when he stopped reading.

Derek bowed his head.

"What do you think it is?" Jenny asked, leaning toward him.

He shook his head. His eyes welled up but he fought it, willing himself to retain his dignity. He would not answer that question willingly, though he knew that he should.

"Derek, a giant spike isn't something just anyone can… What do you think?"

Derek looked up at her. He held her eye contact, silently pleading, desperately urging her not to make him say it.

"Derek?"

"Who do you think did it?" he spat. "A woman who had the knowledge to help us build an army, and she's dead the day she writes this letter. Who do you think?"

"No, Derek, we don't know –"

"Get out of denial, Jenny, for the love of God!" Derek stood, withdrawing a handkerchief and dabbing his sweaty brow. He turned his back to her, his hands on his hips, an expression of frustration worn across his perspiring skin.

Jenny closed her eyes, dipping her head and covering her face.

This isn't Eddie, she reassured herself. *This is whatever has taken over, whatever has taken control. This is not Eddie.*

She kept thinking it over and over, as if repeating it made it true.

This is not Eddie, this is not Eddie, this is not Eddie.

Despite her mental protestations, she was not entirely convinced.

"So, what do we do now?" Jenny prompted.

Derek turned toward her and nodded to the list.

"We do what we must," he began. "We find those names on the list. We train them. We protect them. Until it is time."

"But, Derek, how do we protect them from someone who could do this?" She lifted the newspaper, indicating the picture of the woman on the front with a solid spike stuck through her chest.

Derek shrugged his shoulders and shook his head.

"We do what we can, and what we must. Nothing more, nothing less."

He placed a reassuring arm on Jenny's shoulder, the gesture somehow providing a momentous boost of comfort.

But it still wasn't enough.

CHAPTER EIGHT

anuary 8, 2003

"You're not listening, son!" belted the booming voice of Father Douglas.

I proper hate this fat, bald twat, Martin told himself, doing everything he could not to voice his opinion.

The heat was unbearable. His perspiration soaked through his shirt. His knees bent with exhaustion, his back ached from rigorous movement. He could barely see in front of him, such was the ferocity of the sweat dripping from his brow.

But this bastard saw none of that.

He saw none of Martin's continuous efforts, none of the frequent attempts at getting these spells right. None of the constant retrying, and retrying, despite the relentless berating of Martin's conceived lack of effort.

"Curl your hands around in a circle; quickly, boy!"

Martin did what he was told.

He furiously rotated his arms, trying to create this fire ball he could supposedly create.

How the hell was he meant to make a fire ball?

I mean, a sodding fire ball! Out of nothing?

Was this bloke mistaking him for Edward King or something?

Martin didn't feel he could ever amount to the status of the legend he had heard so much about. He was not the heir of hell. He didn't have these inherent tremendous powers.

He was a scumbag. A failure. A kid with no future, raised as an illegitimate catastrophe, an irritating fiasco of a dead, disabled woman.

"You don't believe you can do it," snarled Douglas, circling Martin like a shark. "That's why you don't get it, my lad. You think all you can see is what is visible right in front of you. You are a let-down. A nothing."

Martin went to retaliate but resisted. He had spent so much of his time at school fighting against teachers who told him he wasn't worth shit, and it got him nowhere.

He needed to do this. For the world, if not himself.

Though he truly did not understand why it couldn't be someone else.

Why him?

I'm no one.

"What are you thinking about?" Douglas demanded, rushing up to within inches of Martin's bowed head, spewing odorous, panting breath from his haggard old face. "About how much of a failure you are? Think it and it will become true."

"No..." Martin shook his head, then stopped himself once more.

The fate of the world.

Derek.

Derek believed in him.

Cassy believed in him.

They sent him here because they thought he could do something.

They were wrong.

"No, what?" growled Douglas in an exaggerated sneer, nothing but contempt consuming his face. "No, you are a failure? No, you can't do it? No, you don't believe what you can see?"

"What is your problem?"

Martin couldn't help it. No one had ever pushed him like this. He had never let anyone. Not a soul.

No authority figure, no friend, no person, nothing.

Why should Douglas be any different?

Martin tried to calm himself. Did all he could. Told himself to suck it up. Told himself to believe.

"That's what I thought," Douglas laughed mockingly. "Just a talentless nitwit. Someone with no past, no present, and no future. A nothing."

Martin leapt forward and planted his fist into Douglas' face, sending the old, incessant tormentor sailing back onto his arse.

It felt good. It felt so good. But as soon as Martin did it, he regretted it. He knew it wasn't the right choice to make. However much Douglas deserved it, it was the rise Douglas was trying to get.

Martin had grown up enough in the past few months to recognise when someone was simply trying to get a rise out of him.

Douglas stayed on the floor. He wiped his lip, dabbing a small patch of blood where a scab had fallen off his mouth.

"I'm... I'm sorry," Martin stuttered.

"No, you're not," Douglas smirked with hostility. "That was the first bit of emotion I got from you, don't ruin it."

"Why do you always do that?" Martin cried out. That wall he'd built, the resistance to this kind of ridicule; it was tumbling down.

"You think it's a coincidence your mum just happened to be chosen to be one of the devil's three?" Douglas proposed, using the wall of the church to climb back to his feet. "You think the devil just happened to gravitate toward her? You don't think there's something about *you*?"

"There ain't nothin' about me, mate." Martin shrugged. "No one does nothing for me my whole life, and now you're suddenly telling me I'm cracked up to be the world's last defence."

"I can't tell you who you are in all this," Douglas passionately defied, stepping closer to Martin. "I can't tell you, because then all of this, all the things we know you can do – will come from a place of false belief. You need to know yourself, before you can be told."

"I ain't got no idea what you are on about!" Martin shouted, gesticulating with his hands in pure exasperation. "All you keep saying is just noise to me, I don't get it. I don't get what you want from me."

"And you won't."

"I don't know what the hell that means! I am no one! No – one!"

Martin turned his back to Douglas and marched toward the exit from the churchyard, and paused. His hands rested against his hips with annoyance, his foot tapping and his head shaking.

"You're right," Douglas mused. "You are absolutely right, boy. You are no one. And, the way you think, that will be how it stays forever. A big fat nobody."

Martin kicked his bag in frustration, sending it sailing across the yard. He turned back toward Douglas with one fist clenched, and the other hand jabbing toward his supposed mentor with furious rigidity.

"Fuck you!" he screamed. "And fuck all of this!"

He kicked open the gate and marched away.

Where to, he had no idea. Somewhere. Maybe where this guy wouldn't lecture him about him being nothing. Where there was not a weight of expectation on him. Where he no longer had to possess this knowledge that the world was going to end.

Douglas watched him go, deep in contemplation.

"Are you sure he is who he says he is?" he serenely asked.

"Give him time and patience," came Cassy's voice from behind him.

"Unfortunately, those are two things we don't have."

CHAPTER NINE

*J*enny despised early mornings. Not being able to lie in was something she shunned. She treasured her sleep, and her mornings when she didn't have to get up for work were invaluable.

But on this day, she didn't mind waking up early.

Because on this day, Lacy had a morning off as well. Lacy didn't have to get up at the crack of dawn, pull on her nurse's uniform, and force herself to the hospital for another mundane shift.

And she looked so damn beautiful in Jenny's arms. Curled up as the little spoon, nestled into Jenny, fitting so perfectly into the slot of her body.

She fleetingly recalled a hazy memory of Eddie meeting Lacy for the first time. Having faced a negative reaction from her parents to her coming out, she had dreaded what would happen next. But Eddie was more supportive than she could have possibly imagined. If it weren't for him, she probably wouldn't have been comfortable enough in herself to actually enter a relationship with Lacy.

Of course, her parents had eventually come to accept her.

They were a generation that weren't used to people being honest about their sexuality. It just took time.

But with Eddie, it hadn't even been a question.

The voice of experience talking, she scoffed sarcastically to herself.

She had been so young. Eighteen years old. Twelve years ago.

Jesus, was it that long ago? Twelve years?

Yet here they were. The woman Jenny loved most in the world lay asleep next to her, still filling her with giddy joy.

Those fluttery feelings still swarmed around Jenny's belly; butterflies of ecstatic elation any time Lacy's name was mentioned.

Lacy was so much cooler, so much calmer than Jenny. But that was good. Lacy soothed Jenny's anxieties.

"Are you watching me?" whispered a spirited voice from between Jenny's arms.

"Maybe…" Jenny playfully retorted.

"You know, some people might think that was creepy…" came an equally playful voice from Lacy as she turned over to face Jenny. "But me, I think it's just sweet."

Lacy leant in and placed a soft, sweet kiss against Jenny's lips. They rested their foreheads against each other and left them there, breathing each other in.

"I love you," Jenny told Lacy, stroking her hand down the side of her face.

"I know," Lacy answered, knowing such a response would infuriate Jenny. Leaving it just a beat, she finally replied, "I love you, too."

They shared another delicate kiss.

"Have you got much to do today?" Lacy asked.

"Yeah." Jenny pondered over her day's schedule. "Me and Derek, we have a list of people we need to recruit. We're kind of working our way through that."

"How's it all going?"

"Oh, you know…"

Jenny turned over and sat up. The loving moment was gone. Her thoughts turned back to Eddie and the task at hand. Back to the apocalypse, the evil, the empty salvation.

"What is it?" Lacy asked caringly, sitting up.

"It's just…" Jenny trailed off. She didn't want to bring this into their home life. Their bedroom was a place for love and relaxing, not a place for heavy conversations about the fate of humanity.

But she was deeply troubled about this war. Issues of ethics and tactics and humanity always sat in the back of her mind. She needed to vent in some way.

But there were some things too tough to say aloud.

"Talk to me, Jen," Lacy pleaded. "You know I'm here for you, for anything."

"No, I don't want to trouble you."

"After this long, you really think that's still an issue?"

Jenny sighed.

Lacy was right. Of course she was. She always was.

That was the most annoying thing about her. Always the voice of reason.

Jenny mustered the courage to say what was troubling her. She forced the words to her lips, willed herself to be mentally resolute, urged herself to fire these thoughts out of her mind.

"Derek thinks…"

"Derek thinks what?"

She sighed. Another hesitation.

Just say it.

"Derek thinks there's no way to save Eddie."

"My God." Lacy raised her eyebrows. "Really?"

"He thinks…" Jenny wiped away a stray tear. "He thinks

there's no way back for him. As in, this is it. We are going to have to kill him."

She covered her face. Lacy was out of the bed like a shot, getting to Jenny as quickly as she could, spreading her arms around her and holding her tight.

Lacy let her just cry for a few moments. Let her feel the emotions she was feeling.

Then she decided she needed to be honest. Or it would just come back to bite her.

"Maybe he's right," she uttered, waiting for the inevitable reaction.

"What?" Jenny pulled away and stood back.

"I'm not saying there's no way to save him. But maybe, him not being able to be saved – maybe it's something you need to prepare yourself for."

Jenny folded her arms and shook her head in fury.

"So, you're on *his* side?"

"God, Jenny, I'm not on anyone's side. I think you should do everything you can to bring him back. If you think he's in there somewhere, do it. I'm just saying…" She shrugged, looking around herself, trying to find the words. "Just, maybe… you should be prepared. You know, just in case."

Jenny's head dropped. Her eyes closed. Her face scrunched up.

She had been so strong for so long. So mentally guarded. This whole thing was a nightmare. A complete and utter nightmare.

"I can't give up on him."

"I'm not saying that."

Lacy rushed back to Jenny, placing her hands on her arms, resting her forehead against hers.

"I know how much he meant to you – means, to you. But I was there."

Jenny sniffed. She looked back to Lacy.

"I saw him shift too, and..." Lacy again struggled for words. "And I don't know how you come back from something like that. This isn't just something within him. He turned *into* that something. Maybe you just need to be ready for the fact that this may not be Eddie anymore."

Lacy's hands ran through Jenny's hair. Jenny lifted her hands and grasped them around Lacy's arms, holding tightly, taking every bit of comfort she could.

Before Jenny knew it, she was scrunched up against Lacy's chest, with Lacy's arms back around her.

Lacy took Jenny back to bed and allowed Jenny to lay in the comfort of her arms. They stayed like that until the morning alarm finally went, and Jenny knew it was time to meet with Derek.

CHAPTER TEN

eptember 8, 1986

THIRTEEN YEARS, three months until millennium night

JENNY LAY ON HER BED, a magazine propped before her. She couldn't say what magazine it was, or even what the article was about. But she still convinced herself she was reading it nonetheless.

Somehow, she had always been aware of these feelings, but she was torn as to what to do about them. She'd had them her whole life, but it was only now, at the tender age of thirteen years old, that they were beginning to make sense.

She jumped at a *rat-a-tat-tat* against her window, and abruptly sat upright.

Eddie's innocent face appeared at the window, tears in his eyes.

Jenny rushed to the window and opened it, quickly

ushering him in. It was pouring down with rain and Eddie was drenched.

"Oh my God, Eddie, how did you get up here?" she gasped.

"I climbed the drainpipe," he stuttered between broken tears, clutching one of his hands over his eye.

Jenny rushed to her wardrobe and withdrew a towel. She wrapped it around Eddie and guided him to the bed.

Still, he clutched his eye, crying so much his whole body was convulsing.

"What is it?" Jenny asked, reaching for his hand. He flinched his head away.

"Dad was drinking again," he sobbed.

Slowly and carefully, she placed her gentle hand against the fist Eddie pressed against his eye, softly lifting it down.

She practically choked on her breath as she cast her eyes over a huge, shining black eye.

"Oh my God, Eddie!" She gulped. Her whole body stiffened.

He withdrew his hand again, adamantly returning it to cover his eye.

"You've got to do something about this. You can't let him get away with doing this to you. You have to say something."

"Say what?" he barked through gritted teeth. "And to who?"

She instantly froze, aware that his outburst could well have woken her parents. She paused for a moment, waiting to hear if there was movement.

Nothing.

They were safe.

Without needing to say a word of instruction, she drew her duvet back and allowed Eddie to lay down. He lay on his side so that the pillow would cover up his blackened eye and he would be able to withdraw his hand.

Jenny pulled the duvet over them, laying opposite him so they were both facing each other.

She took a tissue from a tissue box beside her bed and used it to dab his visible eye. She wiped away his tears, then threw the tissue to the floor and smiled at her best friend.

"Why does this have to happen to me?" Eddie deliberated, his tears drying up. His hair, still wet from the rain, was soaking the pillow. But Jenny didn't care.

She could easily change it in the morning.

"It could be worse," Jenny smiled, attempting to liven the mood.

"How?"

"You could be Mrs Jenkins. Married to a bald husband, with fourteen cats and shrivelled-up old lady tits."

They both chuckled at the expense of their maths teacher.

"True," Eddie confirmed, a smile finding its way to his face. "So what's up with you? I feel like I just keep having all the problems."

"That's not fair, Eddie. Things are really tough for you."

"Still. What's new?"

Jenny sighed. She contemplated.

Maybe she should tell him.

But how?

How does someone approach something like this?

"Eddie…" she sighed. "Have you ever, like, thought you might, like, feel something, but, maybe you aren't sure if it's, I don't know, right?"

Eddie's eyes narrowed.

"I have no idea what you mean."

Jenny hesitated and dropped her head.

"Never mind."

"No, go on, Jen. This sounds like it may actually be something interesting."

"Well," she tried, lifting her head up. "What do you think, of, like… people who are… gay?"

Eddie shrugged. "Never really thought about it. Why?"

Jenny closed her eyes and shook her head. She loved him, but sometimes he could be really stupid.

"Oh!" Eddie suddenly cried out, realising. "Are you? I mean, do you think, like… you might be?"

"I don't know, maybe."

"Are you sure?"

"No. I mean, how can you be sure of something like that? But I feel like it. I've always felt… I don't know."

Eddie remained silent. Jenny couldn't read him. Couldn't tell what he was thinking.

"What if I was? Would that make me a bad person?"

Eddie took a long pause to think about this, in which time he peered at Jenny. Her face turned weak, her heart skipping a beat.

Finally, Eddie replied.

"You'd still be you," he decided. "And whoever you are, you're still pretty awesome."

Jenny smiled.

That's when she knew he would be her best friend forever.

Dear Martin,

We are doing our part. We hope your quest is going well in doing yours.

We are finally in possession of the list Stella Clutchings sent us. A list that will give us the names of the most powerful people in paranormal science in the world.

This is our chance. Our piece of the puzzle. This is what we can do to help back you up.

You will never have to fight this fight alone.

Any time you are on the front line, look back over your shoulder. You will see us, fighting with you. Covering your back. Giving you an army to wage this war with.

Only this comes with a warning.

Eddie has started. Whatever he and the devil are doing, they have started. Essential people have started dying.

And the deaths are committed, almost certainly, by the hand of whatever Eddie has become.

We should really stop calling him Eddie now. He is no longer Edward King. Only, I don't know what other name to call him.

Just know that whatever he brings our way, within you lies the balance. Within you lies what we need to face him.

To face 'it' I should say.

Stay safe, my friend.

I have all the faith in the world in you.

Yours,
    Derek

CHAPTER ELEVEN

$\mathcal{J}$anuary 15, 2003

THREE YEARS since millennium night

TOURISTS MOSEYED up and down the cracked paving slabs, marvelling at the magnitude of the architecture around them.

Martin scoffed.

The Church of Nativity was a tourist location to them. A religious pilgrimage. A lovely family holiday.

They had no idea the significance of this building. All the streets they were walking up and down, *road 90,* where they may have travelled up the coast, the fellow holiday makers they flung their arms around – all of it would be gone. Engulfed in ravenous flames, all nearby souls destroyed, nothing that the God they travelled here to pray to could, or be willing, to do about it.

No, they had no idea that this church was currently home to an angry boy who could hold the key to stopping all of this.

Or so he was told.

He didn't feel like the key to humanity's salvation. He didn't feel like a messiah, a hero, an apocalypse-denying legend.

He felt like a fool.

A teenage scumbag with no family, no hope, and not a possession to his name besides the clothes on his back.

He perched on a set of steps, watching a visiting mother spit on a handkerchief and rub it on the face of a toddler. A nearby father clung onto another child, laughing and joking with him, happy. Making memories.

It was something Martin would never have.

He never knew exactly what happened to his mum following the ritual that brought forth the heir to hell from within Eddie. Naturally, he'd known she'd died. But he had never known what she had endured in doing so.

It occurred to him that, although he may never have this precious family dynamic, he was not necessarily unlucky. So many people, unlike him, had something to lose.

Maybe that was why he'd been chosen for this. Because he had nothing to lose; no emotional attachments. No home, no friends or family who would miss him if he disappeared to Israel to undergo training with some overbearing, balding priest.

But many people did. And they stood to lose it all.

That was what was at stake.

He sighed and shook his head to himself. He couldn't stand another session of being taunted, told he was nothing, ridiculed about his insignificance. Father Douglas was right, and that's why it hurt so much.

It was something he would never be able to change.

Shoving his hand into his pocket, he felt a ruffled piece of paper. He withdrew it and unfolded it, reading it.

It was another letter from Derek, which had arrived a few days ago. A letter he had stuffed into his pocket with hopes of reading later.

It forewarned him that Eddie had started.

I have to stop calling him Eddie. As does Derek. He is not Eddie.

The heir of hell had started.

Time was running out, and Martin was getting nowhere. Besides the dent on his self-esteem, Father Douglas had nothing to show for the time he had spent with him.

Maybe Cassy had gotten it wrong? Maybe she had him confused with someone else?

Then he read those final words Derek had written.

STAY SAFE, *my friend.*

I HAVE ALL *the faith in the world in you.*

NO ONE HAD EVER CALLED him his friend.

No one had ever had faith in him.

Martin couldn't decide who was the bigger fool; him or Derek. Derek, for his unfaltering, positive belief that something good would come out of an awful situation. That Martin would amount to something.

Or whether it was Martin; the bigger fool for believing Derek.

The family he had noticed at the bottom of the step now passed him. A young boy swung between the parents.

But there was a young girl.

Where had she gone?

"Hello," came an inquisitive child's voice from beside Martin.

Looking to his left, he saw the wide eyes of the young girl he had noticed earlier.

Why was she standing there, just watching him?

Her family had paused. From a distance, they were watching. Letting their daughter talk to him, but being warily cautious from afar.

"Hi," Martin mustered, confused. Why was she talking to him? It defied social etiquette. Martin was antisocial at best, and not one to ever communicate with strangers besides a grunt when he bought some food.

"You look sad," she told him.

Martin smiled and gave a slight laugh.

"I am," he admitted.

"Why?"

Sighing, he glanced to the family watching, then to the clear blue sky above. To the birds in the trees, the sun in the sky, the laughter of distant children in the air.

"Because everything's going to end," Martin told her, in the midst of a knowing, resolute smile. Despite meaning it literally, he knew it would not be taken so.

"Why is everything going to end?" She tilted her head.

"Because all of this, all the people, all the buildings, all of it – it's going to be gone. And I can't do anything about it."

He held eye contact with this little girl, who looked momentarily upset. It looked like tears were bubbling in her eyes, a slight quiver in her lip.

Then she looked back at her family.

Her sadness ceased.

She turned back to Martin with a smile. Unexpectedly, she placed a hand on his shoulder.

"I think you can," she nodded.

She wrapped her arms around Martin, gave him an abrupt, tight squeeze, then ran back to her family. Her father gave Martin a slight nod and they carried on walking, enjoying their holiday.

Martin watched them go until he could see them no longer, then watched the space in which they had left.

An act of kindness, from a young child to a stranger. For no reason other than because she could.

That was what he was fighting for.

That was what was at stake.

He shovelled the note in his pocket, stood up, and marched back to the Church of Nativity.

CHAPTER TWELVE

*J*anuary 16, 2003

THE DUST WAFTED from the browned pages of the old book, forcing Jenny to cough. How could a book be so dusty? When she had started this venture with Derek, she'd had this stereotypical vision of all books about demonology being big, dusty slabs of writing with broken leather bindings and unappealing, crammed writing inside – she never realised how accurate her expectation would be.

Having seen Eddie's bookcase, and Derek's bookcase, she knew that there were loads of books that weren't so tatty and outdated. New editions, new found accounts, intriguing memoirs.

But no! She ended up having to bring home *Demonic Forces in Today's World.*

'Today's world.' *Hah. More like 'ancient world.'*

She flicked to a random page and read the title:

'VAMPYRS IN CITIES.'

JENNY WAS new to this supernatural world, having entered it solely to save her best friend, and would be the first to admit she knew little about it; but was still fairly certain that 'vampyrs' weren't an actual thing.

Not as far as she knew, anyway.

"Hey," came Lacy's chirpy voice from the doorway.

Jenny looked over her shoulder and smiled.

"Hey, you," she replied.

No matter what she was doing or where she was, just a simple waft of Lacy's voice or glimpse of her smile was enough to make Jenny go weak at the knees.

Even after all this time.

Lacy glided forward and leant over Jenny, scooping her arms around Jenny's neck. She kissed her on the cheek and firmly embraced her.

"What you doing?" Lacy enquired.

"Oh, you know," Jenny answered, as if she had a clue what she was actually doing. "Research. Reading. This and that."

"This book looks a tad old."

"Yeah, it is. I think it even dates to before Derek was born."

They giggled. Lacy slid to Jenny's side, stroking a gentle hand down Jenny's bare arm.

"Hey, Jen," Lacy nervously peered up at her girlfriend. "I have a question to ask."

"What's that?" Jenny replied, still peering at the small writing of the book.

Lacy positioned herself so that she was on one knee, Jenny's hand in her hands, gazing up at her.

"Jen…"

Jenny paused what she was reading and turned toward Lacy.

"Yeah?"

"Will you… will you marry me?"

Jenny's eyes grew wide. She shifted her entire body toward the woman she loved, clutching onto her hand.

At first she was astounded, then she was excited – then, she grew confused.

"But… how?" Jenny offered, flustered.

"How what?"

"How would we get married? Lacy, we're gay."

"They are starting to debate allowing civil partnerships in Parliament. Or, if not, we can go to Belgium, some-place in Spain called Aragon; they've even married same-sex couples in a part of Canada. We can travel."

Lacy's face grew vulnerable. She was still poised in that same position, looking up at Jenny, clutching onto her hand. Not only was her leg starting to ache, she had expected Jenny's first words following her proposal to be more positive.

Then Jenny's fluster faded to a grand, elated smile – and Lacy felt reassured.

"I…" Jenny shook in excitement, euphoria overcoming her. "Of course, Lacy. Of course!"

Lacy's smile grew tenfold. She jumped up, as did Jenny, and they embraced in a close, tight hug. Jenny's hands gripped onto Lacy; not just grabbed, but gripped – clutching her tightly, ensuring she would never leave from this position.

They pulled back for a moment to look each other in the eyes.

They laughed. Smirked. Rested their foreheads against each other's.

Then they kissed. A long, passionate, loving kiss. Their first as fiancées.

"Oh my God, who do we tell first?" Jenny eagerly burst out.

"I don't know! Our parents?"

"I've got to tell Derek, and oh my God, when Eddie finds out, he is going to flip –"

She froze.

For a fleeting moment, her positive demeanour dropped. She looked to the floor, bit her bottom lip, quivering ever so slightly.

Lacy grabbed Jenny's face in her hands and forced her gaze to fall on her.

"We're getting married," Lacy emphatically reminded her. "Oh my God, when should we do it?"

"Well, we'll obviously want to wait."

Lacy paused, looking back at Jenny with clear perplexity.

"What?" she prompted.

"Well, the world is ending; obviously, we can't do it yet," Jenny insisted. "Besides, I'd want Eddie at my wedding, wouldn't I?"

Lacy's expression didn't falter. Her eyebrows remained narrowed, her lips stuttering over what to say.

"But – what if he can't be?"

"Why would you say that?"

"I just think –"

"Look," Jenny interrupted, feeling an argument coming on. "Let's just celebrate being engaged first. Then we can carry on with this, right?"

"Okay..." Lacy reluctantly confirmed, her irritation still obviously evident.

"Come here," Jenny instructed, spreading a smile across her face, wrapping her arms around Lacy.

She held her loving partner close. Treasuring the moment, knowing it could all end soon.

CHAPTER THIRTEEN

*J*anuary 21, 2003

CLOUDS HOVERED IN THE SKY, bearing a thickening grey omen overhead. They were ominous but reliably dense, somehow reminding Martin of his ma. They took him back to a thought, a hint of memory he had lodged in the depths of his mind, from when he was a child. He and Ma had just left the cinema; she could still walk and they were happy.

The clouds above had been a gloomy haze, fully formed, with the smell of fine rain in the air; but no rain falling as yet. His mum had just paused in the middle of a busy street, looked up, and smiled.

"What you doing, Ma?" his young boy's voice had asked.

"I love the rain," she had answered, smiling peculiarly at the threatening cloud constellations passing above.

She had always loved the rain, Martin remembered as he bowed his head.

"Fine," Martin grunted, standing wearily in the middle of the church courtyard, his voice bouncing off the stone walls. "Teach me. But just don't treat me like shit again, yeah?"

Father Douglas grinned a knowing grin, as if there was some deep knowledge or wisdom he was aware of, that Martin wasn't. Like it was a joke Martin wasn't party to.

"You see, boy, that's the problem," Douglas eagerly gesticulated. "All these things I say, that I shout at you, all I'm doing is echoing your thoughts. You have to think – is it really me you are afraid of listening to, or is it your own mind?"

Martin shrugged, sighing with sheer exasperation, looking around himself for imaginary answers.

"See," Martin replied agitatedly, "what does that even mean?"

"It means your thoughts are too loud." Douglas strode toward Martin, placing his hands upon Martin's shoulders in a firm, passionate grip. "Shut them up."

"How am I meant to shut my thoughts up? They're just kinda there, you know?"

Douglas remained within inches of Martin, his hands resting resolutely upon the young man's shoulders. His eyes willed Martin's to understand, to react.

"That is why you can't do it. That is why I'm not bringing this out of you, what you are is not reaching the surface."

"I don't –"

"Your mind is a mess, boy!"

A mess? Well what do you expect? I'm a homeless orphan forced half way across the world to be abused!

"I –" Martin stuttered, throwing his arms in the air, pulling out of Douglas' grasp and walking around in an energetic fume.

"What? Speak, boy!"

"Stop calling me boy, to start with!" Martin cried out, turning to Douglas and flailing his arms in the air.

"What else?" Douglas smirked.

"What else?" Martin echoed in disbelief. "Stop telling me I ain't shit; that I ain't amounting up to nothin'."

"That bothers you?"

"*Yes!* I have got *nothing* in the world, you prick. *Nothing!*"

Martin collapsed against the wall, ignoring the sharp pain of the solid stone banging against his forehead. He held in his tears, held them in as hard as he could, refusing to crack, refusing to give in.

"Stop holding it in," Douglas demanded. "This is why you fail. Your emotions control you, you don't control your emotions."

"You make no sense!" Martin screamed at his mentor, flinging himself around, his voice reverberating around the courtyard multiple times.

"Let it out!"

"Let what out?"

"Why you are such a coward."

"*I am not a coward!*" Martin fell to his knees, bowing his head, gritting and grinding his teeth, clenching his fists into tight balls of fury, digging his nails into his palms. "I have *nothing*, you hear me? I ain't got no parents, no friends, no home, nothing. And you stand here telling me I don't mean shit?"

His tears forced themselves out like bullets. His cries liberated from the pent-up rage that had boiled through him his entire life. Everything came soaring out: his dad, his mum, the accident, the death, the beating by Bandile, the degradation by Douglas, the beating up by his best friend, the exclusions from school, the constant defiance of anyone who tried to help him.

It forced its way out.

Then it stopped.

His tears ended. Evaporated. Turned to meaningless condensation.

Douglas crouched before Martin and placed an affectionate, caring hand on Martin's back.

"How do you feel now?" Douglas asked.

Martin lifted his head, wiping his eyes.

"Better," he answered.

"Good. Now this is out of you, you might just be able to think clearly. You might just be able to do something magnificent with your life."

Martin nodded.

Martin smiled. Not a pretend smile he'd shown to teachers at school – a real smile. The first real smile he had given in years.

CHAPTER FOURTEEN

anuary 22, 2003

DEREK'S ORGANISATION made Jenny feel slightly inferior.

Across the entire far wall of his study was a giant pin-board, illuminated only by the powerful lamp light Derek shone against it in what was otherwise an unlit room.

This board displayed a map of the world, with pins on certain locations, led by strings to various pictures and notes of information that represented the different people on the list. The locations were all educated guesses for where these people could be – but Jenny was still impressed.

Most notable was the name of Stella Clutchings; that had a big red cross marked over it. The first victim of the heir of hell – or the 'heir', as Derek had taken to referring to him.

Jenny still referred to him as Eddie.

Because that is his name.

"So if we believe that the heir was here a matter of weeks

ago," Derek was saying, in the midst of one of his engrossed lectures of what they were to do, "Then the heir must be travelling to somewhere close in Europe for his next. Unless the heir's powers are such that he doesn't need to follow a logical pattern. After all, the heir would likely return to hell, making such an assumption redundant."

"Why do you keep calling him the heir?" Jenny demanded.

She stood in the doorway of the room, hands on hips, blocking any light from seeping through from the hallway behind her.

"Why, because that's what it is," Derek paused, sneering at her without deliberately intending to. "It is the heir of hell we are facing."

"No, it's not," Jenny exclaimed, taking a step forward. "It is Eddie."

Derek sighed. He bowed his head and closed his eyes. He would need to consider how to approach this; Jenny was obviously hurting, and this was a struggle for her.

But so am I, dammit. I'm hurting too!

If they were to succeed in killing this demon, they needed to be realistic. He only wished Jenny could see this.

He raised his head, taking a calm, soothing tone; determined not to act irrationally or aggressively, ensuring this did not turn into an argument or a heated debate.

"Because, Jenny," he began, "it is not Eddie we are facing."

Jenny shook her head and looked away.

"Don't get me wrong," Derek continued, before she could interrupt. "I miss Eddie more than anything. But Eddie is dead. What this is, is no longer Eddie. It is a piece of evil that grew from within him, and destroyed him. We are no longer facing our friend."

"You just don't get it, do you?"

Derek grew irritable, and despite his better intentions, his irritation surfaced. He threw a stack of papers from his hand

and turned toward her, jabbing his pointing finger into her personal space.

"What? What is it I don't get, Jenny?" he spat petulantly. "That Eddie was a great man? That Eddie does not deserve this, that we love Eddie, that this is a bloody atrocity and we all would dearly love Eddie back? Or is it that I was the one who trained him, and helped him hone this thing inside of him, and if it wasn't for me we wouldn't be in this bloody mess of a situation?"

Jenny shook her head, waving her arms in surrender. "I'm sorry," she told him. "Sometimes you're just so black-and-white about this stuff that it doesn't seem like you actually feel anything."

"Oh, believe me," he growled venomously through gritted teeth, "I feel everything. I just don't go wearing it on my sleeve. Because what good will that do? One of us has to have our head on."

Derek turned back to the map and rubbed his sinus. He rolled his sleeves up; a gesture Jenny knew as a sign of Derek's petulance. His appearance was always immaculate, no matter what. Even now he was wearing a shirt, tie, and waistcoat. But for him to roll his sleeves up to his elbow and allow, even for a minute, one bit of scruffiness into his demeanour – that small, insignificant gesture indicated he was done with this discussion.

"So, what do we do now?" Jenny enquired, folding her arms. "I mean, what's our next step?"

"Our next step is to reach the next person on the list. They are written in order of power. We need to recruit our army."

"And where do we start?"

Derek picked up his list and read the next name aloud: "Jamile Arshad." Tracing his finger across the string that led from this name to the map, he announced the location of the man they needed to recruit next.

"Canada."

This made Jenny smile.

Canada was a place that had allowed a civil partnership. One of the first places, in fact. Somewhere she and Lacy could go to should they need to leave the country to get married.

Then she realised – Derek didn't know. How could she not have told them?

"Oh my God, Derek," she announced, grabbing his arm. "I haven't told you yet. I completely forgot."

"What is it?"

Jenny lifted out her left hand, revealing a gold ring with an impressive diamond perched upon it.

"What is this?" Derek asked, confused.

"We're engaged!" Jenny cheered, waving her hands in the air in excitement. "We are getting married. Me and Lacy."

Derek looked back at her with a muddled gaze.

"I mean, I know we might not be able to do it in this country yet, but they are debating it. If not, then there are other countries where civil partnerships are slowly becoming legal. I can't believe I forgot to tell you about this! Aren't you excited?"

Derek's face bore no expression. He stroked his hand down his goatee, then, eventually, his eyebrows furrowed.

"Excuse my questioning," Derek began, "but... is this the best time?"

Jenny's happiness slid away like an upturned bucket of water.

"What?"

"I mean, that's delightful, yes – but isn't it a rather inopportune moment?"

Jenny's jaw dropped. Her head shook despondently.

"I cannot believe this."

"Forgive the impertinence, Jenny, I was just saying–"

"Well don't 'just say.' And yes, I do think this is the right time. I think this is the perfect time."

Derek dropped his head. He knew he'd said the wrong thing and guilt spread over him.

"And for your information," Jenny continued, one hand on her hip, and the other jabbing a stiff, pointed finger in Derek's direction, "I told Lacy this wasn't the right time to actually have the wedding yet. I just agreed to get married. Because I love her. And if the world is ending, I would like that to be damn well known."

Silence overcame the room. Derek closed his eyes, shaking his head, lifting his arms helplessly in the air as an indication of him being unable to justify his reaction.

"Jenny, I'm sorry –"

"Forget it," she snapped. "Let's just get on with it."

She sat down at the desk, resting her head on her hand, crossing her leg and pulling an expression of disgust as if she were an insolent child.

Deciding it was best to just carry on, Derek continued to explain the plan.

Jenny didn't listen to a word.

CHAPTER FIFTEEN

*J*anuary 25, 2003

THE SNOWY MOUNTAIN stood still beneath the clouds, puffs of white floating slowly like a mask of absence. The trees gathered together like soldiers led into the distance beyond the mountains; a jungle one could so easily lose themselves in.

Jamile Arshad had done so many times.

He loved living so near to Alberta, with its glorious mountains big enough to rival even God's presence. Its smooth lakes remained blue, despite the pollution inflicted on so many of the world's bodies of water. The trees, the grass, the snow, the humid moisture in the air, the rocks that led down to the water's edge – it was heavenly.

It was magnificent.

And Jamile felt so lucky to have lived there his entire life.

When he had first discovered his gift, it hadn't been easy. People had died attempting to climb these mountains;

although this number had decreased significantly with the recent knowledge of mountaineering most escapists had.

Still, it was a strange way to learn that you could communicate with the dead. Often conversations between Jamile and wayward mountaineers would take an entire afternoon of discussion before the mountaineers would realise they were dead.

This day was just like any other. Sat beside the water's edge, he could hear a distant sobbing. When he looked over, a small boy wearing what looked like a private school uniform knelt by the edge. He wore shorts and, on a day like that, shorts were an unusual choice.

"My friend," offered Jamile. "Are you not cold?"

The boy turned slowly, dumbfounded that someone might be talking to him. As he revealed his face, Jamile could see water dripping from his hair, a redness in his cheeks and an inquisitive, taken aback stare in his eyes.

The boy looked over his shoulder a few times, trying to figure out who Jamile might be looking at.

"Yes, I can see you," Jamile grinned. "Strange, isn't it? You're ignored by everyone, so much so that when you're not ignored, you kind of wish you were?"

The boy just gazed back at Jamile, stumped.

"Did you drown?"

The boy faintly nodded.

"I thought so. The dripping hair gave it away. Strange, really – that the way you die impacts so much on the appearance you take when you are dead."

"I'm…" the boy muttered. "…Dead?"

"I'm afraid so."

Jamile stood, placed his hands in his pockets and meandered down to the water's edge.

"I have a gift, see," Jamile continued. "I can see people like you. People who are stuck here. I can help."

"You can help me?"

"Sure."

"Can you... help me find my mummy?"

Jamile sighed and shook his head. "Afraid not. I can help you find peace, but your mother – that is one thing I cannot find, as it goes."

"Oh. That's a shame." The boy stood beside Jamile and peered out across the lake, gazing at the same beautiful scene Jamile had gazed upon his entire life.

"So how did you drown?"

"I didn't."

Jamile frowned. How strange. He was normally completely accurate about these things.

"How did you die then?"

"I haven't," the boy grinned, turning his head toward Jamile. "Though I did kill my host, so maybe that's what you mean. He died."

"And... who exactly was your host?"

"Maybe you've heard of him," the boy gleefully joked. "His name was Edward King."

Jamile froze. His eyes widened. His blood raced.

He was in serious danger.

He turned on his heel and sprinted, accelerating as fast as he could, hurtling forward in no particular direction.

It was no use.

Within moments, the boy had transformed into a creature so large it covered the entire landscape in shadow. Glancing back at the beast, Jamile gagged at its vile appearance. So triumphantly intimidating was it, Jamile's legs became too weak to move and he fell.

A lifetime of speaking to the dead and he had never come across anything like it.

As he cowered on his back, crawling backwards, the

shadow of the creature looming over him, he feasted his eyes upon the beast that hung over him.

It was terrifying. Its fanged teeth dripped with thick red, its claws were hugely curved and ready to tear Jamile apart, and its eyes…

Oh, it's eyes.

They were bloodier than any part of him. Pupils consumed with dark red, nothing but pure, unaltered evil ruminating in waves toward its prey.

"Please…" begged Jamile, knowing it would do no good. "Please… you must still have Edward King inside of you… you must remember… you must fight this…"

The grin of this monstrosity was the last thing Jamile ever saw.

Its claw elongated into a pointed arc, firing through Jamile's chest. Its teeth ripped his neck into pieces within seconds, spraying buckets of blood over the snowy tops of the nearby trees.

Jamile's instant demise was a violent atrocity, a brutally humiliating wave of mortification that echoed through the valleys of Canada so that anyone who was tapped into the happenings of hell could feel it.

They could feel a man of Jamile's power surging through the air, then gone in a matter of seconds.

Then the heir to hell disappeared.

An unrecognisable corpse remained.

CHAPTER SIXTEEN

*T*he orange tint hovering above the hazy white clouds, signalling the descent of the evening sun.

The stone temples above stone walls around stone houses.

The stone walls of the courtyard, with aged cracks spewing small mounds of moss.

Sand in the air, floating from nearby surfaces.

The sound of a hymn. The waveforms of distant song barely audible.

Prayers lingering in the air. The condensation of church mist. The echoes of tiny voices bouncing off the stone walls inside.

"Martin," spoke a soft, gentle voice from the lips of Father Douglas. "Can you hear it?"

Martin closed his eyes. His mind still. Focussing on the elements that encompassed him.

The voices. The hymns. The humid haze. The orange glow. The taste of church air.

He could feel everything. Every connected beat, every piece of energy between every lingering life.

From inside of himself, his thoughts were quiet. A mind at peace. A definite clarity of vague feelings.

"I can," Martin confirmed.

"Good," acknowledged Douglas. "Then we will start."

Martin's eyes sprung open, but his body remained completely still. Sat on a wooden chair, his hands resting symmetrically upon his knees, his focus was placed entirely on the object before him.

A pencil.

Laid still on the floor.

Ten yards away from Martin's fixed stare.

"Keep listening," Douglas spoke, circling Martin and the pencil. "Keep feeling, detect everything. Keep your mind calm. Think of nothing but what you feel."

Martin remained comfortably rigid, keeping his mind focussed on his environment. From the close to the distant, from his beating heart to the motionless pencil.

"Keep your eyes on the pencil," continued Douglas. "Keep your focus on it."

Martin's eyes barely blinked, gazing firmly on the weightless object that remained immobile.

"Now channel that energy, channel that focus, that awareness, toward the pencil. Direct everything you have into that pencil. But do not try to move it."

Douglas paused behind Martin.

"You will not be able to move it. Just focus on it. Feel it. Take it in, soak the energy surrounding it up."

A day ago, Martin would have told someone spewing this complex pencil-obsessive diatribe to shut up and stop being such a pretentious twat.

But now he felt it.

The pencil before him sank into his body, tingling his senses. The lead, the tip, the inscription of HB marked into the side; it flowed through him.

"Now, my boy," Douglas grinned, crouching behind Martin, both the pencil and Martin in his peripheral vision. "Nudge the pencil."

Martin took a deep breath in and let it out. He willed his mind to remain calm.

Getting it calm was the easy part; retaining that calmness enough to undertake an impossible task was something else.

"Picture yourself nudging that pencil," Douglas whispered encouragement. "Picture your finger doing it. Feel your finger doing it, but do not move your finger."

Move it but don't move it? Jesus.

No.

Remain calm.

Don't be sceptical now. I can feel it. I can do this.

In his mind he saw his finger reach out, a large fist with a raised point, edging closer to the pencil.

Brushing the pencil with this imaginary finger, he could feel it against the tip, feel it against his skin.

He pushed.

The pencil did not move.

He let out an exasperated breath, moving his head away.

"Do not lose focus, son," Douglas asserted, and Martin abruptly resumed his gaze. "Nothing works the first time. If you are ready to give up on the first attempt, you are not ready to be successful. This may take one, ten, a hundred, maybe a million times. You've just got to believe that, eventually, you will move that pencil."

Martin resumed his focus, getting in tune with his surroundings, feeling his environment, feeling the pencil before him.

Shutting up any critical thoughts, he listened to the pencil, listening to the absence of sound it was hammering into his ears.

Listening to the air around himself.

Willing himself to feel it.

Whatever that means.

The pencil. Nudging. His hand reaching out.

I can see the pencil moving.

The pencil moving.

The pencil.

Moving.

THWACK!

The pencil flew off the floor at an exceptional speed, soaring toward the far wall of the courtyard with such ferocity it smashed into tiny pieces of lead.

Martin's jaw dropped.

He rose from his seat, though he was completely unaware of himself doing so.

His hands shook. He was stuck in disbelief.

"Oh my God!" he exclaimed.

He turned to his side, where Douglas wore an elated grin, a grin spread across his face.

"There you see, my boy." Douglas held his arms out warmly in celebration. "I knew once you quietened your mind…"

Martin pumped his fists in the air and walked around excitedly, at a loss as to what to do with himself.

I just moved a pencil with my mind!

"I – I – I can't believe it!"

Without any warning or realisation what he was doing, he flung himself onto Douglas with a large, congratulatory hug.

He stood for a while, his hands in his hair, staring at the pieces of pencil spread around the floor.

"Right," spoke Douglas. "Now you've moved a pencil, how about we start on conjuring fire?"

… What?

CHAPTER SEVENTEEN

*J*anuary 26, 2003

JENNY'S FINGERS drummed irritably across the table. Noticing Lacy's death stare, Jenny promptly ceased and shoved her hand into her pocket.

Jenny was slouched in her chair, her head resting on her fist, staring half-heartedly under drooped eyelids at the screen Lacy was displaying toward her.

"So there's this lovely place in Canada," Lacy beamed, showing a beautiful, snowy cabin on the computer screen. "It looks so nice. And a winter wedding would be just magical."

"Uh-huh," Jenny grunted.

She couldn't believe Derck's impudence the other day. She played the scene back over in her mind, again and again, each time playing out a different version of what she could have said in retaliation.

"I also found this lovely place in Germany," Lacy continued, opening another window on the computer. "It's quite far off for our families to go, but if we left it a year or so for people to save, it should be all right, right?"

"Mm."

"I mean, we're not asking too much, are we?"

"No."

Is this the best time?

How dare Derek.

Jenny didn't have to volunteer her time. She didn't have to give up her job, her social life, her freedom. It's true she was doing it for Eddie rather than Derek, or even the entirety of humanity; but the absolute cheek to voice such a ludicrous opinion.

I mean that's delightful, yes, but is it the opportune moment?

The opportune moment?

Jenny couldn't think of a more opportune moment. The world was going to hell. What difference would it make?

"Jenny, what is going on?" Lacy demanded, staring daggers at Jenny, whose eyes had absentmindedly glazed over.

"What?" Jenny mustered, shaking herself out of her funk.

"I'm trying to talk to you about wedding stuff and you're not even here. It's like you don't even care."

Jenny ran her hands over her face and knelt forward. Lacy was right. Jenny was not giving her due attention or putting her enthusiasm into this, and it wasn't good enough.

"Sorry, Lace, I'm just a bit pissed off about something," Jenny admitted.

"Okay, well, maybe you can forget about it."

"But I can't forget about it, it's just–" Jenny stood and paced back and forth, grunting an exasperated growl. "Derek, man. He's doing my head in."

She leant against the windowsill beside the computer Lacy was trying to use to show her various wedding venues.

"What has he done now?" Lacy sighed, turning her head away and trying not to let her annoyance show.

"I told him about us, I mean, our getting married," Jenny ranted. "But then he went on about what an 'inopportune' time it was. I mean, I just said we are getting engaged. He doesn't actually expect us to have the wedding before we've finished all this, does he?"

Lacy frowned.

"Doesn't he?"

"I mean–" Jenny continued, unaware of Lacy's folding arms and shaking head. "Yes, it's not an opportune moment, but it will sure lift our spirits to have something to celebrate."

"You just want to get engaged to lift our spirits?"

"No, no, of course not," Jenny protested. "I want to get engaged because I love you."

"Jen…" Lacy trailed off, gathering her thoughts, making sure she was careful with how she articulated them. "I know the world might be ending and all that – but, just in case it doesn't, I'd still like to plan for our future."

"Yes, exactly!" Jenny exclaimed. "That's what I told him."

"And what exactly do you mean – of course we aren't having our wedding yet?"

"Well…" Jenny froze. Seeing the hurt etched over her lover's face, it finally dawned on her that she and Lacy weren't understanding each other. "I mean, I want to get married – but not yet, right? This has to come first."

"*This* has to come first?"

"Yes!"

Lacy bowed her head, covering her eyes with her hand.

"What is it?" Jenny asked.

"It's nothing," Lacy lied. "It's fine. Maybe we'll never bother. I'm just fed up with hearing about Derek and this quest. Can't we just concentrate the time we have together on us? On our wedding? Without having to involve any of the other load of things that's going on?"

"You're right," Jenny nodded. "You're right. I'm sorry. My head's not here, that's my bad. I'm totally focussed now."

She turned around and knelt beside Lacy, resting her hands on Lacy's lap as she peered up at the computer screen before them.

"Right, well, this is Germany, a location where another gay couple got married," Lacy indicated with her hand. "I think it looks really lovely."

The phone rang.

Jenny looked remorsefully to Lacy.

"You don't have to get that," Lacy suggested.

"You know I have to," Jenny urged, stroking her hand down Lacy's hair in hope of her affection proving that Lacy did still come first. "I never know what it might be."

She marched out of the room. Lacy listened to distant talking and, within a minute, Jenny was back in the room putting her coat on.

"I'm so, so sorry," Jenny claimed, putting her arms around Lacy.

"What is it?"

"Someone else has died. Some guy in Canada, actually. I need to go see Derek now."

Lacy didn't respond. She allowed her silence to hang in the air.

Jenny, unfortunately, didn't have time to fix it. She knew she would have to do something to make up for it later; maybe flowers, or some kind of gesture.

She gave Lacy a kiss on the forehead and rushed out the door.

CHAPTER EIGHTEEN

eb 1, 2003

LAUGHTER CONSUMED THE COURTYARD. It was like a box to an eternity of magic had been opened, and Martin could barely keep it in.

He felt himself surge with power, casting spells and spewing elements with ridiculous ease.

Father Douglas sat in his chair, rocking back and forth with a knowing smile. This child could amount to all he was supposed to be yet.

Martin let out a cocky bawl of laughter as he twisted his hands in a contorted circle quicker and quicker, fire emulating from his fingers. Once he had built up enough fire he lunged it forward, launching a cylinder of flames at the wooden target propped before him.

The spray of flames engulfed the target, plunging it into a wall of blaze.

"Oh no, fire!" Martin joked, amusing himself. "Well, fear not!"

He moved his arms in a frantic motion once more, this time raising them upwards in unison, circling them again and again.

Sprays of water flung from his fingers, raining upon the cobbled ground. The drops grew and grew, expanding until they reached a large ball of liquid wrapped around each of his palms.

Flinging his hands forward once more, he threw a stream of water onto the fire he had previously created.

Bowing his head and closing his eyes, concentrating on his surroundings, he rested his mind.

Then his eyes shot open.

In response, the drenched wooden target before him went sailing into the far wall in a gust of wind, smashing into pieces.

Martin smirked again.

He deserved to be cocky.

Unbeknownst to Martin, a familiar figure watched on. Behind and above Douglas' chuckling pride, from the heavens above, a beautiful, graceful figure smiled, despite her eyes being consumed by concern.

Cassy was pleased with his progress. He had done well, she didn't doubt this.

But she felt like she was exploiting him.

This boy had no idea the war he was waging, or the reasons he was involved.

"What's troubling you?" came a wizened woman's voice beside her.

Cassy turned to Gabrielle and forced a smile, dropping her head, and resting her eyes in a momentary second of weakness.

Gabrielle was a magnificently elegant woman. With

luscious black skin, perfectly groomed hair flowing down her shoulders, and a peaceful, white dress adorning her as it had for thousands of years.

She was used to the trepidation of her disciples.

The most significant hesitancy she had witnessed came a little over two thousand years ago, from a woman who gave birth to the man who changed everything.

Now, they were witnessing a similar time with the messiahs they were training.

But never in her eternal existence of representing the heavens had she been aware of such feelings of opposing malevolence coming from hell.

The fallen angel Lucifer grew stronger now his antichrist grew in power. Their messiah was on earth, just as their previous messiah had been two thousand years before – only this time, their messiah wasn't there to bring love.

This new messiah was there to be the world's defence in the biggest war of mankind.

"Don't fake a smile with me, Cassy," Gabrielle pleaded, placing a comforting hand upon Cassy's arm.

Cassy was a grand angel, a real asset in their battle against hell.

But Cassy was still young in her ascension. She was inexperienced. Gabrielle had thousands upon thousands of years' experience against her, and it made her all the calmer in dealing with troubled times.

"I'm sorry, I just…" Cassy trailed off, weakened in her trail of thought.

Her thoughts felt like she was betraying her mission. Gabrielle noticed this, as Cassy knew she would. But it didn't make Cassy feel any less guilty about such feelings.

"Speak honestly," Gabrielle insisted. "There is no point in disguising how you feel."

Cassy watched Martin again, on earth. Enduring the triumph that would precede the inevitable pain.

Heaven was a safe haven from such things. It was unfair that Martin should fight whilst Cassy stood by and gave meaningless advice.

"I feel useless."

"We do not have the whims that hell does," Gabrielle reminded Cassy. "When they intervene with human nature, it is at their peril. Heaven is above such things. We do not alter free will, it is not our way. All we can do, all *you* can do – is guide."

"It's a feeble excuse."

"But true, nonetheless."

Cassy meandered to a chair that formed out of cloud. She sat on it, and Gabrielle placed herself beside Cassy, lending a sympathetic ear.

"Does Martin even have a clue why he was chosen for this?" Cassy lamented. "He probably thinks his being picked for this was random. He doesn't have any idea how he was conceived, does he?"

"Do you think it would benefit him if he did? Make it any easier? Make the sacrifice any less painful?"

"No, I guess not," Cassy sighed.

Or would it?

Would it not help him to know?

She knew it would have helped her.

"You think too loud," Gabrielle acknowledged. "Yours and Edward's presence on earth was an abomination. You couldn't have known."

"But that's not fair. You killed me because of a deal with the devil. You damn well interfered with human free will then! I endured over a decade of hell because of who I was. And you expect me to just accept it? Like you expect Martin to?"

"When the time was right, we told you."

"Yes, when I finally reached heaven."

"But you are a piece of heaven. Edward is a piece of hell. The devil made him, so we had to make sure to balance the equation, we had no choice. Surely you must understand, once you have removed yourself from your feelings or personal relation to the issue, it was the right thing to do."

Cassy shook her head vigorously.

"Except it wasn't, was it?" Cassy gestured in an accusatory manner toward Gabrielle. "Because when you balanced it out, the devil brought Eddie back without you knowing. And now here we are. About to pay for it with the potential destruction of humanity."

"This is why Martin is so important!"

"He's a pawn!"

Gabrielle leant forward passionately, the first real input of emotion Cassy had ever seen from her. "After Edward lived, we had to balance it again – we *had to!* There *had to be* a solution for this uneven world."

Cassy closed her eyes for a moment of contemplative solitude. She opened them once more, gazing again at Martin enjoying the multitude of powers he had managed to control without any knowledge of why he, above anyone else, had the inherent power to do so.

It wasn't fair what they did to her. Conceiving her to balance life on earth. Just a pawn in their game.

It wasn't fair how Eddie, such a loving, caring person, had been destroyed by this part of him.

It wasn't fair that Martin now had to bear the prison.

It wasn't fair.

None of this was fair.

"We know that everyone who has been born of God does not keep on sinning, but he who was born of God protects him, and the evil one does not touch him. We know that we are from God, and the whole world lies in the power of the evil one."

1 John 5:18-19

CHAPTER NINETEEN

*J*anuary 8, 1988

TWELVE YEARS before millennium night

A LUCID, translucent mind sat amongst a sea of disinterested faces. Eddie's eyes swept over them, fading beneath half-hung eyelids. The lesson bored the rest of the class, yes, but this was something else.

Eddie was tired.

He was so damn tired.

Night after night of screaming and shouting, banging against the wall, inches from Eddie's tired head, was having an inevitably negative impact. Every night he'd tried to sleep to cries of "It's your fault!" "It's that kid's fault!" "I never wanted to have him anyway!" Every night he huddled up in a ball, not daring to make a sound for fear of having the wrath turn on him.

There's nothing that makes you feel worthless quite like hearing your father insist to your weakened, beaten mother that you were an unwanted mistake.

The only escape were the nights he crept out, his parents too wrapped up in their busy fights to notice him tiptoeing past their bedroom door. He would find himself at Jenny's house. Sometimes he came in the front door, where her parents were always welcoming. But, when it was especially late at night, he would climb the gutter to Jenny's room and tap on her window. They would share a bed, Eddie falling asleep almost immediately after finally finding the rest he craved.

Jenny rarely slept that well with him in the bed beside her, but that was okay. She would never turn him away. She cared too much.

And, sitting in class just a few seats behind Eddie, he could feel Jenny's worried eyes on him. As his eyes dropped with fatigue, hers avidly watched his drooping head.

Other students sniggered. Some tried to concoct ill-prepared pranks, such as tying his shoelaces together or nicking his book. It would never work, as Eddie would jerk awake at the exact point those selfish idiots would flinch away.

Then, within moments, his head would be lulling once more.

It never used to be like this. He used to be so lively. He would take care of his sister and she would follow him everywhere. His parents would take them on days out as a loving family. They had the kind of close family dynamic other families craved.

Those days were long gone now.

He had changed a lot from that eleven-year-old boy

who'd lost his sister. He was now a troubled fifteen-year-old young man, in need of help.

Jenny had no idea how to get it for him.

"Edward!" barked the teacher, picking on the student who looked to be paying the least attention.

Eddie's head abruptly lifted and he shook himself awake. In all honesty, it was a feeble attempt – within seconds, his eyes were drooping again. Even though his head was up, pointing in the direction of the irate teacher, it didn't matter.

He wasn't there.

"If you could perhaps wake up for one moment," Mr Radburn rattled on, "that would be delightful. What do you say, Edward? You with us?"

"Uh… yes, sir," Eddie grunted, saying whatever he thought he should say.

"Perfect. Now, perhaps you could answer the question for us."

"What question, sir?"

"The question I just asked."

He was clueless. Stumped.

What's more, he didn't seem aware enough to realise it. Or perhaps he didn't care. Jenny wasn't sure.

"Sir!" she shouted out. "He's just tired, please, I can answer the question."

"No thank you." Mr Radburn frowned, astonished at the impudence of her daring volunteering. "And you can stay at break-time for speaking out of turn, young lady."

Jenny went to roll her eyes, then thought better of it. Instead, she willed Eddie to respond. To do something to get Mr Radburn off his back.

"Mr King, I will try again," he spoke with a poor imitation of an army general. "What was the answer to my question?"

"I didn't hear it, sir."

"Just as I thought." Mr Radburn narrowed his eyes and

approached Eddie, a handful of rulers grasped between his fingers. "You are pathetic."

Eddie bowed his head in shame.

Eddie didn't need to be told that. He knew it already.

Jenny wished she could just reach out an arm, place it around Eddie, and assure him that he was worth far more than this idiot teacher was declaring.

As it was, she daren't speak out of turn again.

So, regretfully, she kept quiet.

"Alas, Mr King, I will ask the question again."

Mr Radburn continuously whacked his handful of rulers against the desk, emphasising every other syllable he spoke. He knew it was intimidating, and Jenny was sure the old man probably got off on it.

"Remind us, if you would be so kind," Mr Radburn sarcastically spat, still pounding the rulers against the nearest desk. "Within the realms of geometry, we have the Pythagoras theorem. What does this tell us about the hypotenuse?"

Eddie looked blank. His face was vacant. Even if he was awake enough to answer the question, or even understand it, he clearly didn't have a clue.

Surely Mr Radburn knew that?

What kind of sadistic pleasure is he getting out of this? Jenny considered. Her belly twisted in sickening agony. She wished her best friend's misery would end.

"I don't know, sir," was Eddie's vacant response.

"You don't know!" exclaimed Mr Radburn, thwacking the rulers against Eddie's desk, making Eddie jump.

A few other students laughed at Eddie's expense as his distant mind flinched at the beating of the rulers on the desk.

"And why is that?" Mr Radburn bent over, inches from Eddie's face, laying into him with a snakish grin and a reptilian stare. "Because you're stupid? Or because you're an idiot?"

Eddie's eyes glared back at Mr Radburn's.

Those eyes widened, filling with blood.

Eddie looked awake now, all right.

But Jenny felt uncomfortable by the look Eddie was giving.

She had seen that look before. It made her stomach twist into knots.

"Could you answer that question, huh?"

Mr Radburn slammed the rulers down on the final "huh" of his sentence.

For a moment, there was a deathly stare between Eddie and the teacher. A stand-off, like a duel of who would back down first.

That's when the inexplicable happened.

The rulers in Mr Radburn's hand snapped.

No, *snapped* would be too loose a term.

They shattered. Miraculously burst into pieces, soaring into various directions of the classroom, making Mr Radburn yelp and fling himself backwards onto the floor.

Everyone in the classroom shrieked, shoved their chairs backwards, covered themselves up.

That was, everyone but Eddie.

Eddie just remained motionless.

Staring at Mr Radburn.

Mr Radburn, who was poised helplessly on the floor, gaping at Eddie. He stood up, brushing himself down, and returned to the front of the classroom.

Without any acknowledgement of what had happened he resumed teaching, picking on other students to answer the questions.

He made a few even stay behind after the class to help pick pieces of ruler up.

He did not make Eddie stay behind.

In fact, Jenny couldn't recall another moment where that teacher had been cruel to Eddie.

Eddie just descended his head back to the table, closed his eyes, and continued the rest of the lesson in an unconscious silence.

Occasionally, Jenny would think about that moment.

She would wonder how the rulers shattered in that way.

She would wonder why Mr Radburn had been so terrified of Eddie following the incident. What exactly he had seen in Eddie's eyes, or what he thought had caused the incident.

She would wonder whether Eddie even really knew what had happened. He didn't look aware of his actions. His eyes didn't feel like his own.

After a while, Jenny's memory of the incident faded, and she questioned what she really saw.

Then the memory faded to a distant image, like memories often do.

CHAPTER TWENTY

eb 2, 2003

THREE YEARS, one month after millennium night

THE SIDES of the newspaper scrunched in Derek's hands.

He couldn't believe it.

Another one.

"What's the matter?" Jenny innocently asked, laying a cup of tea down for Derek, then sipping on her coffee.

Without looking at her, Derek held the newspaper out to Jenny. It only took her the first few lines to realise what had happened.

DENTAL RECORDS PROVE IDENTITY OF MAN BURNT TO DEATH

. . .

YESTERDAY IN CANADA, one of the worst cases of arson in the country's history left a man completely unrecognisable. The man, who was later identified as Jamile Arshad, was later recognised by dental records, from only a few teeth that were left not charred with the rest of his body.

"SHIT," exclaimed Jenny.

He threw the newspaper across the room in a burst of rage.

Derek stood with his back to her, facing the wall of his study that held his map. His head was bowed, with one hand on his hip and the other running through his hair.

"What are we going to do?" Jenny asked.

Derek didn't reply.

He withdrew a chair, sat down, and knelt forward, burying his head in his hands to conceal his face.

"Come on, Derek, we can't just sit around. We need to figure out our move. We can't let Eddie – sorry, the heir – just kill everyone before we even recruit them."

"It's not as simple as that," Derek mumbled.

"How? We need to get these people and–"

"And what?" Derek rose his voice, leaping from his chair and turning to Jenny full of hostility.

Jenny was stumped. She had never seen this reaction from Derek before. Derek was the cool, calm guy who had all the answers. Not the one who got annoyed with her for asking the important questions.

"Derek, come on. Don't lose your cool now."

"Don't lose my cool?" Derek repeated in angered astonishment. "That's two dead. The next recruit is…"

His sentence lingered off into the air.

He was tired of speaking. Tired of hypothesising. Tired of fighting.

"We don't stand a chance," he grumbled, immediately regretting it, and hoping Jenny hadn't heard him.

"Come on, we just need to figure out who's next to be targeted and save them from getting killed. Right?"

"How are we meant to figure–"

He froze mid-sentence.

"The list," he whispered in rapid realisation. "The list!"

"What about the list?" Jenny asked, not following Derek's trail of thought.

"The list Stella sent me, it was in order of who was the most powerful and most important for us to recruit first," Derek pointed out.

"Yeah?"

"Stella was first on that list," Derek declared. "Jamile Arshad was second."

"So you think they're being killed in order?

"Well, of course. It makes sense. The heir would kill them in the order of the biggest threat, wouldn't he?"

Jenny flinched at the mention of Eddie as the 'heir,' then quickly shook herself out of it.

"Right," she acknowledged. "So we find out who's next on the list, then we let them know or protect them or something."

"But that's the thing. How on earth are we meant to protect them?"

"What do you mean?"

"Surely, if we go to protect them, we'll put ourselves in the firing line and we'll be dead, too. We won't stand a chance."

Jenny nodded. Derek was right. They were helpless.

"Well, look," she suggested, "let's just find out who is next, then we'll figure out what to do from there."

She realised she was making the plan, not Derek. It made

her feel unexpectedly uncomfortable, her having to be the one to encourage him.

He rifled through papers on his desk, pushing various notes and scribbles aside until he eventually withdrew the list.

He stared at the piece of paper.

He read the next name on the list.

He couldn't move.

He grasped the note, his hands tightening it into a screwed-up ball. Mortified.

"Who is it?

Derek didn't answer.

"Come on, who is it?"

Derek's eyes closed and his head bowed. His reluctance, his frustration, his hindering pessimism; every bit of it spread across his face.

"Derek?"

Derek lifted his head, looked to Jenny, then looked back to the list.

"Who is it?"

"It's – it's Father Douglas."

CHAPTER TWENTY-ONE

The church was serenely quiet at night, just how Father Douglas loved it. It was his home, his sanctuary. He treasured it like a child.

It was where he fed his congregation, where he homed those on a pilgrimage to the birthplace of Christ, and it was where he trained humanity's hope in harnessing his gift.

As Douglas blew out the final few candles at the chancel, allowing the stone walls to be illuminated by a few fading lights, he cast his eyes upon the lonely boy who sat on the front row.

That was the only way he could truly describe Martin. Yes, he had degraded him and attacked his character, but that was to give him the fuel to become what he was now becoming. In truth, Martin was clearly lonely, and in need of someone to care for him.

Douglas could care for him, but only as he did God's other children.

Martin did not belong to him.

Martin did not belong to anyone, not even his real parents.

They were not the ones who created him.

Douglas leisurely strolled up the nave, passing the aisle between the pews until he finally stood behind Martin. They both cast their eyes upon the large cross standing prominently before them.

"It's funny," Martin spoke. "I don't even believe in God."

"Really? After all you have done? Are you not astonished enough to believe in God's power?"

"I know what I've done is awesome and all that. But it could be given to me by anything." Martin looked over his shoulder at Douglas. "Not necessarily God. I see no evidence for that."

Martin stood and zipped up his jacket. Churches were cold places, and this was no exception. Douglas, however, was used to it. He embraced it. It meant he was home.

"I think I'm going to go to bed," Martin revealed.

"Well, son. I hope that if there is one thing you do choose to believe in, that it is yourself." Douglas placed a reassuring hand on Martin's shoulder. "Because you have truly proven that power."

Martin smiled, gushing slightly.

"Thank you, Father Douglas. For everything."

"Don't thank me. Just do your duty, and I will do mine."

"I will."

With a final smile, Martin walked to the stone spiral, staircase that led to his room.

Douglas remained in the same position, watching the space from which Martin had departed, lingering in the same spot.

An odd feeling of resolution overcame him. He could feel the end coming closer.

It was nearly time.

Soon, Martin would truly be alone.

Douglas broke out of his vacant stare with a rapid shake

of his head. With a knowing smile, he took a few small steps toward the altar, blessing the water; ensuring Martin had a weapon if he needed it.

Douglas finally took his position in front of the cross, looking up at the representation of his faith that had always given him comfort.

He empathised with what Martin had said. He had spent his whole life teaching God's word. He had dedicated all his preaching to teaching the lessons of the Bible.

But there was still so much he was yet to understand.

There were so many dark parts of the Bible, so many words of hate and prejudice that people could use to justify awful actions. Throughout history, the Bible had given ammunition to people to torture and burn atheists. In the Crusades, they spitefully took on other religions in the name of Christianity.

The Bible preached love, but it also preached lessons that had grown outdated.

But he believed in his mission.

His fate.

After all, it was unmistakably his fate to be at this church, in time to meet Martin, to bestow the tools needed to access the part of Martin that the boy didn't even know he had.

Douglas knelt before the cross.

Bowing his head, he kissed his hand, and made the sign of the cross over his chest.

Whatever sceptical thoughts he had grown in his old age, he believed in heaven. The power of good. And, to him, this symbol he knelt before was the power of everything he preached, everything he did. It represented those life teachings he was given.

"It's ironic, really," Douglas spoke doggedly, "that you choose to do this in a church. Your power has become such that not even the house of the Lord will repel you from carrying out the devil's wishes."

A deep, sinister chuckle echoed lightly down the aisle of the cold, stone chairs. A human chuckle, coated in terror.

Faint footsteps echoed closer.

Douglas did not turn around.

He knew what was coming.

He had felt it.

He had no choice.

Once more, Douglas raised his head, gazing toward the tip of the cross, up to the heavens.

I will be there soon.

"Hello, Father Douglas," spoke Edward King.

CHAPTER TWENTY-TWO

"Oh Douglas, you fat fool," sang the sickening voice, a human sound mixed with tones of devastating malevolence. Its tone still retained the character of its owner, but its pitch had morphed into an unnatural boom. "Is it you?"

Douglas bowed his head, taking to his knee, making a cross upon his body.

In a sudden instant, his body was flung from the floor, soaring across the dusty air of the church. Within seconds he was hovering before his feared opponent, poised statically in the air, unable to shift a single muscle of his paralysed body.

He stared into the eyes of the heir of hell.

He recognised the face. It still had the features of the legendary exorcist. Eddie King, the man who removed Balam from a young girl. The man who banished Lamashtu from his body. The man who fought the devil in hell and escaped.

But the face was not that of a man anymore. Its eyes had turned to a fully dilated red. The hair had grown to a thickened black, his teeth full of sharp spikes and fangs, his pale, faded skin scarred with the grey streaks caused when human skin morphs into that of a demon.

His arms ended with thin wrists, protruding into vile paws feeding long, twisted claws sharp enough to slit a throat with a faint scrape. His body, covered with a sharp, black suit – for decoration only, Douglas was sure – had spouted muscles in places muscles had never been. Its feet protruded from his ankles with the sinister tap of hooves.

Yes, it bore a resemblance to Edward King. But this thing was nothing of that person Douglas had thanked God for not so long ago.

What struck Douglas with even more fright than the sickening appearance, was the mere feeling of being in the presence of this thing. It reeked of hatred, with powerful, malicious sin swelling from its pores.

"But you are a good man..." Douglas pleaded, helplessly hovering, attempting to appeal to the human part that was no longer there.

"A man?" the contorted face of Eddie replied. "Do not insult me. Man?"

He shook his head with a venomous shake, exuding wrath with its disgust.

"Man will be our slaves. What I am is so much more."

"The heir of hell? Is that what you're calling yourself?"

Eddie's twisted paw rose and Douglas flew through the air, pounding against the metallic cross standing prominently against the chancel. His spine cracked, and he felt his legs fall loosely from his bones. He howled in pain, knowing it did nothing, then curtailed his voice.

He must not let Martin know what was happening.

Martin was the man the heir of hell was after.

Douglas needed to do all he could to die quietly, fearing Martin might show himself at the sounds of distress.

Eddie flew across the air with spiteful sophistication until he was only inches from the pained expression swept across Douglas' visage.

"Tell me who he is!" Eddie's face demanded.

"I don't know what you are talking about."

Eddie's hand clasped into his fist, prompting numerous cracks to reverberate from Douglas' feeble body. Douglas could feel the various knuckles and toes of his body snap and shatter into pieces.

He stifled his screams, bit his lip, grinded his teeth, did everything he could to stop the yelps escaping his quivering jaw.

"We know heaven conceived another child. We know he is hidden."

"There is no child..."

"Liar!" The scream came out in various screeched, deafening pitches, pounding against the walls of the church and resounding back against them again and again.

The scream would have been heard for miles.

Martin would have heard it.

Please, just kill me before he gets here...

Eddie flung his arms open wide and Douglas' body responded with various stabbing pains shooting through his chest. Douglas knew something inside of him had exploded – something that would cause a slow, painful death.

His face scrunched into excruciating pain.

"Why are you trying not to make any sound?" Eddie mused. "What is it you are hiding?"

Footsteps pounded against the stone steps from the nearby spiral staircase.

Martin.

All at once, various punches of agony fired around Douglas' body. He lost the sight of his right eye, feeling a splattering of blood against his face, just as the bones in his arms shot into hundreds of pieces.

He couldn't take it anymore.

His weak voice screamed out into his beloved church.

"Go to hell!" Douglas bellowed.

The last thing Douglas saw as death overcame him was Martin's worried face appearing in the far doorway.

"So that's what you are hiding?"

"Father Douglas!" cried out Martin.

No. Martin, no!

This was not what Douglas wanted.

It was not Martin's time.

Now Martin would have to pit his inexperienced powers against the heir of hell.

Now Douglas would have to die before he even saw Martin lose.

Then, with one gigantic explosion of torture, his nervous system shattered.

He was to helplessly watch the final moments of his life fade away.

CHAPTER TWENTY-THREE

"*C*ome on, come on, you son of a bitch!" Derek barked at the phone.

He'd lost count of how many times he had punched the number in. He'd tried everywhere he could think of: the church's reception, the personal landline to Douglas, the tour guide booking line.

But at this late hour, it felt like a lost cause.

Everything feels like a lost cause lately.

He had to keep trying. It was all he could do.

He had to do something.

He couldn't just sit back and leave Father Douglas to die.

Nor could he leave Martin in danger.

The last thing they wanted was for the heir to discover they had been training Martin, or discover who Martin was – or, even worse, discover what Martin may be able to do.

Martin was the world's last hope.

He was the only hope.

This couldn't happen. They couldn't lose him.

They couldn't reveal him, not until Martin was ready.

The repetitive ring of the dial tone gave further indication that there was nothing Derek could do.

Maybe it was too late.

Maybe Douglas was already dead.

He slammed the phone down and lifted it back up, pressing it against his ear and punching in the number once more.

And he listened.

Listened again to the infuriating dial tone.

That sound was torture. A relentless reminder that there was no hope. Douglas and Martin were on the other side of the world, and Derek could do nothing about it.

Jenny wearily approached the study. Derek looked to her with distant hope.

"Any luck?" he weakly asked. He was tired, stressed, and fatigue was setting in.

"I've booked us flights for the morning. We leave at nine fifteen, then we'll get there four fifteen in the afternoon, their time."

"What's the time difference?" Derek demanded, not meaning to come across as impatient as he sounded.

"They are two hours ahead, so quarter past two our time."

Derek let out an enraged breath of frustration. He leant back, defeated, slamming the phone back down for what felt like the thousandth time.

Israel was over twelve hours away. Anything that was going to happen was likely happening now.

If it hadn't happened already.

It could well have been yesterday. Or the day before.

For all they knew, Douglas and Martin's dead bodies could be laying on top of each other unnoticed in the back room of the church.

"Any luck on the phone?" Jenny asked, sitting in the vacant chair next to Derek, leaning toward him.

"No." Derek shook his head.

"So what do we do?"

Derek shrugged. "Pray, I guess."

He bowed his head, closing his eyes. Attempting to find some kind of positive comfort in this hellish situation.

"Derek, I've never seen you like this," Jenny admitted.

"Yeah, well," Derek snapped, "it's not easy always knowing the answers. Sometimes you run out; but the questions just keep coming."

"You know you've done your best, right?" Jenny assured him. "With Eddie, with me, with this fight. You shouldn't feel bad about anything; you've done what you can."

Derek forced a grateful smile but his eyes said otherwise.

"It doesn't change the truth that I've failed. The heir will find Douglas, and Martin with him, and will discover what he's done and kill him."

"Maybe we should have a bit more faith in Martin," Jenny suggested. "Maybe he's made more progress than we know."

"Maybe," Derek nodded.

Maybe Martin had made great progress, and they were underestimating him. Maybe he was full of uncontestably commanding power. Maybe he was surging with the good he needed to defeat Eddie.

Martin was, after all, a far more headstrong young man than he had ever been given credit for.

And he had the sight in him.

Just like Eddie had.

Derek told himself that there was hope, that Martin could do it. Or, he could be sensible enough to not get involved, to not battle the heir, to not let his emotions get the better of him. He'd see Eddie fighting Douglas, and he would bury any loyalty he had toward his mentor away and remain uninvolved.

The heir could have such a direct, tunnel vision of hate

that it bypasses Martin and gets Douglas without any acknowledgement of Martin's existence.

It could all work out well.

Douglas could even be saved.

The heir could be wounded.

Yeah, Derek thought. *This could all be far better than I am imagining.*

Martin will win.

There was only one thing plaguing his mind.

His gut told him otherwise.

CHAPTER TWENTY-FOUR

*T*he repetitive sound of a distant phone ringing finally ceased.

Martin focussed on everything else.

On the sight, the sound, the smell, the feel.

But all he could feel was terror.

All he could smell was death.

The distorted face of a man he had once met, the man who had vowed to save his mother from an inevitable death, gazed back at him with a vague satisfaction.

Then that face was gone. Twisted into a spiral of dark, menacing shapes.

With a cry of sheer pain, the body of Edward King contorted, twisted, shifted, morphed, and turned. The clothes were ripped and shredded as its body loomed larger. Once it was almost the size of the church, its features finally appeared. A claw at least three times the size of Martin, a hairy torso subtly alight with the small flames of hell, and hooves in the place of feet, mounting sharp instruments of death in the place of its toes.

What had been the body of Edward King was no more. It

was now a large, powerful, indistinguishable hell beast, set on destroying anything in its path.

All Martin could hear breathing around the church were the croaked, sadistic growls of the heir of hell.

All he could see was a demonic creature so large and consumed with hate that it could wipe out anyone in its path with a simple glance or swipe of the claw.

But Martin had to avoid focussing on that.

He had to, if he was to stand any chance of surviving.

Father Douglas' eyes turned to Martin, widening at the sight of his mentee standing stumped in the doorway.

Douglas had not been afraid before. He had welcomed death like an old friend, happy to be on his way to heaven.

But now he knew that, following his death, it would likely be Martin's, too.

Then all would be lost and his death would be in vain.

"Run," whispered Douglas.

Martin squinted, unable to hear him.

"Run!" Douglas shouted, his eyes full of desperate pleading.

Martin shook his head.

Martin no longer ran from his problems.

Foolish boy.

Does he not realise everything rests on him?

The beast turned from Douglas, who remained stationary in front of the cross he had given his final prayers to. His body was paralysed, but his mind was moving a million miles an hour; darting through various frantic thoughts of what he could do to protect his apprentice.

Martin couldn't help but be intimidated. The beast was terrifying. Its carnivorous dominance was more than Martin could fully comprehend. Its strength was such that it knocked out the solid stone of the pillars of the church, just by the simple act of barging forward. Its eyes were deadly, its claws were sharp, and its teeth were curved into razors.

It took a simple step forward for the beast to be towering over Martin.

"Martin…" Douglas pleaded from behind the beast, in a whispered shout. "Do not reveal your powers! Do not let him know who you are!"

Martin wasn't sure why Douglas was suggesting such a thing.

As much as this power-demon made him shake, he would not stand down. Despite his quivering knees, his thrashing heart, and his pounding blood, this was what he had trained for.

Finally, his life could mean something.

He did not fear death.

The creature boomed a deep, sickening laugh; the first thing it had done that had given it a remotely human quality.

Martin put one foot forward and curled his arms in a circular motion.

Conjuring fire would do the trick.

Realising what Martin was preparing to do, Douglas willed himself to wave his arms in a hysterical indication to stop.

The main advantage they had at the moment was that Martin was secret.

Even if Martin survived this, if he revealed who he was…

The demon had come there for Douglas.

He needed to make sure that's where it ended.

He closed his eyes. Concentrated. Lifted a hand up.

With a weak tense of his muscles, he managed it.

He reached his hand in the altar and withdrew a fistful of holy water. He threw his arm feebly forward, spraying a line of liquid over a small patch of the beast's feet.

The beast roared, shooting around, focussing its attention on Douglas.

"Yes, that's it," Douglas confirmed. "Look at me."

Its feet tinged with a slight hiss, a small puff of smoke rising from them, and the beast quickly withdrew its foot.

Martin started marching forward, but Douglas flinched his hand, indicating for Martin to stay where he was.

He could sense Martin's hesitance. He could feel Martin's wish to jump forward and protect Douglas, to ensure his mentor didn't die.

"Please, Martin, don't," he muttered, reaching out to Martin with his weakened stare. "Just let me lead him."

A large gloop of salvia dropped out the beast's mouth and landed in a puddle before Douglas' feet, encasing them in red.

Douglas dragged his arms forward, pulling himself along the hard, stone surface toward the door, opening it, dragging himself into the yard.

The creature merely walked into the wall, smashing it to a wreckage beside his feet. The solid structure that had remained so unbeatable for thousands of years, destroyed in a mere moment.

Douglas reached the centre of the courtyard and stopped.

He could see Martin in the distance, looking confused. Looking lost, hopeless, wanting to intervene, torn as to why he couldn't.

Douglas closed his eyes.

"Dear Lord, please save my soul," Douglas whispered.

The beast's contorted, expressionless mouth manifested into a cocky grin. Its muscular, enormous torso, ravaged with bloody hair, loomed sinisterly over its prey.

"Even though I walk through the valley of the shadow of death, I will fear no evil."

From the distant path into the church, Martin crept forward, raising his hands in preparation to attack.

Douglas vehemently shook his head, willing Martin to stay back.

"For you are with me."

Douglas imagined himself kissing his hand and making a cross on his chest.

"Your rod and your staff, they comfort me."

He smiled.

"You prepare a table for me in the presence of thy enemies, you anoint my head with oil, my cup overflows."

Douglas lifted his head up to the demon, staring into the eyes of masochistic abyss.

"Surely goodness of mercy /shall follow me all the days of my life, and I shall dwell in the house of the Lord forever."

Douglas' eyes narrowed.

"Give me your best, you piece of shit."

The demon swiped its claw across Douglas' neck. His head flew across the wind, and splattered against the far wall.

The last thing Douglas heard was Martin's scream.

"No!"

CHAPTER TWENTY-FIVE

*M*artin sprinted at a pace he never knew he had, his feet treading heavily against the stone floor, echoing around the hollow church. He leapt through the crumbling brick that had been the wall of the holy church and burst toward the beast.

As he manoeuvred his hands in circles, he scrutinised the beast's malevolent eyes. Such ferocity encapsulated in two circles of red. Martin had to do all he could not to be scared.

He threw his hands forward, exuding flames powered by pure anger.

The beast set alight.

But it did nothing.

It stood still, an ominous grin circling its fangs. The flames from Martin's spell flew off its coarse skin, rising into sparks of amber.

The beast relished the flames like a gift.

The heir rose its claws, turning Martin's fire into flickering flames of its own. The blazes travelled along its body and to its paws until it was nurturing two hectically organised fireballs, each twice the size of Martin.

Martin ran in the direction of Douglas' headless body, swallowing a mouthful of sick as he passed his mentor's remains.

Flames sprung from the heir's claws and thrashed against the steps, Martin narrowly escaping the blaze that brushed his heels. Douglas' body turned to black ash, and the rest of the courtyard became engulfed in a humungous, beating fire.

In a moment of quick thinking, Martin conjured a circle of wind and used it to propel him into the air, away from the flames licking his feet.

He landed upon a side of the church roof, nestling himself into a high window ledge.

The heir turned its snarling eyes to Martin, who glared back, taking cover. The heir leapt onto the side of the building, spearing its claws into the walls, dragging itself up. It only took three stretches of its arms to be within swiping distance of Martin.

Martin's legs seized, his knees thrashing against one another. The ground below him was small, too far away for a safe landing. Even if he could safely jump, the ground was manically ablaze.

The heir grew closer and swept its arm toward Martin. He narrowly ducked the deathly blow, and decided he had no choice.

Martin jumped to his peril, but aimed his hands for the side of the beast. He grappled hold of a large bone on its sharp spine, clinging on with everything he had. The heir retaliated by letting go of the building, falling into the pit of flames.

Martin had to think quickly. He twisted his arms around to form a ball of water, lunging the vast puddle below him so that, when he landed, it could act as protection from the flames. He flung his arms out to his side, spraying the water into every direction until he had reduced the fire to a few remaining flickers.

Before Martin had any time to get cocky at his successful landing, the beast swiped again toward him, catching the boy and sending him flailing against the far wall of the courtyard, onto which he landed face first, attempting to use his hand to support himself.

Martin dropped to the floor, groaning in pain. His ribs were consequently in agony, and the fingers on his right hand couldn't move properly.

It hurt. But an injury was nothing compared to the death he would face if he did not stop fighting.

The beast marched toward him, reaching out its arms and exhibiting its intimidating claws.

Martin twisted beneath the heir's legs and ran back inside the church. Pushed forward by a gust of wind from a swipe of the heir's claws, Martin shook at the chaotic sound of plummeting stone. The dust from the rubble turned to a mist in the air, forcing Martin into a coughing fit.

He dove behind the altar, scrunching himself into a tiny ball, hoping he would be too small to be found.

That's when he saw it.

A few yards across from him.

A trapdoor. Some kind of secret passage behind the chancel, beside the sacristy.

If he could only get to it unnoticed.

The wary snarls echoed behind him. The tapping of elongated nails and the thudding of the hooves made it clear the beast was searching Martin out.

Martin could feel it sniffing. The air of its vast nostrils fanned the back of his neck

Surely it would sense him.

This was the heir of hell.

The heir of hell.

He shook his head.

I was a fucking idiot to think I could take on the heir of hell.

No time to think of that now.

Come on, Martin.

Need to get to the trapdoor.

Douglas. He's dead... He's dead...

Grieve later. Run now.

Douglas...

He peered around the altar, watching the beast twisting its head. Its deep breathing filled the church walls with a cold, echoing gust.

A sudden stabbing pain fired through Martin's chest.

He grabbed his wrist with his usable hand. Something was hurting. He was in pain. Too much to bear.

He couldn't fight.

He needed to get to that trapdoor.

He peered around the other side of the altar, glancing at the rear of the resting creature. He lifted his hand out, pointing at the far pew.

If I could just cause a distraction...

He focussed his mind.

Listened.

The breathing of the beast brushed against the walls of the church. But once Martin focussed, it wasn't the only sound he could hear.

The distant laughter of children. The faint breeze travelling through the air. The cold against his teeth, the dust in his lungs, the ash in his hands.

The pew flew across the church, smashing against the far wall, giving Martin a momentary distraction that might just give him the respite he needed.

The creature shot its head in the direction of the sound.

Martin flung himself forward, peeling toward the grate and diving into the pit.

He landed flat out on his back, the hard stone floor slamming against his bones, and he had to stifle a pained moan.

This was what he was up against?

This was the thing he was supposed to beat?

Are they fricking kidding?

He pushed himself against the far wall, ensuring he was out of view if the heir chose to look through the trapdoor. The only light came from the above grate, meaning he could consume himself in darkness against the shadow of the wall.

He stayed there until he heard nothing.

Until the small amount of light faded.

Eventually, the deep breathing left. The dark, sinister presence faded from his bones.

He could feel it. He was alone.

In too much pain to stand.

His hand deformed, his back in agony, his ribs in furious, torturous pain.

Closing his eyes, he tried to concentrate on something else.

Focussing on quietening his mind, like Douglas had taught him.

Douglas.

Oh God, Douglas.

Blood seeped through his fingers.

Eventually, he passed out.

Dear Martin,

Hope you are feeling better than you described in your last letter. I was disappointed to find that your relationship with Father Douglas was growing strained, but it may just be a matter of crossed wires.

Douglas is a brilliant man. He has done amazing things for the field of the paranormal, training many an exorcist and many a psychic.

He is the kind of man who can take someone with erratic powers and help them harness it.

Unfortunately, I have never had the pleasure of meeting him in person, but hopefully I will be able to soon. I have still corresponded with him over the years, seeking advice when I have needed it.

He has always known the right thing to say.

Even though what he has had to say may not have been a pleasant thing for me to listen to.

Whatever he is telling you, saying, making you do – it will be for a reason. This is a man who thinks carefully through the purpose of everything he does.

Listen to him.

Learn from him.

In time, he will grow to respect you and you will grow to respect him.

Hopefully, by the time this letter reaches you, your relationship will have grown and you will find him to be as good a mentor and as good a teacher as you could hope him to be.

Sending you good thoughts on this journey.

All the very best,

Derek

CHAPTER TWENTY-SIX

*A*sh consumed the air like a poisonous gas. Vacant onlookers gathered at the church's lower steps; the commotion, the thrashing, and the flames had attracted quite the attention.

Martin didn't care. They could stare all they wanted.

They'll all be dead soon, anyway.

As he lifted his t-shirt over his nose and mouth, shielding his lungs from the wet smoke hovering in the atmosphere, Martin peered through the grate of the trapdoor. He lifted it up, climbed out of the pit, and lunged himself onto the stone floor; an action that left him seething in pain. He lifted his top up and flinched at the sight of a large, dark-grey bruise spread along the right side of his ribs. He tried touching the wound with his hand and recoiled with pain.

There was a deafening ringing in his ears he couldn't escape. His brain pounded against his skull, and a lump on his forehead throbbed at every pulse.

His nose flinched and his skin felt tight, dried blood cementing it in place. His jaw hurt to move, his back ached, and shooting stabs of pain fired up and down his leg.

Once more, he dragged himself to his feet, using the altar as leverage. A whimper escaped his lips. His muscles wobbled, convulsing with throbs of anguish.

Come on you fucker. If you can conjure a fireball, you can withstand a bit of pain.

In truth, it was far more than just a bit of pain.

But the one thing he had learnt at school, the one lesson he paid attention to in GCSE Psychology – was that the words you use affect your mind-set and influence your unconscious. Perhaps, if he played down how much agony he was in, it wouldn't hurt so much.

Well, whoever had come up with that stupid theory was wrong.

It still hurt.

Taking longer than he wished, but going as fast as he could, he dragged himself into the debris of the courtyard.

The sunny blue sky had vanished. Grey clouds lingered overhead and drips of rain fell, sinking through cracks in the ground.

A few steps and his muscles gave way again, forcing him to collapse into a heap.

The courtyard looked like it had been launched into a ball of fire, then drenched with a rapid tsunami.

Wet ash stuck to the stone surfaces. Black, burnt scars stuck to the ancient, cracked walls with stubborn displeasure. Part of the wall had been smashed to a dusty rubble of rock. A pile of stones collected upon the ground beneath the side of the wall the beast had launched itself upon.

There was no sign of Father Douglas' body.

Of course, there wouldn't be. He had been burnt to pieces.

The ash that hovered in the wind, dancing around in black flakes, consuming the air with the lingering destruction of the fire – that was Douglas. That was all that remained of him.

That was, until Martin looked behind him. Something was rammed into a burnt-out hole in the wall of the church.

Something shaped like a head.

But the face had been reduced to grey, tinged flesh. The parts of the visage that had not so long ago been prominent features of an old priest's face were now charred peelings of faded skin and skull.

A circle of hair surrounded Douglas' bald spot, stubbornly clinging to blackened skin. Occasional red marks interrupted the black-and-grey scar tissue that had formed around the skull.

An unrecognisable mess remained in place of a face.

The man who'd taught Martin to calm his mind, to conjure the elements. The man who had found a way to access the troubled mind of a manically conflicted teenage boy. The man who had such a profound influence that Martin had actually begun to believe in himself, believe that he was something, that he could actually make a difference in this stupid, ridiculous war.

This was all that remained.

None of the warm, wise heart that Martin had only just gotten to know. None of the knowing eyes or proud smile. Just a distorted chunk of charred flesh.

Martin collapsed into a heap on the floor, curling up into a ball, and bawled like a child.

It was fine. No one was around to see it.

If his mates back at school saw him now, they would laugh. Laugh at his pathetic tears.

But they weren't his mates.

They had never been his mates.

He had no mates, no family, nothing.

And the only man who had begun to change this had played his part and was gone.

Martin launched an angry fist into the stones, smashing his knuckles and peeling back dead skin. It hurt, but he didn't care. The pain helped.

He punched again, relishing the beautiful agony.

He lifted his head to the heavens and screamed.

Why do you sit by and watch us wage this war for you?

Martin collapsed onto his back, staring up at the darkened sky that dripped solemn raindrops upon his suffering face. The rain grew faster and, before Martin knew it, he was pummelled with a bombardment of bullet drops of water.

It pounded his face.

But he liked it.

His mother had always loved the rain.

He had always loved the rain.

As he allowed his mind to wander, his thoughts led to the image of the ghastly beast he had fought.

"Fucking hell…" he muttered.

That used to be Edward King.

That used to be a man.

A great man.

That was what he was meant to be training to fight?

That's what the world was sending him up against?

Tears flooded once more, mixing with the rain water into nothing.

He was the frontrunner for a war that could never be won.

"We know that we are from God, and the whole world lies in the power of the evil one."

1 John 5:19

CHAPTER TWENTY-SEVEN

ctober 8, 1989

TEN YEARS, three months before millennium night

NO MORE BEING BATTERED or bruised. No more listening to the echoes of dismay beating through the bedroom walls. No more inexplicable marks prompting faked concerned looks from teachers.

Today was a new start.

Everything Eddie owned was in a sports bag. A few clothes, a book, and a picture of Cassy.

That was it. Sixteen years on this earth and these were his accumulated possessions.

Jenny's warm smile greeted him as he crossed the threshold into her parents' house. Her happiness to see him move in helped slightly to ease his nerves.

But only slightly.

His stomach still churned, twisting into knots, uncomfortably tingling.

"Hey." Jenny put her arms around Eddie and hugged him. "So glad you're here."

"Eddie!"

Before Eddie could say another word, Jenny's mum appeared behind her and engulfed him in a large, affectionate hug.

"We are so glad you are here," she greeted.

Jenny's dad appeared in the far doorway, nodding a welcoming nod at Eddie, who returned the gesture.

"Thank you so much for letting me stay here," Eddie gratefully spoke.

"Oh, speak nothing of it." Jenny's mum waved her arms in defiant dismissal. "I have watched you grow since you were a little boy, and become such good friends with Jenny, it's already like you're my own."

"Still," Eddie offered. "They'd have put me in a foster home otherwise. God knows where I'd have ended up. It's really nice of you."

"Come here, you silly pudding." Jenny's mum embraced him once more.

"I'll show you to where you're staying," Jenny suggested.

Jenny's mum finally let Eddie go. She placed a strong hand on his shoulder and nodded in silent understanding.

Jenny led Eddie up the stairs into what used to be the guest bedroom. The bed was perfectly made, the duvet tucked in at the sides and fancy, thick, floral pillows perched against the headboard. The wardrobe smelled like fresh wood cleaner, the carpet immaculate, and the curtains a comforting shade of blue.

It was a small room, but it was far more than he'd become accustomed to.

There was no stench of booze, no arguing parents on the

other side of the wall, no bedsheets left unwashed for months by parents too busy wallowing in their own self-pity.

The room was a dream. A hint of lavender in the air from the various scented cleaning products, smoothed-down bedsheets, and an empty wardrobe for his things.

It was more than he felt he deserved.

"So, what was it like?" Jenny asked, sitting on the bed and staring up at Eddie. "Watching them go, I mean?"

Eddie dumped his bag and lay beside Jenny, gazing at the ceiling. Even the light had a clean, pretty lampshade around it, with some kind of flower pattern. He'd spent more than enough time watching a weakly flickering light, often choosing the dark instead.

"I don't know," Eddie shrugged.

Jenny turned to him, draping her arm over his body, loosely cuddling in that way they always did.

"You've got to feel something over it. It's not something many teenagers go through."

"I guess." Eddie sighed. "I don't deserve this."

"Deserve what?"

"Deserve this house, this room, your parents being so nice, being able to stay here."

"You give me one good reason why you don't deserve it."

Eddie went to speak, but ended up spewing vacant sounds. It was a tough question.

I've just gotten used to far less, I suppose.

"Look, Eddie," Jenny began. "Your parents were lovely parents before, you know, what happened. But now… sorry to speak so badly of them, but they are scum."

"That's unfair. They've had a lot to deal with."

"Yes, but so have *you*. Who was there for you?"

Eddie turned his head toward Jenny and beamed.

"You were."

Jenny blushed, rolled her eyes, and sat up.

"You still haven't answered my question," Jenny observed.

"What question?"

"What was it like to see your dad led away? In a police car?"

Eddie sat up, contemplating what to say. He stood and meandered to the window, gazing at the garden below. The grass was cut, the trees were trimmed, the flowers were pretty. There was even a bench in the corner.

"I was kind of numb to it, I guess," Eddie admitted. "It was more the cheers and the jeers from the neighbours and all that, you know? Because they will forever judge me on what my dad's done."

He bowed his head. Stifled his tears. Willed himself to be a man.

"Well, you're not going to have any nasty neighbours here, I can promise you that," Jenny offered, a chirpy bounce in her voice. "Though I can't promise I won't jeer you," she joked.

Eddie turned, leant against the windowsill, and studied his best friend.

After everything; all the shit, all the grief, all the torn feelings, the fights, the tears, her sexuality, his self-defence mechanisms, their days together, the nights he'd crept in to her room.

After every single piece of grief they had faced, nothing had changed.

"Thank you, Jenny," Eddie acknowledged.

Jenny smiled back. It was all he needed.

CHAPTER TWENTY-EIGHT

eb 3, 2003

THREE YEARS, two months since millennium night

BIRDS SANG in the early hours of the morning as Jenny burst through the front door.

Thoughts of Martin plagued her. They still couldn't reach him, and had no idea whether he was safe.

Had Eddie – sorry, the heir – gotten to Father Douglas first?

Had Martin seen it?

Had the heir found him?

Most pertinently, the biggest conundrum she faced, the most perplexing thought:

How am I going to save Eddie if he keeps killing?

How am I going to bring him back once he is too far gone?

She knew what Derek's answer to that would be.

"He's not Eddie anymore. He's past saving. He is something else."

Well, screw him.

She would not give up on Eddie, even though everyone else had.

She would not give in to these despondent feelings of lost hope. She had far more faith in Eddie than that.

If only she could get to him.

See him in the flesh. She could talk to him. Once she had preached to his better side, reminded him of who he once was, who he still must be deep down; maybe, just maybe, she would manage to bring him back.

Derek hadn't known Eddie for anywhere as near as long as Jenny had.

He didn't know.

She had memories of him. Memories of him at his weakest. She had seen what he had overcome, seen what he had managed.

However he now looked, it would not make a damn bit of difference.

She would bring Eddie back.

But she had to find him first.

She sprang into the living room, not bothering with the light. She grabbed her gym bag from the corner of the room; a bag she had not used for quite a while now, having had numerous other things on her mind other than exercising.

She tipped the bag's contents onto the floor.

"Hi," came a feeble voice from behind her.

Like a shot she sprang around, only to see the soft outline of her girlfriend on the sofa.

Jenny switched the light on and stared at Lacy in astonished confusion.

Lacy sat with her arms folded, her legs crossed and a

deadened, narrow-eyed expression. Bags sat under her eyes with uncomfortable prominence.

"Lacy –" Jenny gasped.

"It's quarter past four in the morning," Lacy pointed out. She did not shout, speak accusingly, or act out of control; her voice was calm and measured, but full of sinister fury.

This was worse than if Lacy was shouting.

This was Lacy upset in a way Jenny had never seen before.

"I'm so sorry," Jenny pleaded.

"I haven't heard from you since this afternoon. I had tea ready at eight, but it went cold. I was one minute away from calling the police."

Jenny bowed her head and closed her eyes in shame. She had screwed up, she knew it.

Then again, she had good reason.

"I'm sorry, Lace." Jenny lifted her head and approached her partner. "I'm sorry, but we had a real big issue. Someone was killed, and it might be someone who had Martin with him, which means–"

"Enough!" Lacy screamed, and turned her face away.

Lacy was the cool and collected one. She was the voice of reason, the one who kept Jenny calm; the one who pointed out why Jenny was being irrational.

She had never been angry like this before.

It smashed Jenny's heart into pieces.

"Lacy, honestly." Jenny crouched down in front of Lacy. "I would not have screwed up like this if it wasn't really, really important."

Lacy's eyes shook, growing red and wet.

"I was really important, once."

Jenny bowed her head once more. Desperately exhaled. Tried to cling onto that piece of her that belonged to Lacy, that piece of her no one else could ever touch. Tried to find a way to show that piece to Lacy.

"Look, Lacy, there's a lot at stake here," Jenny cautiously asserted. "I should have let you know."

Lacy huffed.

"Let's just go to bed," she decided, "and we'll deal with this in the morning."

Lacy stood up and made her way toward the door, but froze once she heard Jenny's next two words.

"I can't."

Lacy poised at the door. Hostility etched over her face, her fists clenching, her muscles tensing.

"What?"

"I know this is just going to make things worse, but... I have to go to Israel."

"*Israel?*"

Jenny looked around the room, frantically trying to think of the words to say. She needed to leave quickly if they were going to get to London in time to get their plane. She didn't have time to stay here and explain everything, to go into the detail needed to justify herself to Lacy.

But Lacy deserved that.

And Jenny didn't want to make things any worse.

"When I get back, maybe we can talk about this. There are real reasons I have to go, reasons I just don't have the time to go into right now."

"Of course, you don't have the time for me."

"Lacy, please, the whole world is at stake. I need you to understand."

Lacy peered back into the eyes of the one she loved. Almost half her life had been spent with this woman. So much love shared, so many memories created, so many warm evenings spent cuddling and making love.

She tried to show that, but couldn't.

Lacy saw Jenny waiting for a response, waiting for reassurance that it would all be okay, that Jenny could explain herself when she got back and that would be fine.

But Lacy couldn't give her that.

So she said nothing.

She turned and walked away, trudging up the stairs and into bed, where she lay awake for the rest of the night.

Jenny packed her bag and, within minutes, was gone.

CHAPTER TWENTY-NINE

*T*he Vatican had already covered the whole thing up.

Various builders, repairmen, and people who do God-knows-what flooded into the building. A sign was lodged onto the entrance to the Church of Nativity, saying that it would be temporarily closed due to a few health and safety issues and repairs.

Martin scoffed. Health and safety issues?

It had been a little more than a few health and safety issues.

Martin watched as the hurried operation quickly implemented a slick overhaul of the remains of the courtyard. Within hours, the sheer amount of people and their obvious impeccable training had managed to restore most of the church, and in complete incognito. Though people may had heard the noise and smelt some smoke the previous night, the sign on the entrance indicated that there had been a few issues and their feeble, happy minds would be content with that explanation.

The less they knew, the better.

Martin took a stroll away from the rubble and repairs. The grey skies had left and the sun had returned. Even though the locals were in jackets and coats, Martin was in shorts and a t-shirt. The temperature was cold to them; but to Martin, this was a warm winter. Far warmer than he would be used to back in England.

He walked for hours. Past tourists, locals, restaurants, beggars, religious nut-jobs – everyone he had come to be aware of living in this part of the world. Passing stone steps, cobbled streets, and various run-down businesses and homes, he somehow found himself crossing the main road beside a large hill and arriving at the coast.

There was no one else around. Just him and the sea.

A cool breeze flickered his t-shirt and he wished he'd brought a jacket.

Still, he could have been killed a few hours ago. Best be grateful for what he had.

Martin didn't need to turn around to realise he was no longer alone. He could feel the presence beside him.

Despite having been seeking solitude in his meandering to the sea, he was grateful for the company he found himself in. He had never felt more alone, and it was good to be able to know there was still one person following him and protecting him.

"I'm sorry," was the first thing Cassy said.

Martin absently nodded.

"For what? You didn't kill him."

"Yes, but we should have foreseen it. Father Douglas was such an obvious target, it was foolish for us to not have thought."

"Yes, but again, Cassy, you didn't kill him. Eddie did. He's the one to blame."

"That thing is no longer Eddie."

For the first time since he had felt her beside him, he turned and looked at her. She was as angelic as ever, beaming white light, elegance personified.

But, for the first time, he witnessed a spark of hesitance over her face.

Her brother was clearly her weakness.

He turned back to the sea and peered into the horizon, where the ocean melted into distant ocean.

"What am I going to do now?" Martin asked.

"Derek is on his way," Cassy informed him. "Derek is gathering an army, an army that you will undoubtedly lead."

Martin sniggered ironically. "I can't lead an army."

"Really, Martin? After everything you have accomplished, everything you have found that you can do, you continue to doubt yourself?"

"I just got my arse handed to me."

"Yes, but you survived. You fought and lived through a battle with the heir of hell. That's more than you can say for anyone else this creature has faced."

A sudden tinge of pain in his ribs reminded him of what the battle had cost him. True, he had survived. But he had come nowhere near winning.

The power of the thing… The evil that exuded from it…

They are asking too much.

"Why do you call him that?" Martin mused.

"Pardon?" replied Cassy, not quite understanding.

"Eddie. You either call him the heir of hell, or the creature. Why not Eddie? Is it because you can't bear to face what this thing is?"

"This thing is not Eddie."

"Yes it is!" Martin punched the air in frustration and spun around to face Cassy.

145

"You have done brilliant things, Martin, but you still have a lot to learn. Just make sure you're listening."

"I'm the one who's not listening?"

Martin stormed away from her, toward the sea. He halted when he realised he had nowhere to go. He shifted his weight from one leg to the other, his hands on his hips.

Cassy stayed where she was. Watching him. Studying him. Wishing she could tell him everything.

"Why me?" Martin turned around and gesticulated to emphasise his question. "That's what I keep wondering in all of this. Why me? What is so fricking special about me?"

Cassy peered into his deep, sorrowful eyes.

"I only wish I could tell you."

"I'm going to need better than that," Martin aggressively chuckled. "You want me to wage a war, risk my life, lead an army – you are going to need to give me more than a request to take a leap of faith."

"Sometimes you have to take a leap of faith."

"Oh yeah? And when was the last time *you* took a leap of faith, huh? When was the last time you risked it all for the sake of the world?"

"The day I appeared at your side and told you to kill my brother."

Martin didn't move. He remained conflictedly static, stumped to the spot.

Heaven had taken a leap of faith in him. They had bestowed so much into him, putting all their hope on his shoulders.

But he had never asked for it.

He never asked for a leap of faith.

All he ever asked for was a quiet life. With his ma, maybe even with his dad. A younger sister, maybe. A good job, a sweet woman, and a nice house.

Not this.

"I'd better go," he grunted.

With a final menacing glare in Cassy's direction he staggered forward, fists still clenched and muscles still tense.

He didn't need to turn around to know that Cassy had gone the moment he walked past her.

CHAPTER THIRTY

eb 4, 2003

DESPITE BEING RESTORED, the church felt empty. It was strange how just one other person had made the grand chambers feel so full and welcoming. Now Martin was on his own, without Father Douglas, the immaculate architecture just felt empty and dark.

He sat on the pew farthest away from the altar at the rear of the church, staring angrily at the cross standing prominently at the front of the church.

Martin had never believed in God. Or maybe it was that he did believe, but just thought God was a dick.

He silently snorted, amusing himself with his blasphemous cogitations.

Footsteps echoed from the entrance. Martin turned around to see Derek approaching, wearing a sympathetic smile. He was impeccably dressed, as always, and was accompanied by a woman he'd met a few times. He remembered her name was Jenny.

"Martin, my boy," Derek greeted him.

Martin wearily approached Derek, who grabbed hold of Martin's hand and shook it firmly.

"Are you okay?" Derek asked out of clear, genuine concern.

Martin shrugged. How was he meant to answer that question?

Jenny stepped forward and gently hugged Martin.

"I'm really pleased you're okay," Jenny softly observed.

"Thanks," Martin replied. He appreciated the concern, although he felt very far away from being 'okay.'

Martin guided Derek and Jenny into one of the smaller rooms of the church. Martin offered a coffee, but Derek insisted on making it, protesting that Martin needed to rest. Within ten minutes they were sat around the table, each of them with a coffee in front of them and a gentle breeze floating from the open window.

Martin didn't realise how much he had been sweating. The cool night breeze felt good against his warm face.

It was at this point he realised how long it had been since he'd had a shower.

"Well, I know this is only coffee, not necessarily the good stuff," Derek observed, raising his cup. "But I would still like to propose a toast." He beamed affectionately toward Martin. "To Martin. Who fought the heir and lived. And to Father Douglas, who was a great man."

Jenny echoed Derek's raising of the cup and sipped hers. Martin gave a gentle nod of acknowledgement.

"I'm so sorry about what you have had to endure," Derek preached. "It was an error on our part that we didn't foresee such an obvious attack."

"That's what Cassy said," Martin grunted, not sure what he intended to accomplish by pointing that out.

"You've seen her?" Jenny piped in, astounded.

"A few times. Now and then."

Jenny raised her eyebrows in bewilderment. "I grew up with her. I was there when she died, it's…" she petered off. She had no words.

"Right," Derek slammed his hands against the table and looked to Martin, then to Jenny, then back to Martin. "Excuse me for being forthright, but we have little time to lose. We need to get down to business. Decide our next move."

"Our next move?" Martin echoed.

"By now I'm sure you are aware that your role in this is to lead the army, to be the frontrunner in the war against hell."

"Yeah, about that –"

"Please, Martin, I know you will feel trepidation over such a task."

Martin frowned, wondering what *trepidation* meant.

"But please, don't fear," Derek continued. "I'm sure the whole prospect must be quite daunting. Just give it time. When the day comes, you will be ready. When the day comes, you will be the one guiding and reassuring me."

Martin gave a contented nod. No one had ever put it like that before. Everyone just went on about what was expected of him; no one had ever told him that it would take time, or that it doesn't matter if he doesn't yet feel ready.

"So what do we do until then?" Martin asked.

"Until then, my friend, we gather our army."

Derek withdrew a piece of paper and placed it on the table before them. On it were a list of fifty or so names – with the first three crossed out.

"This, Martin, is a list of the most powerful people in the field of the paranormal in the world. The heir has been working his way through them. It is now our task to collect the rest before it is too late."

"Won't it be difficult to convince them?" Martin mused.

"On the contrary; these people know what is coming. They are powerful; they will have felt it. All we need to do is recruit them."

Derek grinned.

"My friends," he gestured grandly, "it is time to gather our army."

CHAPTER THIRTY-ONE

eb 6, 2003

CALIFORNIA, United States of America

THE STUDIO AUDIENCE poised on the edge of their seats, peering at the remarkable woman on-stage, jaws dropped in astonishment.

"And so," Elisha Port continued, "your husband, Michael."

The bewildered woman beside Elisha covered her tear-stricken face with both hands, peering through her eyes at Elisha.

"He is well. He is in heaven, at peace," Elisha continued. "And he has one more thing he would like me to say to you."

Elisha's bracelets jangled as she reached out an arm and placed it on the woman's leg. Elisha's dreadlocks were tucked behind a bandana, her large body filling out a bulky multicoloured robe she had worn for every single television show she had performed over the last forty years.

This was the moment. This was the moment she waited for, the reason she did this job.

"Your husband wants me to say that he is okay. He also says, watch out for the jelly-fish, love, otherwise things could get awkward again."

The woman choked on her pleasurable grief. Her tears mixed with smiles, contently resolute, despairingly ecstatic with the news.

"Is that okay?" Elisha asked.

"Yes. Thank you. Thank you so much."

"You're very welcome. Please, if you'd like to take your seat."

The woman, bursting with sobs, blubbered her way back to her seat to appreciative claps.

Elisha took centre stage and addressed her audience.

"Thank you so much for joining me on this journey," she concluded. "Thank you, and good night."

With a nod, she left the stage to a deafening applause. People whooped, cheered; some gave a standing ovation.

She paused in the wings, sipping on a water bottle.

"Hello, Elisha," came a young man's voice. A teenage boy leant against the wall.

"Hello," Elisha replied.

"My name's Martin," said the boy. "You know what I'm here for?"

"I wouldn't be much of a psychic if I didn't. Please, let me get my bag and we can go."

Martin nodded. She returned with her luggage within five minutes, and together they left for the airport.

* * *

RICK WOOD

10 Feb 2003

Mumbai, India

Traffic poured past like a gushing water of misery, men on motorised bikes weaving in and out of impatient cars. The grey buildings stood in regimented lines beside the road. People scurried past, not looking at her leant against the wall, shivering beneath her blanket.

The streets were all Aisha Mustaaq had ever known. Fourteen and homeless. Discarded by her family for being an abomination.

All the things she'd had to do, she had done to survive.

Things she had never wanted to do.

Things she would never admit to herself.

Her body stiffened at the sight of a man hurriedly approaching her. As soon as he opened his mouth, his words came tumbling out, too quick for her to fully understand them. Aisha was hungry and tired, two things that delayed her senses, and her fragile state of mind struggled to take in the man's diatribe.

But it only took her a minute to realise what this pervert was after.

The man was grabbing at her, throwing away her blanket, his hands flailing over the parts of her body she had been taught to keep private.

No one around her did anything.

She begged him not to do it, tried telling him what would happen if he did, urgently pleading with him to listen.

"Please, I don't know how to control it!"

If anything, her resistance only spurred him on quicker.

As soon as his hand entered her, that's when it happened.

154

Why did it always have to happen?

The man's body launched backwards, soaring across the air, and lethally collided with an oncoming car.

The car sped away and she was left to weep over another body she had unwillingly taken.

"That's quite a gift you have there," came a British accent from behind her.

She spun around, her hands risen, ready for a fight. But this man was not like any other she had met. He was warmer. Kinder. With a smile, more genuine than anyone who had ever approached her. His attire was remarkable; a grey suit with waist coat and black tie, dressed in a smart, Western fashion.

Luckily, he appeared to be able to speak her language.

"My name is Derek," he told her. "I'm here to take you to Britain. To give you a home, to put your powers to good use."

"Leave me alone!" she shouted. "Or I'll end up hurting you!"

Derek shook his head.

"Try it," he stated matter-of-factly.

She flung her arms out toward him.

Nothing.

It didn't affect him.

He crouched beside her. "One of my friends, who used to be a very good man, helped me learn how to resist such things."

"You – you know how to control this?"

Derek confidently nodded.

"I do. Will you come with me, Aisha? Let me teach you?"

Finally.

This was her salvation.

* * *

12 Feb 2003

Nakhon Sawan, Thailand

Paradise Park was truly that – paradise. The morning sun paraded around the blue sky, coating the scene in unfathomable beauty.

This was good for Tee-Yong Sin.

Plenty of tourists. Plenty of money.

He wandered through the crowds, peering over all the faces of holiday-goers. Of happy families. Of hopeless idiots.

A woman, speaking some European language, possibly French, perched on the railings. She was obese, with a juicy bum crack sticking out from beneath her vest. She stuffed an overfilled sandwich into her mouth.

Her bag sat on the floor beside her, unguarded.

Tee-Yong grinned. With a flick of his hand, a wallet floated from the bag, into the air, and across the park, landing in his pocket.

He bit his lip and smirked. Too easy.

"You know," came a female voice from behind him. "Some people call that stealing."

Tee-Yong shot around. A Caucasian woman with a British accent stood behind him.

"Who are you?" Tee-Yong demanded.

"My name is Jenny. How would you like to put this power to good use, rather than nicking everybody's personal belongings?"

Jenny took the wallet out of his pocket and walked over to the fat lady, placing it back in her bag unnoticed.

"Do you mind?" retorted Tee-Yong with strong irritation. "I'm working here!"

Jenny looked him dead in the eye with a knowing grin.

"Not anymore you're not."

Tee-Yong raised an arm and pointed it at Jenny.

Nothing.

He tried again. Did all he could to enter her mind, but for some reason, he was blocked.

"What?" he exclaimed. "How can you…"

"How about you come join me for a coffee?" she proposed. "And I'll tell you about all the many people like you I've met – and how you can join them, actually do something good with this gift."

CHAPTER THIRTY-TWO

*a*n army. They were raising an army.

And he was to be part of it.

Cameron Goliath felt like a child in a sweet shop. So many opportunities, so many ways to go, decisions to make. This was his dream.

To use his gift to help the world.

To this day, it had been a tragic curse. A hellish hobby he'd had forced on him.

It was as if he had an overbearing parent, insistent that he was to learn a musical instrument. He did not want to learn it, but he was given no choice – he had strict, domineering parents who told him he had an ability he needed to use.

After all, if someone has a talent, it is their responsibility to use it.

It's just that most people's talents were things like playing musical instruments. Or drawing. Or painting. Or sewing.

Oh, how he'd love to be a sewing master.

Instead, heaven bestowed on him the powers of telepathy. The ability to enter and manipulate someone else's mind. It may sound like a brilliant gift – but honestly, would you want to befriend someone who could, unbeknownst to you, enter your mind and twist your thoughts to their wishes?

"I will get the next plane to London," Cameron told a friendly man named Derek on the phone.

Placing the phone down, he paused.

Smiled.

Finally, he was part of something bigger.

Then he heard it. Inside his head.

You think you are meant for something greater?

He dropped to the floor, shooting his eyes around the room, examining every crevasse and corner. There was nothing. He was alone.

Except, in his head, he wasn't.

How could this be?

Normally he was the one inside someone else's head.

Only this time, someone had penetrated his.

"Who is this?"

Cameron Goliath, I am giving you an option.

"Where are you? Show yourself!"

Give yourself up and I will make this less painful than it need be.

"Go to hell."

Laughter boomed against the corners of his mind.

Only if you come with me.

The wall to his house ripped apart in a sudden, drastic motion.

The last thing he saw was a raised claw dripping with blood.

CHAPTER THIRTY-THREE

eb 18, 2003

MARTIN COULDN'T DENY IT – the buzz in the air was electrifying.

The hall was filled with roughly twenty esteemed and accomplished soon-to-be warriors. Paranormal experts, exorcists, psychics, telekinetics, clairvoyants – you name it, they were there.

And it was all down to him, Jenny, and Derek.

He had played his part. He had recruited a third of these people. Within two weeks, he had tracked down and brought home the essential experts from his portion of the list. All nationalities, all cultures, all languages. The common cause overruled whatever background they had come from.

They were there together, and they understood why.

Martin weaved in and out of the lively gathering, deliriously marvelling at the variation of powers. Some people were enthusiastically chatting, whilst the more introverted were against the walls sipping coffee. Some people knew what was being said to them before it was said, some knew more about the person they were talking to than that person did, and some just made themselves a drink without having to touch a spoon or a cup.

It was remarkable.

It was a world he had never been privy to, one he never thought existed.

Despite the impossible challenge, it left him with a tinge of hope. So many people willing to fight. So many people putting their powers to a good cause.

And he would be leading them.

He was less powerful than most of them, yes, but Derek had assured him that, in time, that would change. These people would see what he could do and would be astounded. People who could move a brick with their mind would see him conjure fire out of nothing and their jaws would drop.

Hush abruptly swept through the room, people halting their conversations, and turning to a raised platform at the front.

Derek stood upon the platform, gazing into the sea of faces that gazed back.

Everyone stared at him. Attentive, listening, ready for what he had to say.

Derek didn't speak straight away. Instead, he moved his eyes in awe over the crowd eagerly staring back. The extraordinary image of experts of every creed and colour, turning to him for his guidance.

He couldn't help but grin.

"Friends. Men, women. Black, white, brown... purple even. Psychics, clairvoyants, exorcists, priests, every known role within the world of the supernatural. Europeans, Americans, South Americans, Asians, Australians. I welcome you to the United Kingdom. I welcome you, to the stand against hell!"

He lifted his arms and shouted his final words and every single person in the room cheered.

Martin's spirits uplifted. He felt high, his heart rising to his throat, a head fluttering with wondrous excitement. His arms tingled, his head buzzed, his exhilaration grew overwhelming.

He clocked Jenny across the room, looking back at him. He could tell she was feeling the same.

"We have gathered you," Derek continued, speaking with a grand, booming voice, "from all corners of the world. For one common purpose. The one common enemy. For one united army.

"The world looks to us. We rally together in secret, but we will go down in untold history as the people who stood up to hell. As the people who stood up to *the devil.*"

Cheers rang out again.

"Whatever your powers, your gift, or your purpose. Whatever your motivation, your reason, or your history. We are now one, an army together, ready to rise, ready to say no to the destroyer of humanity.

"There will be casualties. There will be times without hope. There will be battles lost, lives gone and hopeless, shattered remains.

"But I know, with all that everyone here has already accomplished in their respective fields, that we will not be dismayed. That we will not back down. That we will not give in.

"I ask each of you now, together, to turn to the person on your left. Now turn to the person on your right. Now turn to every soul around you in the room, make eye contact, shake hands, take an unspoken vow; that you will stand by them as brothers and sisters. That you will join with them together.

"That you will swear an oath.

"That today we stand together.

"That together, we will face this evil… *And we will win!*"

Cries of jubilation and exhilaration reverberated around the room.

Derek stood down from his podium, immediately greeted with various shaking hands, nods, and congratulations.

He greeted everyone in turn, ensuring he paid due respect to every person who had stopped their lives and joined them.

Martin couldn't help but watch on with grateful warmth.

Everyone was looking to him to lead them.

But in truth, Derek was his true saviour.

CHAPTER THIRTY-FOUR

eb 19, 2003

LIGHT WAS an absent memory to Cameron Goliath. His speech had gone; his screams had taken his hoarse voice from him. His wrists were bleeding through the tightness of restraints and his naked body grew weary under the burns and wounds inflicted upon him.

He opened his eyes, realising he had passed out again. This time he found himself atop a mountain, clouds beneath him, snow furiously pounding his body.

He was frozen cold, his body violently shaking. His open wounds grew sore as the cold flakes of snow snuck into their crevices.

In the distance, beyond the thrashing snow, was a silhouette. It was still, motionless, but Cameron had no doubt it was looking at him.

It took him a few minutes to realise this silhouette was not of a man. There were hooves, claws, horns, all faded into the vague visible creature. Its snarls carried across on the wind. Cameron's pain grew even more excruciating.

"You have been contacted by a Derek Lansdale, have you not?" boomed a voice mixed with the snarls.

Cameron frantically nodded.

"Yes! Yes! I have!"

"Why?" echoed a long, drawn-out syllable.

Cameron looked around himself, darting his eyes to the distant nothingness surrounding his torment. His pain grew agonising, his temperament faltered and he prayed that, whatever it took, he could find a way out of this unbearable moment.

"I don't know..." he moaned. "He said something about recruiting me or something..."

"Recruiting you? Recruiting for what?"

"I don't know!"

He was not lying, he wouldn't dare lie. He felt cowardly, but it was too much. At the end of a man's pain threshold was when he would reveal who he truly was. But, in that moment, Cameron didn't care.

If being a coward would end the anguish, then he would be a coward.

"What has the boy got to do with Father Douglas?"

"What boy?"

"His name was Martin. How has he come by these powers?"

"Martin, Martin..." Cameron racked his brain. "Oh God, you mean the boy... he is supposed to be the saviour, the one to lead whatever Derek is recruiting for..."

"Are you telling me, Derek Lansdale is building an army?"

"I... I don't know!"

"And this army is to be led by a sixteen-year-old boy?"

"I don't know, please, I don't know! Just let me go, I'll tell you whatever I can!"

The beast took a few sinister steps forward and its jaw

came into view. Dripping saliva, cracked teeth and dark-red stains exuded from his wicked mouth.

"Oh God…" Cameron begged. The more he saw of this creature, the more frightened he grew.

"How much does this boy know what he is capable of?"

"I don't – I don't even know what he's capable of, how could I know?"

Again the beast stepped forward, its bloody eyes and malevolent presence looming dangerously closer.

"Are you telling me you know nothing more?"

"Exactly, exactly!"

"Then you are of no use!"

A claw lashed out from the beast's body and ripped from Cameron's groin to the top of his head, separating him into two bloody heaps. His intestines fell like a dropped pudding, spreading over the snow with splatters of red.

The beast turned its head away.

So Derek Lansdale had found a boy with powers like his own.

He was going to use him to lead an army he was recruiting.

There was only one way this boy had such a gift.

He was his opposite.

Which meant he must die.

CHAPTER THIRTY-FIVE

*E*ven an English summer wasn't summer. Aisha was ridiculously cold. Mumbai had always been so humid, even the streets she'd slept on had a hesitant warmth. But the late afternoon summer's breeze filled the garden, raising the hairs on her arms.

"I'm a psychic," Elisha declared, bracelets jangling around her arm. "Been doing this for many, many years now."

"Seriously?" Tee-Yong Sun asked, sticking his bottom lip out with an approving nod. "Can you tell us something about Aisha?"

Elisha smiled. She loved being tested, being able to prove doubters wrong. She turned to Aisha, narrowing her eyes, taking her in. Elisha's expression grew excitedly curious, highly anticipating what secrets she could discover.

"Aisha is your name," Elisha announced, her thick California accent sounding dominant to Elisha's frail mind. "You're fourteen. And you live on the streets. I'm sorry to hear that, Aisha."

Aisha forced a smile, looking down.

"What do you do?" Elisha asked Tee-Yung.

"I'm a telekinetic. I can move stuff with my mind."

"Really?" Aisha eagerly lifted her head. She'd never met anyone like her before.

"Yeah, watch!" Tee-Yung instructed, turning cockily to see what he could move.

He fixed his gaze on a bench in the corner of the garden. With a sly smile and a flick of his head – that bench tumbled over and flew halfway across the lawn.

"Whoa!" Aisha gasped in awe.

"So what do you do?" Tee-Yung enquired as he turned to Aisha, strutting like the dominant lion of the pack, smug at his success.

"I…" Aisha drifted off. What did he call it? A telekinetic? "I'm a tele – I'm like you."

"Seriously?" Tee-Yung stood back, impressed. "Show us then."

"I – I'm not so good with the control," Aisha admitted, dropping her head. "It just kind of happens, I don't necessarily make it happen."

"Hey, I'll help you."

"Really?"

"Yeah, come on, stand next to me."

Jumping to her feet with enthusiasm, Aisha took her place next to Tee-Yung and followed his instructions.

"Right, you've got to stand like this," Tee-Yung began, moving his legs shoulder-width apart. Aisha followed. "Then move your arms like this."

He circled his hands, generating as much speed as he could. Then, in a sudden, unexpected motion, he threw his hands out. The bench went hurtling toward the far wall – then stopped mid-air as Tee-Yung froze his arms. As he opened his palms, the bench dropped to the floor.

Aisha mimicked him exactly. Circled her hands, getting

faster and faster, throwing them out, then – nothing. Absolutely nothing.

She felt like a fool.

"You've got to quieten your mind," came a firm voice from behind her. She abruptly turned around.

Her jaw dropped.

"Oh my God, you're him?" she gasped.

"Him? Is that what they call me?" the man replied.

"No. I mean… you're Martin. You're the one who's supposed to lead us."

Martin forced a weak smile and vacantly nodded.

"Supposedly, yeah," he chuckled to himself.

Aisha looked to Tee-Yung, who was in just as much awe.

"Elisha, you're a psychic, tell me," Martin began, resting himself against the bench Elisha sat on. Despite being an experienced, older woman, she too was dumbfounded at the ease at which Martin spoke to them. "What is her state-of-mind?"

"In one word?" Elisha began, focussing on Aisha. "Chaotic. It's noisy, full of stormy thoughts."

"Hear that?" Martin directed at Aisha. "Do something for me. Close your eyes."

Aisha closed her eyes.

"Clear your mind of everything."

She willed her mind to go blank, free of thought, free of anxiety. It was tough, but she wanted to impress Martin so much that she willed herself to try.

"Now listen to everything. Feel it, smell it, take in your surroundings. Listen to the wind, feel it brush against the hairs on your arm. Listen to the distant voices, feel the smell of the breeze. Feel everything."

She tried.

She could.

Everything. The flicker of wind brushing against her face.

The bustle of people inside the house. The smell of distant smoke from someone's barbeque.

"Now try again."

Aisha's eyes opened.

She focussed on the bench.

Move. Come on, move.

Every piece of energy and focus she had, she put into moving that bench.

Ever so slightly, the bench wobbled.

She grinned with delight, throwing her arms in the air, jumping for triumphant joy.

Martin smiled back at her.

"There you go," he spoke as he wandered aimlessly back into the house. "You'll be moving mountains in no time."

As he disappeared back into the house, Aisha watched him go, welling up with pride.

CHAPTER THIRTY-SIX

eb 25, 2003

THE EVENING AIR had calmly settled. Inside, the various members of Humanity's Hope (as they had decided to call themselves) gathered for evening tea.

Martin wasn't hungry.

It was a peaceful, tranquil night and he enjoyed being outdoors, on his own, far more than he enjoyed being stared at. If he had to hear "so you're the boy who's going to lead us" one more time he was going to scream.

Instead, he used an adjacent field, where no one thought to go. He propped his wooden target into the ground and measured out thirty yards with his pace.Again and again, he conjured various forms of fire and launched them forward. He managed to create balls of fire, streams of fire, and flickering flames. But one thing he was failing to master was his aim. He was getting the edges of the wooden circle, but not the centre mark he aimed at.

After trying again, he huffed and dropped his head. He was exhausted. But he needed to be able to do this, otherwise he was going to look like a sham to everyone else. They all looked to him to be this amazing, talented leader who could do far more than they could. As it was, he felt like a fraud.

"Father Douglas has taught you well," acknowledged a voice from behind Martin, making him jump.

He glanced over his shoulder to find Derek approaching, coat and gloves on, greeting him with a warm smile.

"Do you mind if I join you?" Derek asked. "Or would you rather be alone?"

"Don't care," Martin shrugged. "Join me if you want."

Derek perched against a tree stump to the side of Martin, his hands nestled in his pockets, looking upon the young man.

"You doubt yourself too much," Derek announced. "That's why you're not hitting the target."

"Nah, that's not what it is."

"Are you so sure? Father Douglas taught you to quieten your mind, yes?"

"Yes."

"Well, how can your mind be quiet, when you are adamantly thinking so many bad thoughts?"

Martin nodded. It was worth a try.

"Believe you can do it," Derek passionately exclaimed. "Then you will do it. It is as simple as that."

Martin turned to the target and readied himself.

Right, believe I can do it.

He closed his eyes to calm his mind, then opened them again. His eyes locked onto the bullseye before him.

I can do it.

I can do it.

I can do it.

He threw his hands forward, sending a fire ball quickly

hurtling at the wooden prop. Sure enough, it hit the bullseye with immaculate precision.

Derek laughed heartily and threw his hands in the air.

"See, what did I tell you?" Derek grinned.

"All right, all right, you were right, I get it," Martin agreed, playfully rolling his eyes.

He walked over to Derek and sat beside him, gazing into the night air.

"Did you ever train Eddie like this?" Martin wondered.

Derek's smile faded. His eyes fell to the ground and his expression turned solemn.

"Sorry, I didn't mean to," Martin quickly adjusted. "You don't have to."

"No, it's okay," Derek decided. "I need to start getting over Eddie's death and move on, and that means talking about it, I guess. To answer your question – yes, yes I did do this with Eddie. Though most of his practise he did with Jenny."

"I don't know much about Jenny, I don't really speak to her much."

"Oh, lovely woman. If not a little bit blinded by her love for Eddie."

"Were they…?"

"Oh, Lord, no. Jenny is a lesbian. But they knew each other since they were babies. They grew up together, they were there for each other in everything. I think Jenny, more than anyone, is struggling with what has happened."

A moment of comfortable silence lingered in the air.

"She misses Eddie very much." Derek's head dropped. "We all do."

"Jenny seems to think there's a way of saving Eddie, bringing him back. Do you think she's right?"

Derek forced a wry smile and looked up to the stars

above. Those stars always made him feel so small, so insignificant.

"Jenny would like to think that she's forever the optimist," Derek spoke. He turned to face Martin. "But in truth, I would have to say she is in denial. She can't bear to lose Eddie to what that evil part inside of him has become, has manifested into."

"Do you not think we can save him?"

Derek took a deep moment of contemplation, staring at the ground. He turned his eyes to the sky once more, then back to his hands. He gathered his thoughts and took a deep, inward breath.

"Jenny is clouded by love. And I only wish I thought as she does."

Martin nodded, understanding.

They sat there for a little while longer, then both found their way back into the house where the rest of Humanity's Hope were gathered.

CHAPTER THIRTY-SEVEN

 eb 28, 2003

IN HELL, all you can hear are screams. All you can hear are shrieks of pain, rape, and torture. An eternity of suffering for the damned, pounding your eardrums with vicious ferocity.

Eventually, you tune it out.

But if you are the heir of hell, you enjoy it. Soak it up. Use it for ammunition.

The heir strode through the flames, over the lava, through the pits of fire licking at its body.

Once it reached the throne of its father, its god – the devil – the heir stopped. It dropped to its knee and bowed its head.

The throne was a lavish, scorching seat of animosity. A welcome aroma of burning flesh rose from the imposing amber structure. Mixed with the gold and blazes of the chair were the bones of humans and creatures conquered. Its extravagant spine sprung from its solid arms, snarling faces the rest for the devil's hands.

"My father," the heir's voice rumbled.

"My son," the devil grinned, closing its eyes, and taking in the pleasure of its rightful heir kneeling before him. "You may rise."

The heir did.

"What news do you bring?" the devil demanded.

"They are forming an army," the creature replied. "Derek Lansdale, once a friend of Edward King, has recruited upwards of forty people with differing gifts to wage war against us."

The devil roared with laughter. Its manic cackles recoiled around the horizon's abyss.

The heir couldn't help but derive pleasure from the ridiculous audacity of the humans.

"They think they can raise an army to rival us?" the devil snorted between laughs like a demonic hyena.

"They do, my Lord, they do. What's more, they have a boy born of heaven to lead them."

"It's *him?* He is the one they dare conceive?"

"He has grown a few powers. Feeble powers. Conjuring elements. The army look up to him, like this child means they stand a chance."

The devil narrowed its eyes in evil scrutiny.

"Go forth to them, bring them out. Taunt them. And show them what chance they really stand. Show no mercy. Slaughter everyone."

"As you wish, Father."

With that, the heir was released from hell and found himself on land once more.

It was in a field, surrounded by houses.

Next to a park, with a nearby swing set that felt like some significance to the man he once was. A faded memory of a girl and a boy on this swing set crossed his thoughts.

A crying boy. A loving girl.

This is where he would lead them.

Looking to the sky and closing its darkened eyes, the heir sent a wave rippling through the air. A wave one would only feel if you had not been conceived by powers of this earth.

There were only two creatures on this earth who had such ancestry.

The heir, born of hell.

And a young boy, born of heaven.

Soon, that young boy would bring his army to this field. After sending visions of death, torture, and destruction, the army would refuse to let it be. They would surely come.

It was a matter of time.

Then the heir would bring forth the devil to this world.

And they would end it.

It was so close.

So close, the heir could taste it like flickering flames on its tongue.

"Come on Martin," it echoed through the air to its nemesis. *"Come and die."*

"And he said to them, 'I saw Satan fall like lightning from heaven.'"

Luke 10:18

CHAPTER THIRTY-EIGHT

$\mathcal{M}$ arch 1, 2003

ONE IN THE MORNING.

People slept, spread across various floors and sofas in various rooms. Some even in tents in the garden. Somehow, Humanity's Hope had all managed to cram into the generously sized house that belonged to Derek.

Martin, like most nights, did not feel like sleeping.

He had been out for a midnight walk, gazing at the stars, surveying the infinite space and galaxies. Wondering if, out there, there was another world facing the same predicament.

Did every world have the same devil, or were their deities different?

It made it all seem so irrational, so nonsensical.

But racking his mind about such grand thoughts set off his migraine. They were big thoughts for a mind with such small space remaining.

With a sudden surge of pain, those thoughts ended.

Something shot through him.

He was paralysed.

A painful euphoria swept over his mind. He lost control of his arms, his muscles tensed and, before he could realise what was happening, he had risen ten feet above the ground.

That's when he saw it.

A playground.

Flames exuding from the swings.

Running. Screaming. Begging. Torturing. Maiming.

Genocide.

His body thumped to the ground with a torrential force, slamming his delicate face into the painful slab of the bumpy pavement.

Martin went numb to the pain, spitting blood without conscious thought of doing so.

His conscious self was resting. He only saw through his unconscious mind.

He saw through the eyes of a beast consumed with passionate, detestable hatred.

From his claws, fire sprayed over swarms of people, screaming, sprinting for their lives. Mothers tried to protect their children, boyfriends grabbed their girlfriends, cowards left their friends behind as they ran for their own selfish lives.

None of them survived.

Each one burnt to a crisp, suffering an agonising, scorching death. Some laid down and died, some ran in circles, some fell to their knees and screamed. In the end, their fates were all the same.

More people appeared.

Martin didn't know where from.

But he slaughtered them, too. His arms reached out and ripped them to shreds with his gigantic, demonic claws.

Every soul that didn't run fast enough was torn apart.

Decapitated, sprung limb from limb, opened and left to slip on their own bodily juices.

Any who did run quickly enough to get out of his grasp were sent up in flames.

It was mayhem. Death stank the air, hundreds of bodies piled upon a sea of skulls as far as the eye could see.

Then it all froze. The fire, the death, the mutiny – it stood completely still. The whole of the setting appeared to be like a photograph, halted.

All except for two people.

Young people, maybe in their early teens. Sitting on the swings. A boy, and a girl.

They looked familiar.

The girl... *Jenny.*

Younger, yes. Before she became a woman; her skin clearer, her hair brighter, and a child's body – but it was Jenny, without a doubt.

Then who was it next to her?

"Do you think we'll still be friends like this when we're older?" came the innocent young boy's voice. Dried tears stained his cheeks.

"Of course," replied Jenny.

Who was this boy?

Martin opened his eyes.

He was back on the drive.

But it wasn't over yet.

The very last image he saw was that of a swing set in a field.

The young boy and girl.

The boy cried.

The swing set launched on fire.

Then it all went dark.

He didn't remember the numerous times during the night he opened his eyes, screaming until his lungs grew sore. He didn't recall the times Derek and Jenny stood over him, shouting at him to stay calm. He didn't even acknowledge the moment his bloodshot eyes sprang open and his pupils dilated, just as he shrieked into Jenny's face that she was going to die.

It was light when his eyes peacefully opened.

He propped his head up, to find himself laid on the living room floor, a crowd of faces watching. Light gracefully adorned the room, filling it with a peaceful amber glow.

Except Martin's mind was anything but peaceful.

In an instant, he remembered everything.

With no idea where they came from, Derek and Jenny were at his side, ushering him to lay back down.

"No, no, you don't understand," Martin argued.

They tried to comfort him, tell him he needed to rest, assure him it was all okay.

"It is not okay!" he exclaimed, shoving them off his arms. "You need to listen to me."

Derek and Jenny remained stationary, staring at him with sceptical apprehension.

"I saw something. I... I saw through his eyes. Through the heir's eyes." He turned to Jenny. "I saw through Eddie's eyes."

Martin saw Jenny's eyes melt into pain.

"What did you see?" Derek urgently prompted, finally taking him seriously.

"Death. Fire. A lot of death. He – he killed everyone."

"Martin, this happened to Eddie, and it's a startling experience," Derek knowledgably, yet cautiously, informed him. "It is a vision. It gives you some kind of sight, some kind of awareness. You say you saw through his eyes?"

"Yes. I saw him, except..." He shook his head, willing the fuzziness of his recollection to fade. "Except I wasn't watching him. I *was* him."

"Do you have any idea where this was?" Derek pleaded.

"No. No, I don't."

Derek bowed his head with an exasperated exhale.

"Actually," Martin decided, racking his brain to make the memory clearer. "Actually, I did see something."

"What?"

"Swings. I saw, I saw a swing set."

Derek frowned at Jenny. "A swing set?"

"Yes. Yes, it had a boy and a girl on it. The boy was crying."

Jenny peered across the room in contemplation. The thought struck her. Her hands instantly clasped over her mouth, gasping, and she rose to her feet in shock.

"Oh my God." Her arms shook.

"What?" Derek rushed over to her, putting his hands on her arms. "What is it? What do you know?"

"The swing set…" she whispered, peering again across the room, racking her brain.

"What about it, Jenny?"

"With a boy crying. It's a memory."

"Yes, we know it's a memory."

"No, Derek, you don't get it. It's a memory from Eddie. It's one of Eddie's memories. The creature was having one of Eddie's memories. Surely this means, he must be in there somewhere…"

Derek's fingers grew stiff with agitation. No matter how many times this conversation arose, it was still the same argument.

And now was not a time for it.

If the heir was assembling, it would be sending a message as to where it was. A message targeted at Jenny.

A memory that only she shared with Eddie.

If anything, she was the most vulnerable. The creature was luring her. Using her love against her.

But that was a conversation Derek was to have with her at a later date.

"I think we should go there and face him," Martin declared.

Derek turned to him with caution. "If you're sure. I do warn you, Martin – when something tragic occurs, it leaves a mark. The evil behind awful acts lingers there for decades. If the heir has chosen this place, it could be for a reason – he could be intending to use the evil that remains."

"I don't think it is," Martin insisted. "I think he's chosen it because it's a place that's important to him and Jenny. After all, the flashback had Jenny in it."

Martin nodded in understanding. "I don't know, what do you think?"

Derek paused. He turned his head slowly to Jenny.

"Jenny, do you know where this swing set is?"

"Yes," Jenny acknowledged. "Yes, I know exactly where it is. I know where he is."

CHAPTER THIRTY-NINE

*J*enny slumped in the corner, hunched over, her legs shaking, biting her nails.

The house exploded into an organised chaos. The soldiers of Humanity's Hope bustled back and forth, every person preparing themselves for war. Preparing spells, armour, weapons. Anything they needed for fighting or protection.

To Jenny, the excitement hung in the air like poisonous gas.

A few people strode past her on phones, calling loved ones, telling them how much they cared for them. Trying to say their goodbyes without giving away they were saying goodbye.

They were all physically, mentally, and strategically preparing.

Preparing to kill.

Preparing. To kill. Her best friend.

Eddie...

The vision. Martin had seen through the eyes of the beast, exactly through its eyes. The creature had shown everything it planned to do, everything it planned to destroy, all the maiming and the torturing it was going to commit.

But it had also shown a piece of the man she loved. The man she had grown up with, grown close to.

Eddie had come through, but only fractionally – seeping through the chaotic vision of Martin's mind. Behind all the destruction there was a single memory Martin had mentioned. A memory only Jenny could know.

A memory from 15 July 1984.

A memory of her and Eddie at eleven years old, shortly after the death of Eddie's sister. Eddie cried that day. Her memories were hazy, but she could still see his weeping eyes as clearly as if he was sat next to her.

It was a memory Jenny treasured. An image of them both as children, sitting on a swing set, Eddie crying.

The creature had the same image.

Eddie had the same image.

It was a message. It must be. What else could it be?

A message from Eddie, trapped within. Somewhere in there, trying to show Jenny he was still around.

Begging to be freed. Begging to be helped.

But Derek wouldn't have it. Derek was so adamant Eddie was dead, such an idea wouldn't even be a conversation he would be willing to have. It would be dismissed immediately.

Martin was headstrong, yes, but he was young. And he admired Derek so much he followed him absentmindedly, just as Eddie had done.

Neither of them would listen to her.

Now here they were. Humanity's Hope, dashing back and forth around the house, preparing to kill the beast.

Kill the heir.

Kill her Eddie.

If there was even a single piece of Eddie left in there, even a minute, tiny chance that he could be saved, then this expedition was wrong. All wrong.

She had to do something about it.

She knew where he was. She knew where Eddie was.

So did they.

But they weren't leaving yet. They needed to mobilise, organise, plan tactics.

This would leave enough time for her. Enough time for her to get to him first. Enough time to appeal to Eddie within the beast, to lure him out, to defeat the disgusting, demonic, destitute casing this hell-beast had wrapped him in.

Then it hit her. An instant moment of clarity.

How to save Eddie.

She remembered what Derek had said to Martin.

"When something tragic occurs, it leaves a mark. The evil behind awful acts lingers there for decades. If the heir has chosen this place, it could be for a reason."

Derek had told her how a tragic incident leaves a mark. The evil that was there lingers for years. Eddie had many tragic incidents in his life...

The death of his sister. The death of Kelly. The visit to hell.

And that swing set. That swings set he so often visited with Jenny, baring his soul. When tragedy hits, the resonance lingers – which means a part of Eddie could linger at that swing set.

Maybe, just maybe – instead of evil lingering at this swing set, it was a part of Eddie. And that part of Eddie could aid Jenny when fighting the demon. And this was Eddie giving her that message.

She just needed to appeal to that part of Eddie.

She grabbed a pen and paper and wrote furiously.

. . .

DEREK – I've gone to get Eddie,

REMEMBER how you told us that every act of tragedy leaves a mark – well, what about Eddie's marks? What if we revisit those incidents where Eddie had experienced tragedy?

THAT IS where we will find Eddie's true soul still lingering.

THIS IS what I'm going to do.

Jenny

SHE PLACED the note in the spare bedroom, next to a pile of her clothes and a washbag she had left at Derek's. Hopefully, once Derek realised she had gone, he would search here, read the letter – and realise what she was doing.

Realise that Eddie could be saved.

Without a second thought, she marched to the door.

"Where are you going?"

She froze.

She turned to her side. Martin sat in the study, watching the commotion.

"Erm…" Jenny thought quickly. "I'm just getting some air. Getting some water and stuff, you know. Whilst all the powerful people prepare, I'm going to go get the essentials. Derek sent me."

"Fair," Martin nodded. "Seems like a plan."

She looked into the eyes of Martin, gazing back at her

with that wounded look she had seen in Eddie so many times.

Funnily enough, Martin reminded her so much of Eddie when he was younger. So beautifully damaged. Torn into pieces that reformed into something magnificent.

She wished Martin had known the Edward King she had known.

Not this beast he had been instructed to kill.

"I'll see you later, Martin," Jenny smiled at him, stifling a stray tear she felt brewing in the corner of her eye.

"Later."

She opened the door and left.

The driveway was also a scene of hectic preparation. People practising spells, talking each other through various techniques, people praying, taking a last look at the sky.

She barged past all of them.

Eventually, she was clear of the noise, of the energy of an army assembling.

She made her way to her car and got in.

For a moment, she was stuck. Her hand held the key, hovering over the ignition.

A sinking feeling filled her chest.

Like something bad was going to happen.

She shook it off, turned the engine and sped away.

CHAPTER FORTY

*T*he door swung open, smacking against the wall.
Jenny barged in. She had little time to lose.

She swept through her house, searching for the items she was after, her frantic mind unaware of where she had left them.

Lacy appeared at the bottom of the stairs.

"You're home?" she asked optimistically.

Jenny turned to her and shook her head despondently.

"Sorry, Lace, I've got to do something," she pled.

"Of course." Lacy folded her arms and nodded. She pursed her lips; another look of disappointment.

Jenny finally found what she was after, in a draw in the cupboard under the stairs. She pulled it open, grabbed a photo album, and shoved it in a bag. She closed the door, pulled the bag over her shoulder, and made her way to the door.

Lacy stood in the doorway, blocking Jenny's exit, her arms folded.

"Lacy, look." Jenny reached her arms out, rubbing Lacy's shoulders with her hands. "This is likely to be the last thing.

Honestly, the last thing. If I'm successful in this, then… well, it will all be over."

"It's never over," Lacy muttered, shaking her head.

"Yeah, but this time, it really is."

"Jen, I haven't seen you in days. You've been sleeping God knows where–"

"I've been at Derek's. Helping with the army. With Martin."

"Then the two minutes you do actually come home, when you're not running off to Israel, or God knows where, you're now running off telling me it's the last thing."

"But it is, I swear."

Lacy unfolded her arms, dropping them rigidly by her side, her hands clamped up into fists. She looked away from Jenny, her head furiously shaking and her teeth grinding.

Finally, her eyes locked onto Jenny's.

"Jenny. I love you. Isn't that enough?"

"Lacy, God, I love you," Jenny pleaded, placing her hands on the side of Lacy's face. "But there's not going to be a tomorrow if I don't–"

"If you don't what?" Lacy pushed the hands from off her face. "You're not Eddie. You're not Derek. You don't have magical powers. You don't have a big knowledge about demons. You're not anything."

Jenny's mouth dropped. "What do you mean, I'm not anything?"

"I mean, you are a human, a normal person. Leave saving the world to the experts. Your place is here, beside me. That's where you belong."

"I'm *not anything*?" Jenny spat. "I'm Eddie's best friend. If it wasn't for him, I wouldn't be comfortable enough in myself to have even gone out with you in the first place! We owe so much to him."

"No, Jen. We owe so much to *us*."

Jenny closed her eyes and bowed her head. Humanity's Hope were arming themselves. They would be attacking soon. She didn't have much time.

"Lacy, I'm sorry, but we really are going to have to finish this another time. I promise, when I get back."

"No."

"I really need to go. Please, Lacy, just get out of the way."

Eddie. The beast. They are going to kill him.

"Please just get out of the way."

"No, Jenny. I won't."

"Please."

The swing set. There's hope. But I have to get there first. I have to.

"I'm not moving, Jenny."

Jenny barged into Lacy, knocking her against the side of the doorway, and marched into the front garden.

"Jenny!" Lacy shouted, grabbing hold of Jenny's arm, swinging her girlfriend around to face her.

"Lacy, please, when I get back. I've got to go to the swings, it's the only way."

"Jenny," Lacy begged, tears dripping down her cheek. "If you leave now, don't ever come back."

Jenny's heart melted. She had never seen Lacy cry.

Lacy's defiant, weakened stance propped against the door. Staring at Jenny. Pleading to her with her tears, pleading to Jenny not to make this decision.

Begging with her eyes for Jenny not to go.

Jenny didn't have time for this.

But it was Lacy. She always had time for Lacy.

"Jenny. Don't go."

Jenny closed her eyes and shook her head. She couldn't bear to look at Lacy.

So she didn't.

She strode away from the house and into her car. She drove away without looking back.

Lacy slumped against the doorway, dropping to the floor. Inconsolable. Her tears like bullets, and her heart like fragments of shattered glass.

*D*erek felt a sting of pride. Humanity's Hope were almost set. Less than an hour and they would be marching into battle.

He only hoped they were ready.

He wandered through the house, looking over the various warriors he had recruited, readying themselves.

"When are we going?" a young man enquired to Derek.

"Less than an hour, we will make our way. Just make sure you are prepared. Do me a favour, and please let everyone know." Derek smiled and nodded at the young man.

Nodding, the young man retreated to do as he was asked.

Martin appeared at Derek's side. Both men stood in a strong, content stance, their body language echoing each other.

"Are you ready?" Derek asked.

"No," Martin shook his head. "This just feels... I don't know. Premature."

"Premature?" Derek stuck out his bottom lip to feign being impressed. "Someone's been improving his vocabulary."

"Yeah," Martin sniggered. "Took the apocalypse to make me read."

Martin looked around, peering through a few door ways.

"Jenny back yet?" he asked.

"Back? From where?" Derek gave Martin a quizzical look.

"She said you sent her out to get water and stuff."

Derek's face dropped. His eyes grew wide.

He rushed to the study, peering around every face. He ran to the living room. The kitchen. The bathrooms. The bedrooms. Upstairs. Downstairs. The garden. The front garden.

She was nowhere in sight.

"Martin," Derek ran up to Martin, gripping Martin's shoulders and shaking the young man more than he intended to. "What exactly did Jenny say?"

"Erm, I don't know… I just saw her popping out, asked her where she was going. Said she was going to get water and stuff; that you sent her."

Derek stumbled backwards, his feet giving way, a stark realisation dawning over him. He found himself sat back on a step, Martin continuously asking what was wrong.

The vision of the swing set.

She had thought that was Eddie speaking.

She had thought that was Eddie calling her.

"Shit!" Derek shrieked, his hands gripping into tight fists. His whole body shook in a quiet rage. He did everything he could to contain his emotions, but his anger and concern overcame him until he was visibly irate. "Stupid, stupid girl."

"What's happened?"

"She's gone after him. Alone."

"Why the hell would she do that?"

"Because she thought the swing set was a piece of Eddie still in there. She thinks she can talk him down."

Derek sprang to his feet and wandered back and forth

aimlessly, running his hands through his hair, his mind running through solution after solution, each one equally unfavourable.

"Well, ain't that a good thing?" Martin pointed out. "What if she can?"

"No, you don't get it." Derek paused and leant against the wall, dropping his head. "Eddie didn't give that memory to you in your vision. The heir used one of Eddie's memories against us. It's a taunt. A way of letting us know where he is so we fall into his trap."

Martin finally understood.

"And now she's walking right into it… She'll die."

"Yes, in no uncertain terms, that would be fairly accurate."

In a quick, unexpected move, Derek rushed over to the phone and dialled a number.

CHAPTER FORTY-TWO

*L*acy didn't care what time it was. She didn't care how pathetic she looked. She didn't even care about the tear marks she left smeared across the wallpaper.

She just didn't care.

She slumped against the wall of the hallway, her head between her knees, manically weeping. Her cries were loud and continual, her grief never-ending.

For so long, she and Jenny had been indestructible. The one couple who all other couples envied. The two who remained strong, complement each other, brought out each other's positives and banished the negatives.

Now what?

She couldn't remember life without Jenny. Back then, she had only existed. This was the love of her life. The only person she had ever cared for enough to keep close.

And that person chose to leave.

Lacy had given Jenny a choice, there and then, to stay or to go. And Jenny had made her decision.

She had made her decision.

The shrill song of the phone ringing echoed throughout

the house. She ignored it. She didn't care. Whoever it was could leave a message.

But what if it was Jenny?

Jenny made her choice.

But what if it was Jenny, saying she was on her way back? Saying she was wrong?

Lacy jumped up and rapidly withdrew the phone from the wall.

"Jenny?"

"Lacy?" came Derek's voice.

Lacy's heart sank.

"Yes, it's Lacy."

"Listen to me, this is really important," Derek told her. "Is Jenny with you?"

"No."

"Has she come home at all?"

"Yes."

She heard Derek breathe a huge sigh of relief.

What was going on?

"Lacy, how long ago did she leave?"

"About ten minutes ago, why?"

"Listen to me, Lacy – Jenny is going to confront the heir."

"The heir?"

"Eddie. She is going to confront Eddie. But not Eddie the man – the monster, the creature he has become."

"Why?"

"Because she thinks she can talk him out of it."

"Can she?"

"No, Lacy, listen to me. It is a trap. Eddie is not in there anymore. It will slaughter her on sight."

Lacy's head filled with anarchy, shooting a hundred perplexed thoughts around her mind.

Is that why she was in such a rush?

She thought she could save him?

"Listen to me, Lacy; if Jenny does return home again, keep her there. Then phone me. It is really important that you phone me."

"Okay."

The line went dead.

Lacy slowly edged through the house and into the living room. She sat herself down, trying to make sense of it all, trying to understand what was happening.

Eddie was the heir of hell.

He had killed and slaughtered people already, she knew that.

Now Jenny was going after it.

Jenny will die.

She got up, paced back and forth, her hands stuck to her forehead, racking her brain.

Think. Where would she go? Where is she going?

Then it hit her.

One of the last things Jenny had said before she left.

"I've got to go to the swings, it's the only way."

The swing set Eddie and Jenny used to go to as children. It was Jenny's safe place. The place she went to think, to worry, to feel at ease.

That's where she was going.

Shoving a coat around herself, Lacy grabbed car keys and ran out of the house. She didn't care she was wearing pyjamas; she didn't care she had told Jenny not to come back. She didn't care about any of it.

She loved her too much to let her die because of her own foolish wish that Eddie was coming back.

Eddie was never coming back.

But Jenny was. She must. She had to.

Lacy opened the car door and switched on the ignition, went to go, then – how do you get there?

She knew what it looked like, but she had little idea where it was. It wasn't somewhere she had ever driven to.

But she knew where Jenny used to live.

Where Eddie used to live.

She would go there. Drive to every part of their history if she had to.

She slammed her foot on the accelerator, determined.

She was not going to let Jenny die.

CHAPTER FORTY-THREE

*F*ine rain hovered in the air with a wary uncertainty. Grey clouds lined the sky, an ominous foreboding of further rain to come.

Jenny pulled up her car and ran out so quickly she forgot to lock it.

She didn't care. She didn't care how wet the rain was making her, how much she was perspiring out of despair, how much her legs hurt to carry her as fast as she was going.

She just didn't care.

She slipped in a puddle, dirty water splashing up her trousers. She scraped her palm on the painful cement of the path as she stumbled forward, ignoring the flinching pain.

After only seconds of running up the path adjacent to the field, she reached the park. Memories consumed her thoughts.

As a child, her parents taking her and meeting Eddie's parents for a chat, racing each other to the slide.

As a teenager, her and Eddie's safe space where their solitude could be kept and they could endow comforting words upon one another.

As a woman. Desperately seeking the better side of the man she once knew.

Lightning flashed in the near distance. Thunder menacingly rumbled, continuously growling. The rain poured faster, pummelling and bombarding Jenny with painful missiles of water.

She reached the swing set.

She was already drenched. She could barely see a few yards in front of her, such was the ferocity of the weather. Her soaked clothes stuck to her skin, the coldness of the rain making her shake profusely.

The rain hurt.

But she didn't care.

"*Eddie!*" she screamed, beckoning him out.

Flashes of jagged-edged lightning and water beating the ground occupied her surroundings.

There was no one near. Anyone sensible would be indoors, sheltering themselves from the downpour.

Not Jenny.

"*Come on out here, Eddie, I know you're there!*"

She turned and turned, surveying the environment, seeking out the monster she summoned.

"Please, Eddie," she whispered, mostly to herself, her throat hurting from her shouting.

But that whisper was enough.

A distant growl mixed with the sinister thunder.

"... *Jenny?*"

Jenny's eyes darted around herself, seeking out the source of the rumble, looking for the face of the demonic beast.

The face of her friend.

A large shadow engulfed the swings, overwhelming Jenny with darkness. Her jaw dropped and her eyebrows raised in horror as her eyes fell on the man before her.

"Eddie…" she gasped, tears cascading down her cheeks at the sight of the friend she had lost.

He lifted a ravenous paw, as if it was about to strike; his eyes growing huge, malevolent pupils preying over Jenny.

"*Stop!*" she bellowed, standing her ground, peering up to the beast.

Eddie paused. A slight etching of confusion faded its way over his deformed face. A snarl protruded from his nostrils, his eyes glazing over with innocuous perplexity.

"I am not speaking to the beast I see now," Jenny barked through gritted teeth, refusing to be coerced into feeling anything but love. "I am speaking to the piece of Eddie that still dwells within!"

Deep, booming laughter rang out over the field, mixing with the thrashing of the rain.

"Laugh all you want, you foul beast" Jenny barked once more. "I am speaking to my best friend!"

Her lips were pursed into a snarl, her eyebrows furrowed into a menacing glare, her face scrunched into an expression of pure intimidation. Her torso leant forward aggressively, her fists clenched by her side. She let out all her anger, all the bottled-up rage, all the ferocious guilt and spewing hostility she had kept inside.

She would not stand down. She would not be scared by the demon that was trying to shine through Eddie's handsome face.

She would not let it win.

"Eddie, I want you to listen to me!" she screamed over the sound of the pounding rain, now turning to vicious hail. "Fight this, Eddie. Fight this! You know who you are, you know what you can do. You have defeated Balam, you have defeated Lamashtu; you have even defeated the devil. Now defeat this. *Defeat it!*"

His facial features turned beastly as he ducked its head,

bringing a sinister grin toward Jenny, stepping toward her, dangling its malicious intent within inches of her. She could feel its tepid breath snorting through his nose, spraying over her face and blowing her hair back.

Still, she stood her ground.

Still, she would not falter.

"You can get as close as you want," she spewed. "But you will not make me back down. Not until I get him back."

His eyes were now level with hers. Its suffocating stench choked her, made her throat tight.

She remained firm, stood where she was.

"Come on, you prick. Is that all you got?"

Its claws trickled against the pavement, making a terrifying click as each one left an indented scratch. But the creature shivered, showing a hazy lack of confidence Jenny had not yet seen in it. Its claws began to retract.

There was hope.

"Give him back to me!"

It sneered, at first. Then that sneer got lost in the air, along with any deformed feature of a demon that remained.

"Give back Eddie! Give me back Edward King!"

It chortled, leering its playful laugh over Jenny. Its lingered laugh grew quieter as its fangs shortened.

In a moment of lightning, it was indescribably human in shape.

Edward King stood, looking back at Jenny, with fear spread across his face.

A solitary tear slid down Jenny's cheek.

"Eddie?" she offered, cautiously keeping her distance. "Is that you?"

CHAPTER FORTY-FOUR

pril 5, 1991

EIGHT YEARS, eight months before millennium night

EDDIE ANXIOUSLY TAPPED against the underside of the table. He sipped his coffee without consciously being aware of doing so.

Why was he so nervous?

He wasn't the one who was being introduced to their girl-friend's best friend.

Yet he knew how important this was to Jenny. How much she had done to get there. What an incredible journey she'd had.

The bell on the coffee shop door rang and Jenny strolled through. She held hands with a woman who followed behind her.

This made Eddie smile. He wasn't sure why. Maybe it was

because of how much apprehension she'd had about revealing her sexuality, the initial unacceptance from her parents, or the years of coming to terms with who she was. But for her to now have the confidence to walk in public with her hand in another woman's hand; it was remarkable. It made him beam with pride.

Eddie stood and greeted Jenny with an embrace.

"This is Lacy," Jenny introduced.

Eddie grinned warmly as he gave Lacy a heartfelt hug.

"It's so great to meet you," Eddie told her. "I've heard so much about you."

"Likewise," she smiled.

As the waitress came over and noted their drinks, Eddie stole a look at Jenny's girlfriend. She was petite, slim, and incredibly cute. She had purple-dyed hair, which made Eddie feel like she was a bit rebellious – the complete opposite of Jenny. She was a few months younger than Jenny, still seventeen. She wore a hoodie and baggy jeans and protruded a cool calmness.

Once Jenny had finished ordering and the waitress had left, she immediately started fretting.

"Oh damn it, I forgot to say no biscuit on the side," she anxiously remembered. "What if it's ginger? What if she doesn't know I'm allergic to ginger?"

Lacy placed a soothing hand on Jenny's leg.

"It's okay," Lacy told her. "If there's a biscuit, I'll eat it. Then it won't get anywhere near your coffee."

"Okay," Jenny smiled, turning to Lacy and nodding.

Wow, Eddie thought. *Someone who can calm Jenny's irrational craziness.*

As much as he loved Jenny, she did get worried about the most ridiculous things. Eddie was glad that she had found someone who could comfort her; show her that she didn't need to be so worried about everything.

"So how did you guys meet?" Eddie asked.

"Well, we both went to the uni open day and ended up sat next to each other in the presentation," Jenny began. "And, honestly, I don't think I heard a word of the presentation. I was too distracted by the incredibly fit girl next to me."

"Oh, was she on the other side of you, or...?" Lacy joked, and they all laughed.

"Amazing," Eddie acknowledged. "So, what are you looking at doing at uni, Lacy?"

"I'm looking at doing my nursing training."

"A nurse? Wow."

"Yes," Jenny nodded. "Far more worthwhile than a useless English Literature degree."

"Hey, at least you're getting a degree."

They continued chatting and joking for hours. Eddie instantly adored Lacy, seeing what a perfect fit she was for Jenny. Someone who could calm her, guide her to thinking clearly. It was perfect.

He was so happy for her.

He was sure that these two would be together until the day they died.

CHAPTER FORTY-FIVE

M arch 1, 2003

THREE YEARS three months after millennium night

SCREECHING her car to a halt beside the first payphone she saw, Lacy sprang out of the car and ran as fast as she could.

The mixture of rain and hail attacked her body, and she briefly regretted being so hasty as to run out in her pyjamas. The regret didn't last long, as she picked up the phone and punched in Derek's number.

Nothing.

She had forgotten to put change in.

"Fuck!"

She sprinted back out of the phone box and opened the car door. Opening the glove compartment, she took out her purse and grabbed a bunch of coins.

In the few seconds it took her to run back into the phone

box, she was drenched. Water fell from her hair, down her back, and beat against the floor, leaving her shivering from the cold damp.

But she didn't care.

She shoved the coins into the payphone, not looking at how many she was putting in, just ensuring she had shoved enough in to be able to make the call. she dialled the number, put the phone to her ear, and waited.

Turning around, she took in the scene of the street. It was dark and the weather was like a ferocious animal uncaged. Wind carried rubbish around in circles, lamp lights barely lit the street, and not a soul was in sight.

"Hello?" came Derek's voice.

"Derek, thank God!" Lacy shouted, alert. "Listen, I can't find my way to the park. I know where it is, I just don't know how to get there."

"Well, where are you now?"

"I don't know. Somewhere in town, I think. How close are you to leaving?"

"We're ready, just going now. We won't be long. Less than ten minutes."

"Okay, but please, just tell me how to get there first."

She realised she was crying.

"How far are you from the war memorial?"

"Erm, just passed it."

"Right, head down past the museum, park your car, then get out to your left and down the path, it's there. It's minutes away, you'll be fine."

"Okay, thank you, Derek."

She slammed the phone back into the receiver and ran back to her car, ignoring her change.

She turned the ignition and switched the windscreen wipers to full. She could barely see anything. She resorted to putting her high beams on, not caring who she startled or irritated.

Accelerating as quickly as she could, she did a hasty three-point turn and headed back down the street she had driven.

She rubbed water out of her eyes, her palms so wet they were making her vision worse. She lifted her drenched t-shirt and rubbed her eyes with that.

Despite not being able to see where she was going, she sped as fast as she could. She shot straight over the war memorial roundabout, ignoring a horn from a car that had to brake suddenly for her.

Going past the museum, she screeched her car to a halt on the side of the road.

She sprinted out, running past a few shops and down a narrow path. Her foot went into a divot in the path that had turned into a deep puddle and she went flying onto her front.

Groggy, she lifted her head up. She could feel the mud on her face and she could see it dripping against the soaked floor. Her arms, her vest, her trousers, were all covered in brown-and-black gunk.

Not caring anymore, she stuck her hands into the soggy surface and dragged herself to her feet.

She hobbled forward, her legs in too much pain to run.

Deciding she needed to just ignore the pain, she did her best to speed up. Limping and shuffling, she accelerated forward.

Then she froze.

That's when she saw them.

In the distance, far across the field, next to the swing set.

Two figures.

Two figures masked by the rain and sleet.

One of them was Jenny. Lacy could tell the curve of

Jenny's body, however cased in shadow or obscured by hectic rain it may be.

It was definitely Jenny.

The thing in front of Jenny looked... It looked like Eddie. It was Eddie. It had worked. Lacy couldn't believe it.

Then she saw its shadow, which did not match the man stood before it. The shadow was of a huge, carnivorous beast.

And its claw was lifting in the air, as if ready to swipe.

"Jenny!"

CHAPTER FORTY-SIX

*T*he front line.

Martin knew it was where he belonged.

Leading Humanity's Hope into battle.

Still, he couldn't help it. His hands were madly quivering, his arms seizing, his knees buckling. Thoughts entered his mind and spun around like a tornado.

What if he died?

What if he died without managing to actually do anything with his life?

What if he was the world's only hope, and this battle had come too soon, before he was ready?

He was defeated last time, quite substantially. There was no doubt in his mind, he had stood no chance.

And what was different now?

Sure, he had forty-odd people with various gifts marching behind him.

But did they have any idea what they were really getting themselves in for?

Only he had seen this creature. Only he had fought and

fled from it. Talking the talk is great, being willing to give your life to a cause sounds heroic, but when it comes down to it – how many of these people were really ready for what they were about to see?

"What's the matter?" Derek turned to Martin, breaking him out of his helpless thoughts.

"I don't know, Derek," Martin replied. "This doesn't feel like the right time. I'm worried."

Derek lifted his fist in the air, indicating for everyone to stop. They had reached a fence, cutting them off from a large field.

Martin peered over his shoulder. Despite being under the cloak of darkness and torrential rain, the army looked strong. Everyone took their place next to the fence, peering across the empty park.

Growling reverberated in the distance. Snarling, screaming. Something was there.

Derek took out a set of binoculars and peered toward the other side of the field, where the swing set sat. Next to it was the silhouette of something formidably large.

Derek couldn't say it out loud, but he was terrified. For the first time in this venture, he was genuinely mortified.

But he had to think clearly. Had to be objective. His life was insignificant compared to the long-term aim of this war, and he had to remember that.

His life belonged to something bigger. Something greater.

"Martin," he spoke. "You are the one destined to lead us into this war. If you think this is too soon, you say the word, and we will withdraw."

"Really?" Martin gaped.

"Look around you," Derek instructed, placing a firm but reassuring hand on Martin's shoulder.

Martin looked around him. All the faces of all the people

they had gathered, these experts, people who had spent a lifetime committed to the pursuit of controlling the forces that remain invisible to us.

All of them were looking at him.

Eyes of experience and voices of wisdom, all directing their gaze to him.

Waiting for him to lead.

"You see that?" Derek continued. "It doesn't matter where they are from, who they are. They know the goal, and they know who you are."

"But I'm not ready."

"Ready?" Derek scoffed. "When will you ever be ready? It is time to stop talking about 'if' or 'when.' It is now. You are not *going to be* the leader, Martin – you *are* the leader. And it's time for you to take that responsibility."

Martin glanced over his shoulder. Everyone's eyes were still on him.

He looked into those eyes, taking his time to understand the faith they were putting in him. Some of the eyes were weak, some scared, some terrified even. But despite whatever these people had inside them, whatever fears they held – each and every eye that looked at him was expectant. They believed in the cause and in the leader. They knew what they were risking, and they were fully willing and able to do so.

"So what do I do?" Martin shrugged.

"If you say we aren't ready," Derek proclaimed, "then you give the word, and we will withdraw. We will move every person back and continue our training and preparation."

"But what about Jenny?"

Derek looked back to the distance. The rain pounded against the shadow of the raised claw of a demon, a faint outline mixed with the torrential weather.

It was getting ready to strike.

It was now or never.

"Then…" Derek tried to produce an answer, providing blank noise until he could form the words. "Then Jenny doesn't survive. A necessary loss. A tough loss, but a necessary one."

"We can't…"

"I adore Jenny, but Martin, there is a big picture here. We have to be unattached. We have to think clearly – what is the right thing to do for the world?"

Martin closed his eyes and bowed his head.

Who was he to make this decision? He wasn't even an adult yet. He wouldn't even be able to drink at the celebratory party if they won.

He didn't feel ready. He knew that, knew they were marching into something they couldn't win.

But he couldn't let Jenny go.

If only for the memory of Edward King, he could not let that manifested evil destroy the one person who had retained an unaltered faith in him.

He knew what the answer was.

He knew what they were going to do.

"We attack," he declared to Derek.

Derek nodded a firm, hesitant nod.

"Okay. Give the signal."

Martin climbed over the fence and took a few steps forward.

This is it.

Turning over his shoulder at the expectant eyes, he gave a firm nod.

Then he turned back. Raised his arm.

And screamed.

As he charged forward, the screams of his legions charging behind him sprang him forward. The bombardment of their feet against the ground shook the fragile earth, carrying them toward their fate.

He was not alone.

Derek was at his side, running.

Humanity's Hope were running at his trail.

Everyone was behind him.

Time to restore that faith.

CHAPTER FORTY-SEVEN

*J*enny's eyes broke at the sight of the man she loved so much.

Eddie lifted his arm, his nails extending into sharp claws. His eyes were fully dilated, filled with red. He lifted his claw to swipe at her.

He was going to kill her.

Eddie was going to kill her.

But surely, if that was true... he would have done it by now?

"Please, Eddie," she begged. "Please, I know you are in there. Stop this."

Jenny fell to her knees. Unsure whether it was anxiety, exhaustion, despair, whatever it was – she just couldn't stand up anymore. Her knees were too weak.

Her temperament was too weak.

"Please Eddie, don't do this," she whimpered. "Don't tease me with showing me your face, then use it to kill me."

Her eyes flooded, her cries disappearing with the rain that continuously attacked her. Water was running furiously down her face, down her body. Her trousers were ripping from the frailty of the water, and her t-shirt had torn some-where along the events of the night.

In a quick thought, she dug her arm into her bag, and produced a photo album.

The claw remained poised in the air, ready to swipe, ready to do permanent damage.

Jenny grabbed a photo out of the album, dropping it, then scooping it out of the puddle. The rain destroyed the material of the photograph almost straight away, but this did not deter her.

She held the photo up to Eddie's eyes, hovering it before him. His breath was still deep and croaky, blowing her hair back in ferocious gusts of wind.

"Look, look!" she pleaded. "It's you and me. As babies. With our parents. We met when we were babies, do you remember?"

The claw was still poised.

He hadn't killed her.

She was still alive.

There was hope.

She dropped the photograph into the chaos of the weather and it faded away. Reaching into the album, the grabbed another one, lifting it up to him.

"This is us again, at this very swing set. Weren't even teenagers, but already had such an understanding. You loved me. I loved you. This was how it was, how it always was."

Eddie's eyes focussed on the photo. Motionless, displaying a vacant, unfeeling expression.

Jenny couldn't tell if it was working. It was difficult to make out any kind of expression in an expression that hadn't changed one bit.

Whatever was going on inside, it was staying deep and buried.

I have to bring him out. I have to.

She clung to the next photograph, shoving it in his face.

"Here we are again. Me, you and Lacy. Remember Lacy? You said she was good for me, kept me calm. And you were so right. Me and Lacy, we have survived for so long."

Her eyes broke, tears strewn down her face, her whole body shaking with anguish.

"I don't think I could have survived my first relationship if it weren't for you," she furiously sobbed, barely able to articulate her words, her face too scrunched up with torment.

"Please, Eddie," she tried. "Please come back. I can't survive without you."

Eddie's eyes met hers, and she could tell he was there. She could feel him close by, his love and affection warming her frozen body.

It's working.

She dropped the photograph and went searching for another one, pulling it out and thrusting it forward once more.

"And here, it's us again. Me, you, and Cassy. Do you remember Cassy? Your sister?"

The beast didn't move.

Eddie didn't move.

"You loved her so much. You never recovered from her death, but still, you freed her. Freed her from a prince of hell. She'd still be being tortured right now, if it weren't for you."

She wiped her eyes along her arm, though it made no difference. The rain and the tears were too furious.

"Now you need to free yourself. From an heir of hell. You've done it for so many other people, you just need to do it for yourself. Please, Eddie, come on. I know you're listening. I know you're in there."

From the corner of her eye, she saw Lacy. Far down the path, limping forward, covered in mud.

She came. Lacy understood and she came.

Jenny held up a hand, warning Lacy to stay where she was.

Eddie went to turn his head, but Jenny quickly got his attention back.

"No, Eddie, look at me. Please, face me."

Lacy paused, watching from afar. Jenny could see her eyes were about to break, that she was terrified.

But Jenny knew what Lacy didn't. She knew that Eddie was in there, and she was succeeding, she was reaching him.

"Eddie, please. I miss you so, so much. You've been there my whole life, and now I've had to survive without you, and I just can't. I can't survive without you. I may as well be dead without you."

She reached her hand out and gently placed it on the hideous, corrupted face before her.

Eddie didn't flinch. He didn't move. He allowed her to touch him, allowed her to feel the skin of what he had become.

"See, Eddie, it's just us two. Just us."

She heard a rumble in the distance, like loads of people were running. Defiant shouts accompanied the heavy steps.

Humanity's Hope. They were here.

"Please, Eddie, we don't have much time. That sound, it's an army, come to kill you. You need to come back to me now. Otherwise, it's too late. It needs to be now."

She had now placed both hands on the side of his sticky, blood-drenched hair, staring into the eyes of a malicious creature, seeing only love and fear.

"Come on, Eddie," she whispered closely to him. "It's time to come home."

The beast snarled.

"This is where you brought me. Our swings. Where we did all our talking. I know you love me."

She peered into his torn eyes, seeing her best friend looking back at her.

She finally saw in his eyes what she had been so desperate to see.

He was there.

Eddie was there.

"Oh my God, Eddie, you're back!" she celebrated, smiling uncontrollably. "I can't believe you're actually back."

His eyes lingered on hers for one more moment.

His arm reached out, sending a long, sharp claw through Jenny's heart.

Within a second, he had transformed back into the huge beast he really was.

The claws, the fangs, the fur. The dilated, blood-red pupils. The deep, croaking snarl of its breathing. The pure hatred in its eyes.

It reached out its jaw and sent its sharp teeth straight through Jenny's neck, ripping her throat apart. It let out a growl that reverberated through the air and lifted its head back, throwing Jenny's bloody flesh from his jaw, a spray of red staining the grass beneath her body.

Jenny's eyes remained wide open, staring at the eyes of the heir of hell.

She collapsed to the floor in a pool of thick, red blood.

By the time the heir was done, the pieces of her body lay scattered, with barely anything left.

CHAPTER FORTY-EIGHT

*L*acy had never run so fast in her life.

Agonising pain shot up and down her leg, but she didn't care. She ignored the limp and powered forward.

The beast went to attack her, too, just at the point Humanity's Hope intervened. In an instant, the park was filled with fire, water, wind, levitation, flashing lights, miraculous sounds – everything one could think of.

But Lacy didn't hear a single bit of it. It was merely a distant ringing her ears tuned out.

She skidded to her knees beside what remained of Jenny. She managed to grasp her head, leaning it on her lap.

"Come on, Jenny, come on," she whimpered

She knew it was denial.

She'd had her throat ripped off and her torso torn upwards.

"Please, Jenny," she muttered through despairing tears.

She couldn't tell the rain had drenched her. She couldn't tell her pyjama trousers were ripped. She couldn't even tell her arm was bleeding out of a gaping open wound.

What was left of Jenny didn't move.

Jenny's eyes were wide open, staring at the sky, unfaltering. But still, unmoved.

A large chunk of bone stuck out of the gaping hole that took up half of her neck. A large slit went up her chest, blood seeping out, body innards slowly sliding along the wet grass.

Lacy bowed her head and leant it against Jenny's.

"I'm so sorry," she whispered. "I'm so sorry I was mad at you. I'm so, so sorry."

It was no good.

Jenny couldn't hear her.

Her damp sobbing was gone with the rain, floating away with the triumphantly violent wind.

Lacy looked up. The beast was in front of her, bombarded by the army Jenny had assembled with Derek.

Already, there were so many dead.

Multiple corpses lay strewn over the field. The inside of their bodies lay nearby in a bloody heap.

The beast was simply working its way through them.

"Who are you?!" Lacy screamed across the park at what used to be Eddie, going completely unnoticed.

Lacy turned her head in a quick motion as she threw up. Her head collapsed to the soaking grass. Her tears flew out like frantic waves in a hurricane.

She was gone.

Jenny was gone.

It had really happened.

But it couldn't have. How could she be gone? How could she be here one moment, then not the next?

Lacy lifted her head and looked back at Jenny's deadened eyes staring dormant back at her.

She gently brushed her hand down Jenny's face, closing her eyes.

Lacy's muddy trousers were covered in blood. Clumps of

red stuck to her, having escaped from the open slit in Jenny's body.

Lacy couldn't move. She averted her eyes, fixating on a blade of grass that lay untouched.

If she looked away, it wasn't true. She couldn't see the proof. She could pretend it hadn't happened.

If she never looked back, then maybe this would change.

Maybe Jenny wouldn't be mad at her. Maybe Jenny wouldn't be dead. Maybe Jenny…

"I'm sorry," Lacy muttered. Her final parting words to the woman she had loved for almost twelve years.

CHAPTER FORTY-NINE

*A*isha watched as Elisha's body turned to a fiery mess. Within seconds, the beast had lit her on fire, committing her body to a bitter end.

Aisha fell to the floor, collapsing to her knees.

What the hell was she meant to do against this... thing?

Elisha couldn't do anything.

Everything she'd done... Every accomplishment, every smile, every ounce of love she'd given – gone. In seconds.

Tee-Yong threw himself forward, furiously circling his arms, raising bricks from a nearby construction site into the air, mixing them with chains from a swing set and charred remains of surrounding corpses – and he hurled them at the beast.

It did nothing.

The heir snarled an arrogant snarl, booming a conceited smile at the feeble attempt of this puny human.

Its claw stuck through the chest of Tee-Yong, ripping his body apart, then threw the leftovers across the field until he was out of sight.

"No!" Aisha cried out.

All around her was death.

Fire.

Blood.

Guts.

Remains of people just like her, except with exceptional powers.

She was meant to rival this thing?

She couldn't even stand on her feet without her legs wobbling.

Finally mustering the strength to run, she got to her feet and turned. She ran. Where to, she didn't know, she just ran.

Past the hopeless battle waging around her.

Past the people she had just begun to call friends.

This was the first time she missed home. Missed the streets. Missed the sick bastards who tormented her as she tried to sleep.

Martin. She saw Martin.

Finally, some hope.

Except, there wasn't. His eyes were feeble. Helpless.

Even he didn't have faith they could win.

Almost everyone was dead.

She sprinted as fast as she could, and didn't look back.

CHAPTER FIFTY

*B*odies were falling, and falling fast.

Martin could hardly believe it. All around him was death. Entrails hanging from people whose faces he knew. Powerful people.

Spell after spell attacked the beast. It pushed the heir back inches, then the heir leapt forward yards.

Across the park, Martin could see Jenny's open body in Lacy's weeping arms.

His heart sank. The reason he had risked all of this. The reason these people had marched to their deaths, in defence of him, trusting what he decided.

Jenny had been dead before they'd even arrived.

Martin looked across the field to Derek, who wore a similar pained face.

Their eyes met each other's for a solemn moment. In that moment, it was as if everything went into slow motion. Bodies were flung at sluggish speed and every second Derek's lost eyes met his were deliberate torment.

"We need to pull back!" Derek shouted across the field at Martin.

Martin was stumped. Rooted to the spot. Paralysed.

How could such decisions be his?

No one they recruited was left. They had been slaughtered, ripped apart, without even standing a chance.

As the beast lifted its claw to meet another victim, Martin stood forward.

"Enough!" he bellowed.

The beast paused and turned to Martin.

He removed his jacket and stepped forward.

"It's me who's meant to kill you, not them," Martin declared.

Derek clambered forward. "Martin, what are you doing?"

"Check for survivors, get them out of here," he demanded, without diverting his glare from the heir.

"But–"

"I thought I was in charge, weren't I?" Martin snarled at Derek.

With an obedient nod, Derek searched the bodies for signs of life, managing to help one or two to their escape.

The beast didn't care. It swivelled its full attention to Martin.

As Martin stood in the rain, water parading upon him, sickening death strewn over all the fields, he truly felt everything they had lost.

And one last glance at Jenny's remains being dragged away by Lacy was all he needed to give him that final piece of motivation.

He felt ready.

"So, it is true?" boomed the voice of the heir. "You are what we thought."

Martin paced in a circle around the beast, furrowing his brow, clenching his fists.

"Yeah, I'm the one who's supposed to kill you, an' all that," Martin announced cockily.

"You're young. You're pathetic. And you're supposed to go up against the antichrist?"

Enough trash talk.

Martin remembered what had been taught to him.

Remembered the teachings of Father Douglas.

Last time he faced Eddie he had been hasty; he had been ill-prepared, like a child taken by surprise.

This time he had enough awareness to fully access his gift.

In a single second he closed his eyes, and dragged that second out for as long as he needed it. He quietened his mind, shut down every thought. Every niggling doubt, every worry, every anxiety – gone.

Every time he had claimed with self-deprecation that he wasn't good enough.

Every time he had felt lonely that he had no friends, no family.

Every time he had felt he couldn't do what was expected of him.

It went. Disappeared in a puff. Leaving his mind in total blankness. Vacant wisdom filling his empty thoughts.

Then he soaked up the environment. Took in everything.

The smell of fine rain mixed with a rotting stench of death.

The feel of water punching and punching him in the face, in the gut, in the chest. Every ounce of water that rebounded off his skin, he felt it soak him.

The sound of the thunder, lightning, poisoning the sky, echoing a looming premonition of doom.

The taste of rainwater mixing with his blood and saliva.

Opening his eyes, he took in the last aspect of his surroundings. What he could see.

A scared little creature. Something that claims to be evil

but made of man. Something that will never amount up to what it was meant to be.

Martin screamed.

He threw his arms forward, spewing fire in a rapid repetition of flames beating against the beast.

He held one arm in the air to continue this fire, then opened his other palm again, and again, and again. Each time he opened his palm another sharp spike flew toward the beast.

Ripping his arms away to look at the damage he had done, he realised it was nothing.

The beast was unscathed.

The beast struck, and Martin fell onto his back, knocked unconscious.

Everything went black.

CHAPTER FIFTY-ONE

"*You* really, truly are a remarkable young man."

Martin's eyes opened to a flicker of white. As he opened his eyes further, he had to cover them to shield him from the sheer brightness of the scene before him.

Once his eyes had adjusted, he found himself sitting on the floor of a forest. There was no rain, no wind, nothing. Just a bright, beaming sun shining down upon him, next to brightly covered trees and the perfect smell of recently mowed grass.

"What?" Martin mumbled.

Cassy reached out her arm, taking Martin's hand in hers and helping him up.

"Where are we?" Martin asked. The last thing he remembered, he was throwing fire at the heir of hell.

"Oh, right now?" Cassy stuck her bottom lip out and thought. "Right now, you are lying unconscious in a field, the heir of hell approaching you, just before you are about to die."

"I'm about to die?" Martin repeated hysterically. "Then let me go back, I need to defend myself!"

Cassy smiled wryly and placed a comforting hand on his back. She guided him to a log, where they both sat.

"What you have done," she told him, "is incredibly brave. You have decided you are ready, you have the power, you have decided you have it within you and you have stood up to the beast. You really, really are a magnificent young man."

"And what? Now I'm going to die?"

"No, you're going to return momentarily. I just thought we could have a nice chat first."

She clasped her hands together and looked around the beautiful scenery that lay before her. Wildlife, green and purple leaves, various kinds of plants. It was an incredible scene.

Martin, however, wasn't paying attention to it. He was staring at Cassy, waiting for her to continue.

"About anything in particular?" he retorted.

Cassy chuckled and looked to him with that warm, graceful stare that put him instantly at ease.

"As gallant as you are," she continued, "it is not time yet. The heir will attack the world and you will stand between it then, yes – but right now, I'm sorry. You are not ready."

"I'm not ready? What about all that believing I'm ready shit?"

"That's just part of the journey you have to go through, and you needed to go through it."

"I... I don't get it."

Cassy looked deep into Martin's eyes, peering into the window of his soul. She respected him too much for him not to be told the truth.

It was time.

"Do you have any idea why it is you who is involved in this? Why you?"

"Honestly, not a bit."

"Wouldn't you like to know?"

Martin glared at her. "You mean you knew? All along, you knew?"

"I have always known," Cassy admitted. "But I have had restrictions placed on me, the same way you have. You could not have trained under the pretence of fate; you had to do this of your own free will. Now, I think it is time."

Martin shook himself out of his annoyance and cleared his head. This was important. This was the answer he had been after for so long.

"The devil, as you probably know, is a fallen angel. He was once a warrior of heaven, like me, but he was cast down to hell for his wicked ways. Since then, he has always been clamouring for control over earth, the in between, the only place neither heaven nor hell owns. Heaven cannot intervene because interfering with free will is an abomination, but hell does not care about such things. But more recently, we broke that vow, Martin. And we broke it twice."

"What do you mean?"

"The devil wanted his own messiah, same way heaven had theirs two thousand years ago. So, he decided to make it happen, and he conjured from nothing a soul, and planted it within a woman.

"In 1972, the devil had a child conceived by evil with a woman on earth. In 1973, that woman gave birth to that boy. His name was Edward King."

"You mean, Eddie wasn't really a human?"

"He was half-human. His mother's side. But as for the evil that lurked within him, there was nothing that could stop that from coming to the forefront.

"So, in retaliation, heaven had a child conceived out of good, with the same woman. A sister, born in 1975. By the name of Cassy King.

"Me."

Martin stared at Cassy in astonishment. No wonder she was an angel – she was a child of heaven!

"Unfortunately, things didn't go well, and when hell found out about heaven's conception, a pact was made. We would both kill our children to avoid a war coming to earth.

"As a result, both me and Eddie were hit by a car whilst riding our bikes in 1984. We both crossed over to the other side, and heaven thought that was it.

"But when heaven wasn't aware, hell reached into purgatory, latching a demon called Lamashtu onto Edward King, and pulled him back to earth. Eddie lived, Cassy died. Evil was now on earth without a balance to the equation.

"But then heaven did find out. And that's where you come in."

"Me?"

Martin couldn't figure it out. How on earth did he fit into this?

"Unbeknownst to hell, we conceived another child out of good, in the year 1986. A child who would balance the equation, one who would be the warrior for good on earth, should this evil rise.

"His name was Martin."

Martin's jaw dropped. His eyes fixated on Cassy, then drew away as he let her words wash over him. Slowly, they sunk in.

But he was still speechless.

"You see, Martin, this is why you need to believe in yourself," she told him, placing a hand on his shoulder and turning him toward to her. "Because despite one of you being conceived by evil and one by good, you both share the same amount of power from each source. You, Martin, are just as powerful as Eddie is. Only your power comes from heaven, not hell.

"You just need to access it.

"And that is why you aren't ready. Your skills need to match his, and right now, they don't. And you need to escape; otherwise he will win, and you will die before you ever have a chance to fulfil your potential.

"If you die, there is nothing else that will protect earth. Hell will open, and everything within it will be let out."

Martin stood. He felt lightheaded, oddly giddy. Feeling as light as a feather, he jigged his body in readiness, surging with energy, bursting at the seams with a want to fight.

"So how do I escape?" he asked.

"I will distract the beast," Cassy declared. "Once he is distracted, you leave."

"Okay," Martin vehemently nodded, adrenaline rushing through his unconscious body. "I'm ready."

CHAPTER FIFTY-TWO

*M*artin's eyes shot open.

He rolled to his side, dodging a claw that went digging into the ground.

Jumping to his feet he dove, avoiding a swipe at his legs.

He spun on his heel and ran, sprinting away from the beast, away from a certain death.

But soon, he found he wasn't running anywhere. His feet had risen from the ground. His legs were scarpering at high speed, but in the middle of the air, against nothing.

Behind him, the beast roared.

It had him.

Then a bright, shining white light decorated the sky, bursting forward with extreme intensity. The beast flinched its eyes away and Martin was able to drop to the floor as it loosened its telekinetic grip.

Glancing over his shoulder, he saw her. Adorned in her white dress, her glowing hair, the strong light behind her.

Cassy stood directly before what used to be her brother.

The beast narrowed its eyes.

Martin couldn't move. He knew Cassy was an angel, but… this was the heir of hell.

What if he killed her?

No. Cassy is doing this so I can get free. She wouldn't want me to stick around.

He ran.

But the roar of the beast once against floored him, paralysing him. He turned and watched as Cassy stood before the creature that stood so much taller than her.

She held out her hand.

"No." She shook her head. "You will not pass me."

The beast swung its claw out and Cassy flew into the air to dodge it by mere inches.

Martin couldn't go. He couldn't leave her.

As if sensing his hesitance, Cassy turned over her shoulder and made seizing, defiant eye contact with him.

"*Go!*" she demanded.

Come on. Pick yourself up and run. Do it now.

"*Why do you wish to protect this child?*" the beast mused.

Martin leapt to his feet. With another insurgence of adrenaline, he forced his way forward.

"*He is my equal, isn't he?*" were the final words Martin heard echo from the beast's mouth.

Once he reached the fence at the far side of the field, he looked over his shoulder. The rain was still moving quickly, and he couldn't see well enough into the distance to know what was going on.

He couldn't see if Cassy was okay.

"Cassy…"

It took all his strength to will himself on, to push himself forward.

She wouldn't want you to die because you stuck around to see what happened. She's doing this for you, you idiot. Just move!

238

He leapt over the bench and splashed his heavy feet through the flooded road before him.

He ran, and ran, and ran.

Soon, the rain faded and dawn approached. The hazy morning sky cast a little light over the drenched scene. Roads, fields, houses, were all flooded from the torrential night's rain.

Martin was out of breath, no idea where he was, no idea where he had run to.

No idea what had happened to Cassy.

Furiously panting, he leant against a wall and fell to the ground. He ended up sitting in a puddle, but he didn't care.

He had the truth now.

He knew what his purpose was. Why he had been chosen.

He knew what his potential was.

Next time they faced each other, he would be ready.

He swore to himself he would be ready.

CHAPTER FIFTY-THREE

*M*arch 18, 2003

LACY DIDN'T MANAGE to make it all the way through her eulogy. She tried, and Martin knew everyone appreciated that, but the tears were too much.

Being the gentleman that he was, Derek had stood next to her in case, and offered to carry on. Taking the note, he finished Lacy's final words.

Then everyone stood in complete silence.

The coffin travelled behind the curtain and, as the flames that cremated Jenny's body pushed the curtain outwards, Martin struggled to keep his composure.

Glancing to Derek, he saw him doing his best to do the same. He had never seen Derek cry. Martin was sure that in the corner of Derek's eyes there was a reddened dampness, trying to seek its way out. But that's all Derek gave.

Martin couldn't bear to look at Lacy. He could hear her over the deafening silence. She was inconsolable. It made him distraught to even try to imagine the pain she was in. Not just the death, but the tragic circumstance. The culprit who committed the murder. The good Jenny was trying to do at the time.

Following the funeral, Martin stood at a distance, watching beside a far tree in the graveyard.

He watched as the service ended and people lingered.

One by one, they left. Gradually finishing their goodbyes and petering away.

All but Lacy.

Lacy didn't move an inch.

Martin felt Derek's presence at his side and they shared a silent moment of understanding. A shared knowledge of the terror that had been committed that never needed to be verbalised.

"Come on," Derek put his arm on Martin's shoulder in an attempt to guide him away. "Let's leave her alone."

Martin nodded to show his hesitant agreement and, with a final glance at Lacy kneeling over the grave, he followed Derek down the path away from the graveyard and past the church.

* * *

STOOD in the middle of Derek's spare room, Martin and Derek stared at the pile of clothes Jenny had left upon a desk. The only remains of her presence in his house. Despite the bin bag clutched in Derek's hand, he made little move to remove them.

"Did you know?" Martin asked. "About the equation. Did you know?"

"I had an inkling," Derek admitted. "But I had no idea the lengths of it, nor had I had any confirmation. I will certainly say, however, that it has made things make far more sense now."

"Well, at least that's one thing this battle gave us," Martin offered, then felt bad. The amount of people who'd had to die was awful. There was nothing that justified that.

They paused by the side of the church.

"What happened was a tragedy," Derek reassured. "But do not let it make you cast doubt on what you think is right. I trust you."

Martin took a deep intake of air, held it in his lungs, then let it out.

"There's a big fight ahead of us, that's for sure," Martin announced.

"Yes."

"Got to say one thing for Jenny, though. She never lost faith in Eddie. Even right at the end, I don't think she had a single thought in her mind that the heir could do it."

"Yes. Foolish girl." Derek forced an empty chuckle. "But this does confirm one thing."

"What?"

"Eddie can't be saved. It's not an option. The heir of hell has to die."

Martin nodded in silent agreement.

Those were the words that stuck in his mind, engrained in his thoughts.

Edward King has to die.

With one large brush across the desk, Derek pushed Jenny's remaining items into the bin bag. Her clothes, a washbag – and a folded-up note addressed to Derek that he would never read.

BOOK FIVE: THE WORLD ENDS TONIGHT

RICK WOOD

THE EDWARD
KING SERIES

BOOK FIVE

THE WORLD
ENDS
TONIGHT

"Let not your heart be troubled; you believe in God, believe also in Me. In My Father's house are many mansions; if it were not so, I would have told you. I go to prepare a place for you. And if I go to prepare a place for you, I will come again and receive you to Myself; that where I am, there you may be also."

John 14:1-3

CHAPTER ONE

une 15, 2002

TWO YEARS, six months since millennium night

KELLY HESITATED. She edged through the room, wandering aimlessly, her thoughts twisting, contorting into troubled questions. As she dawdled past Derek's ageing book collection she allowed her fingers to gently trace their dusty spines, leaving a finger trail amongst the dirt of Derek's library.

"Eddie really looks up to you, you know," she spoke, a soft absence in her voice.

"Well, I believe, someday," Derek replied, "we will all look up to him. He's destined for great things, as I am sure you realise."

Managing a feeble nod, her body slumped against a

nearby desk. She folded her arms and huffed, unaware she looked so troubled. She got lost in her heavy thoughts, her perplexed conundrum, glaring gormlessly at a faint coffee stain ingrained in the carpet.

"Why don't you tell me what it is that's troubling you?" Derek asked, stroking his neat beard inquisitively. He leant gently against the bookcase, making sure not to disturb his excellent collection of old and sacred texts.

"I don't know..." Kelly muttered with a vacant shake of her head. She glided to the books, gazing at them absently, then drifted to the window, her eye contact remaining free of Derek's.

"He thinks the world of you, you must know this," Derek assured her. "He would do anything for you."

"I know. And I believe that."

"So, what is it?"

"It's... night terrors."

"Is Eddie struggling to cope with your sleep issues?"

"Oh no, Eddie's being brilliant. Out of everyone, he's the only one who has experienced first-hand what I went through. He knows how to help me."

"So, what's the problem?"

"It's Eddie's sleep. He's getting really bad night terrors, sometimes worse than mine. They are getting more and more frequent."

Derek paused. This threw him. It wasn't like Eddie to have night terrors; the last time Eddie had a sleeping problem was because he was being disturbed and troubled by the demon Lamashtu. In fact, these issues were what prompted Derek to meet Eddie. A chance encounter, though some could argue it was fate.

But Eddie had disposed of the evil entity latched onto his soul, Derek had made sure of that. Since then, Eddie had trained his mind to become calm, a sea of serenity, a resolute gathering of complicated thoughts that never seemed to trouble him. So it was strange for him to be having them now, especially as an exorcist at the top of his game.

Then again, Eddie had gone to hell. To rescue Derek. And God knows how much trauma and insomnia Derek had suffered as a result of that experience.

Surely the ordeal had put a strain on Eddie's psyche just as much, even if he hadn't shown it.

"I'm going on a journey," Derek announced. "To find answers. To find out why Eddie has these powers; to find out more about these prophecies. Hopefully, when I return, I will have more knowledge to guide you."

"But what should I do in the meantime? He's so… vacant, sometimes."

Derek leant against the desk beside Kelly. Normally he would react strongly to anyone leaning on his desk, especially when there were organised papers that they may be obstructing.

But when it was about Eddie, it didn't matter.

"Have you spoken to him about this?" Derek asked.

"Briefly. I mean, not really. It's just tough when he spends so much time supporting me."

"Maybe you should try talking to him."

"He'd deny it. Tell me nothing's wrong."

"Maybe there isn't."

"But how could there not be, when he's going through this?"

Derek shifted uncomfortably, mulling over useless ideas, dwelling on trails of thought that led nowhere. He couldn't deny it – he didn't have the answers.

Everyone always looked to him for them. Expecting him to know what to do. But in all honesty, sometimes it just came down to lucky guesswork.

"What do you think I should do, Derek?"

Derek stood, pulling his tie up, tucking his shirt in and rearranging his suit jacket. Tidying himself up was an act Derek had come to recognise in himself as an avoidance technique. A way of distracting himself from having to deal with whatever was in front of him. He felt strongly about always appearing smart, but fidgeting with his clothes were a sure sign of his discomfort that anyone else would just pass off as his 'tidiness.'

He told himself to stop it.

He looked into Kelly's melancholy eyes. She was so young, so innocent. Derek couldn't have been happier for Eddie and Kelly as a couple; but there was no denying that she didn't have the life experience Eddie had, and maybe that made it a struggle to cope.

Truth was that Eddie could deal with his night terrors and any issues that came his way better than Derek could, and better than Kelly could. Kelly needed the support, but Eddie... Eddie was something far more than they were.

"Eddie is the best man I know," Derek told her. "He is strong, and knows the difference between right and wrong more than any of us. Maybe talking isn't something Eddie necessarily needs to do."

She nodded, forcing a weak smile.

He was right.

Of course, he was right.

"Trust in Edward King. We owe him that much."

CHAPTER TWO

*J*uly 25, 2002

TWO YEARS, seven months since millennium night

BANDILE HAD KNOWN, ever since that sweetly menacing little girl had visited the side of his deathbed, that his decision on that fateful night would be his fatal undoing.

He had wrestled with the ifs and buts of his decision, entertaining notions of what it would mean if he had said no.

But that hadn't been an option. He was young and selfish, and did not want to die.

If he'd have greeted death and denied the devil, maybe he would have been rewarded by a place in heaven.

But he was young, foolish, and cowardly.

Though, if he was honest with himself, the only thing that had changed was that he was no longer young.

The devil had saved him from death and bestowed all the riches that could be brought to him. The devil had given him the gift of foresight, as selected though his prophecies were. He'd been given everything every man had ever dreamed of

Unfortunately, it had come at a cost.

And any idea of saying no disappeared as soon as they had come. He had to follow his duty. He had to follow the path set out for him by hell. It was not something anyone could defy.

One does not simply contemplate facing the wrath of a creature made of pure evil.

Now there he was, part of the Devil's Three. Along with a disabled woman and a dead man, he had formed the triad that had called on the devil to restore the antichrist into its rightful body.

And they had succeeded.

Bandile was on his knees, in disbelief at what he was seeing. He was a big man, having had to work with his hands in hard labour to survive growing up in huts in South Africa, and had grown muscles that filled his black frame, giving him a lean, intimidating posture. But even now he found his lip quivering and his body trembling at the sight of what was happening.

Edward King, the man with a reputation as a noble exorcist with heartfelt intentions, was diving the sharp end of a knife into the throat of the girlfriend, Kelly – who had been captured by Bandile to be part of the Devil's Three ritual as 'the suffered.'

Eddie pulled the knife away and Bandile, along with all other transfixed eyes in the room, watched intently with dropped jaw. Kelly's helpless eyes looked up at the man she loved as blood sprayed haphazardly from her neck and all over the room, fizzling out into a gushing puddle dripping along the floor.

Derek Lansdale, the man he had fooled so easily, watched on in shock, gasping.

"How could you…" his feeble eyes cried, crumbling as his body collapsed into an inconsolable heap on the floor.

"It was the only way…" Eddie whimpered.

Eddie's body stiffened, his joints contorting in various directions. His shed his skin like a snake's, peeling off and floating into ashes. His features moulded into a malevolent mess, red eyes looking over the room, claws and beastly features bursting out of him in a painful transformation.

Bandile glanced around the room. Two young women, supposedly friends of Eddie, backed up against the wall. Jason Aslan, who had been 'the dead' as part of the ritual, disappeared into floating pieces.

Eddie's skin was now dark and blood-red, with veins sticking out all over his body.

Bandile was not going to waste any more time in this room. He had done his part.

He turned toward the window that already had a few cracks tearing up its surface and leapt toward it, smashing through and leaving the disrupted living room, tumbling onto the painful bumps of a small hedge below.

He jumped forward and ran.

And he did not stop running.

He endured all the weather. From the beating of the furious sleet, to the frozen temperatures of night, to the harsh heat of the following day.

This continued for longer than he could tell. He had no distinctive home, and was scared to return to any places he'd once haunted, though he wasn't entirely sure why. He couldn't make sense of much in those early days, his mind awash with tormenting, chaotic thoughts shooting through his brain and exploding into fragments. He grew paranoid, anxious, even seeing things he wasn't entirely sure were there.

For days at a time all he would do was run, run, run. He would steal food, sleep under discarded newspaper in shop doors, beg for mercy from those who tried to rob him only to find he had nothing.

Then he ran some more.

Finally, he broke down. Collapsing on his knees in the middle of a busy town centre, he held his hand out for food, glaring with dizzy vision at the people who bustled past him. They all ignored him. He had nothing.

He stole. He fought. He wept.

He was a shattered wreck of a man.

His strong, muscular body deteriorated rapidly under the stress of his mind and the heavy strain upon his body. He starved, his dry throat parched, begging the devil for quenching that would never come.

He never once considered praying to God. He knew he would not be welcome there anymore.

The devil had offered him salvation. This was anything but.

His ribs became visible through his chest.

His bones ached.

He became accustomed to the headaches of dehydration, the emptiness in his stomach, and the pains in his chest as he yearned for anything to sustain his miserable existence.

He longed for the devil to do something.

Bandile had done his bidding. Was he not coming to offer some salvation?

He knew he deserved no mercy, but he at least deserved a reward. A place in hell, away from the torture, somewhere the devil could hold him high and rave about his triumphant contribution to the cause.

Then, one day, shivering in the doorway of a broken-down factory on a cold, lonesome night, he heard footsteps approaching.

He closed his eyes, hoping that whoever it was would leave him alone. Wished that they were not going beat him, or humiliate him, or mutilate him.

Then again, he decided, perhaps they would grant him the sweet release of death.

"Pafetick," one of them declared, in a screechy, anarchic voice. "Fort ee woz meant to be some big man?"

"Shut the fuck up," came a gruffer, more assertive voice. Bandile felt the owner of the voice come down to his level, but he closed his eyes tighter, wishing to be left alone. "Oi, open yer fuckin' eyes."

Bandile did as he was told.

The owner of the first voice was stood, his head tilted to the side. He was topless, and unhealthily skinny. Every inch of his body was covered in tattoos, all of them either tribal, or scary laughing faces, or of the crucifix hanging upside down. A pattern of engrained ink ran along his lips, like the shadow of his teeth, adorning his face with ceremonial tattoos, even covering his eye lids and his ears with black patterns.

The other man, crouching down to Bandile with an arm rested on his shoulder, had a large beard. He wasn't as heavily tattooed, but still had his forehead marked with upside-down crucifixes and tears marked down his cheeks. He wore a long, brown coat that made him look homeless, and the hand that rested on Bandile was beneath a tatty, fingerless leather glove. Bandile noticed a swastika decorated his knuckles, and he immediately grew wary of a racist attack.

"Wh – what do you want?" Bandile begged.

The crouching man shook his head.

"My name is Dexter, and this behind me is Bagsy," he

introduced with a rough, gruff, common voice containing a mixture of accents. "We've been waitin' f'you. Nah you're 'ere under a fuckin' doorway. What is going on?"

"I – I don't understand."

"'E sent us mate!" screeched the one called Bagsy. "We been waitin' for yous to lead us!"

"To lead you?" Bandile echoed.

"We worship him, in his name," Dexter explained. It took a few seconds for Bandile to realise they meant the devil.

Satan worshippers... Bandile thought to himself. *And they want me to lead them?*

"The antichrist has risen," Dexter continued. "The heir of hell is here."

"Really?" Bandile responded, not knowing whether to be worried or pleased. He had seen it happen, but had since disbelieved his eyes.

"Yeah, an' we're worried 'bout these hoomans who fink they can do 'im in. They be raisin' an' army, or so we 'ere."

It took Bandile another few seconds to adjust to their voices and understand what they were saying. He assumed by 'humans' they meant Derek Lansdale, and assumed that by 'do them in' they meant… Well, to bring about a fatal end, or something to that effect.

"Okay," Bandile confirmed.

"So get up, you're comin' wiv us," Dexter told Bandile, grabbing him to his feet. "An' we ain't got no time to lose."

CHAPTER THREE

*M*arch 20, 2003

THREE YEARS, three months since millennium night

DEREK WATCHED from the study window as the unsettled trees collided against each other in the frantic wind. Tree branches bombarded the air with venomous strikes. The rain bashed against the house, a salvo of attacks against the window, beating against it like a broken drum.

He wanted to sleep.

More than anything, Derek wanted to sleep.

"And the reports are coming in this hour of more mysterious disappearances," came a voice over the radio Derek had forgotten he had left playing. "Many of the world's greatest, most noble figures have vanished without a trace. In more than eighty reported cases across the world, law enforcement officers have said that there were no signs of struggle, and the world is yet to come to an explanation that satisfies all the conspiracy theorists that–"

Derek turned the radio off.

Glancing a sight of himself in the reflection of the window, he flinched at the pronounced bags beneath his bloodshot eyes. His collar was open, his tie hung three buttons down, and his shirt was half-untucked. He had never allowed himself to deteriorate to this state of scruffiness in his life.

But he had a meeting. He couldn't go to bed yet.

So he waited, watching the violent weather attack people running by, sending bins flying against the debris of a nearby field.

"Derek," came a well-spoken, elegant female voice from behind him.

He did not jump. He was expecting this.

The news report on the radio had left him in no doubt as to what was happening.

He turned around confidently, bestowing his eyes upon the most beautiful creature known to man. A faultless woman, with lusciously smooth black skin, long, black hair, and a white dress that glided off her curves as if by magic. Gabrielle was an angel through and through, there was no doubt about that. And, for someone who was thousands of years old, she did not show it.

"I suppose you've come for me, have you?" Derek prompted with an air of irritation in his voice.

"Yes," Gabrielle confirmed. "Are you ready?"

Derek turned back to the vile storm. The weather was no coincidence. The end was near and the environment was furiously retaliating; though most people would be gazing at the spring gale thinking it was an ordinary storm, with no idea of the omen it was announcing.

The heir had risen. The devil would follow. And then the depths of hell would be unleashed.

It made sense to go with her.

To be evacuated. To run. To save himself, along with the other people deemed good enough to rescue.

But Derek hadn't been one for making sense lately.

"I'm not going with you," Derek decided.

"Please, Derek, don't do this–"

"I'm not doing anything. I'm just not going with you." He stared absentmindedly out the window without turning back to her. "You can leave now."

She took a stride forward. He could feel her pained eyes reaching out to him, beseeching him. He had no doubt she understood his reasons, but she would still try and argue the contrary. It would do no good. Any attempt to persuade him would be futile.

"Please, Derek, you must come with us."

"What, go with you so I can watch everyone who isn't worthy enough die?"

"This was how it was always going to be! You read the books, you saw when the prophecies ended. The rapture is coming, and God is evacuating his own worthy. And you have been honoured enough to be chosen as one of them. Please don't stay on earth to die."

"I'm not staying on earth to *die.*"

"The apocalypse is coming, we can't stop that. There is nothing more heaven can do. Surely you can understand this?"

"Then maybe heaven isn't trying hard enough!" Derek screamed, hauling his entire body around until his heavy arms pointed in the direction of Gabrielle. He was suddenly panting. His heart punched rapidly against his chest as if bashing against a cage.

An uncomfortable silence followed where all that could

be heard was Derek's heavy breathing. He was infuriated. Incensed.

"With all that we've done, all the fights we've entered, all the lives we've lost!" Derek spat. "And you are telling me that heaven – that *your Holy One*, is just packing it in?"

"This isn't the first time something like that this happened, Derek."

"Oh, please."

"You think you're the only world out here with life on it? You think you're the only world where something evil has risen up and taken hold? We've done this many times. We've seen what it is like to fight it, and we have seen how pointless it is. We are not abandoning earth, we are being rational."

"That's not what it feels like."

"Derek, please–"

"Just *go!*"

Derek's fists clenched, a surge of fury firing up and down his spine, his gut filling with hate like poison. He could see it dawning on Gabrielle's face. It was useless.

Derek was not going.

"This is your decision? You are just going to stay on earth to die?"

"No, I am going to stay on earth to fight. Dying is something that happens in life. Your God created life, and he created death, so surely he'll know that."

Gabrielle sighed and turned toward the door, pausing one last time.

"Are you sure you will not come with me?" she asked.

"God and heaven may have given up on earth," Derek retorted. "But I haven't."

With a flickering white light she was gone, leaving Derek to glare at the empty space where she had stood.

Suddenly, he felt very alone.

CHAPTER FOUR

*E*ternity begins with an earth-shattering moment.

The jolt of two eyelids shooting open.

The squint against blinding light. The flinch away from the vast luminosity encapsulating any mortal person's vision.

Eddie fell to his knees, producing a mouthful of bloody vomit, coughing it over the rough surface he knelt upon.

His stomach was in inscrutable pain, twisting and throbbing into bumps of harsh acid, churning his vacant insides like butter.

But there were no insides. He felt hollow, empty. But still heavy. Like he felt the weight of burden pinning him to the floor like dead weight.

Where am I? his mind weakly wondered.

He rotated his head, taking in his surroundings. The walls felt like they were closing in. He was boxed into a room that had barely a few yards between each wall. The walls themselves were made of large, dirty stones, fading from grey to dark grey. Against the walls was a subtle blue illumination, shading the walls with the colour of the ocean.

Beneath his bare feet was straw. Many pieces, covering a bumpy rock surface. No matter where he walked his feet hurt, whether it was from the sharp spikes of straw or rough bumps of harsh gravel.

Noticing something on one of the stones in the wall, he stepped forward, surveying it intently.

They were scratch marks. Five definite corresponding lines where someone's nails had dug in and dragged. The more he looked, the more detailed carvings he noticed. Words such as, "save me," "God help us," or, "no hope here," were carved at various points of the wall, only visible when Eddie got close to them, squinting against the dark light.

At first he went with his instinct, frantically scouring the walls for a weakness. There was no door. But maybe if he could find a weak stone, something he could move...

He went through every stone he could reach, pushing it, prodding it, grappling with it.

There was nothing. No escape whatsoever.

He looked upwards, peering into the sky above that just faded into darkness. He was no doubt in a pit, but if the pit had an opening, it was far out of his reach. The sturdy walls disappeared into the darkness above, narrowing into nothing but distant black.

He leapt up, pushing his fingers into the cracks between the stones, hoping he could somehow climb, manoeuvre his way upwards – but doing so sent a shockwave through his body and sent him firing on his back.

He groaned in anguish. It hurt.

Something about the stones was stopping him climbing. They were cursed somehow.

He'd been in purgatory before. He'd been in hell before. But he did not recognise this place.

And he was certain that it was not heaven.

The shock he felt when touching the stone continued to fire through him, like something was inside his body, writhing like a wild creature.

A sickening convulsion of his body churned into a stiffened twitch. Every muscle in his body contorted into a fixed clench, like his whole body was a tightened fist, pressing against itself.

He screamed, allowing the pain to escape his lips.

It did nothing.

It was still agony.

He struggled against it, fought against whatever was holding him still, whatever was holding him captive.

With a defiant shriek, he collapsed to the floor. He curled up into a ball, shaking, quivering, overwhelmingly alone. Terrified, but at the same time, hesitantly curious.

Where am I?

This was not his world.

This was not somewhere he belonged.

He dropped his head and closed his eyes, trying to will the migraine away. But the soreness of his cranium only grew greater, harder, his stolen mind beating against his fragile skull.

When he lifted his head up there was something there. Like a screen, but with fuzzier edges. In front of him, a blurred image blaring down.

He watched it intently as the image drew into focus.

It was Kelly.

Oh my God, Kelly.

The screen grew, wrapping around his face, and played out an image like it was through his eyes. Like he was the one committing these actions.

His hands held onto a knife.

His hands plunged it downwards, into Kelly's throat.

He watched as she cried out in pain, looking up into his eyes with a helpless lack of understanding.

The moment went into slow motion. He lived it again.

And again.

And again.

Just as he already had numerous times.

Watching that look in her eyes as he did it, as the person she loved and trusted most in the world betrayed her. Then she went limp. Flopped into a heavy body uncomfortably spread out upon the floor.

The final thing Kelly saw before she died was him killing her.

It all came back. It thwacked him like a punch in the gut.

The image changed. He felt his arms stiffen, grow, his nails elongate into claws, and within seconds he was a vast, snarling, carnivorous hellbeast.

Then he snapped out of it. He was back in the dark, dank dungeon, completely perplexed.

That's when he realised.

He wasn't Eddie.

He was, except not all of him.

This body he looked down at was not his own body. It was an image of his body. He could see it clearly, but it was not his body. It was his mind inventing what he needed to make this experience make sense.

He was merely a soul. The remains of what was.

Eddie was in hell or on earth. Rising up as the heir and slaughtering innocent people. Preparing for the devil's ascension. Getting ready for the rapture.

And this is what he had been sent. That one piece of Eddie that was good, that had been left.

His soul.

That thing that had to be used so he could be conceived by hell.

Trapped.

If only I could get out, find a way back, I could put this piece of good back in my body, I could...

No.

It was useless.

There was nothing he could do.

He peered around himself. It was empty. Nothing but stone walls rising up into a dark abyss until there was nothing left.

There was no entrance. No exit. No way in or out.

Nothing he could visibly see.

He had no powers.

He wasn't Eddie, he was just a soul. His body had changed. His face had changed. He had no real hands he could pour spells out of. He had no way to fight.

He had to rely on his friends. Derek. Jenny. Lacy.

They could do it.

Surely, they could do it.

And the dawn of realisation struck his mind like lightning.

He was stuck in a cycle. Watching the pain of his loving girlfriend die again and again. Realising he could do nothing to stop it or save it. All because it was some part of a sick game.

Some part of Eddie's sick game.

The heir of hell's sick game.

A way to keep him trapped. Keep him going crazy. A way to ensure his maddening state only worsened as he found no resolve that he could use to escape.

And it was working.

He had no idea how long he had been trapped there.

All he knew was that his body was being used as a vessel for hatred. An entity occupied it with malice and cruel intentions.

If there was a low point, he had far surpassed it.
He only hoped his friends would not have to suffer.
He knew Derek would try.
He knew Jenny would try.
His faith had to be put in them.

CHAPTER FIVE

*C*ircling a few fading ice cubes in a half-empty whisky glass, Derek sighed at the few drops of therapeutic booze he had left. The ice cubes collided with each other so ungracefully, just three little circles left crashing around in his tumbler.

He downed the rest of the glass, grabbed the whisky bottle from the side of the chair, and filled himself back up again.

He looked down. Open collar, loose tie, shirt untucked. A prickly beard sticking untidily off his chin like the wild hairs of an untamed animal.

It suddenly struck him what he had once said to Eddie.

"One must be presentable, whether you are meeting the mother or taking on the very depths of hell itself."

Derek scoffed.

The irony.

So much said to guide a wayward man, such advice that he had now neglected.

Realising he was starting to pity himself again, he took another large swig of his whisky to numb his mind, relishing the sharp uncomfortable sting scalding the back of his throat.

He had never been one to wallow in self-pity before.

But his advice had never resulted in the death of so many before.

He was not the one who gave up, who wavered in their disbelief of others, who gave in and let a single crease of shirt be unfolded.

But recent events had debilitated him. They had gone some way to wearing down his resolve. This only incensed him further, knowing he was better than that, knowing that he wasn't a weak man.

He was everyone's rock.

Well, sometimes he got tired of being a rock.

Tired of training Eddie.

Guiding Martin.

Being heaven's bitch in each and every one of their battles.

He retched at the thought of the glorious angel of Gabrielle being sent from his Almighty, with the intention to fetch him away from earth. To remove him from a war he had been waging for years. Because he was supposedly special. Because he was worthy.

"Hah!" he grunted, and took another big gulp.

Worthy?

He shook his heavy head, dropping his pounding, drunken mind, and directing his absent gaze to the crumbs ingrained in his carpet.

How was he worthy?

He remembered the words he'd said to Martin. What he had told him.

They had lingered by the side of the field, waiting for Martin to decide whether or not the army should fight the heir.

Derek had declared that they would follow Martin.

Derek had believed in Martin.

Derek had known it was the right decision.

Turns out he had known nothing.

Now they were all dead. The army they had gathered, the powerful, supernatural forces recruited from around the world. Dead. Slaughtered. Pulled apart by a demonic, genocidal maniac.

The world had lost the only people with the power to resist what was to come.

And all because he'd told Martin to keep going.

He had to be Martin's rock. Martin was inevitably inconsolable following the army's death. Following the loss of Jenny. But Derek couldn't let that cause him to falter.

There was too much resting on his young shoulders to let him think he was to blame.

"It is not your fault," Derek had reassured him. "And you can't let it be your fault. Self-doubt is a bigger enemy than the heir; you need to believe in yourself."

Derek snorted.

What bullshit.

The only part of that Derek truly believed was that it wasn't Martin's fault.

Because it was his.

He had told Martin to make the decision. He had followed the call of a delinquent seventeen-year-old without thought or hesitation. Because he thought it was right.

Now look where they were.

He finished his whisky. Grimaced as he poured too much down his throat. Withdrew the bottle once more and filled himself up to the top. Stared at it. Circled it, watching the whisky temporarily stain the inside of the glass as it whipped around seamlessly.

He closed his eyes.

"Sorry, Jenny," he whispered.

He lifted his head back and chugged a large gulp of whisky down his sore throat. He relished the sting, relished the pain, relished something breaking this absent knowledge of what they needed to do.

"Sorry, Eddie," he whispered.

Glared at his glass.

Swilled it in another circular motion.

Downed it.

Filled his glass up.

Downed it once more.

Closed his eyes.

Tried to dream. Tried to think. Tried to rid his tired head of all the justified negativity.

After a few more glasses, he passed out.

CHAPTER SIX

*M*arch 21, 2003

THREE YEARS, three months since millennium night

AN ABRUPT CRASH into the wooden bench sent broken shards of wood bashing against the back wall of the house. The garden was a mess of splinters, wooden wreckage lying across the grass like small pricks of failure.

Martin sighed. It wasn't working. He'd been at it for hours.

But if he was to become the heir's equal…

He must have a range of spells.

Fuck a range of spells. Cannot be arsed.

But he knew that, despite how assertively he may think that, he did not believe it.

It took hard work. Patience.

The only problem was that Martin had never been one for patience.

"Right, again," he demanded of himself.

He stuck his right hand out, spinning his finger in a small, circular motion. The faster he got, the more a spark ignited, a golden flash echoing his movement. As the flashes grew more frequent he increased the radius of the circle he was creating more and more, until he had created a circle of light that turned from flickers to a fully formed circular edge.

Watching carefully, ensuring he picked the exact correct time, he plunged an open palm forward. The circle flew across the garden with apt precision and, for a moment, Martin was hopeful.

Half of the circled wrapped itself around the bench, then the other half ignited into a fiery mess, exploding planks of wood to shatters in the process.

"Argh!" Martin growled, turning his head to the sky and collapsing on the floor. "For fuck's sake!"

I've been at this for hours!

He'd gotten the basic spells down; conjuring elements, throwing fireballs, plunging a gust of wind into an opponent. But the last time he faced the heir, these spells had proven useless.

He had to learn something better.

He had to *be* better.

It was just so bloody difficult.

After huffing with exasperation, Martin lifted his head to glare at the remains of his attempts.

A restraint spell. Conjuring a circular edge out of condensed fire, throwing it forward and trapping your opponent. If he could do this, he could temporarily hold the heir, then hit it with lethal attacks.

But who was he kidding?

The heir would not allow itself to be trapped in this shitty excuse for power.

Martin allowed his mind to wander, stumbling upon memories of school. His so-called friend, Simon. Kristy, the girl he fancied more than anything.

He wondered what they would be up to now.

Simon would probably be down the park underage drinking or hanging around outside McDonald's, intimidating passers-by.

Kristy would most likely be getting off with whatever guy she let take her around the back alley of Primark.

Even so, Martin felt a pang of jealousy.

They were still living out their lives, exploring their youth, taking the time to discover who they were. If they did something dickish, it would be all right, because "they are just kids."

Such reasoning didn't apply to Martin.

Not anymore.

He couldn't be just a kid. He was only just approaching eighteen, but had a responsibility that no adult in this world could understand.

He dragged himself reluctantly back to his feet.

If at first you don't succeed...

Once more he rapidly rotated his arm, creating a circle, making the elements fit just right. Then once he had a perfect solid base of gold, he threw the circle forward, watching it crash into the bench and smash the final remains to oblivion.

...then scream and cry and tell everyone to fuck off.

What if this had never happened? What if he had never gone to Eddie about his mother? What if Cassy had never come to him and placed this burden on his shoulders?

What would he be doing?

Intimidating some old lady. Starting fights with anyone

who gave him a dodgy look. Convincing himself that he didn't need stupid, pathetic school.

Yes, this was a horrible fate, but at least it stopped him from being a dysfunctional yob.

Oh, what he wouldn't give to be able to go back to ignorance… To deny that any of this was real, to return to his incessant prickishness, to continue hating everything and everyone. To be able to throw a teenage tantrum, kick off at a teacher, shout at everyone that it wasn't fair that he was being made to learn maturity.

He would never have had to witness death. He would never have had to see Father Douglas' demise, Jenny's body being ripped apart, or the violent end of the entire army they had gathered.

An army.

What a mistake.

This burden was his, and his alone. Derek was a huge support, but even so, ultimately, it was up to him.

Heaven conceived him.

No one else.

So he needed to get a grip.

Stop daydreaming ridiculous fantasies.

It was over.

That old life was over and he could never go back.

This was his life now.

Waiting to fight.

Waiting to die.

Or, just waiting.

"Fuck it."

He lifted his arm out and began the circular motion once more.

CHAPTER SEVEN

*E*ddie's mind spun with empty thoughts, absent ideas racing manically around his vacant mind.

He had no idea how long he had been lying there, but he knew that it was making him go crazy.

As he imagined the devil would be intending.

His back ached less, as if he was getting used to the uncomfortable bumps he had been laid upon. He didn't know what was worse; feeling the pain, or being there for so long he became accustomed to it.

What struck him most was the complete absence of anything. No stimulus, no interaction, nothing to do but sit and ruminate – it stirred his mind into a fever. If he wasn't careful, he was going to lose his sanity.

If he had sanity.

Does a soul have sanity?

Yet another thought that could swim around its mind until it drowned in the sea of unanswered questions.

A faint whirring attracted his attention. A small spinning from behind his head.

He sat up, opened his eyes, and peered at a small image unfolding before him.

Upon this screen was a field. The weather was torrential, rain beating furiously down upon the soggy grass.

But the lightning and the thunder rumbles weren't what attracted his attention.

The screen was through the eyes of something. Of someone. And beneath these eyes were a mass of people, full of supernatural gifts, hurling different spells at him, conjuring vast amounts of elements, bombarding him with everything they had.

Before he had been able to muster an idea as to what this screen was, it had shot forward and wrapped itself around Eddie's eyes. Eddie could now see through the screen as if he was physically in it.

Because he was in it.

At least, part of him was.

His hand reached out, revealing a sharp claw, bigger than several human heads. Below this claw was a mass of puny humans, all of them fighting, attempting to oppose him.

He resisted anything they threw at him with tedious ease. His claw swung down in retaliation and swiped through several throats, splattering blood into the rain as the bodies turned limp.

This was him.

He was doing this.

He could feel it. Every swipe he took, he could feel the soft tissue of their throats ripping at the tip of his fingers. Thick, red blood seeped through his claws. The stench of death was overwhelming.

And the rage.

It soared through his body like a hundred volts of electricity, purging him of any positivity, soaking him until he was drenched with a detesting of everything.

It belonged to him. All of this belonged to him. This body, this anger, these raging thoughts – they were his.

Eddie ripped himself away from the scene that had wrapped itself so securely around his face, diving to the floor, doing all he could to tear himself away from the trance.

He lay on the blank floor shivering, covering his head to protect it from being consumed by this vision again.

He knew what it was.

He knew he was looking through the eyes of the heir of hell. He knew he was slaughtering innocent people with the ease of slicing butter. He had no control. He was in there, feeling everything, but in the backseat; whatever was driving him was not of this world. It was something completely and entirely evil.

But how many did I kill?

As if something wanted to torture him with the answer, the screen changed. Eddie lifted his weak head, ignoring his painful migraine, and watched, allowing it to wrap around his vision once more.

It was done. Now it was a sunny day and the field was covered with bodies. A few of the corpses were intact, but most weren't; it was like a butcher's bin. Body parts, bloody heaps of unrecognisable limbs, dead rips of skin. Everything was unidentifiable. And he had done all of it.

Derek.

He saw Derek traipsing despondently through this field, looking around himself, recoiling at the horror.

So much death.

Derek couldn't see him.

Derek didn't know he was watching, hiding.

Derek paused, closing his eyes, dropping his head. Like looking at the suffering was too much. Like he couldn't bear to see it.

Like he couldn't bear to see what Eddie had done.

The man he had trained. The man he had nurtured, taught, watched evolve into a powerful soldier of good. Now the cause of so much pain and misery.

It was more than Eddie could take, and he was about to look away until he saw that Derek wasn't alone.

Someone was there. Someone bright. An elegant, white dress folding their body into beauty; long, blond hair, a beam of positivity.

She wasn't of the mortal world, Eddie could see that.

Then he realised. He knew who it was.

The girl who died when he was a child. The girl he had freed from Balam. The girl who had set all the terrible events of his life in motion.

"Cassy…"

Now there she was. A grown woman, except… she was more than that. Accepted by heaven as a soldier for good.

Working with Derek.

Working with Derek in the fight against humanity.

Working with Derek, against Eddie, in the fight against humanity.

His heart stung. He collapsed to his knees, unable to control tears from escaping his eyes.

The little sister he had loved so much. He'd lost her as a child. He had fought to save her. He'd battled for her soul, to have it freed from hell.

Now she was taking the last stand against the brother who had done everything for her.

Because she knew it was right. Because she knew that it was what this Eddie would want her to do.

And he did want her to.

He wanted her to make him stop.

"No more…" he whimpered, wanting to go back to the monotonous absence he had been suffering. To return to the tormenting, vacant room so he didn't have to watch those he loved weeping over the mess he had made.

Anything but this.

Anything to relieve this pain.

But he could not escape it. Everywhere he turned, her torment was decorated over his vision. Her face as she cried at the anguish caused by him.

"Cassy, it wasn't me!" he begged, wishing she could hear her.

Her head rose. A flicker.

As if she was reacting.

As if she had heard something.

"Cassy? Can you hear me?"

She froze. Her eyes widened. Something was taking hold of her.

"Cassy!" he cried out with everything he had, his vocal cords straining under the pressure of his scream. "Free me! I'm trapped, I'm here!"

The image disappeared. As if someone could see what was happening.

The sounds, the feelings, the smells. It all went. Eddie was back to the dungeon again.

He didn't know if she had heard him.

But it was worth a fraction of hope.

CHAPTER EIGHT

The field was stained with the remnants of loyal fighters. Everywhere Derek looked he saw death, torture, and mayhem. He tried to raise a mental barrier to it, conceal his emotions, put a block on his emotions.

But it was tough.

It was so, so tough.

Walking amongst the remains was unbearable. He'd had the call that morning that the church was sending people to conceal it, to cover it up. To make sure no one went near it. The authorities had been paid enough to keep the public away, and Derek expected them any moment.

But part of him wished they didn't arrive.

So what if everyone saw this? Surely people should know what was coming, and what they were up against.

If only to ensure that they knew the devil was real, and that he was coming – so very, very imminently.

"Hi," came a soft feminine voice from behind Derek. He didn't need to turn around to know who it was. He remained dawdling, stepping over a mangled bloody lung, between a contorted leg, until it was too much. He had to look up to the sky, if only to stop looking at the destruction spread across the field.

"Do you know what I don't get?" Derek began, turning to Cassy, her angelic state shining over the darkness of the field. "Is why your stupid God allows this to happen."

"It is unethical to mess with free will."

"Unethical?!" Derek exploded. "You're talking to me about what is unethical? Standing by and watching people fight in his name when he could bloody do something is ruddy unethical!"

"Derek–"

"And then your stupid head angel comes down with plans to evacuate when all of you could come down and fight and rid us of this damn mess!"

"Derek, calm down," Cassy spoke, not raising the temperature of her voice one bit. She placed a reassuring hand on Derek's back, watching his face tear with emotions he couldn't handle. "This isn't you."

"I have been here for years, doing his work, and I have said nothing. I have called on him to remove demons from innocent people's bodies. Why do I need to do that? Why do I need to call on him to do this, when he could so easily do it himself?"

"But he has fought back, Derek. He gave the world you. And Martin. And sent me to guide you. That is him playing his part, and it is quite a stretch as to what he could do without messing with free will."

Derek shook his head, turning his angry eyes to Cassy's elegant gaze.

"It's such a cop-out."

"Derek, please don't let this get the better of you. You've been a strong and stable leader. For all of us. Myself included. You need to keep the faith."

"Keep the faith?" Derek echoed, disdain soaking his voice.

"You've got to–"

Cassy's eyes grew wide and she grasped her chest as if she'd just taken a heavy punch in the gut.

"Cassy?"

She fell to her knees, her eyes practically bursting out their sockets, reaching out a helpless hand. Derek rushed to her side, placing a hand on her back, trying to steady her, but the pain was evidently vast.

As she scrunched her face and her body up, battling the agony, she moaned an exasperated wail.

Then she froze. She uttered a quivering gasp, her lips shaking, her eyes open wide.

"Oh, dear God," she gulped. "Eddie…"

Derek's brow furrowed. He kept his arms around her, steadying her; but his gaze grew into a longing need to know what she was seeing.

"Cassy," she spoke, in a voice slightly altered, as if it was deeper; it was her speaking, but with a different tone entirely. "It wasn't me."

She choked. Closed her eyes. Then opened her mouth once more.

"Cassy, can you hear me?" she spoke in the same man's voice.

She fell to the floor, rolling around, groaning, then froze once more. Her eyes shot open.

"Free me! I'm trapped, I'm here!"

Derek recognised that voice.

But no…

It can't be…

Then, with a final flourish of her fluttering eyelids, Cassy fell flat out on the floor, her body no longer tense.

"Cassy," Derek prompted, kneeling beside her. "Cassy, are you okay?"

She shook her head. "It's Eddie…"

She reached her hands out and used Derek's body to help her clamber to her knees.

"What about Eddie?"

She ignored him. Instead, choosing to push herself onto her feet and aimlessly wander away, unconsciously stepping over various entrails. Her hand rested on her forehead, her eyes scrunching together as if dealing with a horrific headache.

"Cassy, please," Derek pleaded, walking after her. Whatever she had seen, he needed to know.

If it was to do with Eddie, he needed to know.

"It's Eddie," she tried to explain, stumbling over her words. "But not Eddie..."

"What does that mean?"

"It was Eddie's soul, I'm sure of it."

"His soul?"

Cassy turned to Derek, fixing her eyes on his, watching as his insides entwined into a sickening muddle just as much as hers had.

"He – he's there."

"There? Where's there? Where is he? Is he going to do something else? Is he going to kill more people?"

"No, it's... not the heir of hell. It is Eddie."

"But Eddie *is* the heir of hell, Cassy."

"No." She shook her head. "His soul still remains good. I've seen it."

CHAPTER NINE

anuary 1, 2000

MILLENNIUM NIGHT

"THAT THE BEST YOU GOT?" Eddie taunted the demon before him with a cocky grin.

Balam rose out of Adeline's body, hovering in the air. Its three heads – that of a human, a bull, and a ram – each snarled and snapped at Eddie. Its human head lifted its frown into an aggressive growl, its bull head snorting readily, and its ram head beating against its own chest in desperation to kill this bastard.

It had been a tiresome exorcism on the night of the new millennium, and Eddie was growing weary. But he knew that now he had ridded Adeline's body of Balam, he could return Cassy from hell. There was no doubt Balam had Cassy's soul, captured for torture, kept in hell for what Balam must intend to be an eternity.

Eddie was determined to do this. Determined to save her from this prince of hell's evil clutches.

He would die before he gave in.

Balam growled again. This time not to intimidate, but to show aggressive displeasure at being well-matched. Eddie had already ridded young Adeline's body of Balam's possession and, for this reason, it felt increasingly weary. It had struggled to defeat Eddie and was giving its last attempt at fighting by throwing a series of flames forward.

Eddie lifted his arms in a swiping motion and forced the flames to cease, to drop to the floor in a handful of ash. He threw his arms in the air, exploding a ball of wind before him, forcing Balam to thwack against the far wall, dropping to the floor pathetically.

"Free my sister!" demanded Eddie, a scream filled with rage and resolve.

He rose his arms, forcing Balam into mid-air, rotating and rotating its body, faster and faster, until the ram screamed, the bull helplessly snorted, and the human face begged for mercy.

"Free my sister!"

Balam's body bashed against the wall, again and again. This would be too much humiliation for this proud prince of hell to take, and Eddie hoped this would be enough to open Balam's clutches and to take Cassy's soul back.

"I command you, bitch of hell. Release her!"

Balam screamed out, its voice getting caught on the wind of its spin. The room was a tornado of chaos, objects turning to weapons against Balam as they were caught in the middle of the whirlwind it created.

Eddie chuckled as the ram head squealed in agony, enjoying seeing this thing suffer.

"It is done!" Balam cried out.

The body of Cassy rose out of his muscular, scarred chest, rising into the centre of the room.

Balam did not stick around to see the two reunited, and neither would he want to. With a fit of aggression, his body instantly sank downwards into the ground. The room disappeared as it plummeted and plummeted, further and further, until it found itself slamming its aching back against a large stone, back in the pit of hell.

It lifted itself off.

It was livid.

Fought. Defeated.

Embarrassed that he'd had to free his servant.

Back in hell to let the devil know that he had let heaven's child go. That he had been defeated by hell's own creation. That the prince of hell was not worthy of its king.

The chains Cassy had been kept in lay absently without an owner across the rocky cliff. Balam had enjoyed torturing many souls across an eternity of human civilisation, but never had enjoyed torturing a human spirit the way Cassy's had been tortured – after all, this was the daughter of heaven. Heaven's conception, forced to face an eternity of pain.

Now, nothing.

Balam's pride was severely wounded. A huge dent in the ongoing belief that it was better than anyone, or anything. Especially those peasants on earth.

Now it had been defeated by hell's child.

It swore then and there that it would have revenge. When they brought out the heir of hell, when it rained fire upon the weak earth, Balam would rise. It would find this Cassy girl and return her to hell.

There, Balam would continue to torment her. To wriggle inside her until it made her bleed, to slash her with a thousand continuous flicks of a sharp whip, to rip her in two and feed on her insides then watch as they agonisingly grew back. To humiliate her, to rape her, to watch as she squealed under his three heaving heads.

When the time was right, Balam would return to earth.

Balam would march on up to heaven and snatch her out if it needed to.

Cassy would face an eternity of his rage and torment.

And at that point, Edward King would have fulfilled his true destiny, and there would be no way to stop him.

CHAPTER TEN

*M*arch 22, 2003

THREE YEARS, three months since millennium night

MARTIN WATCHED with his mouth agape as Derek and Cassy frantically paced the study, musing over possibilities that were completely nonsensical to him.

"It could be a trick."

"It could be fake."

"Or it could be real."

"What if there was a way to reach him?"

"Could we bring him back?"

"Would he come back right?"

"Would it matter?"

"Of course it would."

"Are you sure what you saw was real?"

"The devil couldn't play a trick on an angel, you're not mortal."

"It must be genuine."

"It must be real."

Eventually, Martin sighed, growing frustrated, and tried to interject.

"Guys?" he offered.

"Where was he?"

"I have no idea."

"Guys?" he tried again.

"But why now?"

"Where has he been all this time?"

"*Guys!*"

They both froze, turning their muddled stares toward him.

"What the hell is going on?" he asked, exasperatedly waving his hands in the air.

Derek and Cassy sat, realising they needed to calm their ideas and fill Martin in. Slowly but particularly, Derek explained what had happened in the field.

"What do you think it is?" Martin mused. "I mean, are we sure it's Eddie?"

"If it was something you or I saw," Derek answered, "then no, I could not be sure. However, I am certain hell could not interfere with a servant of heaven so easily. If they could, the angels would be entirely wiped out by now."

Martin nodded, trying to make sense of what Derek was saying.

Had she really seen Eddie?

Because Martin had battled this thing and it was nothing like the Eddie he had briefly met – it was evil. Eddie had turned into it – not just metaphorically; Eddie had literally changed into a demonic beast. Derek had witnessed Eddie physically transform after the ritual of the Devil's Three, then disappear to hell. Eddie had become this thing.

So how could he still be out there when his body wasn't?

Martin had faced it. Just after Jenny had appealed to the Eddie within; and if anyone could appeal to the Eddie within, it would have been her.

So where had the true Eddie been then?

The thing had slaughtered everyone they had gathered for an army. All the most powerful experts in the fields of the paranormal and supernatural had been wiped out within minutes.

Eddie wouldn't do that.

Unless this wasn't Eddie they were dealing with. That piece of the devil within him could have taken over, pushing Eddie to the background. Could he really still be in there? Could he really be stuck, watching everything the heir of hell was doing, helpless to stop it?

After all, the body and soul cannot exist without each other. Maybe hell had to bury Eddie somewhere deep down so they could keep the heir.

"Right. Well, what does this mean then?" Martin asked, realising he had been amid silent thought for a while.

"I think it means we have a chance of bringing him back – the true Eddie, that is," Cassy answered. "Maybe that is the only way to defeat the heir. He's too powerful for any of us to kill, so maybe we have to beseech the Eddie within."

With an infuriated sigh, Derek abruptly stood from the table and turned away, vigorously shaking his head.

"Derek, mate, surely you see Cassy's right?"

"It's not that," he grunted, refusing to turn around.

"Then what?"

He leant against the bookcase, loosening his collar, dropping his head.

"It's Jenny," he answered.

Martin shot a confused glance at Cassy.

"What about her?"

Derek took a deep inwards breath, then let it go slowly. He turned back toward them, doing all he could to gather himself, to retain some composure.

"It's just – oh, God… I've been a fool."

Martin shrugged at him, prompting him to explain.

"If I'd have only listened to Jenny," Derek observed, "then maybe… She was so adamant Eddie could be saved, and I wasn't having any of it. If only I'd have listened, she'd still be alive." He closed his eyes and hung his head. "They'd all still be alive."

Martin looked to Cassy, hoping she would have something reassuring to say, but she didn't. At first, Martin wasn't inclined to argue either, instead agreeing with Derek that they should have listened.

Then he remembered all Derek had done. Not just for him, but for their fight.

"You made the call you had to make," Martin reassured him. "You made the decision with the info you had, and I dunno if I'd have done differently."

"He's right," Cassy confirmed. "None of us had any idea. You can't beat yourself up over it."

Derek absently nodded.

Martin knew Derek knew they were right. But he also knew that it would not stop Derek from beating himself up or doubting himself. It must be tough to constantly be the strong one, and to put this decision entirely on his shoulders wasn't right.

Martin only wished there was some way he could let Derek know that.

Martin decided that a change of conversation would help.

"Right. What do we do now?" he asked. "With us knowing this, what do we do?"

Derek turned to the window and looked out at the vast horizon, the setting sun in the amber evening sky.

Derek shrugged. "I have no idea."

CHAPTER ELEVEN

*T*here could be no doubt about it – he had seen them.

Derek and Cassy.

Alive.

How could Eddie reach them?

Laying in a sinisterly dark room, lit with a hazy blue tint, with nothing but his ruminations and incessant thoughts to accompany him, it was a question he lingered on for a while.

Maybe if he tried, just closed his eyes, and really tried, he could get through to someone.

Jenny would be his best bet. He was closest to her, they grew up together; they could practically read each other's minds already. What's more, he knew that out of all of them, she would be the one who could recognise him trying to make contact.

She would never give up on him, he knew that.

So he knelt, closing his eyes and concentrating, ignoring the bumpy floor digging into his knees.

He concentrated the way he would when conjuring an

element, preparing for a fight, readying himself for an exorcism.

He listened to the absence. Smelt a distant linger of smoke. Felt slight movement he made hitting the stone walls.

Everything melded into one piece of nothingness.

He just had to think. Had to reach out. Had to hope that she would hear him.

Jenny.

I'm talking to you, Jenny.

He pictured her face.

Her long hair, her infectious smile. Lacy by her side, holding her hand, always loyal.

Jenny frantically searching for a way to get Eddie back.

Eddie knew that's what she would be doing.

He looked for her in her home. Thought about her making a cup of tea, or sitting on the sofa watching a movie with Lacy.

But he couldn't see her there.

A vague outline of Lacy appeared, but no Jenny.

So he tried harder.

He could not fail.

He had to get through to her.

Jenny, can you hear me?

Nothing.

Maybe if I spoke it...

"Jenny, please, can you hear me?"

He waited.

"Jenny, this is Eddie. It is actually me. But I need to know you can hear me. Come on, please..."

He waited.

And waited and waited.

He didn't know what he was waiting for, but he knew he'd know it when he had it.

He had such great powers, such a gift; if anyone could do this, it would be him.

Surely.

"Jenny, come on, I know you're there, do you hear me?"

He felt nothing.

"I'm alive, Jenny. I'm here, but I need your help."

He listened intently.

Really straining himself to hear any sound, any feeling, any smells or touches that reminded him of her.

Something. Like the graze of her hand against his. Like the sound of her voice in the distance of his mind. Like the look in her eyes when she saw he was upset.

But all he had were his desperate thoughts, continually and unsuccessfully reaching out for her.

All he could feel was a longing, blank space.

"Come on, Jenny."

No.

It was useless. Futile. Pointless.

He collapsed onto his back.

It was no good.

He was stuck there.

CHAPTER TWELVE

*T*he devil's throne spiralled lavishly into the air away from the spewing lava and choking ash of hell. He sat upon it, casually poised upon a gigantic set of skulls that allowed him to look over all the eternities of suffering and torment.

Watching over the demons enjoying their torture of various souls made him giddy. Like a child unwrapping a birthday present, excited to see what was in store. Loyal demons swarmed the surroundings, unleashing terrific tirades of torture over every inhabitant trapped in a world of volcanic sorrow.

One of his most trusted demons approached, slithering toward him on the endless serpent tail that attached itself to its muscular torso. Its dragon wings were thrice the size of its body, with sharp claws savagely fixed to their end. Each of its three human heads had a body that attached itself to its slithering lower parts, each with horns pointing triumphantly into the air of ash. Along its body were sharp spikes that could slice an enemy in half before it even knew what was happening.

The devil had seen it. Humans had been decapitated before they had even laid eyes on this monster.

It was magic. Brilliant beauty decorated in bloody bunting.

What was more prominent than the intimidatingly sinister movement and ferocity in its eyes was the immense evil it exuded. To be in the presence of this demon was like being in the presence of pure hatred, something the devil drank like water.

"You called for me?" spoke the demon, Geryon.

"Yes. And you came."

The devil smiled, watching his loyal servant a moment longer, enjoying the detestable, exuberant hostility encircling Geryon's face.

"What can I do for you, my Lord?" Geryon requested.

"The soul of Edward King, the living good of the heir we cannot kill," he began. "It's trapped. But it's finding ways to reach out."

Geryon nodded, listening intently and obediently.

"He has even tried to reach out to his friend, Jenny." The devil burst into hysterics. "But she's dead!"

He practically fell off his throne, such was the extremity of the hilarity he found in the situation.

The soul of Edward King was just so... pathetic.

Trying to reach out to the one person he couldn't because he had already killed her!

It was a beautiful kind of irony.

Geryon did not falter in its expression. It remained dementedly serious, patiently awaiting further instructions, a permanent grimace tattooed to its cheeks.

"What would you like me to do with him?"

"You are the guardian of hell, Geryon," the devil answered, still cackling. "Guard him."

"As you wish."

"He cannot escape. You keep the door shut. Do not let him pass. Do not let him send messages or signals of any kind."

"Yes, my master. It is done."

Geryon turned and slithered away, its large claws clicking against each other with a looming tick. Its huge dragon wings flapped grandly, taking the demon into the air and on its path.

The devil sat back in its throne.

"You think it stands a chance of escaping?" came the familiar voice of the heir of hell approaching from behind him. The devil could detect a tone of worry in the heir's voice, a longing not to let the soul out of his cage.

"No," answered the devil. "But time is of the essence. Enough waiting. Ready yourself. We are going to open the gates of the underworld and finally claim the earth for our own."

"Very good."

"My heir, my son – we are going to unleash hell."

CHAPTER THIRTEEN

*S*ettling the chewed pen down on the table, Derek decided he needed to stop being so agitated. It wasn't him. Whatever dreadful, terrible, fatal mistakes he had made, he needed to be calm and collected; even if just for Martin's sake.

He looked at the young boy beside him.

Not even an adult yet.

Such expectation weighed upon him. Quite literally, the weight of the world. The boy was supposed to be humanity's last salvation. He was heaven's hand in this disaster, their roll of the dice. It was he who would fix this.

If he could.

Martin wasn't destined to do this, he had only been given the powers. There was nothing guaranteed he would even make a difference.

There was no prophecy about this. In fact, all prophecy books Derek knew of ended in the coming months. No one could predict anything beyond that.

Which could be incontrovertible evidence that this is where it ends.

But Derek couldn't accept that.

Then, suddenly, with a little spark of light tingling in his brain, an idea grew. A radical, ridiculous idea, but an idea nonetheless.

"How is your restraint spell coming along?" Derek suddenly inquired, suppressing a smile caused by the impromptu attack of his idea.

Martin sat back and shrugged, rubbing his eyes. He was evidently tired. In fairness to him, before all of this he had never worked a day in his life. He had walked out on school and refused to do anything. But the way he had dedicated himself to his role in all of this was nothing short of heroic.

Derek only hoped Martin realised that.

"Dunno, man," Martin muttered, shaking his head. "It's... not, really. It's more of a throw a circle and clatter the bench. Not really getting the hang of it."

"You will."

Martin scoffed.

"Oh, trust me, you can scoff all you want. You will."

"Yeah, what do you know?" he grunted, turning his head away. He was slouched, his hand resting on an anxiously bouncing knee, his face curled up into a scowl.

"Not much," Derek admitted, watching Martin intently. "But enough."

Martin went to reply, then thought better of it, instead choosing to let out a big sigh.

Derek recognised the teenager in him. Even saw a bit of himself at that age – the need to argue and defy anyone who tried to oppose his sceptical mind. However much was expected of him, Martin was still young, and this was how kids his age would react. With a tantrum; if that's what one could call it.

And Derek couldn't blame Martin if he was starting to

lose faith in him. Derek had been wrong a few too many times, and too much death had occurred as a result.

Derek abruptly stood, placing his hands on his hips. He meandered over to a cupboard, opened it, and withdrew a whisky bottle with two tumblers. He poured them and handed one to Martin.

"What's this?"

"Whisky."

"I've never had it before."

"Then today will be your first. Just sip it."

Martin took the glass from Derek, watching as Derek took a very slight sip from his glass. Martin took a swig from his and reacted with a repulsed face, completely disgusted.

"That's why I said sip it," Derek pointed out jokingly.

"Why are you giving this to me?"

"Because we are going to make a toast."

"A toast? To what?"

Derek hesitated. He peered at Martin. So young, so boisterous. He was like Eddie when Derek had first met him – completely unaware of what he was capable of.

"What do you reckon we should toast to?" Derek mused.

"There's nothing. We have nothing."

"No, that's not true." Derek shook his head. "We have the trees outside. We have the air in our lungs, for now. We have each other. We have the knowledge, you have powers, we have a life of memories, some happy, some sad. We have plenty we could toast. Just pick one."

Martin defiantly placed the glass on the table and shook his head.

"I can't believe you're trying to be positive after all–"

"My belief in God came *after* I had proof; before then, I was a passionate atheist, as I believe one should be until they see a reason to be otherwise. I hated how people believed in God because it gave them comfort. Why should you need

God? Look around you at this world, this wonderful life, these wonderful things. There is always so much to be thankful for."

Martin stared at his feet, mulling something over in his mind.

"No, we don't need a God. We need what we have. So, tell me, Martin – what should we toast to?"

Martin shrugged, then lifted his glass. "To Eddie, I guess."

Derek smiled.

"To Eddie."

They took another sip, and Derek couldn't help but be amused by another disgusted expression on Martin's face.

It was time.

Derek had to announce his plan.

"I'm going to perform an exorcism."

"You what?" Martin answered, full of confusion.

Derek sat beside to him, placing his glass on the desk, facing his prodigy straight-on with sufficient intensity.

"I am going to perform an exorcism on the heir."

"What?" Martin yelped, shaking his head with angered disbelief at yet another ridiculous, doomed-to-fail plan from Derek. "How the fuck are we going to do that? In case you ain't noticed, the heir ain't easy to pin down!"

"That's where you come in. And your restraint spell."

"Derek, I ain't able to do that restraint spell, it's shit!"

"Then make it not shit."

"I don't know what you are on, mate, but this is the most ridiculous plan I've heard yet."

"No. It's not. It's what I've overlooked. It's a possibility I never entertained and, however improbable or preposterous an idea it seems, it's the best one we have. We can't kill it. How could we kill it? But if, like Cassy saw, Eddie's soul is there somewhere, we need to access it. Bring it back. And the only way to do that is with an exorcism."

Martin stood, running his hands through his hair.

"This is just another plan to get us all killed."

"This isn't some ruse to get us killed, Martin, but yes, that is a bloody strong possibility!" Derek retorted, rising to his feet, doing his best to avoid becoming frustrated.

Martin looked back, seeing in Derek's eyes that he meant it. That he was absolutely determined to go through with it.

"I think you're a nutcase."

"Maybe," Derek replied honestly. "But it's time we had faith in Eddie. If I'd have done so earlier, Jenny may still be alive."

Martin didn't reply. He was torn. Torn between whether to go along with this or not. Despite being so nonsensical, part of it made sense.

"Yes, Martin. It is time to have faith in Eddie. Have faith that we can get to that part of him that is still good."

"And if we can't? If we don't manage to finish this exorcism and he kills us?"

Derek shrugged. "Then we won't be any different than if we did nothing."

CHAPTER FOURTEEN

*A*s a tear glistened in the corner of her eye she knew it wouldn't matter. She wished she was home, in her mother's arms, even in her neglectful father's arms.

But she had already felt herself becoming resolved to death.

Maybe on that first night, things had been different. She had remained optimistic of being found, or even freed. She had begged her captors and they had even given her hope.

It felt foolish now.

Kicking and screaming had done nothing.

If anything, it had only spurred them on more.

And, watching as they stood grinning at her, she knew the end was near.

And she was grateful for it.

After all the deprivation of water, the sexual humiliation, the cries of "we gots ourselves a virgin to offer!" night after night after night, the nightly torture, the further loss of hope as every passing day went by – she felt ready for the sweet release.

She hoped her mother found her body.

That way it could give her a way to move on. A way to ensure she did not keep hoping against hope that she would return.

"It's time," declared the one she had assumed was the leader. He was a large black man the other two often referred to as Boss, but had also been referred to as 'Bandile.' "Let's make the sacrifice now so the heir can grow stronger."

"But the more she suffers, the more strength she'll give…" spoke the one next to him with a large beard. She'd heard them call him Dexter.

Then the one that had introduced himself as Bagsy on that torturous first night stood to the side of Bandile. Watching her intently. His sadistic eyes not blinking. He didn't appear to listen to a word the others said – he just kept chewing her up and spitting her out with his eyes. Those eyes made her stomach churn. Those eyes were the eyes she saw right before anything awful was about to happen to her.

"The one heaven has conceived," continued Bandile, "is being kept in the home of Derek Lansdale. We know where he is."

Dexter turned his head with a sudden gasp toward Bandile, child-like excitement adorning his face with a wide, creepy smile.

"You lie!"

"I do not lie. We will kill him tonight."

Dexter's eyes refocussed on her.

"And this one?"

Bandile shrugged. "Finish her already. I got bigger stuff to do."

Bandile turned and strode out the room, Dexter following – giving Bagsy an approving nod as he did.

Bagsy, not removing his playful eyes from her for a second, tiptoed toward the door and locked it.

"Juz yoo an' me!" he sang out, the tattoos of his face

creasing under his repulsive acne. He looked sickeningly unhealthy. Every time she had seen him he had worn nothing but grey shorts, revealing his heavily inked flesh. Satanic symbols and intimidating skulls mixed with snakes, grinning sinister faces and tears dropping from his eyes, marking his entire body with tattoos designed to put the fear of God in you.

Except, this man was clearly not a man of God.

He was from something else.

He crept toward her, his joints seeming to point in every direction as he moved, like an insect about to eat its prey. He moved to within inches of her face and she could feel his toxic breath wiping over her, fluttering her hair back as he let out a long, sickening exhale over her eyes, which she shut tightly.

"Do not close yous eyes to meez," he whispered in a voice that went up and down in pitch with such a lack of harmonisation that it became chaotic. "My love, we haz too much to do."

"Please…" she whispered. "Just kill me."

He reached his arms around her in an embrace that felt like she was being wrapped in barbed wire. He cut her rope open with a knife, allowed her binding to drop to the ground, setting her free.

She gasped.

"Are you… are you letting me go?" she asked, feeling a sudden rush of optimism flood through her body.

With a slow nod accompanied by the sound of clicking bones within his contorting neck, she turned and looked around herself for an escape.

He raised an arm and pointed a thin finger toward a far door.

She sprinted forward, stumbling with eagerness.

She was going to see her mother.

Once more she would be reunited.

She could see her tearful face now; she could practically smell her perfume, feel her arms around her.

She dove at the door, clamping her hands around the handle and pulling it.

It was locked.

She turned.

Bagsy stood directly behind her. She hadn't even heard him move. A low, sinister chuckle trickled past his infected lips.

"Please…" she begged, feeling that sudden rush of hope falling out of her.

In a foul swipe, he swept the knife forward and stuck it inside of her, sinking it into her ovaries.

She felt the knife tear up her, ripping through her belly and up to her chest. Everything dropped.

She could hear the wet thump of her insides dropping to the floor.

The last thing she saw before her dead head hit the ground was the wide grin of Bagsy's face as he revelled at her torment.

CHAPTER FIFTEEN

*N*ovember 16, 1999

ONE MONTH until millennium night

SHARDS OF GLASS smashed through the window and floated along the gust of wind. Manic screams and wails of all pitches consumed the room – every single one of them coming from the same young boy's body.

"I command you demon, be gone!" screamed Eddie, his youthful energy surpassing Derek's. Eddie's mentor stood at the side of the room, shielding his face from the large pieces of furniture firing at him.

Eddie made a mental note to remove loose items from the room before his next exorcism.

"From all sin Lord, from your wrath, from sudden and unprovided death, from the snares of the devil I beg you to clutch this servant of God away from this wretched villain!"

The boy screamed as his body rose into the air, his bare, torn chest rising slowly toward the ceiling. Only a loose set of rags covered the child's dignity, revealing deep wounds and ravenous cuts that would leave devastating scars up and down the child's legs and torso.

"From all lewdness, from lightning and tempest, from the scourge of earthquakes, from plague, famine, and war, save us from everlasting death and defeat this demon, oh Lord!"

The boy's head lifted, its demented eyes completely black, its sweaty hair entwined with dried blood and unrecognisable ectoplasm.

Eddie looked over his shoulder at Derek.

Derek had taken part in nearly a hundred exorcisms. This was Eddie's twelfth.

Yet there was a feeling of inherent experience in Eddie that he had somehow surpassed his guide. Derek stood out of the way, protecting himself from the chaos of the room, whilst Eddie embraced it. Took it on, willing the demon to do its worst.

"By the mystery of your holy incarnation, by your coming, by your birth, with the holy baptism of fire, free this child from this demon's clutches."

The flying objects of the room, the soaring glass, child's toys, ripped clothes, all of it froze. Poised in the air with a sudden pause. The boy's body hovered momentarily, then thudded back down to the bed.

This was it.

This was nearly it.

The boy's head lifted, directing its fiery stare at the boy's saviour. Eddie looked back just as intently, not withdrawing his glare, refusing to be the one who gave in.

"By your cross and passion," Eddie spoke, this time in a calmer voice, enunciating every syllable like he was spitting bullets at the demon. "By your death and burial, by your holy resurrection, your wondrous ascension, the Spirit, the Advocate, on the day of judgement – please, Lord. Please. Deliver this child from evil."

"You may think you have won," the demon choked in a deep, croaked whisper. "But you fight for the God you defy."

Eddie stepped forward, presenting his defiant snarl.

"Don't try and trick me, demon, I will not be fooled."

"One day…" the demon muttered, shaking the boy's head with slow, pressured movements. "You think I'm the one who needs to be exorcised?"

"On the day of judgement–" Eddie persisted.

"On the day of judgement, it will be you that leads us!"

"On the day of judgement," Eddie repeated, even more forcefully. "We sinners will beg you to hear us as you hear us now."

He held out his cross and took his final stride toward his enemy.

"Give us peace and unity. Remove this demon and free this child."

The boy's face wrapped up into a visage of rage, defiant to the end.

"Leave this boy be, I ask you, my Lord. Remove this demon."

The boy's body stiffened to a rigid plank, its fingers curling. With a high screech, the child convulsed, stiffened more and more until, in a sudden snap, his body relaxed.

The room fell to tranquillity. A lucid calmness cast itself over them like a sunrise.

The boy breathed slowly, staring at the ceiling. Free at last.

Once the boy had been reunited with the mother and Eddie and Derek had received her gratitude, they made their way to Derek's car.

"What I don't understand," Eddie spoke, "were the things this demon was saying."

"Demons will say anything to defy you, Eddie. You need to learn not to listen to them."

"But if each demon keeps saying it?"

"Then they all know who you are and are saying the same thing to make you question it. Don't be fooled."

Eddie sighed, leaning against the car in quizzical thought, Derek's answer clearly not good enough.

"Eddie, a demon is a devious thing, full of nothing but evil. Its sole purpose is to hurt us. You don't think they have some kind of organised defiance against someone as powerful as you?"

"I don't know. I guess."

"Eddie, you need to understand, there is no demon that can defeat you. There is nothing. And they will clutch at anything to change that."

Eddie nodded, soaking up the reassurance, starting to feel better.

"How is it you believe in me so much?" Eddie asked.

"Because I have seen what you can do. I have witnessed it."

"Yeah. It's just... I don't know."

Eddie turned to get into the car, full of doubt, until Derek put a hand on his arm to stop him.

"Well I do," he defiantly asserted. "You may have doubts in you, but I won't. My belief in you will never falter, Eddie. I promise."

CHAPTER SIXTEEN

arch 25, 2003

THREE YEARS, three months since millennium night

ONCE AGAIN MARTIN stood unwillingly in the garden, numbing his mind into frantic concentration.

Glaring at the object before him. The garden bench was now wrecked pieces of wood, so he was forced to find an alternative, coming to him in the form of a dining chair. One that Derek had eagerly carried out from the kitchen.

First things first.

Concentrate on all the elements.

Sight.

The chair before him. Rustic, with a light-brown furnish. Clear green grass beneath it soaking up the rays of a bright sun.

Sound.

Birds singing. Nearby children playing. When really straining, there was even a faint hum of distant traffic.

Smell.

Flowers. Sweat.

Touch.

He flexed his hands, flowing them through a soft breeze, feeling the brush of gentle wind glide through his fingers.

Taste.

A faint taste of that morning's toothpaste.

Ready.

He concentrated on all of this, soaking it up, feeling the sun bash against his skin, listening to the birds, happy tweets of horny animals.

He moved his right arm in a circular motion.

The breeze.

His perspiration.

He moved it quicker.

The blades of grass sticking between his toes, the soft sink of soil beneath the sole of his foot.

He widened the radius of his arm's circular motion. A gold flickering circle had emerged, vague sparks bursting away like an electrical charge, the circle itself taking on a solid form, more and more solid with every circular motion, getting stronger with the increased speed of his arm.

The sun.

The blue sky.

The chair.

The wooden chair. Brown. Old. Uncomfortable. Sitting unknowingly across the garden, waiting for an attack.

The circle had taken its form. It had turned into a solid object he had conjured from pure awareness, from a complete absorption of his surroundings.

In a sudden thrust, he threw his open palm out, flinging the circle he had created toward the chair.

To Martin's astonishment, the chair did not explode. It remained sturdy. What's more, the circular magical binding flung itself around the chair.

Martin closed his fist and the circle tightened. It squeezed securely around the chair so that if the chair was alive there would be no way to escape, completely restricting the movement whilst leaving it intact.

Martin fell to his knees in inexplicable exhilaration.

It had worked.

The damn thing had worked.

It's actually doing it...

Martin closed his eyes and turned his face away, then opened his eyes again, expecting it to be a hallucination or a hopeful mirage.

It was still there.

Flicking like an uncaged wire of electricity, its voltage giving off sparks, it gripped firmly around the chair.

It's real...

So much working, so much trying, and he finally had it.

The flickers told him that the restraints weren't perfect yet, but that was fine, he could perfect it later. For now, he had actually done it.

He got up to go find Derek and tell him the great news.

Then a thought suddenly halted him. His smile faded, his body tensing again.

He remembered.

I'm going to have to use this spell on the heir.

Throwing a small circle around the chair was one thing. The heir was something else.

The flickers would have to go, as they would be a weakness the heir could easily penetrate. The size needed to be bigger, far grander – huge – to be able to fit around this creature. It would need to fly faster, otherwise, the heir would just beat it away.

Yes, it needed a lot of work.

Far more work.

But Martin had managed this. He had finally done it. A week ago he was getting incredibly frustrated, now he had the spell working.

But to get it to where he needed it to go…

It was an impossible task. It would take ten times as much as he'd put into it so far, at a minimum.

With a reluctant sigh, he stood. The positivity of his triumphant celebrations were over. Back to work.

He focussed on the object once more, taking in the elements.

CHAPTER SEVENTEEN

*A*nother dusty, flat slab of a book heaved open upon Derek's desk.

This plan was all good and well, but would it succeed?

An exorcism.

An exorcism that doesn't call to God, but to a soul.

How would it even work?

Filling his whisky tumbler up, he took a sip, not even feeling the sharp sting of its high alcohol content, such was his concentration. He placed his reading glasses on, grimacing at the thought. It had only been the last few months he'd had to acquire them, and the thought of growing old saddened him.

Then again, the luxury of growing old is one many of us may not be afforded...

Flicking through the pages of *The Rites of Exorcism,* he re-acclimatised himself with the process of removing a demon from a helpless body.

It had been a while.

He had given Eddie the knowledge then found himself no longer needed to perform these acts. Eddie had managed to banish a demon from a body in twice the speed and with less effort

But it was time to return to it. To his roots. To how it all started.

He opened a chapter about the reasoning behind the process of an exorcism and found himself reading the words he had originally read when he began his endeavours to rid the world of hungry demons possessing their prey, almost two decades ago.

AN EXORCISM'S purpose is to tear two entities apart. Within possession, the soul of a victim has a demon latched onto it. You must separate the demon from the soul.

THE BODY CANNOT EXIST without the soul, and the victim will be buried deep within. The exorcism consists of calling on God's strength to identify this soul and help pull it away from the demon.

DEREK LEANT BACK.

Thought deeply.

Pondered the various reasonings and thoughts behind these words.

By this theory, Eddie's soul would still be there.

It said that the body cannot exist without the soul. Therefore, the heir of hell's body cannot exist without Eddie' soul.

So it must be in there somewhere.

Buried very deep, maybe – but there.

It said that a possession means the soul has a demon latched onto it.

The issue was that Eddie's soul hadn't been latched onto by a separate entity. They were both the same thing. The heir of hell was not possessing Edward King – it *was* Edward King.

Normally an exorcism takes a demonic entity that has attached itself to a separate host. Could it still work, considering the heir and Eddie were not separate, but one and the same?

Could the process be performed in such a way that it separated the soul from the rest of the body, even if the soul belonged to that body?

Then again, an exorcism's purpose is to remove the evil from the good.

A soul is inherently good. Hell cannot create a soul, only heaven can.

Therefore, it must be in there.

And by that logic, it could be separated.

Could be.

Derek mulled this over. He'd have to tear apart two things that are fastened together as one and the same. Unless the devil had to remove the soul when raising the heir. Unless the soul had already been ripped away and was being kept somewhere separate.

If it had already been ripped away, it would be looser, and easier to snatch off... but it would mean penetrating whatever protection the devil had put around it.

It was complicated, no doubt about it.

The one thing it confirmed was that Jenny was right.

There was still a piece of Eddie in there.

His soul.

That was the part they needed to appeal to.

That was the part Derek needed to reach.

It may not work.

Then again, it might.

He downed the rest of his whisky.

Slammed the glass down upon his coaster, the surface of which was peeling away.

The task was a daunting one to say the least.

To restrain the most powerful demon to ever have existed. Then to exorcise that demon. Then to plunge past the devil's defences. The devil's barriers.

Bloody hell, Derek. This is madness...

He had no choice.

He turned to the chapter on the prayers and became reacquainted with the ancient skill of the rites of exorcism.

He would need to know them thoroughly if he was to commit to this.

CHAPTER EIGHTEEN

*H*eaven was such a wonderful place, but it could be lonely if you kept looking to earth. Seeing what so many people don't have.

Particularly for Cassy, who stood watching Martin trying again and again to produce the spell they needed to capture and fight the heir.

To exorcise it.

Being honest, Cassy wasn't entirely sure it was the best idea. It was radical, no denying that; but was it doable?

Then again, was killing the heir doable?

Cassy had felt Eddie's soul. She had felt it rip into her. He was there, she knew it.

But an exorcism, to rid the heir of its own imprisoned soul.

The only other option was to kill the heir, and they had already realised that would fail.

Even with the powers heaven had bestowed upon Martin, he was far less experienced than his opponent. And even if he had full control and ability over his inherent powers, he would only reach a stalemate with the heir; heaven and hell would always cancel each other out.

"You look solemn," came a familiar voice behind her.

"Why do you think that is?" she replied.

Gabrielle appeared at her side. Her long, black hair glided over her immaculate white dress, her luscious black skin smooth as silk.

"Come, join the others," Gabrielle prompted.

Cassy shook her head, holding back tears.

"This is no good," Gabrielle insisted. "There is nothing we can do for them now. They are on their own."

"Why?" Cassy demanded, lifting her head defiantly to Gabrielle. She had never so much as challenged her, respecting the thousands of years Gabrielle had been doing God's work. Compared to her, Cassy's wings were so young. She just didn't understand.

"We offered Derek a way out. He turned it down."

"Yes, because he's doing our job. We should be fighting."

"You know God forbids it."

"But *why?*"

"Because it is not our job to meddle, you foolish child!" Despite being an angry retort, her voice was still soft and in control – something only a wise angel could achieve.

"I just don't get why we are supposed to stand back and watch as the devil unleashes hell on earth."

"Because that is the difference between us and hell. The devil interferes directly with human dealings. We give them the tools, but to hold divine influence would be ungodly."

"Ungodly," Cassy scoffed.

She peered at an image of Martin, repeatedly trying his restraint spell, again and again. Each time growing increasingly frustrated because it was either not big enough, too many sparks, or had a lack of power – whatever it was, she understood why he was getting infuriated.

A delinquent child plucked out of immaturity and plunged into a war he didn't understand. What he had done, including all his hard work whether he succeeded or failed, was remarkable.

And where were the servants of heaven reassuring him of that?

"We need something for Martin," Cassy proposed. "Some kind of divine intervention. Even if he masters this thing, he's going to come up against a brick wall with the heir. The heir has had years of sitting back and driving Eddie's thoughts. Martin is a child plunged into this. He will lose."

Gabrielle remained silent. She looked to earth also, watching Martin, feeling her pain.

"We have conceived him from heaven. What more can we do?"

"I don't know, some kind of weapon, maybe?"

"Cassy, this is not up for discussion. We are here to do His bidding; that is it. Now please, come."

Cassy shook her head. "I'm not coming."

Gabrielle's face faltered with a flicker of distress.

"There is going to be a rapture, Cassy. The earth is doomed. We have evacuated the most faithful, now it is time for us to move out of the way."

"Move out of the way? The devil rises and we are just going to move out of the way for him?"

"Cassy, are you coming?"

Cassy looked back into Gabrielle's eyes, those piercing, strikingly beautiful hazel eyes. So much wisdom, so much experience.

Who was she to challenge that?

But when you know in your heart what you must do...

"I am not," Cassy decided.

"You are not coming?"

She looked to Martin, then back to Gabrielle.

"No," Cassy confirmed. "I am going to stand with Derek. With Martin. I am going to do what I can. Without interfering as you are so adamantly against."

"Cassy, once we have shut the door to heaven from earth, it will remain shut until it ends, if it ever does. Those gates will not reopen; you will not be allowed back in."

"Then I best hope it ends."

With a hesitation, Gabrielle nodded. There was no way to change Cassy's mind.

She stepped forward, putting her arms around Cassy, holding her in a tight embrace.

"Take care," Gabrielle instructed.

"I will."

Keeping her arms around Cassy, Gabrielle leant back and looked intently into her eyes.

"If you are going to put your faith in Eddie, as I see Derek is planning to do, you must keep that faith. The only chance you have is if Eddie plays his part too."

Cassy nodded. She felt herself crying. Gabrielle had been more than a friend. She had been a guide. It broke her heart to leave her; but it broke more that she was going knowing Gabrielle was not joining her. Her eyes welled up and she held Gabrielle tightly, wrapping her arms around her and bringing her in closely.

"You are a sweet child," Gabrielle spoke.

Before Cassy could respond, Gabrielle turned away, walking a few steps until she faded away.

And with that, the stairs to the gates of heaven faded.

Cassy couldn't fight. She couldn't interfere.

She was stuck in the world of mortals with a helpless fragility.

She did not know whether it was the right decision.

But she knew it was where she belonged.

CHAPTER NINETEEN

*A*pril 2, 2003

EVERYTHING CAME DOWN TO THIS.

Or, at least, that's what it felt like.

As Martin watched Derek sit at his desk, studying his book, he couldn't help but feel like it was the end.

They had been waiting for the heir to strike with a sense of foreboding helplessness. That at any time he could just rise up, bringing the demons of hell with him, and unleash their tirade on earth.

What could they do to stop the heir now?

The heir had wiped out their army. The most powerful supernatural influences in the world were dead. Yes, powerful people still remained on earth, but they would all be second choices; all with far less ability than the ones that were already so easily slaughtered.

Now it was up to the powers heaven had bestowed on Martin and the knowledge Derek had.

So there Derek was, studying the rites of exorcism. Even though Derek had performed hundreds of exorcisms, and witnessed almost as many whilst training Eddie, there he still was. Strengthening his knowledge. Being thorough.

That's why Derek was Martin's inspiration.

He was relentless. An ethic of constant hard work, something Martin had never had growing up; but something he had attempted to emulate.

Teachers at school nagged him. Punished him for doing nothing. They never gave education a purpose or a relevance, never gave him the patience to discover it's okay to make mistakes so long as they are learnt from.

But Father Douglas had. Douglas had stripped his dignity down to its bare bones and helped build the muscle around them.

And Derek.

Derek had never expected more than Martin could give.

And it was the same now.

If they died giving the world over to hell and all its creations, but went down with the biggest fight they could muster, he knew Derek would still be proud.

Martin grew restless and began wandering the study. Looking over the dusty, broken leather of Derek's old books, the journals kept in a cupboard, and the drawers full of junk.

He realised he had never seen inside those drawers. Out of curiosity, he opened one.

He froze.

"Derek?" Martin spoke, alert.

"Yes?" Derek asked, not turning away from his book.

"What is this?" Martin asked, pointing to a revolver in Derek's drawer.

"What?" Derek glanced over his shoulder, noticed the gun, grinned, then returned his gaze back to his book. "It's a six-shooter revolver."

"Why do you have it?"

"Don't worry, it's just for show. The chambers are empty."

"Oh," Martin answered, feeling comforted. Then it struck him that it was still a gun, loaded or not.

He closed the drawer, deciding that there were many layers to Derek that he would never truly be able to unfold.

A warm hand rested itself on Martin's shoulder. He recognised the soft touch, and turned to see the beautiful face of Cassy.

"Cassy?" he prompted, surprised to see her.

Derek turned, equally perplexed.

"Cassy?"

"Hello, Derek," she said knowingly, smiling back at him.

"What are you doing here?"

"Is that how you greet me?"

Derek chuckled heartily, but it quickly faded.

"The evacuation is complete. I thought that included all of the angels."

"It did. I told them I wouldn't go."

"You what?"

Derek rose, stepping forward, staring at her intently.

"My place is not hiding away in heaven with a God who does nothing to help. My place is fighting with you." She turned with a graceful smile toward Martin. "With both of you."

Martin grinned. He was astonished.

"If you'll have me, that is."

"Of course," Martin answered, beaming at Derek.

"So where are we with this?"

"Oh, yes." Derek quickly readjusted and picked up his bulky book. "I've been studying the rites of exorcism again, looking to see if there was anything else we could do, any stronger prayer I could serve."

"And?"

Derek shrugged.

"I have a question," Martin announced. "If the angels are hidden away with God, will the exorcism work?"

"What do you mean?"

"Isn't an exorcism calling on God to remove a demon from its victim's body?"

Derek nodded.

"Well, in that case, ain't God going to be hidden away? I mean, how would he answer?"

Cassy looked to Derek, realising that she hadn't thought of this either.

"Maybe," Derek confirmed.

"But how?" Cassy interjected.

"Because we are not going to be calling on God to free Eddie from the demon's body. It would do no good, for the reasons you have stated, but also because we are not removing a demon from its victim. Instead, we are removing the victim's soul from its demonic body. We will need to reach out to that soul with our prayers, rather than to God."

"I don't understand."

"We will not be praying to God to exorcise the demon. We are going to be calling on Eddie himself."

CHAPTER TWENTY

*T*he room filled with silence. A few moments of contemplation reflecting upon Derek's statement.

Cassy looked from Martin, to Derek, then back again, perplexed.

They were going to call on Eddie?

It was either genius or reckless – Cassy was still undecided. It hadn't been attempted, calling on anyone but God to remove something – but in theory, it should work. If Eddie's soul was trapped away somewhere, they would need to call on it, grant it access to return.

Then it struck Cassy – the overpowering flaw of this idea.

"So, your hypothesis is that you could exorcise the soul from the demon's body, detach it and create a new entity," Cassy thought aloud to Derek. "So you would then have two conscious beings – the heir of hell, and Eddie's soul. Correct?"

"Spot on," Derek confirmed, nodding enthusiastically.

"The only issue," Cassy continued, "is Eddie's soul. We don't know what form it would take."

"What do you mean?"

"The human soul is not a human. The soul's conscious mind has the ability to project its own body with its own mind, so it can see itself as human – but it is not."

"Not what?" Martin interjected.

"Human. The soul, in its truest form, is merely a ball, made up of elements and supernatural components. You could very well remove the soul from the heir so that Eddie, as the soul, can defeat the heir. Only issue is…"

"… He wouldn't be able to defeat him in the form of a soul," Derek finished, bowing his head and closing his eyes in disappointment. "He would just be a ball of energy."

"I really do not understand what you guys are on about," Martin announced.

Derek and Cassy exchanged a glance, sub-consciously deciding who would explain to Martin in laymen's terms what the issue was.

"If we managed to exorcise Eddie's soul," Derek told him, "the soul would not return in a recognisable form, and wouldn't be able to defeat the heir."

"Oh," Martin uttered, leaning against the desk, his face turning to that of disappointment.

Cassy's initial excitement faded with the prospect of what they could have done. What other option did they have? How else could they defeat the antichrist, but with a piece of himself?

"Is there really nothing we can do about it?" Cassy asked.

Derek's pointing finger jolted upright, a complex thought striking him.

"What?" Cassy asked.

"There is a way," Derek announced.

"Okay?" replied Cassy, made anxious by Derek's tentative look.

"But you're not going to like it."

Cassy knew instantly where this was going.

"No, Derek, no," she insisted, standing and waving her arms. "I am an angel. We fight in heaven's name. There is no way."

"What?" Martin asked.

Derek turned to Martin and explained to him, knowing he couldn't look at Cassy while he suggested what he was about to suggest.

"There is a way to turn a soul into human form that I read about a while ago. Only, it's… it's not…"

"Not what, Derek?"

"Not something God would approve of. To turn a soul, something made out of heaven, into a mortal form, goes against the rules of heaven. It could only be done with devil worship."

"Why doesn't heaven approve?"

"Because that soul already had its turn in mortal form. It's not allowed to be returned; it is supposed to pass on."

"I can't believe you're even suggesting this," Cassy interrupted, feeling her temperature rise and her blood boil. "This is sacrilege! God would not approve."

"With all due respect, where is your God now?"

Cassy was silenced. As true as his point was, Cassy was not prepared to stand there and entertain the option of using evil in any way.

They would lose far more than just the world if they allowed Satanism into their battle.

"I'm not suggesting that we do it–"

"I don't give a damn what you are suggesting."

"Cassy," Martin tried. "I… I don't know." He turned to Derek. "How would we even be able to use hell to do this? I mean, you may not have noticed, but we aren't really on their side, are we?"

"I don't know, Martin, to be honest," Derek answered. "I was just thinking aloud."

"Well stop it, now!" Cassy demanded. "Stop it, right now! Turning a soul to human form is the devil's work; it is unnatural to how a soul is created. We find the heavenly way to do this. There must be a way – there *must* be."

"And if there isn't?"

The question hung in the air like poisonous gas.

Cassy's fists clenched, her head frantically shaking in defiance of Derek's impertinent question.

"Why don't we sleep on this?" Derek suggested. "We are all tired. It's late. We need to clear our minds and think through this with clear thoughts."

"There is nothing to think of."

"Then what do you suggest, Cassy?"

Cassy bowed her head. Closed her eyes.

"I will go to Gabrielle tonight," she decided. "Hope she hasn't entered heaven's gate yet. See what she says."

"Hah!" Derek laughed forcibly. "And how much help has she been, huh?"

"I will talk to her. Ask if there is anything else that can be done, any other way."

"Yeah, you do that," Derek answered with seething eyes, more hostile than he had intended.

She went to speak, but chose against it. She turned and left, making her way out of the house and into the street, in disbelief of what they could potentially become.

CHAPTER TWENTY-ONE

*D*erek's house was at peace. A full moon cast a serene glow over the house of tranquillity. The house was still and calm.

Except, it wasn't.

The silence of the hallway was filled with absent chaos.

Martin rocked back and forth in his bed, unable to sleep, troubled by thoughts sweeping around his mind like a hive of angry bees.

Derek was finally dozing. His mind was cluttered, but he was exhausted, and much in need of the rest. His long absence from rest had finally forced a light sleep.

Neither of them noticed the lock on the front door being picked with silent precision, creaking open into a soundless hallway.

Bandile treaded into the house softly and carefully, wary not to apply pressure to a creaky floorboard or to knock any ornament or artefact balanced carefully on an unsteady piece of furniture.

Dexter and Bagsy swiftly followed. Dexter's face was full of concentration, obediently following their leader, looking back and forth, observing every shadow and every movement.

Bagsy was less subtle. His grin widened with every step he took, taking sadistic pleasure at the thought of what they were going to do once they found their victims. He secretly hoped that they weren't cooperative – that way he could torture them more. Maim them. Tear off pieces flesh and watch as he forced them to eat it.

Nothing gave him a bigger thrill than a humiliated and helpless victim. It gave him a buzz of adrenaline that no high could otherwise outdo.

Bandile withdrew an Okapi knife. With its brown handle and large, pointed blade, this was a South African knife he had bought fifteen years ago, initially for hunting. He'd even had his wife's first name engraved on the blade, though that name had since faded, along with his memory of her. Still, he held it tightly in his grip, treasuring his weapon along with the sentimentality he attached to it.

He placed a soft foot on the bottom step, feeling it creak and withdrawing his foot promptly. Signalling at the other two with his eyes to indicate that they should skip that step, he placed a soft foot on the step above. Slowly, but surely, they made their way up the stairs and onto the landing.

The moon cast a generous light through an opening in the curtains, casting a humble glow down the corridor. There were two closed bedroom doors that Bandile assumed were home to Derek and Martin.

As much as he would have liked to end his history with Derek with a flourish, it was Martin he was after. The only one who could oppose the heir.

This was Bandile's ticket. His safe ticket through to a high place in hell. His salvation, his promise to the devil that he was worthy of being spared an eternity of torture and torment in their fiery pits. The only way he could ensure that the devil would look kindly upon him. That he would be saved when hell opened and demons swarmed the earth.

He had to prove himself.

Even after all he had done. The Devil's Three was part of a deal – he needed to do something extra, something that provided true evidence of his loyalty.

Bandile placed a gentle palm against the door handle, delicately pushing it open.

There on the bed, his eyes peacefully closed, lay Derek. He looked to have aged significantly in the short time since the ritual, evidence of grey in his hair and further wrinkles on his face.

He nodded to the other two. They stepped forward to detain Derek, as Bandile turned back into the corridor.

Bandile strode to the other closed door at the end of the corridor, to forcibly gain entry to the room that must contain Martin.

Sweaty in anticipation.

Licking his lips as the door grew near.

He clutched his knife. Flexed his fingers.

One swipe and into the neck of Martin is all it would take.

No hesitation.

No point taking him hostage.

Then the devil would see that he was worthy.

He kicked opened the door and stormed into the room, pulling the duvet back, lifting his knife into the air, and–

The bed was empty.

The boy wasn't there.

Bandile searched the room, turning the bed upside down, opening the wardrobe, throwing the desk over in a fit of anger.

He burst out the room and into the next, searching everywhere, opening every door, analysing every corner.

The bathroom was empty.

Every damn room in the house was empty.

Bandile marched back into Derek's room, where the man crouched at the feet of Dexter and Bagsy with a bloody nose.

Bandile tucked his large hand securely around Derek's neck, lifting him up and pinning him against the wall. His arm shook with anger, his face curled up into an aggressive sneer, sickened to the gut with fury that the boy he was after was nowhere to be found.

"Where is he?!" Bandile demanded, growling into the face of Derek.

"Where – is – who?" Derek stuttered, struggling for breath under the force of Bandile's heavy palm.

"The boy! *Where is he?!*"

"I – have – no – idea…"

Bandile threw Derek to the ground.

"Do what you need to," he instructed Bagsy, knowing he would enjoy this task most. "Remove every tooth, every nail, and every limb if you have to. Find out where he is!"

Bagsy's smirk danced upon his face with a fluttering excitement.

"Oh, boss," he sang in a disjointed tune. "You are too kind…"

CHAPTER TWENTY-TWO

*T*urns out having to concentrate on every sight, sound, smell, taste and touch, day in and day out, meant that Martin could tell when something was amiss. A distant shuffle, a barely audible movement, resounded delicately from down the hallway, becoming piercing clang in his ears.

With a curious hesitancy, he crept from his bed and to the door, opening it with a small crack.

Three men. A large black man, a man with a beard, and a man covered in intimidating tattoos. Edging through the hallway, toward Derek's door.

Martin grew alarmed. His whole body stiffened into fight or flight, his mind rapidly firing through his possible next steps.

Fight them?

Hurt them?

Kill them?

They were not demons. They were humans.

Martin's powers were not for killing humans.

It was a line Martin had never thought about crossing.

They opened Derek's door. Led by the large black man carrying a large knife.

Shit.

He looked around himself for a weapon.

Nothing.

He could always get Derek's revolver.

But it was empty.

No.

I am the weapon.

He could conjure fire. He could throw wind. He could manipulate his surroundings into chaos.

But Derek...

There was no way he could guarantee Derek's safety if he was to burst out and start a fight.

He was going to need to be more strategic.

He ran to the window, opening it and looking below. It was a steep drop. Though he was pretty sure he could dangle down, out of sight.

But what then?

How would he get back into the house?

Hearing footsteps heading toward his room, he knew he was running out of time. He needed to make a decision; however instinctive it may end up being.

He climbed out of the window and dangled on the ledge, clinging on with the tips of his fingers. He leant his feet against the wall and reached up a spare arm, closing the window behind, being careful to leave a slight gap he could still use.

He looked down.

If he fell from this, he could land on his neck.

Suddenly the vision of numerous nightmare scenarios ran through his mind.

He closed his eyes. Held on tight. Calmed his mind.

Heavy stomping pounded the floor of his room. Doors

slammed open and shut. Banging of furniture being upturned and items being thrown bashed against the walls, shaking the ledge Martin loosely hung onto.

He felt his fingers slip.

Hearing the heavy footsteps grow fainter, he lifted himself back up, peering into the room.

It was empty.

He opened the window and crept back inside.

CHAPTER TWENTY-THREE

*D*erek blinked the blood out of his eye. He tilted his head, trying to avoid the trail of blood trickling from the top of his head landing in his eye again.

He spat a mouthful of blood to the floor, feeling a tooth dislodge with it. An absent softness announced itself at the back of his lower jaw where the tooth had previously been.

The skinny man with the sadistic grin and devilish inking stomped on his head once more and he saw black.

Absence. A flickering nothing with the heavy close of his eyes.

He came back around again in what he was sure was only a few seconds later. He lay on his back, staring up at a wall that spun in circle after circle.

"Thank you, Bagsy," came a voice Derek recognised. A thick South African accent.

It could only be one man.

A sudden jolt shocked his body into alertness.

"No, it can't be…"

Bandile Thato knelt beside Derek's head. Derek turned to look at his old friend/enemy, feeling the muscles in his neck tighten and his jaw stiffen as he did, his body aching from the pain of numerous beatings.

Visions of Bandile imparting wisdom on him filled the front of his mind; wise words guiding him on what he should do with his concerns about Eddie – all the while manipulating him.

"Hello, Derek," came the thick accent of the man he had once called a confidant.

"You bastard…" Derek muttered, gurgling on a mouthful of blood.

"Where is Martin?" Bandile asked, his voice remaining blank and void of feeling.

"I trusted you…"

"Where – is – Martin?"

"Go to hell…" Derek spluttered, dropping his head away.

Bandile nodded to the one he had called Bagsy.

The scrawny man mounted Derek, holding something high in his hand. Derek tried to make out what it was. It was silver, rusted. Two pieces of metal pressed together, creating a high-pitched ping as they retracted and collapsed. Such a sound had never felt more terrifying.

As Derek's vision readjusted, he made it out. It was a clamp of some kind.

Bagsy held the clamp over Derek's two front teeth, pressing it firmly around them, ready to do his worst.

Derek closed his eyes.

He had to endure.

He had to give Martin a chance.

"I will ask you one more time," Bandile asserted. "Where is the boy?"

Derek scrunched his face up, wincing from the expectation of pain to come. Getting ready. Preparing himself for whatever sacrifice he had to make.

But Bagsy was interrupted.

The door flung open. Martin burst through.

Derek's heart sank.

No...

He had prayed Martin had made his escape. There was too much riding on his existence.

And a smile raising slowly upon Bandile's face told Derek just what was at risk.

Taking the opportunity of distraction, Derek lifted his arm and sank his fist into Bagsy's face, knocking the bony mess onto his side. Derek rolled onto his front, moaning from the pain of the sudden exertion in his increasingly weary state, but managed to push himself to his knees.

Bandile held a knife by his side.

Martin glared at it. Derek could see him concentrating, could see him getting his gift ready.

Derek couldn't let him do it.

To murder goes against heaven. Derek wasn't even sure that if Martin committed such a cardinal sin, his powers would even remain.

Martin raised his hands, nursing a ball of fire in each one, glaring intently at the intruders, readying his fiery weapons.

"No, Martin!" Derek cried out.

Martin looked to Derek, confused.

"You cannot kill them," Derek pleaded. "They are humans, not demons."

Martin appeared thrown by this, dropping his hands to his side.

The bearded man dove upon Martin, taking him to the floor, punching him in the back of the head until his eyes closed and his face faded into submission.

Bandile took this opportunity to raise his knife, ready to plunge it into his victim's neck.

CHAPTER TWENTY-FOUR

*C*assy marched through paradise, venomous rage in her eyes.

A beautiful landscape encompassed the entry to heaven, fruitful trees waving in a silent breeze, the scent of wildflowers complementing the pure air.

Cassy ignored it, staring contemptuously at Gabrielle who appeared from inside the gates to heaven, come to see what the hasty commotion was about.

"Cassy, have you changed your mind?" Gabrielle asked. "I fear it may be too late."

"I haven't changed my mind, Gabrielle," Cassy insisted as she stormed toward her. "I know the gates of heaven are still shut to me; that is not why I am here."

"Then what are you after?"

"We have a plan to bring Eddie's soul back, but we need help."

Gabrielle grew puzzled.

"But – how are they going to manage that?"

"With an exorcism."

"I don't think you understand, Cassy – how are they

going to carry out an exorcism when they are either dead or condemned?"

Cassy was stumped, taken aback by the nonsensical words of her supposed friend.

"What are you talking about?" Cassy retorted. "They are not dead! And to be condemned they would have to commit an act that went against heaven, and whilst we have spoken about this, we have not–"

"Cassy," Gabrielle interrupted. "I don't think you know, do you?"

"Know what?"

Gabrielle waved her arm in a swift, graceful movement, revealing a glimpse of earth.

Cassy saw them.

With a sudden bolt of terror, an entwining twist of her absent guts, she fell to her knees, watching as Derek and Martin were tortured. Hurt. Beaten into bloody messes.

Cassy waved the vision away, unable to take anymore. Her legs felt weak, shaking under the pressure of the burden of what she had seen.

She tried to get back to her feet but fell once more, Gabrielle reaching through the gate to support her.

"And you can just watch this?" she shouted at Gabrielle.

"Cassy, lower your voice; these are the gates of heaven."

"I don't give a damn about the gates of heaven!" Cassy roared, throwing Gabrielle's helpful hands off her.

"Don't you see, Cassy? They only have two ways out of the situation they are in. Either they die, or they have to kill their captors."

"And if they have to kill them, then they are going to hell, right? Is that what you're saying?"

"Not just that, dear child – they would be condemned."

Cassy closed her eyes in frustration, willing herself to be calm as she realised what Gabrielle was saying.

"If they were to kill, they would no longer be worthy of heaven. And any exorcism would prove redundant."

Gabrielle gave a sympathetic smile and a sympathetic nod, which only infuriated Cassy further.

"You are all pathetic, you know that?" Cassy spat. "You called me to be an angel to make a difference in this war. But... You. God. The whole legion of angels – you don't do shit!"

"Cassy, I understand you are hurting, but I compel you to watch your tongue, or He may deem you as being blasphemous."

Cassy laughed. She couldn't help it. She choked on her mocking laughter, in utter disbelief. Her whole belief system, the angel she had become, what she had been made to represent – it all came crumbling down around her.

"Unbelievable. They are fighting in your name, fighting your war for you, and you would condemn them to hell?"

"With a heavy heart."

"To hell with your heavy heart, Gabrielle."

"This conversation is over," Gabrielle decided, turning her back on Cassy and walking back into her sanctuary.

"So that's it, huh?" Cassy cried out. "They are in a situation, you don't want to help, so that's earth done. The whole world wiped out. Because heaven can't be bothered to help them!"

Gabrielle paused, turning around gracefully and, even though she always retained her air of calmness, a slight air of frustration began to creep through.

"The human race has lasted longer than most."

Cassy shook her head and turned away, marching away from the gates of heaven.

"Where are you going?" Gabrielle requested.

"To help them!" Cassy responded, spinning back around before resuming her walk away.

"If you interfere, if you allow these actions, if you condone an act of murder – you will be forever condemned from heaven, Cassy, I hope you realise that."

Cassy continued walking away, ignoring Gabrielle's pleading.

"When heaven's gates reopen, you may have retained your wings, but you will no longer be allowed entry."

Cassy paused. Turning around slowly, she decided this would be her last attempt at reasoning with the unreasonable.

"I think I understand, you know," she spoke slowly and quietly, but with a toxic edge. "God can't involve himself in ungodly acts because He needs His pawns to do it. That way He can keep His hands clean, keep Himself holy. It's always people sacrificing their pledges to Him, He never kills that sacrifice himself."

"Cassy–"

"If he doesn't have the gumption, I will. And I will save Martin and Derek from either fate. And you will look on and say that you tried to help me. Then, by the same reasoning, I will look up and say that I also attempted to help you."

Cassy walked away.

Gabrielle said nothing.

She stood there, watching God's faithful servant disappear into the distance.

It didn't matter whether Gabrielle agreed with Cassy or not.

It mattered that Gabrielle carried out His actions.

His demands.

However difficult that was.

However much she may oppose it; she was an angel, she was His soldier.

She was to take orders.

Cassy rebelled, but she could not.

Still, she found it hard to return into the secluded harmony behind those gates of heaven.

Knowing the gates would be firmly shut soon, she struggled to find her legs striding inside.

Instead, she found herself poised on the outside, struggling with the movement, Cassy's words bouncing repeatedly around her thoughts.

CHAPTER TWENTY-FIVE

*B*andile's knife hung in the air for what seemed like an eternity. Martin watched it, poised for battle, but conflicted by the words Derek had urgently bestowed on him.

He had to ask himself – could he take a human life? Was he prepared to make that sacrifice?

So far he had killed demons, entities made of pure evil, which had not worn down his conscience whatsoever. But killing three people to save his and Derek's life...

Was he prepared to do it?

Yes.

Could he?

...

Derek's eyes widened in what felt like slow motion. Bandile's knife came thundering down with a steady uncertainty that made Martin's heart beat fast.

Martin was pinned down by one of them. Seconds earlier and he would have conjured fire ready to set each of them alight, to burn them to ashes within seconds. Now, he was restrained, and unable to concentrate astutely enough to re-conjure the elements, unable to move his arms in such a way that they would answer.

The question that ripped across his mind was – could he live with himself knowing that he could have prevented Derek's and his death?

Fate had not been in their favour so far.

Then, before the question could be answered, a sudden bright light encapsulated the room. Martin instinctively flinched away, hiding his face, shielding himself from the salvo of light.

As the light died down he opened his eyes.

Cassy.

With her elegant demeanour and a bright-white backlight beaming from the edge of her skin, she stood over them with a look of determination, thwacking the man holding the knife in the air to the floor.

Martin felt himself free of restraints, the man pinning him down having instinctively loosened his grip to shield himself from the light long enough for Martin to burst to his feet.

He circled his hands, flickering embers of fire, readying his attack. He would not be caught again.

Cassy raised her hand.

"No!" she commanded.

"What?" Martin reacted defiantly, enraged that both she and Derek had instructed him not to defend himself. He was eager to fight, and not at all ready to give in.

"Don't," she commanded, a look of begging in her eyes. "You can't. Nothing will work if you take a human life."

"We have no choice!"

"No, Martin, *I* have no choice. I am saving you from yourself."

Before Martin could object any further, she had taken the knife off the bearded man and plunged it into his throat.

He collapsed into a shaking heap on the floor, clutching onto his bleeding neck, blood pouring through the cracks of his hands. He wriggled and thrashed, bashing the furniture of the room with his feet, but knew it would do nothing as he reached his violent end.

Martin watched as the man's life fell through his fingers.

He watched, knowing he could not have done that.

Knowing that causing this pain was not something he could have brought himself to do to another human.

The scrawny tattooed man behind him went to attack but Cassy got to him first, sticking the knife into his gut, then across his throat.

Blood splattered over her translucent heavenly white gown, staining the image of the angelic.

In the instant the man died, her bright-white light faded.

The large black man readied his grand knife, facing Cassy, ready for a fight.

Cassy rose her knife into the air.

"No!" Derek demanded, standing, holding an arm out to Cassy.

"No Derek, it has to be me that does this."

"No, we cannot kill him!" Derek pleaded. "We need him."

"What for?"

"His name is Bandile Thato. He is a devil worshipper."

Cassy realised what Derek's plan was and dropped her knife to her side.

Bandile dove his knife toward her, but Martin leapt to his feet, turning his finger into a definite rotation. Within seconds he had conjured a restraint spell and thrown the gold circle around Bandile. It tightened around his chest and rose him into the air, his legs dangling pathetically. Bandile struggled against his incarceration, but the supernatural binding was too secure for a human to fight.

Martin pumped his fist in the air, celebrating that he had

successfully implemented the restraint spell. Questions still arose as to whether it was strong enough to hold the antichrist, but there were no questions as to whether it would be strong enough to bind a human for as long as they wanted.

Bandile was theirs. Captive and helpless.

Derek stepped forward, looking Bandile up and down. Bandile's lip curled upwards in an aggressive snarl, his head shaking slowly.

"Hello, old friend," Derek spoke.

Bandile's snarl grew, a rebellious insolence wiping across his livid features.

"You're going to do us a favour."

CHAPTER TWENTY-SIX

*B*andile's eyes fluttered like the wings of a moth, adjusting to the dimness of the light. A distant dripping plagued his ears with an incessancy he could do nothing about. His clothes stank like damp, as did the room, and the footsteps of his captors echoed throughout.

His vision finally came into focus. He looked around himself, peering at his surroundings, trying to make an assumption as to where he was.

It was Derek's basement. He was sure of it.

He went to move. He couldn't. He looked down.

Rope circled his chest, spiralling tightly around him multiple times.

Derek and the boy stood before him. Both with their arms folded, feet shoulder-width apart, their faces displaying resolute glares.

Bandile couldn't help but snigger.

Derek was a well-spoken professor, and this other one was a pathetic little kid. And there they were, trying to look tough, like some ridiculous mock-up action men. The imbeciles were anything but intimidating, and he couldn't help but enjoy the hilarity, despite his evident incarceration.

"You two are fucking pitiful," he chuckled.

He turned to his right and saw a woman stood before him. He knew from the white dress and the radiant skin that she was an angel, except... the dress was blood-splattered. Her illumination had faded. She was...

She was being denied heaven.

Because she had killed his cult members. His poor excuse for assailants.

He threw his head back and guffawed.

"You lost your entry to the Promise Land!" he cackled mockingly. "Because you killed Dexter and Bagsy!"

He threw his head to the side, continually belting forcibly distinct jitters of laughter, shouting his guffaws with menacing intensity.

"They were pathetic!" he cackled. "You could have gotten a fucking rat to kill them! And you sacrificed everything..."

He continued to laugh, wailing uproariously. He could feel rope tight against his chest, his ankles restrained to the bottom of his chair, and handcuffs clamped securely around his wrists. He wasn't getting out of this situation, so the only thing he could do was heartily incense them with his interminable hysterics.

"Laugh all you want," Derek attempted to interject. "We have you restrained. You're not going anywhere."

"And what are you going to do to me? Huh?" Bandile taunted them. "Kill me?"

Derek glanced at Cassy and they exchanged a look. Bandile could tell that they had a plan. He could also tell from how Martin was left out of the look that he was seen as the inexperienced one of the trio.

In fact, it wouldn't have surprised Bandile if Martin had been left out of the loop entirely.

"You guys are idiots," Bandile continued. "You fall for everything. And what, you think this little squirt stands a chance against the heir of hell?"

"I'm not going to kill the heir of hell," Martin announced.

"Oh, yeah?" Bandile continued.

"No," Derek took over. "Edward King is."

Bandile fell silent.

Had he heard them correctly?

Edward King was going to kill the heir of hell?

But...

Edward King is the heir of hell.

"What are you on about?" he demanded.

"You are going to do something for us," Derek continued. "Something to help kill the heir of hell."

"Why would I do that?"

"We are going to exorcise the soul of Edward King out of the heir of hell so it can kill the antichrist," Derek continued, ignoring Bandile's irrelevant question. "Only there is an issue."

Bandile grinned. He knew where this was going.

"A soul can't take human form, can it?" he pointed out. "And it is an ungodly act. Heaven won't turn something as beautiful as a soul into something as weak and mortal as a human body. It goes against heaven to return life to a body where there was none. So many reasons they won't do it... so you need a devil worshipper to do it."

"That's right."

"And that is where I come in, my old friend." Bandile smiled widely, watching Derek grimace from his reference to him as an old friend.

"Yes. And you are going to do this."

"Tell me why I would do this, Derek. Please."

Derek sighed and took a few steps toward Bandile, focussing the man he once trusted dead in the eyes.

"If you repent," Derek explained. "Ask forgiveness, then prove this by bringing back the man who can defeat the antichrist, that would be your path to heaven. And it would be your *only* path to heaven."

"Why would I–" Bandile began to object, then stopped.

A thought hit him.

He couldn't care less about a path to heaven. He wanted a throne in hell. It was the only way, the only path after the horrific actions he had taken.

But maybe this was that path.

If he led them to believe that he was going to do this for them... then didn't... meaning they would be full of hope, then left helpless for the antichrist to kill them...

They may just be stupid enough to believe that he wouldn't be deceptive. That he would want this path to heaven.

Derek Lansdale had already proven that he was a gullible man.

"Okay," Bandile confirmed. "I will do this."

Derek nodded.

"Good." Derek glanced at the other two. "Until that time comes."

He nodded and turned, ascending the stairs. Martin and Cassy followed, turning the light off.

Bandile was left in darkness, feeling something soft scurry past his ankles.

CHAPTER TWENTY-SEVEN

*M*oisture hung in the air in that way it always does in church; loose damp that clings to your clothes. The vast, open room loomed overhead with its great architecture, reverberating all footsteps and rebounding voices against its stone walls.

But there were no voices.

And Cassy didn't create heavy footsteps. An attribute of being an angel was that gliding feet took gentle steps.

She made her way to the front of the church and paused.

The tall crucifix stood over her. A symbol of comfort giving her nothing but rage.

So, this is where people came to pray. To ask for forgiveness from a God who doesn't listen and for help from angels that never come.

For Cassy, it wasn't an issue of whether humans should believe in their God. It was a question of whether humans would want to.

Why worship a God that doesn't listen?

A God who chooses to hide those he deems good enough to survive, and lets those he deems unworthy perish.

A God who has buildings devoted to him, but doesn't listen to the people who built them.

A God who gave them the world with painful death. Illnesses. A world where animals have to kill animals to survive.

She was one of his disciples, but even so, she was disillusioned with the concept of faith.

Now she had been banished from heaven. She was an angel without a home, without a purpose. She had an angel's life in a human's body and it was all for nothing.

Thanks to the God they fought in the name of.

But she wasn't here for God.

She wasn't here to ask for his help.

She dropped to her knees and bowed her head, closing her eyes. A moment of solitude, thinking about he who matters most.

"Eddie," she whispered, so faintly only she could hear it. "Please, listen to me."

She tightened her closed eyes. Tears punched the backs of her eyelids, endeavouring to get out, but she refused. She was here to help, not cry.

"Eddie, we need you. Please just hear me."

She lifted her head, opening her eyes. Tears blurred her vision.

"Eddie, you must–"

"You don't call, you don't write…" came a familiar voice singing out bouncily behind her. "The only time you want to talk to me is in a lousy bleedin' church."

Cassy gasped.

Her hands stiffened. Her arms grew rigid, her breath stuck in her throat.

It couldn't be…

"What's the matter, sis? Aren't you gonna say hi?"

Cassy stood, sweaty-palmed, shaking legs. She slowly turned, dreading the sight she was about to see.

There he sat.

On a bench, three rows back. A sharp black suit and a cocky smile that didn't suit Eddie at all. He looked like her brother. He had the same pitch of voice. The same hair, the same face. But his mannerisms were different. The tone of his voice was more sadistically playful. The glint in his eye was neither happy nor charming, but arrogant and conceited.

He had the face of her brother, but she knew that was only to torment her further.

"I'm an angel, you can't hurt me," she spoke, assuring herself more than him. Despite the sentiment of what she said, her lip still quivered and her voice still shook.

"Oh, yeah?"

"Yes. You can't."

"I can't *physically* hurt you, is that what you're saying?"

"Exactly," she spoke, feeling a weak confidence in her fevered chest.

"But that doesn't mean I can't hurt you."

Cassy shook her head. He couldn't hurt her, she knew it. There was an agreement.

Then the sad realisation hit her.

There are no truces in war.

"How about your wise and knowing friend, Derek?" he proposed, sticking out his bottom lip, sitting back and draping his arm leisurely over the side of the bench. "Would be a real shame if I hurt him to hurt you, wouldn't it?"

Her eyes narrowed. She shook her head in terror, glaring at him with fearful malice.

"And your little boy, Martin," he continued, nodding with confirmation. "The little boy made by heaven, the one who's meant to take me on. A pathetic attempt by your pathetic God to make it seem like he gives a shit."

Cassy looked past him, to the far door. Could she get there in time?

"You know why it is I can't hurt you?" he spoke, standing up and sauntering cockily toward her. "Because many thousands of years ago, heaven and hell made an agreement that demons and angels would not fight, so as to avoid a complete mass genocide in which no one would win or lose."

Cassy backed up as he crept closer, bumping into the giant cross with the dead Jesus attached.

"But what if I didn't right feel like obeying the rules? You know, seeing as we're about to break pretty much every treaty we've ever had."

His hands flung to her throat, squeezing tightly. Her arms shook frantically, a sense of doom seizing up and down her spine and in through the pit of her absent stomach. A sense that told her she was truly in the presence of evil.

"Even though you don't breathe," he whispered callously, taking his face within an inch of hers. "It still hurts that I strangle you. Even though you don't have a heart that beats, it would still cause you incredible pain if I were to rip that heart out and squash it beneath my foot."

She closed her eyes, scrunching up her face as if preparing for impact.

Is this what I'm going to contribute? Is this what I came back for?

To be a coward in the face of that which she was helping to oppose?

"Eddie..." she whimpered. "Eddie, please, I need your help..."

It was a long shot, and it stank of desperation – but if Eddie was there, if he was able to control something – he could show her right now.

"Eddie's not here right now," the false face of her brother retorted, grinning wildly.

He lifted her into the air and threw her down the aisle, watching her slide across her back until she hit a pew and collapsed into a heap.

"I've decided to end this," he announced, strutting toward her. "I've decided I'm just going to kill everyone. Got bored, I guess."

She clambered to her knees, dragging her shaking body to its feet.

"But first, I need to know where to find your little friend."

Cassy shook her head, scrambling to her feet and running away. Within a flash Eddie had shot across the church and halted before her, causing her to collapse against his fake chest. He put his arms around her, squeezing tightly, wrapping her in a merciless embrace.

"I miss this. When we just used to cuddle."

"That wasn't you, it was Eddie."

"Oh, I was always there. Hiding. Waiting for my time to shine."

"I will *never* give up my friends. You'll have to break the truce and kill me."

"Not being funny, but I was planning on doing that anyway."

She shook her head.

Please, Eddie. If you are there, just, please...

"How about we take a trip?"

Feeling her chest tighten under the pressure of being squeezed against his body, she winced as she started to feel the first bit of human pain since she had ascended to heaven. Large spikes grew out of his body, digging into her, wrapping around her, ensuring she was painfully secured.

In a shot, he soared them into the air and fired them through the church roof faster than she could handle.

CHAPTER TWENTY-EIGHT

*A*pril 3, 2002

TWO YEARS, four months since millennium night

THE DOOR SWUNG so hard into the adjacent wall that the handle left a dent in the poor paint job. Kelly burst through, punching the door away as it rebounded back against her, sending it swinging on its hinges.

She folded her arms, incessantly shaking her head, storming into the kitchen. She bit her lip, ferociously searching the room for something to occupy her fiery rumination.

Eddie followed, edging slowly into the room with an air of calmness that only incensed her further. He steadied the flapping door and looked at her hopefully.

"Kelly–" he attempted.

"No!" she interrupted, gesticulating her arms wildly in the

air. "No, you do not get to walk in here all calm and try and be the voice of reason!"

"Excuse me?"

"Don't excuse me me, you know exactly what I am on about!"

Eddie raised an eyebrow at her bad use of grammar, then quickly lowered them, fearing further respite.

She sneered at him, refolding her arms and turning away irritably.

He sank his hands into his pockets, and took a moment, gathering his thoughts. He avoided eye contact with her for a few seconds, staring at the corner of the room as he tried to figure out what could possibly be the right thing to say at this moment.

"Look, I'm just trying to help."

"Well, you can't! You don't know what it's like to be possessed!"

"Don't know what it's like? I've been to hell!"

"This is not about you!"

Eddie threw his arms into the air in exasperation. Nothing he could say was right. Nothing.

"What do you want me to say?"

"I–" Kelly stuttered, realising she didn't truly know the answer to that question. "I want you to apologise."

"For what?"

"For what you said!"

"What did I say?"

"You–" she stuttered once more, searching for the right words. "Well, I don't remember, but I still think you should apologise for it."

"Okay," he diplomatically offered with a shrug of his shoulders. "I'm sorry."

"But how are you apologising when you don't even know what it's for?"

"Kelly, that's what you just told me you wanted me to do!"

"Yes, but I don't want a fake apology!"

"Then what the hell do you want?"

"I – I don't know!"

She turned and faced the window. She rested her weight on one leg, using her other foot to tap agitatedly on the floor. Her arms remained tightly folded, her lips pursed together.

After a few hesitant moments, she felt two gentle arms tucking around her waist. She went to push them away but just found them tightening their soft, heartfelt grip around her once more.

"No, Eddie."

"Kelly, we don't even know what we're fighting about."

He kissed her neck.

Damn it, she hated when he kissed her neck.

Within seconds her anger diluted. She resisted at first, adamant that she wanted to stay enraged, her mood dictating that someone should pay, but his embrace was just too inviting. She sank into it, allowing him to wrap his arms around her until she was fully cocooned in his comfortable warmth.

"I know there's no way to put into words what you went through, what it was like," Eddie whispered into her ear. "I hear your screams in the night before they wake you up. The flashbacks are horrific; the things it made you do were horrible, and I think you're incredibly strong for coping as well as you have."

She couldn't help it. His words were so sincere, so inviting. She allowed them to wrap around her heart, coating it with reassurance and undeniable love.

"It kills me that I don't know what I can even do about it, how I could make it go away. There's hardly much comparison out there – there's not really any possessed-by-the-devil-anonymous groups you can go join, are there?"

She nodded. It was true.

"Just know that I will never, ever abandon you. It will never make me run away."

"You promise?"

"Of course. I would never do anything that could cause you even the slightest amount of pain."

She sank deeper into his arms, feeling comforted and reassured in a way she didn't even realise she had craved.

Three months later, he killed her.

CHAPTER TWENTY-NINE

pril 3, 2003

THREE YEARS, four months since millennium night

DEREK STOOD AT THE ALTAR.

To think, once he had planned to be there as a groom. Many years ago, and long faded in his memory now, was the picture of a woman. A woman he loved with every piece of him, to whom he had given a ring and made plans.

But he had given it all up. He had been young and foolish, and chosen this life over her.

Eddie had once seen a photograph of her in his house, one that he had subsequently swiftly hidden.

No other mention had been made of her since the day she left.

Funny, really, how he thought of her now. Wondering where she was. Wondering if, whilst running the vacuum around the house or dropping her kids off at school, she ever thought of him. Just a passing thought, shooting by like something out the window of a train. Brief, but definite nonetheless.

He wondered if she had been granted passage to heaven.

"Can I help you, my child?" came a softly spoken voice from behind Derek.

He quickly dunked his flask into the holy water and took what he needed, placing the flask inside his jacket pocket and turning around to face the priest.

It was not a father Derek recognised. He was a short, podgy man, with a round bald spot amidst a head of messy hair. His face was red and sweaty, no doubt in fear of what was to come.

"No, thank you," Derek replied. "I have what I need."

"You were stealing the holy water," the father spoke gently, but sceptically.

"I see nothing gets past you, Father," Derek observed. "It is for a just cause, I assure you."

"I am sure it is. Bad times are coming."

"They are indeed."

In a hurry, Derek forced a smile and shuffled past the old man, but was halted by a few alarming words.

"If you are stealing holy water, it must mean you are planning to fight what is coming."

Against his better judgement, Derek turned, peering at the father. Priest or not, Derek was already tired of this conversation.

"And what if I am? What do you know of the rapture?"

"It was said it would be the second coming of Christ. That heaven would plant him on this earth once again."

"What if I told you heaven had planted their messiah on this earth, and he was powerful, and he could fight?"

"Then you would pique my interest."

"What if I also told you that what was coming was far too strong, even for someone conceived of heaven, just like Jesus was? Yes, Father, I plan to fight. But I would suggest you hide, or take your ride up to heaven."

Derek turned to leave but was stopped once more.

"Do you not have faith in God?" the father insisted. "Do you not trust that he will do good by us?"

Derek snarled. After spending so much time mulling over the question of why their God didn't do more, he grew livid over such a question. Blind, unaltered, unjustified faith incensed him.

It wasn't a case of believing in God.

He had a child conceived by heaven and a fallen angel on his side. He had fought in God's name against demons of this earth for decades; that much was true.

He had faith that God was there.

But did he have faith in that God?

Faith that God would ever get off his arse and do something other than sending them a warrior in the form of a helpless boy?

God was never someone he felt he had on his side.

"No, I do not," Derek bluntly stated. "But I do have faith."

"In what?"

Derek peered at the priest, who seemed so eager to impart the apparent power of faith into Derek. So desperate to think that his words were wise and not disillusioned.

"I have faith in Eddie."

"But are you not afraid you will have to answer to God?"

Derek turned back to the father and narrowed his eyes into a menacing, sinister glare.

"Do you know what we have had to do to represent your God? The awful, hellish things we have had to do so he can keep his hands clean?"

"My child—"

Derek took a few sinister strides toward the priest until he was inches from his face.

"I would ask God's forgiveness. But after everything, if me and him ever come face-to-face – he will have to beg for *mine*."

Derek turned and marched out of the church, ignoring further shouts and questions designed to bring him back into the pointless debate.

* * *

Sure, the father was trying to talk some sense into a disciple and do what he thought was right.

But Derek truly believed that the father was trying to convince himself more than anyone else. If he knew what the rapture meant, what it truly was in more than mere biblical terms, he would likely deny it.

Which is to be expected. Denial is the most common human trait, despite also being the most counterproductive.

Derek walked for five minutes down a few entwining paths until he met with Martin. They had decided to use the location in which the heir had risen and taunted them last time. Somewhere familiar that the antichrist would find them.

The field of death, or so it felt. Beside a swing set that Jenny saw as significant enough to use in her attempts to get through to Eddie.

She may have failed, yes – but if this was Jenny's idea then they needed to listen to her.

Failing to listen to her was what caused such a catastrophic failure before.

"Ready?" Martin prompted.

"Nearly."

The night was descending and dark-grey clouds hovered

overhead. The field was deserted. Some naïve people would see this as luck; that there weren't any innocent bystanders who could get caught in the crossfire.

They knew better than that. People had an instinct for such danger, even if they didn't know or acknowledge it.

Derek took his leather bag and made his way to the swing set. The place Eddie and Jenny had grown up. The place they had become such close friends, where they had comforted and consoled each other through enduring times.

It was rusted. Left to rot by a neglectful council who didn't care for the sentimentality associated with such landmarks.

He knelt down and opened his bag. A puff of dust rose like smoke, and Derek resisted the urge to choke.

He withdrew the items. Items he had used long ago. Back before Eddie became so prolific at this activity that Derek's own abilities at performing an exorcism had grown redundant.

He withdrew each item with care, raising it to his forehead and closing his eyes for a short moment; before placing it gently and precisely on the floor before him.

A cross. Wooden, with a splintered edge. Old but sturdy, with the faded bumps of a crucified Jesus fixed upon it.

A flask of holy water with the cross marked upon it, taken from the church hours ago.

A Bible. Leather bound, with faded brown pages and illegibly small writing. Part of it was in Latin. It had been a while since he had used the dated language, but he was ready to call on his old knowledge should the process require him to.

Rosary beads, which he did not place carefully with his other items, but instead kissed and placed around his neck, tucking them under his shirt.

And finally, he withdrew salt. He poured a small handful in his palm, which he then poured in a circle around himself.

He bowed his head. Closed his eyes.

"Eddie, have mercy. God, the Son, please give him safe passage in this merciless time."

His eyes welled up. He fought against it. Now was not the time. Now was the fight of his life.

This was it.

Either Eddie was out there, somewhere, able to fight his way back.

Or...

Or... the world ends tonight.

Derek rose to his feet. He took the cross firmly in his left hand. He placed the holy water in his pocket and held the Bible in his right.

"Right you prick," he muttered. "Where are you?"

"But about that day or hour no one knows, not even the angels in heaven, nor the Son, but only the Father."

Mark 13:32

CHAPTER THIRTY

*T*hunder rumbled ever closer with a threatening familiarity, but it did nothing to intimidate Martin or Derek.

They had far more to worry about than the weather.

A trickle of rain pattered against the empty earth. Grey clouds blocked the moon so flickering lamplight was the only illumination available, casting a faint amber glow that deflected kindly off the rusted metal of the park.

"Martin," Derek prompted. "It's time."

"Where's Cassy?" Martin asked, looking around himself. "She was supposed to be here."

"We can't wait any longer. She will get here, trust me."

Martin stood forward, taking in a deep breath. It was a strange feeling, knowing that you could well be dead within minutes. Knowing that everything you have done could be rendered meaningless.

Not just his preparation for this war.

The failed parents' evening reports. The feeding of his disabled mother. The arguments, the tantrums, the fallouts, the girls, the friends, the bullies – everything could mean nothing.

History was not written by those who lose.

He would not be remembered for failing. His name would not go down in history in a world ravaged by demons and death.

This was his immortality.

He had no army. He just had two faithful followers who had never faltered in their belief in him, despite such blatant, undeniable evidence that he was not strong enough.

It was time to repay their faith in him.

It was time to forget all those pointless things in life.

Those teachers can tell his parents he's a lazy little shit. Fine. Who cares?

Those bullies can tell him he won't amount to anything. Where are they now?

Those girls can laugh. Those friends can run. The shouting can get louder and it won't mean a damn thing.

Because this was it.

This is what will define me.

"All right, you fucker!" Martin screamed out, hoping his taunt would be heard. "Come on then! Time for round two!"

He waited, allowing the rain to seep through his t-shirt and drench his skinny body.

"Come on, where are you?"

A figure appeared in the distance. Walking closer, a limping silhouette.

Martin glanced over his shoulder at Derek, who looked equally perplexed, also peering to see who it was.

Martin watched as this figure fell to its knees and clambered back up again. Something was attached to it. Something long and heavy.

It was Cassy.

As she grew closer, her face grew clearer.

But despite her inherent angelic grace, her face was bloodied. Mangled. Distorted. She was hurt.

"Cassy?" Martin shouted. He went to march forward, but a shout from Derek behind him kept him rooted to the spot.

"Don't, Martin – wait."

Cassy stumbled closer and, as she did, her body faded into view. It was wrapped in chains. Big, metallic chains that entwined around her chest again and again, with a longer chain leading into the darkness behind her.

"Oh my God, what happened?" Martin asked. Ignoring Derek's shout, he ran forward.

"Don't!" Cassy screamed, forcing Martin to stumble to a sudden stop. "It's a trap!"

Martin frowned. A trap?

Surely if he was to fight this thing, there would be no traps?

He was ready to fight.

Straightening himself up, he sauntered forward with an air of arrogance, ready for this so-called trap.

A slow growl rumbled across the air, shaking any confidence he had willed to his mind to pour out into the puddles he stepped through.

"Where is he?" Martin demanded, doing all he could to sound strong.

"He's–" Cassy began, but before she could complete her sentence she went flying backwards, back into the cloak of darkness, encompassed in the shadows behind her.

Martin didn't move. He watched, waiting for the next taunt, or the next attack. Waiting warily for the next move.

Staring cautiously into pitch-black. Just waiting for whatever was there to appear.

He looked to Derek, who was the same; poised, still, wary.

The ground rumbled, trembling under a few thudding footsteps. A huge banging became louder, growing closer.

Then, from the shadows, it emerged.

The large beast with hooves, claws, fangs, razor-sharp spikes, and red demented eyes as big as Martin's head.

In the heir's hand was Cassy, held tightly by a claw that could crush her without any effort.

"Let her go!" Martin demanded.

Dripping blood and saliva, the heir's mouth curved into an open grin, a few hearty chuckles booming out.

"You've gotten cocky," the heir declared.

"Let. Her. Go!"

"Finally!" the heir sighed. "Enough of this waiting. Let's get your death out of the way."

CHAPTER THIRTY-ONE

*E*ddie thudded to the floor like his body was made of weights. His chest felt like it was going to burst. His head pounded, beating against the skull he knew wasn't even there.

He willed himself out of it. Told himself to endure the pain. It wasn't real.

He felt such agony when the heir was on earth. And, if the heir was on earth, Eddie knew bad things were happening.

He could feel everything. This was the piece of hell he was attached to. The link the devil couldn't sever.

If he was the heir, he could see through his eyes. See what he was doing.

Only…

Did he really want to see that? Did he want to see the death and destruction being caused by… him?

He couldn't deny that anymore.

It was being done by him.

Just, not the part with the soul attached.

Yes.

He reluctantly bowed his head.

I'm going to have to see this.

He closed his eyes, allowing himself to sink. Sink out of his mind, out of his body, further into the vile casing of the heir. Allowing himself to see through the eyes of...

It was easier than he thought.

He was staring through the heir's eyes within seconds. Feeling his stretched flesh encase his bones.

He was relieved that it worked.

That was, until he saw the scene in front of him.

Oh, God.

He felt something in his hand. Except, it wasn't a hand. It was bigger than that. It was a claw. With sharp nails and...

Cassy.

His own sister.

An angel. Being disgraced, used as a taunt. A bloody, bruised face.

He waved Cassy back and forth in his hand, pulling on a chain in the other, a chain that led back to her. She was wrapped in restraints. And she was crying.

She was begging.

But not with Eddie. She was begging with something else.

With the boy in front of him.

Martin. The piece of heaven. The biblical piece of the rapture – this was the second coming of Christ. This child was that second coming. This was a child conceived by heaven, just as had happened two thousand years before.

The only hope humans had.

And Cassy was begging him. Begging him to do nothing. Not to accept the taunt. To let her die, to let her be shattered into thousands of pieces of bright light that would shine down on them like stars – as Eddie always imagined a murdered angel's fate would be.

Except no angel had ever died before. They had fallen, but this could be the first...

Which, in that case, made it undeniable – they truly were losing.

Martin's faced moulded into a snarl. Full of hatred against this thing before him.

Eddie didn't want to look, but he had to.

He had to.

Because there he was, beyond Martin. The only man who had ever believed in Eddie.

Derek.

About to help fight him to the death. To be the last stand between heaven and hell.

To be the last person fighting Eddie, the man he had helped create.

Eddie fell out of the heir's eyes, out of the heir's body, falling back onto the solid ground of his cell. He couldn't take it anymore. It was too tough.

Derek. The man who had trained him.

Now trying to kill him.

Except, he wasn't.

Martin was the one fighting. Derek was further back. What was he doing?

Eddie leapt back to life, diving into the heir's eyes once more.

Derek had items. What were they?

Eddie peered into the distance.

A cross. Holy water. A Bible.

Those were items used in an exorcism.

Why has he got items for an exorcism...?

It struck him, in a gratifying moment of realisation. Derek hadn't given up on him.

He was trying to get to Eddie. He was trying to remove the soul, save him from where he was trapped, bring him back.

Oh God, Derek.

Derek did still believe in him.

But... how? How could Derek do that?

There was no way out.

Then he heard Derek's voice. So faint that if he even moved he wouldn't have been able to hear it.

"Eddie, have mercy. God, the Son, please give him safe passage in this merciless time."

"Derek..."

Eddie held his position behind the monster's eyes. The position where he planned to stay. He felt physically closer to Derek there – maybe that was where he needed to be to give the exorcism the best chance of working?

He felt invigorated. A new lease on life, a spurt of energy firing through him like a jolt of electricity.

If he could see through the heir of hell's eyes... Then surely... Surely...

Could he do more than just see?

Could he alter the heir's actions? Even take over completely?

After all, it was him. He was seeing through his own eyes, it was the body he belonged to.

He clenched his fists. Held his arms out in the position of the beast, tried to move them, put all his energy into it, urging himself on, willing himself to do it.

But it was no good.

The claw tightened around Cassy and he felt there was nothing he could do.

CHAPTER THIRTY-TWO

Martin whipped his hands around in circles, furiously beating the air until flickers of gold began to generate.

Time to be brave, Martin.

No time for being young, or doubting his convictions. The plan had been made, and it was time to execute it.

Focus, Martin. Fuck everything else, just focus.

The heir of hell's glare intensified. It appeared amused yet angry. Amused that Martin thought he could oppose it, angry that Martin even dared.

"Just kill it!" Cassy insisted. "Ignore me!"

The heir's grip tightened around Cassy's chest, squeezing her into silence and submission.

Martin concentrated on his surroundings, listening to the thunder, taking in the smell of fine rain. He closed his eyes, soaking up every piece of his surroundings. Silencing his thoughts. Focussing on nothing but what was around him.

His eyes shot open. He harnessed a large string of fire in his hands, turning it into a sharp point. He threw it out, landing it on the heir's wrist, forcing it to drop Cassy to the ground.

Cassy stumbled onto her front, then launched herself forward. She ran messily back and forth, trying to retain her balance, and get away from the heir.

Martin retracted his fiery whip and slid it down the back of her chains. She collapsed to the ground once more, wriggling herself out of her incarceration.

The heir snarled. It grew so livid that parts of it set on fire, flames running down its spine to accompany its aggressive snarl.

It ignored Cassy, who continued to run into the distance, peeling off her chains – choosing to focus on the impudent boy before him.

Martin went to throw a whip of fire. Feeling a brief glow of triumphant smugness from the impact of his burning blade, he found any feeling of optimism faded as the heir whacked the fire away.

Its feet beat against the floor as it edged its way forward with intensely large, sinister strides. The simmer of an earthquake followed every placement of its foot. It swiped its sharp claw toward Martin, who conjured a gust of wind just in time to surge himself upwards and out of the way.

He fell onto his back, leaving himself exposed.

The heir curled its claw into a tight fist and sent it soaring downwards into the soggy grass Martin laid upon. He rolled just in time to narrowly miss the strike, feeling the large gust brush against him as the heir retracted its bulky claw.

Martin weakly stared up at the heir, awaiting its next move. The heir lurched forward, glaring, ready for its lethal strike.

"You cannot prevent what's coming!" it screeched so loud it forced a nearby lamppost to wave.

Martin crawled backwards, trying to get to his feet.

The heir sent its clenched paw into the ground, shaking the surface with such ferocity it sent Martin flailing into the air and curling back onto his front.

"You don't get it, do you…"

Martin crawled forward, trying to get to his knees, but another slam sent him rolling across the floor.

He stumbled to his feet and turned away from the heir, sprinting for his life.

He was running away.

Why am I running away?

"I killed Kelly to complete my ascension," the heir reminded Martin.

Martin turned over his shoulder, willing himself to be brave, searching for a way to fight this. But the heir was lifting its claws, storming forward, a rumbling earthquake with each step.

It was going toward him.

And Martin abruptly realised why he was running away.

I can't fight this. It's too strong.

"I killed Jenny to show you that fighting was futile."

Martin tumbled to his side, falling from the shake of the earth vibrating from the impact of the heir's heavy feet.

In the distance he saw Derek praying, Cassy diving to his side, joining in.

Another slam into the surface and Martin bounced up and down, landing on his arm with a painful howl.

He had no more spells. No more elements he could manipulate.

Fire. Wind. That was it. That was all he had mastered.

Only then did it strike him how ill-prepared he was.

It was a ridiculous thought, really.

I wasn't ever going to be able to defeat the heir.

"Now I will kill you to end the world."

The claw of this creature slammed over him, trapping

him like a cage. He tried to find a gap in its claws that he could crawl through but he couldn't. He was stuck. Stuck inside the sharp claws of the heir of hell.

He conjured a ball of fire and sent it into the claw.

It flinched.

But it did not falter.

The claw wrapped itself around Martin and scooped him up like he was a plate of food.

As he was swept through the air he felt the claw tighten, gripping, constricting his chest. He gasped for oxygen, helplessly punching the thick hand wrapped around him.

He was held before the heir's face, made to look into the heir's demonic, bloody eyes.

The grip tightened and tightened.

It suffocated him until he couldn't breathe. He felt his insides squeeze, his muscles compress, his bones crush.

This was it.

This was his resistance.

CHAPTER THIRTY-THREE

The sides of the wooden cross indented into Derek's hand, such was the tightness of his grip.

He watched in horror as the heir wrapped its sharp, curved claws around Martin's body and squeezed, pressing all the oxygen out of his lungs.

Derek needed to do something. He needed to do it quickly.

But what?

He had no powers. Martin was the one who had the gift he was supposed to be using it to defeat this thing. That gift was already proving to be insignificant.

Derek felt Cassy's weak hand on his shoulder. He turned around to see her wounded expression atop her feeble face.

"What can I do?" Derek wept, watching as Martin struggled to stay alive.

"Your gift," Cassy reminded him.

"I have no gift. Eddie and Martin were the ones with the gift, not me."

"That's not true." She knelt beside him and peered

intently into his eyes. "Perform the exorcism. Call on Eddie. Do it now."

Derek bowed his head. They were supposed to have the heir restrained, kept bound whilst he performed the rite of exorcism. To do it whilst the beast was still thrashing around would be near impossible.

If the heir saw Derek performing the exorcism without being restrained, it would kill him in an instant.

But he had no choice.

Clutching the cross, gripping the Bible, he leapt to his feet and marched forward. Marched toward the beast that was slowly killing Martin.

"From all evil, deliver us, oh Lord," he began. "Deliver us, oh *Eddie!*"

The beast roared.

Martin's eyelids flickered heavily. His face grew pale, his arms punching with less and less ferocity.

They were losing him.

"Hear us, Eddie. From all sin, from wrath, from sudden and provided death, hear us."

He held his cross out before him, pointing it directly at the hell monster that consumed Derek in shadows.

"Hold on, Martin!" Derek cried out.

Martin tried to shout back but couldn't. His eyes were distant, staying shut longer on each heavy blink. Derek could see the fading fight on Martin's face, endeavouring to stay conscious, to keep battling. But he was losing life, and Derek needed to act.

Derek needed Eddie to act.

"Hear us, Edward King. From the snares of the devil, from anger, hatred, and all ill will, from lightning and tempest – hear us, *Edward King!*"

The rain mixed with his perspiration, dripping down his face, but he didn't feel a drop of it.

Derek glanced over his shoulder.

Cassy stood a few yards behind him. Nodding reassuringly.

"All holy saints, pass our message on," Derek spoke.

"Deliver us, Edward King," Cassy echoed behind him.

The heir turned its glare toward them.

But Martin no longer fought. His head slanted to the side, his eyes opening and closing groggily.

Derek's eyes faltered, fighting tears, as he saw Martin seconds away from death.

"Be merciful, deliver us."

"Deliver us, Edward King."

"Hear us, Eddie, for all the good in this world, hear us!"

"Hear us, Edward King."

The beast froze momentarily.

Hovered vacantly.

Loosened its grip.

Derek turned to Cassy, who was equally confused, then turned back to the fading face of the heir.

Derek was sure he saw a glint of an old friend in the monster's eyes.

CHAPTER THIRTY-FOUR

*E*ddie could feel the heir's anger bursting through him, surging through his body, filling his veins with gushing blood of hate.

Every part of him was consumed with this urge for destruction. The desire to kill, maim, and torture his way to annihilation. To reach out and suffocate, to rip apart anyone or anything that opposed him.

Through the heir's eyes, he could see Derek. Marching toward him, crucifix in hand.

"No…" whimpered Eddie. "Please, Derek, I'll kill you…"

He felt his right hand tighten, grip around something bumpy. He turned and looked.

Martin.

The young man thrashed out at his claws, but it just felt like a twitch or a tinge of discomfort. After a few seconds, he didn't even feel the slight discomfort anymore. The boy grew pale, his fighting growing less and less.

Eddie was killing him.

He could feel it. The life rushing away from heaven's saviour. The second coming being crushed into submission.

His hand tightened around Martin's chest, constricting his breathing with ease.

Martin's fighting grew weaker.

The thrashing turned to stumbling punches, to light taps.

Martin's eyes closed and his head tilted.

Then Eddie heard something. Something he wasn't expecting to hear.

"From the snares of the devil, from anger, from hatred," Derek spoke, staring the heir straight in the eyes, "and all ill will from lightning and tempest – hear us, Edward King!"

His name.

Derek had said his name.

Derek... Oh dear God...

What was Derek doing?

Then, with stark realisation, Eddie realised.

They knew he was there. They knew Eddie was still there, behind the eyes of the heir of hell. They were trying to get to him, to his trapped soul, trying to free it from its capture. To bring him back into the heir's body.

"All holy saints, pass our message on," Derek continued.

"Deliver us, Edward King."

A soft, angelic voice.

It was Cassy. She was okay.

It's you... My God...

She stood behind Derek, her body hanging weakly, obviously wounded – but alive.

"Cassy..." Eddie whimpered.

He needed to do something. He needed to repay their faith, to find a way back, to do something rather than just watching through the eyes of the devil's servant.

But what?

What could he do?

"Be merciful, deliver us."

"Deliver us, Edward King."

His name.

Cassy was saying his name. Derek was saying his name.

They were doing their part, he had to do his.

He racked his brain. What could he do?

The heir.

Surely, if he could see through the heir's eyes, he could seep into other parts of him? He could feel Martin's body growing limp in his hand. If he could feel it, could he control it?

"Hear us, Eddie, for all the good in this world, hear us!"

"Hear us, Edward King!"

Martin was going to die.

If the heir did not stop squeezing, Martin would be dead in seconds.

It had been a while, but Eddie remembered what he had to do to conjure the elements. To throw fire like he had at the devil to rescue Derek from hell.

It all felt so long ago.

He had to concentrate. Feel. Listen to every sense.

So that's what he did.

He listened. Rain. A pattering of rain with a distant thunder. Every bit of it striking his skin.

His skin. Growing wet. Feeling Martin's body within his tight clutches.

He could smell the rain. See his former mentor and angelic sister willing him to come forth.

He could feel hatred. Nothing but hatred. Surging through him.

And Martin, tight in his hands.

He gripped Martin with the heir, gripping tightly. Did what the heir was doing, so that they became one.

Then he loosened his grip.

He felt the heir's hand twitch. The heir was trying to resist.

Eddie had to concentrate.

The rain. The thunder. Derek. Cassy.

He opened his palm.

Opened it and felt Martin slide out of it.

He looked to Derek.

A glint in Derek's thankful eyes showed a hint of recognition. That Derek could see Eddie in there. That Derek recognised his old friend.

Eddie lifted the heir's arms out to the side.

He held them rigidly, resisting the fight the heir was putting up.

His arms shook, but Eddie was in control.

"Do it, Derek," he spoke. "Do it now."

CHAPTER THIRTY-FIVE

*M*artin fell to the ground with a thud, rolling onto his back with a pained groan.

He wheezed, his lungs rapidly expanding, gasping for air. His muscles shook. His bones felt like jelly, wobbling under the weight of himself. He struggled to get to his knees.

Cassy was at his side. He had no idea when she got there; he hadn't seen her approach, but she was there, her arm around him.

"Just wait, Martin," Cassy prompted him. "You may have a concussion. Let yourself regain your strength."

"But the heir–"

"You'll be all right for a moment."

Martin turned his head toward Derek, who stood defiantly before the heir, a cross held out in his hands.

The heir stood stiffly, with its arms held out to the side like a crucifix. There was something different about its eyes, something different about the expression pasted across its face.

It looked... sincere.

Its arms didn't move. They were held rigidly to its side, the palms open, vibrating under invisible pressure.

"Do it," came a voice from the heir. It was a voice that did not match the face; it sounded more human somehow. "Do it now!"

Martin looked to Cassy, full of confusion.

"Whose voice is that?" he inquired.

Cassy smiled.

"Eddie," she answered. "That's Eddie's voice."

Martin couldn't believe it.

"Martin, we need you!" Derek bellowed. "We need your restraint spell, now!"

The rigid arms of the heir shook as if under an immense pressure, struggling to remain still.

It's Eddie... He's doing this...

Cassy helped Martin to his feet and he regained his balance.

Holy crap, this could work...

Martin stood firmly with his feet shoulder-width apart, glaring at the demon, glaring with an intensity the captive monster could not match.

He lifted his right hand out. He rotated it in a small circle, slowly growing bigger and bigger, extending the radius of his finger's movement.

Sure enough, a gold circle flickered before him, taking form, growing larger and larger.

Martin held his hands out to steady the circle, willing any flickers or breaks to disappear.

The golden circle grew solid.

He threw his hands out, throwing the circle forward until it latched around the demon's body, entwining it in a forced embrace.

The restraint tightened around the heir, forcing him into

submission. Martin squeezed the circle, gripping it like an enchanted lasso.

Martin fell onto his back. What little energy he had had been expended. He collapsed into a heap, his head hitting the ground.

Cassy put her arms around him.

"Come on, Martin," she whispered softly in his ear. "You're too strong for this."

"Did I do it?" Martin uttered between gasps for air.

"Yes, Martin," Cassy answered. "Of course you did."

Martin rolled onto his back.

His eyes searched out Derek, who stared smugly back at him.

His eyes then searched for the heir, who hovered mid-air with a tight, gold circle gripping around its chest, holding securely in place.

Martin had done it.

Derek could perform the exorcism.

Eddie was in there somewhere, they knew it. They had seen it.

CHAPTER THIRTY-SIX

*N*ever mind the damp, the cold, or the bindings around his chest. Nor the knowledge that he was no closer to a throne in hell than he was escaping from his incarceration.

Never mind the starvation, the thirst, or the desperate longing to see light.

It was the incessant, faraway drip that was making Bandile's mind spin into madness.

For as long as he had been there, an undetected dribble of water had been trickling from an unidentifiable location, a tediously repetitive soundtrack to his restricted movements.

He had no idea how long it had been.

Days, maybe.

Or hours that seemed like days.

He had been fed a few pieces of bread and allowed a sip of water – all before they had marched off to what Bandile presumed was their battle with the heir of hell. Their battle to bring back Edward King's soul.

Then they would collect Bandile.

Take him to the battle-ground.

Tell him to place his hand on the soul and use his Satanist values and devil-worshipping history to allow this soul to retake the form of the one they so proudly call Eddie.

He was going to do no such thing.

He struggled against the ropes, pushing at them, feeding his hand through a crack.

Then, to his astonishment, his hand seeped through. He felt it flap freely in the moist air of the room.

Then it struck him.

His plan was to refuse to turn their saviour from a ball of elements to its human casing.

But what if he did more…

What if he could get free…

Then, when Martin came to fetch him…

He could kill the boy, as he had originally intended.

That would be a far better plan.

Reaching his hand upwards, straining his wrist, he grabbed the rope, squeezing it tightly, gripping his hand fully around its thick, chafing surface.

He pulled on it.

It was too tight, too secure for it to budge.

But it wouldn't be if he kept tugging.

And, as far as he was concerned, he had all the time in the world.

So he tugged some more. Pulled on it, lifted his hand behind the rope, twisting his wrist painfully, and pushing from underneath it.

It loosened. Although fractionally, the rope still loosened.

He had a chance.

If he kept doing this, he could get free.

If they came to find him before he managed, then fine, he could just refuse to turn the soul to human.

But if he could do it before they came…

If he could be free when Martin arrived…

He could kill him.

End it.

Earn my place at the devil's side.

With a wide grin he formulated his plan, running his options through his mind.

He pulled and pulled at the rope, gradually loosening it, imagining the cold body of Martin beneath his hands.

CHAPTER THIRTY-SEVEN

There is no fury like a devil's wrath.

The god of the underworld, the ultimate fallen angel, the sick and twisted being of torture and death.

When you piss him off, you piss off hell.

He detested the three puny, pathetic creatures who dared oppose him. The same insufferable humans who'd mustered pitiful attempts against him for years. Those who were ensnaring his heir to reach through to the soul of Edward King.

The soul was trapped in a room that could not be escaped from, guarded by the strongest guard of hell, Geryon.

But this did not dull the devil's rage.

"Enough!" he declared, sat lavishly upon his throne of skulls with flames firing from his body and scorching the black air. "Enough of waiting. It's time."

This was more than a rapture. The rapture had been and gone. The second coming had been attempted, and it had proved unworthy of his antichrist.

Heaven had had its time ruling over the mortal world. Their time was over.

This was the moment he had been waiting for.

The apocalypse of man. The scourge of pitiful, frail humans. It was time to rid them from the world.

It would be a canal feast for his minions of hell.

With an infuriated, hostile nod to his subordinates, he indicated it was time.

Demons gathered at the gates of hell, bouncing with excitement, salivating at the prospect of a buffet of humanity. And, with a grand swing, the gates were opened for the first time in an eternity.

The demons hastily climbed up the entwining roots of earth, soaring upwards, making their way from the fiery core to the surface where the humans dwelled, living out their pitiful lives while waiting for death.

The worthy had gone to heaven. It was time to cull the rest.

Demon after demon emerged, furious, ready for revenge. Bouncing onto the earth in various locations, devouring the helpless fools that stood in their way.

Whilst many demons plunged themselves forward, the devil's closest disciple took its time climbing upwards and surveying the world before him.

This was a demon with a specific target in mind.

This was the prince of hell.

Balam.

This demon had been defeated on millennium night, removed from the body of Adeline by the clutches of the mortal form of Edward King. This man had freed the soul of the heir's sister so she could pass on to heaven, the place of her conception.

The memory made him sick. Made him swelter with rage.

But Edward King hadn't known who Edward King was, or who he would really become.

Millennium night had been when the heir had risen –

only, it hadn't emerged in the instant it rose. It had taken years for the hell within Edward King to surface and complete the Devil's Three, but Balam had been there; Balam had witnessed it.

Balam had been there on millennium night. Although Edward King had banished him back to hell, he had no doubt detected the coming of hell's spawn.

Now was the time he could take back Cassy King for his own.

An angel.

Pah!

There was no agreement anymore. No truce between heaven and hell.

No reason why she should not die and be plunged back into the pits of hell where Balam could finish her off.

He struck a hefty fist through the thick cement, the barrier humans thought would sever their ties between their road and the soil beneath. Balam broke through the cement like it was a weak piece of bread, sending a crack down the centre of a busy road, splitting it in two, sending cars and buildings into chaos.

He stepped forward, scowling at those who did not abruptly part out of his way. Cars screeched to a halt, except for one that sped up. Balam reached his fist out and slammed it into the bonnet of the vehicle, punching straight through, shattering it to pieces.

All around him were lights. Images of lights, busy streets, people swarming around him.

These people screamed and ran.

His human head scowled at their cowardice. His other two heads – one of a bull and one of a ram – peered around at the opportunities for death and destruction. The bull head snorted as the ram head grinned.

His flaming serpent's tail thwacked against a nearby

building, smashing windows and collapsing the brick wall. He grinned mercilessly as people dove out the of building, desperately leaping to their salvation. With a grand swipe of his tail, he lunged any remains of this building into the crack in the ground, sending them sailing, hundreds of lives screaming into the pits of hell.

His faithful bear dove out of the pits, landing at his feet and he mounted it, ready to travel.

He reached his arm out and grabbed a human by the neck, lifting it up to face his eyes, laughing at the intolerable weakness of its weeping face.

"Where am I?" roared Balam.

"T – T – Tokyo!" cried the human.

Balam gripped the human's neck tighter, snapping its head off like a twig.

His bear galloped, taking Balam into the air, onwards to his destination.

Toward the United Kingdom, where Cassy dwelled and fought, protected by her two feeble little friends.

All around the world, similar scenes of chaos descended upon man.

In Hungary the earth opened, swallowing green country-side, turning it to flames.

The perfectly curved body of a demon sprang up; a vile, scaly woman with her mouth covered by a piece of cloth, a spike running down her spine that met a large tail whipping balls of fire back and forth. Tezrian, the goddess of war, surveyed its locale with eyes determined to ensure conflict ensued in her wake.

Umtata, South Africa. A small field full of huts.

The son of Bandile Thato dropped to his knees and prayed as he gawked at the indistinguishable face of Vetis, the tempter of the holy.

Vetis' body was brown like wood, with a white beard

beneath a long, distorted face, and a grey mullet behind large antlers. Its tail whipped and thrashed, destroying lives with an instant scrape of its sharp point. It flew over Thato, its large wings beating against the wind.

The tempter of the holy had already done its job with the child's father. Now it needed to find more innocents, forcing them to deal pain upon those they love.

Across the world, demon after demon descended.

Horns, antlers, whipping sharp tails, fierce claws, and red, fiery eyes.

The cities turned to splattered locations of death. The countryside stained with blood. The smell of fire and rotting hung on the air.

Masses of demons, hordes of monsters, all with one thing on their mind.

CHAPTER THIRTY-EIGHT

*D*erek held the cross out like a sword, directing it at the heir, who hovered helplessly before him.

The heir's eyes were full of malice. Angry snarls as it writhed and struggled against the restraints. Its claws kept retracting and opening again, wanting to be used, wanting to serve a lethal blow as punishment for daring to do this.

Derek knew this spell wouldn't hold him.

He knew it was only managing because of Eddie.

And when the spell broke, the heir's temper would not be easily contained.

He had to be fast. He had to concentrate, to do what he could.

Exorcisms on weak demons could last hours, days, even weeks.

This was an exorcism on the most powerful demon to have ever existed, and it had to be done in minutes.

But Derek hadn't time to consider the odds.

Besides, Eddie had found the power to exorcise a demon in far shorter periods of time. If he was battling from his end, Derek knew that they stood a chance.

If only a small one.

"From all evil deliver us, Edward King."

"Deliver us, Edward King," Cassy echoed, nudging Martin to join them.

"From all sin, from all wrath, from sudden and unprovided death, deliver us."

"Deliver us, Edward King!" Cassy shouted, Martin joining her.

Come on, Eddie.

The demon's anger subsided momentarily, turning into mocking disdain. It chuckled in a pitch so deep it made the ground rumble. Its mouth grew into an infuriating grin.

"What does it say," it boomed, "when you no longer pray to your God, but to a weak man conceived by hell?"

"Eddie is not weak!" Martin cried out.

"Martin," Cassy interrupted, placing a calming hand on his shoulder. "During an exorcism, a demon will always try to say things to taunt you. You have to ignore what it says."

"By the mystery of your incantation," Derek persevered. "By your passion, by your holy presence on this earth, by your own history of fighting hell's creatures, hear me!"

"Deliver us, Edward King."

The demon's low chuckle grew to roaring hysterics. Its laughter shook them, its breath exhaling so forcefully its snorts blew them back with a savage gust of wind.

"You are praying for the soul of a dead man! *I am Edward King!*"

Derek narrowed his eyes.

He must resist the taunts.

This thing was *not* Eddie.

This thing could *never* be Eddie.

It was a vile, monstrous expeditor of hell.

Sure, that may have been what Eddie was conceived to be.

But he had faith in him.

He had to keep faith in Eddie.

Or this would be for nothing.

"By your death and burial!"

"Your death and burial will be following soon…"

"Your Advocate on the day of judgement!"

"I can feel this getting looser… Edward King can't help you anymore…"

"On this, the day of rapture, bring back your faithful soul and rid us of this foul, disgusting beast!"

"Deliver us, Edward King!"

Sparks ignited off the restraints. Fragments began to crumble. Holes appeared.

Martin stood to cast another restraint spell, but the heir managed to loosen a claw that it used to send Martin flying onto his back.

Cassy rushed to his side.

"That you spare us, that your pardon us, that you bring us to your true penance I tell you, Edward King, you can do this. Bring forth your soul and send this creature back to hell!"

"Deliver us, Edward King."

The muscles of the demon clenched, growing larger, bursting against the golden restraint, causing it to flicker and break in more and more places.

"I'm not alone, you know…" the demon announced, sniffing something in the air, like he could sense something.

Derek withdrew his holy water and threw a handful onto the heir's foot.

It tinged with a small puff of smoke. The heir just sneered cockily, continuing to push against its imprisonment.

"You restore my unity, my faith in what is good," Derek continued.

The demon lifted its jaw and grabbed part of the

restraints with its fanged teeth, ripping it away like a piece of meat and throwing it to ash upon the ground.

"Lead all the non-believers in your wake."

A large hole grew in the remains of the spell's binding and it fell.

"That you confirm and preserve us, judge us, help us – listen to us, Eddie! You are strong! *Bring yourself forth and rid us of this bastard!*"

"Deliver us, oh Edward King!"

"Come, Eddie, bring yourself to this unholy world and fight by our sides – we compel you, *deliver us!*"

"Deliver us, Edward King!"

Ash crumpled into a black sooty mound by the heir's feet.

Free at last its face rose, looking ahead with furious vengeance.

CHAPTER THIRTY-NINE

*W*heezing and coughing, Martin rose to his feet. Cassy tried to keep him down but he shook her helpful hands off.

"Derek needs my help!" he hastily observed.

"We need you alive, Martin," Cassy insisted.

"Alive for what? This is it! This is the closest we have come; this is our chance."

The heir had broken out of its restraints. As it did, it lifted its wild head to the sky and let out a tumultuous roar. It brought its heavy head down, glaring at Derek, who continued to stand before him, screaming the rites of exorcism, bellowing and bellowing his prayers to Eddie.

"Eddie, we beseech you, we need you now!"

Martin focussed.

The sound.

The smell.

The rain.

The tired muscles in his legs.

The pounding headache thumping against his skull.

Fuck it all.

The heir lifted its claw to swipe at Derek.

"No!"

Martin threw out a surge of wind that sent Derek sailing across the field, out of the heir's reach.

The heir turned its angry visage toward Martin, snarling at the impudence.

In the distance, Martin saw Derek get back to his feet and give Martin a gentle nod of thanks before continuing with his prayers.

"Yeah, and what?" Martin taunted, lifting his arms out.

He cast his mind back to the time his mate Simon kicked his arse. The time Kristy laughed at him, a girl he fancied so much, a girl he was so blindly falling in love with.

That humiliation he felt.

Never again.

This thing would not humiliate him.

No one will.

He lunged his open palms forward, conjuring a streak of fire.

But the fire hit the heir's chest and rebounded into nothing. If anything, the heir liked it. It had been spawned from a place of fire.It was like petrol to it. It kept it going.

But Martin wasn't ready to give in yet.

With his right hand, he twisted rapid circular motions, creating balls of water. After every few motions he lunged his palm forward, sending another ball of water toward the heir. With his left, he continued to fire flames.

The heir stepped forward with ease, fending these attacks off with simple waves of its claws.

Then a circle of wind encapsulated the heir, frantically spinning like a manic tornado.

"Deliver our souls and the souls of our brethren from everlasting damnation!" Derek persisted.

"Deliver us, Edward King!" Martin heard Cassy's voice from somewhere behind him and instantly joined in.

Derek stood behind the heir, cross in hand, sneer on his face.

The heir went to take a stride toward Derek but found itself struggling, its legs moving like they were wading through water.

Martin's jaw dropped.

It's working... The exorcism is working...

"Grant eternal rest to those departed, and eternal help to those that remain. We beseech you to come and fill this demon with your love and care."

Derek, you're a genius...

Vast circles of wind circled the heir, wrapping around it, tightening it in a tornado it couldn't brush away.

"Deliver us, Edward King!"

The demon tried to move, tried to wave the circling hurricane off him.

But something was doing this.

Someone.

The heir's immobility. Its lack of ability to resist. The turgid movement of its arms unable wipe away the fight.

It was Eddie.

Eddie was in there somewhere.

And he was fighting, just as they were.

CHAPTER FORTY

*E*ddie stiffly held his arms by his side. He could feel them shaking, the heir trying to move them, trying to resist Eddie.

But Eddie grew stronger.

Derek was doing that for him. His faith, his prayers, his reaching out to Eddie was doing all it could to force Eddie into the heir's unconscious.

But Eddie's control of this thing was still only loose, with occasional spurts of dominance. He needed to return to earth, to find a way back to the battlefield. That was the only way.

The heir would not be able to defeat its own soul. It would face its own power, and surely be outmatched.

Yet, the more Derek spoke, the stronger he felt himself getting.

The more he was in control.

The more he grew angry.

Angry at what the heir had done, angry at the use of Eddie's face, angry at the claim that they were part of the same thing.

Eddie was in control now.

And he was furious. Rabid with anger. Drooling with a desire to kill this bastard beast that had taken over his life.

He was the master of this creature. And he was ready to unleash his fury.

Then he saw it.

Something in the sky. Something flapping, something way off.

He stepped out of the heir's body and peered upwards, above the sky of his cell.

A creature.

Eddie jumped onto the stone wall, digging his fingers into the cracks.

The wall didn't stop him. There were no rejections, nothing causing him pain like when he had tried before.

How am I doing this...

He leapt to the adjacent wall, climbing up another few stones.

Eddie took a gasp of relief. His salvation. His way out.

Something had repelled him off the stones when he had originally tried, but now...

His optimism was short-lived.

A fiery fist landed on his chest and sent him hurtling back across the room.

He looked up and saw what had just punched him, denying his escape. A demon. An atrociously vile demon. The middle of its three human heads had a large spike mounted to its centre. Its large wings ended in sharp claws, and its muscular torso descended into a large, snake-like tail with spikes decorating the entirety of its side.

"Who are you?" Eddie demanded, willing confidence to his shaky voice.

"I am Geryon, guardian of hell." It smirked.

A guard of hell. Sent to guard Edward King's soul.

This only confirmed to Eddie how much damage he could do if only he could free himself from this room. They didn't send the most powerful guard of hell to keep him trapped for nothing.

Eddie stood and ran forward, charging the demon, surging toward him, firing ahead with every piece of strength he could muster.

Geryon forced Eddie onto his back with the swipe of its tail. Though he had nothing to bleed and nothing to injure, the lash of its sharp spikes indented him with pain, leaving him writhing on the floor in agony.

Geryon turned and soared back into the air, disappearing into the vague darkness.

Eddie tried to calm himself. Allowed himself to breathe. Concentrated.

He let the anger pour out of him.

Eddie jumped onto the stone, but was instantly rejected. Shooting pains going up and down his arms.

Somehow, he was unable to climb them like he had done moments ago.

He tried again, digging his fingers into the cracks, pulling himself up, but he just fell, landing painfully on his back.

He'd been able to climb…

Now he couldn't…

Something was stopping him that hadn't stopped him before…

Eddie realised there was a way, he just didn't understand what it was.

Something had happened. Something that had let him get closer to freeing himself.

He needed more strength. He needed Derek to keep going. He needed his mentor's wisdom.

He needed Derek to complete the exorcism.

Closing his eyes, he concentrated once more on the heir's

body. He peered through its eyes, holding his arms still by his side.

A tornado engulfed him, a gust of wind wrapping around him.

His body buckled under the pressure but Eddie persevered, holding the heir in place, doing all he could to give Derek a chance.

CHAPTER FORTY-ONE

*A*s soon as Derek had concocted this plan, he had understood the gravity of the exorcism he was about to attempt.

And the surroundings did not let him down.

The wind and rain reacted in such a ferocious way that it felt like they were attacking him in defence of the heir.

Nearby fences uprooted from their static position, flying across the air and encircling Derek. The wind charged at him with such aggression he struggled to stay still. Rain attacked him with a malicious sting, beating his face until he could barely see in front of him.

"By your name save me!" Derek continued to scream, adamantly resisting the weather, holding the cross tightly in front of him. "In your might, defend my cause, hear my prayer, hearken to the words of my mouth!"

Cassy tried echoing but her voice got lost in the thrashing of the wind.

The heir trampled forward, wading through the elements, lifting each foot slowly toward Derek, snarling and growling at the petty resistance before him. It struggled against Eddie's resistance, making slow strides forward.

Derek did not back down.

Martin went to stand, to join Derek in defence, but found Cassy's arm across his chest.

"No," she told him. "You've done your part."

Martin nodded unsurely but obediently, hesitantly accepting her wisdom. He watched avidly as Derek launched his final verbal attack.

"Haughty men have risen up against me and fierce men seek my life, but none see this voice like you do. Edward King, you are my helper!"

The heir swiped its claw toward Derek in a lethal scoop, but as Derek held his cross out, the heir found its hand repelled. This incensed it further, its face a picture of hostility, scrunching up in defiant rage as if to say, *"how dare he resist death?"*

Derek scowled.

Narrowed his eyebrows.

Turned his eyes into a glare.

"Turn back the evil upon this foe and in my faith destroy them, freely to Edward King will I offer you sacrifice, in your name!"

Derek ducked just in time for a swing set that flew past him on the raging gale.

"Because from all distress you have rescued me, Edward King, and through his eyes look upon his enemies, and glory be with you!"

A large roar from the heir was lost with the pummelling of the rain.

Derek could see its frustration growing. It was so desperate to defeat him, but Eddie was there, behind the demon's eyes. Exercising control. Ensuring no lethal blows were given.

With Eddie's resistance and Derek's cross, they provided a fight from the inside and out.

This was the way Derek thought they could beat it.

This was the way Derek *knew* they could beat it.

"As it was in the beginning, as it will be in the end, let the enemy have no power over you, and the son of iniquity be powerless to harm the soul of Edward King!"

The demon tried to roar, but it was stifled.

A sign that it was losing control.

Keep going...

Mentally urging himself, Derek took further strides forward, clutching the outstretched cross.

"Edward King, send him from your holy place, heed my prayer, watch over us and deliver your soul from wretched pain!"

Derek stepped forward still, reaching his arm out until the cross was pressed upon the belly of the beast.

It cried out in anguish, howling in agony, as Derek withdrew the cross to reveal an indentation of red. Smoke floated up in the air, mixing with the wind and rain.

"Your nature is merciful and forgiving. Accept our prayer that you, servant of no one, bound by the fetters of sin, may be pardoned from your dealings and restored as the rightful embodiment of *Edward King!*"

The heir.

Howling.

Struggling.

Falling to its knees, shuddering the earth with its almighty collapse.

"I command you, unclean heir of hell, whoever you think you may be, minion, attacking this servant of heaven, by the mysteries of incarnation, passion, and ascension – *free Edward King's soul!*"

Its eyelids wavered, hanging low, flickering with absence.

It attempted a final snarl but it was too much.

It fell into submission.

This was it.

Enough of the drunken nights. Enough of the crippling self-doubt, self-loathing, and self-pity.

No more believing he wasn't worthy.

No more doubting he'd given Martin the right advice.

Every bit of it had led them to where they were now.

Winning.

Refuting the heir's resistance. Forcing it into a barbarically weakened state.

Then Derek saw it. In the heir's opened eyes. Two weak pupils staring back at his.

That wasn't the look of the heir.

Once again, he saw the look of a lost man. A man Derek used to know.

Derek turned over his shoulder to Martin.

"We're close! We need Bandile, now!"

Martin turned and ran as fast as he could, leaving Derek to continue to beseech the soul within.

"Tell me by some sign in the day and hour of the heir's departure, *your soul, Edward King, deliver us your soul!*"

Derek thrust the cross forward one more time.

"By the love of your friends. By your devotion to your sister. In Jenny's name, in Lacy's name, in *my* name. By the defeat of Balam on millennium night! By all the children you have saved, all the souls you have reclaimed, and the demons you have ridden from this place!"

Eddie's eyes grew solemn through the heir, a clear recognition of Derek's words.

"By Kelly's memory, by Jenny's memory, by *your* memory! By the defeat of Lamashtu, by the abuse of your parents, by every single part of your history that created the fantastic, undeniably great man that you are. We beseech you, *return!*"

Derek looked deep into Eddie's eyes.

"Come back to us, Eddie, come back!"

In a flash, the weather halted.

Rain ceased. There was nothing but puddles. The wind smoothed into a calm breeze. The gust and gales subsided into the lucidity of nothingness.

Cassy ran forward to see Derek.

But he wasn't there.

All that was left was a cross without an owner.

"So, because you are lukewarm, and neither hot nor cold, I will spit you out of my mouth."

Revelation 3:16

CHAPTER FORTY-TWO

*M*artin's feet skidded in the puddles, dirty water splashing over his shins.

He didn't have time to think about that.

He stormed down the street of Derek's house, past worried stares of families boarding their houses up. Martin wondered if they even knew what they were protecting their houses from.

Everyone could feel danger coming. Though not everyone knew how close they were to having their pitiful lives robbed from them.

He fell over a deeper puddle and stumbled to his feet, ignoring the simmering pain of his hands scraping across the floor as he tried to steady himself. He leapt at the front door, shoving the key into the lock.

Stomping through the hallway, he briefly considered how annoyed Derek would be at the wet footprints he was leaving – though he imagined that, under the circumstance, Derek would understand.

He made it to the basement door, swept the bolt across and kicked it open.

He paused.

Refocussed.

He readied his hands, mentally preparing himself to conjure his restraint spell. It was working on the heir – for now – so it would be good enough for Bandile.

He crept down the stairs, having to place his feet horizontally due to the inconveniently small size of the steps. There were no bannisters to steady him. That, along with the unsteady, cracked nature of the stairs, meant he had to truly concentrate to avoid slipping.

Focussing hard on making his way to the bottom step – he didn't want to fall and embarrass himself in front of his prisoner; that would not look good – he leapt into the room and strode toward the chair.

He froze. His body jolting with a sudden convulsion of terror.

The chair was empty.

It displayed a broken rope.

Bandile Thato was not there.

Martin looked around himself, searching every corner of the room. This was purely instinctive, and he knew it – if a man the size of Bandile was hiding in the corner of this tiny room, Martin would have noticed by now.

Diving to his knees he grabbed the rope, searching them for the reason to Bandile's escape.

It struck him that this was counterproductive and he needed to search before Bandile got too far, but he still endeavoured to examine the empty restraints – needing to know how the man escaped

It was denial.

Bandile was a crucial part to the plan – without him, Eddie's soul would remain as just a ball of energy.

Without Bandile, Eddie would not be able to come back, and the heir would win.

He could not let Derek down.

He had to find Bandile.

Just as he bounced to his feet, full of vigour, ready to search every corner and every crevasse of the house and the nearby streets for their prisoner, he found that he did not have to look far.

Bandile Thato placed a few careful steps down the stairs.

Martin went to react, then stopped. In Bandile's rough hand was a revolver, pointing directly at Martin's head.

Bandile's hand didn't shake. His eyes didn't flutter. His lip didn't quiver.

He was ready to take Martin's life, and that thought sent fear firing through his mind.

"Martin," Bandile acknowledged as he reached the bottom step. He was close enough now that he would not miss.

He aimed the gun.

Readied his trigger finger.

Martin raised a hand.

"Look, Bandile, I–"

Bandile pulled the trigger.

CHAPTER FORTY-THREE

erek's eyes opened hazily, overwhelmed by a bright glare. The light faded, revealing a room with a straw floor and an infinite number of stones ascending into darkness.

He rubbed his eyes, willing them to focus. He squinted, scrunching his face up, pulling away as he waited for his eyes to adjust. Eventually, they did, and he pushed himself to his feet, looking around.

It was a claustrophobic box. No door. Nothing above. No way out at all.

"Derek?" came a familiar voice.

Derek's head shot around.

There he stood.

Eddie.

The same messy hair. The same bedraggled body. The same unaltered, undeniably warm, friendly face.

Derek grew immediately defensive, readying himself for a fight, frantically searching over each shoulder for an escape route.

"Derek, it's okay, it's me."

Derek paused. He grew confused, not sure what to make of it.

"I'm not the heir of hell. I'm... Well, I'm not even Eddie, technically."

"You're his soul..." Derek gasped.

Eddie faintly nodded. He returned Derek's cautious gaze, unsure how to react. What to say.

After all, Eddie was part of a creature responsible for a mass genocide. You don't just walk up to someone and say hi after a thing like that.

He didn't expect a warm welcome.

"Oh my God..." Derek whispered, shaking his head in disbelief. "It's really you..."

Eddie faintly nodded again.

After a moment of uncertainty, Derek launched himself forward and wrapped his arms around Eddie in a tight embrace.

Eddie returned the gesture. Every emotion, every feeling of anger, of loss, of sorrow, poured out into their embrace. All the death, all the lack of hope, all the loss they had suffered, pouring into a few seconds of triumph that Derek had finally broken through.

Despite everything, Derek couldn't help but be consumed by an overwhelming sense of warmth toward an old friend.

"It's been so long..." Derek observed, pulling away, looking up and down Eddie in astonishment. "Have you been trapped here the whole time?"

Eddie nodded.

"Where is here? Where are we?"

Eddie shrugged.

"Somewhere in hell, I would guess," Eddie answered. "It's guarded by Geryon."

"Oh, God. *The* Geryon? One of hell's guards?"

"Yeah."

"They must really not want you to escape."

Eddie looked down, fiddling with his hands, nervously shifting from foot to foot.

Derek noticed a blue wash placed over the stones, a soft light faintly decorating the wall.

How strange... he thought. Blue was not a colour hell often used.

"Listen, Derek, it wasn't me. All of this, it–"

"Eddie, I spent so long believing it was – and for that, I apologise."

"Thank you. And the exorcism, I watched. I tried to keep the heir still, and... Thank you."

They shared another moment of contemplative silence. Derek's mind filled with a mix of questions and emotions.

Where were they?

How were they meant to get out of there?

And, most pertinently – how would he take Eddie with him?

"I can't believe it's you," Derek spoke again, unable to get over a wave of doubt that this was real.

Years of knowing they didn't stand a chance. Years of feeling like he was training Martin to march into death. Years of wishing he had done things differently.

The amount of times Derek had laid awake at night wondering, 'what if?'

What if he had seen through Bandile Thato's act?

What if he had managed to prevent the Devil's Three?

What if he had seen this right at the start and told Eddie who and what he was, without being such a coward?

None of that mattered now.

Eddie stood a chance. A real, fighting chance of breaking through.

"So, what now?" Eddie asked. "How are you getting me out?"

Derek looked around absently, realising that Eddie thought he had all the answers. His wave of relief that the exorcism had worked mixed with an onset of terror at the task at hand. He had a feeling that he had won a battle, and a huge battle at that – one that he should be proud of. But, in truth, it had only worked to get him to where he was. Now he had to figure out how to get them out of there.

"I don't know, Eddie," Derek honestly replied. "I performed the exorcism to get to you, and now… I don't know how to get you out."

"But if you're here?"

"I am here, but I just don't–"

"No, Derek, if you're here – that means you found a way in, so there *must* be a way out."

Derek nodded. It was fair logic.

Except Derek had no idea how he had gone from standing in that field launching a tirade of prayers at the heir of hell to standing in the prison of Eddie's soul.

Eddie's soul.

Jenny was right.

He was there. He had been there all along. And getting to him was the way to win.

I've been such a fool.

Derek smiled warmly at Eddie.

"I missed you," he told his old friend.

Eddie smiled a tearful smile back. A genuine appreciation combined with such pain and suffering.

"You too, Derek," he replied. "You too."

"I have no idea how I got here. I'll be honest with you."

Eddie looked around, deep in thought.

"I could climb these walls before. I went through it and Geryon was there. But, I can't… They cause too much pain…"

"Well, how did you manage to climb them before?"

"I... I don't know."

Eddie folded his arms, deep in thought, considering his surroundings.

"I took over," Eddie suggested. "I took control of the heir, I... I got angry."

"Right," acknowledged Derek. "That's a starting point."

CHAPTER FORTY-FOUR

*M*artin flinched, shutting his eyes tightly, readying himself for the impact.

Then nothing.

He waited, expecting a bullet to fire through his cranium and leave him to drop dead in a heap on the floor.

But it didn't.

He opened his eyes.

Bandile stared at the gun, perplexed.

Then Martin realised.

Bandile had stolen Derek's gun.

The one from the drawer in his study.

The one with the empty chamber.

Derek, I could kiss you!

Full of renewed happiness, energy that he had survived what he thought were his last dying moments, he threw his hand out, creating a gold circle with his spinning finger.

Bandile's expression abruptly changed. He dropped the gun, turned his face to terror, and bounded up the stairs as fast as he could.

But it wasn't fast enough.

Martin's restraint spell flew out from his hands, the gold circle wrapping itself around Bandile, tightening until Bandile grimaced with discomfort.

Bandile looked down, struggled against it, fought, tried to move his arms.

But he knew from his previous experience that struggling would be futile. This was a supernatural binding, stronger than rope or handcuffs.

Martin swaggered toward Bandile with an air of cockiness, stopping within inches of his insolent face. Not wanting to show off but, at the same time, immensely chuffed that he managed to get one over this bastard.

"Well," he gloated, knowing he needed to rush, but unable to help himself from having his moment. "That backfired."

Bandile glared intently.

"Well, no, it didn't fire at all..." Martin continued, sniggering – then realised it was too much gloating, and he needed to curtail it. "Let's go make a human out of a soul, shall we?"

He walked forward, making Bandile float behind him, out of the basement and toward the front door.

"You're all going to die, you know," Bandile announced.

"Oh, yeah?" Martin asked, turning back to Bandile with a knowing smirk, still trying to curb his gloating over a brilliant moment of luck.

"The heir of hell is going to kill all of you. The devil will rise. I bet demons have already scorched the earth. You are all going to suffer an eternity of torment."

"You say that..." Martin began, opening the front door, and turning back to the big, muscular man dangling helplessly behind him, "...but I ain't the one who just shot an empty chamber, am I?"

He marched out the front door, Bandile following, floating behind.

Bandile watched as he was taken through the air, squeezed tightly into submission, made to remain helplessly hanging. Watching Martin running in front of him, leading him back to the battle field.

He saw the heir as they approached. Laying helplessly on the ground.

It didn't matter.

He just had to revert to his old plan.

Edward King would not return, he was going to see to that.

CHAPTER FORTY-FIVE

*A*ugust 20, 1999

FOUR MONTHS until millennium night

A HEAVY BREEZE fluttered Eddie's long coat. His forlorn face fell, solemn with the weight of his grief, his mood matching the grey skies hovering loosely above.

Cassy King
Gone But Not Forgotten
1976 – 1984

WORDS ENGRAVED ON STONE, a permanent etching of a sentiment that could never be truly expressed.

Eddie felt Jenny's hand slide into his, aware of her wary glance in his direction.

"She would be so proud of you," she told him. "Of all you've done."

"Yeah…" he agreed, his wandering voice trailing off into sombre thoughts.

A life taken from a child so young – Eddie wished he had gotten to know her. It was a death that caused so many issues. The most prominent being his parents and their drunken, abusive descent into a criminal life that led them to prison, and led Eddie to living with Jenny's family from the age of sixteen.

It seemed like the worst decision at the time, but his moving in with a loving family turned out to be a blessing.

He had visited his parents in prison only once, and that was the last time he had seen them. Just before they stood trial.

They couldn't even look him in the eyes.

"I miss her so much," Eddie told his best friend. "What's worse is that I don't even know where she is."

"She's in heaven."

Eddie shook his head. Jenny didn't know much of the world Eddie was quickly growing accustomed to.

"No," he told her. "Derek and I are thinking that there's more to this death than we know."

They shared another moment of silent sadness, of shared comfortable discontent.

"I just wish I could be reunited with her somehow. That we could be together. Close, like we were as children."

"Someday, who knows? If there is a heaven, you could see her again."

Eddie bowed his head.

He highly doubted Cassy had been allowed to pass on to heaven.

"Derek believes I could find her."

"You speak a lot about this Derek and what he thinks, Eddie."

"He has shown me that I can do things, incredible things; things I hadn't even thought possible. And he says things about me."

"Like what?"

"Like… that I'm going to become extremely powerful. That I am going to be able to change the face of this earth."

Jenny turned toward Eddie and rested a gentle palm on the side of his face. She looked him in the eyes, a genuine caring and affection spread across her smile.

"You don't need anyone to tell me how special you are," she told him. "I knew it from the start."

"Jenny…"

"But Derek is right. You are doing amazing things, and maybe you are destined for something more than the life you ended up with. You're not the dumb idiot who lived on my sofa anymore, are you?"

Eddie shook his head. He slid his arms around Jenny, savouring her closeness. Taking in her comfort and her endless kindness.

Inseparable since the day they met, Jenny had been the constant in his life he could always rely on – and he was so grateful for that.

"I think it's faith misplaced," Eddie spoke honestly. "I mean, I know Derek has faith in me. But aside from being really good at battling people raving on about how they have demons in them, I just, I don't know…"

He dropped his head, but Jenny's hands quickly gripped the underside of his chin and lifted his face to hers.

"It's never faith misplaced, Eddie," she told him. "You changed my life, you changed Derek's life – and there's no reason why anyone of us should ever falter in our belief in you."

"Look, Jenny, I know you're my best friend, it's just–"

"No!" she interrupted assertively. "Don't demean what I'm saying. I'm not lying. Listen to me."

She looked him deep in his eyes.

"Faith in Edward King is never faith misplaced. I will keep saying it until you believe it like I do."

Eddie smiled.

He knew they would be friends until the day they died.

"Faith in Edward King is never faith misplaced."

Jenny

CHAPTER FORTY-SIX

pril 3, 2003

THE HEIR'S body hung limply in the air like damp washing hung out to dry.

Derek's cross lay on the floor in front of it.

Martin brought Bandile's floating body to a halt and turned to Cassy, who sat over a cross without an owner.

"It's Derek..." she told him. "He's been taken to Eddie."

Martin looked bemused. He stuttered over words, trying to conjure a sentence that could coherently convey his thoughts. His mind was a perplexed mess of chaos and hysterics, yet his feet were irrationally still.

Wasn't Derek meant to bring Eddie to them?

"What if he doesn't..." he attempted, before realising he didn't even know the question he wished to ask.

Cassy came to his side.

"I wouldn't worry," she decided. "If the heir is submitting, then it must mean progress. Derek will be somewhere. Hopefully with Eddie."

Martin nodded absentmindedly, his eyes turning to the vacant body of the heir of hell. It hung loosely in the air, its head bowed, unconscious.

Vulnerable.

So still, so easy... This could be their chance.

All it would take would be one measly strike.

"We could kill it," Martin acknowledged.

"Pardon?"

"We could kill the heir of hell right now. End this war. Stop everything. I could get a spell and cut its throat, it would be so easy."

Cassy peered back at Martin, realising the logic of what he was saying – then realising what it would cost them.

"You could," she confirmed. "But what about Eddie?"

Martin looked to the heir, then back to Cassy. His thoughts were an ethical puzzle, searching and grasping for the right answer.

Surely an angel would know the correct decision to make?

"I would guess he wouldn't survive," Martin answered, blurting it out in a faded burst of confidence that allowed him to suggest such a thing out loud. "And neither would Derek, I imagine."

"You would kill my brother? Your mentor?"

"Isn't that what you brought me into this world for? Isn't that what you said to me when you first met me; that you need me to kill Edward King?"

Cassy's face told a thousand stories, none of them clear or good. Martin could see the same conundrum firing through her thoughts, searching for a right answer, and coming up with nothing but unappealing possibilities.

"You're right." She nodded hesitantly, as if she couldn't

bear to say it. "This decision lies on you."

"That's not fair. Why do all the decisions lay on me?"

"Because that's what you were born for. Martin, you could kill the heir right now, end all this, and possibly lose Eddie and Derek in the collateral damage. Two sacrifices to save the entire world."

"Or…?" Martin mused, knowing the answer.

"Or… you could have faith in Eddie."

Martin shook his head, closing his eyes and allowing his heavy mind to drop. His head continued to shake more and more vigorously until he was waving his hands and turning his back on both the heir and Cassy, stumbling a few steps away.

Cassy rushed to his side, grabbing hold of his hand.

"Do not run from your decisions, Martin."

"Oh, fuck you!" he moaned, swinging around and glaring at her. "I'm soddin' seventeen! Most kids my age would be snogging some girl behind the bike sheds at school, not deciding who gets to live and who gets to die!"

"It is a burden, I don't contest that."

"Fuck you, Cassy, fuck you! I'm fed up of people spewing wisdomous crap in my direction like it changes a bloody thing. *I* still have to make this decision. *I* still have to decide. And it's not fair!"

"Fair?" Cassy forced a knowing but frustrated laugh. "I was killed before I reached the age of ten, forced to endure over a decade of torture in hell, then once I was finally exorcised from the prince of hell called Balam, I didn't go on to an eternity of happiness because I was needed as an angel to save my brother! We all have our burdens to bear, Martin, so man up and deal with it."

Martin nodded feebly, peering at the huge, vile body curled in a lump behind Cassy.

He looked over his shoulder at Bandile, hovering with

humiliation a few yards behind them. They had him now. They had a chance of bringing them back.

"I just don't know what to do. What would you say?"

She placed a firm, reassuring hand on his shoulder.

"A wise woman once said that faith in Edward King is never faith misplaced."

Martin nodded.

Then that is what he would do.

He would have faith in Eddie. He would show loyalty to Derek. He would fight for Cassy's family.

Just as the decision was made, a bolt of fire flew into the ground beside Cassy, sending her flailing onto her back. She climbed to her knees with Martin's help, only for him to be struck onto his front at the same time.

A ravenous bear with bloody saliva dripping from his jaw marched across the field with an aggressive eagerness, surging toward them.

Martin could only watch in astonishment as the demon atop the bear was revealed. Three heads: one human, one of a bull, and one of a ram – each snapping their jaws toward him. Its muscular torso gave way to muscular arms with clenched fists attached, bloodied and ready to do harm.

"Oh, dear God..." whimpered Cassy, recognising the prince of hell immediately.

"What is it?" Martin demanded.

"It's... him," she gasped, shuffling backwards, desperate to escape its presence.

Martin stood strong, standing between her and it, confident posture and fiery eyes.

The demon grinned.

Bandile grinned.

Martin got ready to protect an angel of heaven from the sickening prince of hell he instantly understood went by the name of Balam.

CHAPTER FORTY-SEVEN

*D*erek tried searching for an exit, but it didn't take long to see that there was no way out. Stones disappeared into the sky as far as could see and there wasn't much to look at on ground level. A faint smell of smoke, however, lingered in the distance.

Still, Derek looked at the hazy blue light, bemused.

"I don't understand," Derek exclaimed, stroking his beard.

"What is it you don't understand?" replied Eddie.

"Think about it. When they took Cassy's soul, they kept it in hell and tortured it."

"And…?"

Derek turned to Eddie, deep in contemplation.

"Well, why haven't they done that to you?" he asked. "And what's with the blue light?"

Eddie's face twisted into realisation. Derek was right. It wasn't consistent.

"You're right. Why would they keep me trapped in a room like this?"

"It's not torture, is it?"

"The boredom makes you crazy," Eddie pointed out defensively.

"Yes, absolutely – but removing organs and twisting your insides would make you far more insane. So why haven't they done that?"

They both remained silent, considering possibilities. How was the devil benefitting by keeping Eddie trapped in this room?

It wasn't dark or full of fire. It wasn't swarming with demons. It wasn't causing agony from roasting him in a pit of flames.

Unless they needed him to be in this room…

"Of course," Derek declared.

"What?"

"These walls, they need to keep you trapped."

"To keep me trapped?"

"Yes, as otherwise, you may be susceptible to escape."

"Derek, I've missed you, man, but speak English."

Derek chuckled lightly, the first genuine laugh he had given in a long time. It was good to be back with an old friend, even in such dire circumstances.

He approached Eddie with an air of bemusement, a grin spread across his cheeks.

"These walls were designed to keep you in here; that's why they put you here," Derek informed Eddie. "They don't want to torture you, they just want to keep you trapped, so you can't break through them. There must be a reason for that!"

"There's a reason they aren't torturing me?"

"Think about it. There is a soft blue light on the walls. Blue is a calming colour. Why would they want to keep you calm in *hell*?"

Eddie's eyes grew as he finally started to realise what Derek's hypothesis was.

"When I got angry before, that's when I..." he trailed off.

"Exactly!" Derek announced. "Hell thrives on anger and hostility. They have needed to subdue you to keep you trapped. Otherwise, you'll be accessing that part of the heir that is built by hell – that is made of anger – and you cannot be contained by something that you are made of! That is why they won't torture you, because that will make you angry! That is why they have put a faint blue light in the room!"

Derek clicked his fingers, delighted at his own intelligence at fathoming the complicated puzzle.

"So, what, I'm just supposed to suddenly get angry and burst out of here?"

"I don't know, Eddie, these are just thoughts."

Derek studied Eddie carefully as his friend aimlessly wandered, hands behind his back in deep consideration.

"You don't necessarily need to get angry, that wasn't what gave you your breakthrough," Derek spoke. "It was that you were aligning with the side of you that hell created. You need to access that piece of the heir that you are a part of. That piece of the heir will get you out."

"And how do I do that?"

Derek shrugged. Such a huge revelation, yet he was still expected to have all the answers.

"I don't know. But you did it before."

Eddie sighed. He meandered a few more steps and dropped to his knees, sitting on the floor, burying his head in his hands.

Derek crouched beside him.

"What is it?"

"I just... I'm fed up. I miss everyone, Derek. I just want this to be over."

"I know."

"I know I can't see Kelly after what happened, but there

are still people waiting on earth for me. Like you. Like Jenny."

Derek grew confused.

Jenny?

Oh, dear Lord, he thinks she's alive.

"I... Eddie..." Derek attempted. "Did you say you wanted to see Jenny?"

"So much."

"...Jenny's dead."

Eddie's eyes widened. He twisted his head slowly toward Derek, full of a hundred emotions firing back and forth, contorting his gut. It broke Derek's heart to have to tell Eddie this, to watch it torture him and twist his insides like Derek knew it would.

He just hadn't even thought.

"How did she die?" Eddie whispered, as if unable to say it aloud.

"You, Eddie. You killed her."

CHAPTER FORTY-EIGHT

*E*ddie's mind filled with a thousand thrashing cymbals, crashing and collapsing into a chaos of darkness.

In a sudden instant of clarity, he saw it; Jenny's face. Devastated. Overwhelmed.

He was in the eyes of the heir.

"No, Eddie, look at me. Please face me."

Jenny's distraught, tearful face peered back at him. Her clothes were getting wrecked with the torrential, beating rain pounding against her ripped top, but she didn't seem to care. She stared up at him, refusing to back down, refusing to look scared.

In her hand, she clutched a photo. Eddie squinted to see it and, once the image grew faintly clear amongst the bullets of water, he saw it was of him and Jenny.

She was not backing down. She was not trying to kill the heir, not trying to oppose it – she believed Eddie was in there somewhere.

Eddie's heart pounded. Though he knew it was the past, though he could do nothing about it, he willed himself to shrink to her level, to withdraw his claws. As it was he remained stationary, in the heir's body, crying through the heir's eyes.

"Eddie, please, I miss you so much," she continued, pleading, beseeching him. "You've been there my whole life, and now I've had to survive without you, and I just can't. I can't survive without you. I may as well be dead without you."

The words of the memory were like a hundred stinging nettles attacking his body at once. His face scrunched up into uncontrollable weeping. He couldn't believe it. It was the way she was risking her life for him, the things she was saying, the way her love for him overshadowed any feeling of doubt in her conviction that Eddie was, at the core, good, and could be saved.

Her hand reached out and Eddie felt it against the bumps of his face. It wasn't his face he felt it run down, but the heir's, yet he still felt every soft touch. The gentle run of her fingers through the fur of his forehead, down his open jaw, outlining his sharp fangs.

"See, Eddie. It's just us two. Just us."

Eddie wanted to cry out. Wanted to scream at her to turn and run.

He could feel the heir growing intensely angry. He could feel it biding its time, getting ready to kill.

A rumble in the distance signified heavy footsteps coming closer.

"Please, Eddie, we don't have much time. That sound, it's an army, come to kill you. You need to come back to me now. Otherwise, it's too late. It needs to be done now."

I'm trying, Jenny. I'm trying, but I don't know how.

"Come on, Eddie. It's time to come home."

His mouth opened and his tepid breath hovered out, along with a heavy snarl.

His claws twitched.

"This is where you brought me. Our swings. Where we did all our talking. I know you love me."

Eddie looked over her shoulder and, sure enough, past the ferocious weather, he could see it.

The swing set where they had spent many troubled days.

Eddie running away from his abusive parents.

Jenny discovering her sexuality.

Both of them, hand in hand, sharing mutual moments of silence as words were not needed to express how they were feeling. They just knew what would be on each other's minds.

Eddie's eyes opened wide, as did the heir's. Jenny's face lit up as if she recognised Eddie's emotional reaction to the swing set.

"Oh my God, Eddie, you're back! I can't believe you're actually back."

His eyes lingered on her.

His arm reached out, striking a large claw through the centre of Jenny's chest.

Eddie dove backwards, landing hard on the bumpy cell floor.

He no longer saw out of the heir's eyes, no longer witnessed the memory. He couldn't take any more.

He jumped to his feet, screaming, roaring with tearful anger.

His fists clenched, his teeth chattered, his whole body shook. Shook like the anger was causing a seizure, like his fury was coursing through every absent vein and surging into every vacant muscle.

His whole body tensed.

He swung a fist into the floor, sending a crack running down the middle of the room, an amber glow travelling through the centre of his incarceration.

Eddie could feel Derek's eyes watching on in astonishment.

Eddie didn't care.

The one person he loved unconditionally, the one person he needed in his life. The one person who had been there through every punch, every bully, every ounce of pain. Through every moment of anger, of hostility, of solace. She had been there to lend a hand, to dry a tear. She had been there through everything.

Even when Eddie was absent, she was there, battling for his soul, battling to make her way through to him.

And she had died because of it.

That love she had for him had killed her.

And now it was killing him.

Enraged, he lifted his body up, opening his palms and lunging a large spurt of fire forward. It turned the surface of the stone black.

He had made damage to the room.

Eddie leapt onto the wall, digging his fingers into the cracks between the walls.

His anger.

The piece of hell he was a part of.

That's what's letting me do this... Hellish powers work best in hell...

Eddie grabbed Derek under his arm with ridiculous ease, leaping upwards from one wall to the other.

Further and further they went, ascending into the distance, continuing until beneath them was no longer visible.

The further he rose, the more the smell of burning grew. The spit of lava hissed, the smoke choked him, the fires grew warmer.

He was getting close.

Finally, he reached the surface. He threw Derek over and

onto the ground, then climbed himself onto a cracked, rocky surface.

He stood tall and strong, surveying his surroundings. As far as the eye could see were mounds of stone and the fiery pits of hell. Helpless souls trapped on small pieces of rock surrounded by lava. A wave of heat hitting him, fire licking at his feet, screams and wails of torture filling the air.

This was it.

This was hell.

He had escaped his containment and was standing sturdily amongst the land of the demons.

The mound of rock he stood upon shuddered and something pounded downwards. Eddie steadied himself, then peered at the monstrosity before him.

Before Eddie stood Geryon, the guardian of the underworld. Geryon's three human heads scowled, thrashing their pointed, chattering teeth in anticipation of Eddie's death.

"Derek, get back," Eddie whispered, prompting Derek to hide behind Eddie.

Derek shrunk into a ball, on his knees, shielding himself from the twisted beast before them.

Geryon glared at Eddie and snarled.

Eddie snarled back.

CHAPTER FORTY-NINE

*N*o time could be wasted.

Martin leapt forward, throwing fire-ball after fire ball, wave after wave of flamed attacks bombarding the malevolent bastard before him.

Balam's bull head snorted and bashed into the ram, its three heads colliding with a raging intensity. His human head growled, irritated by the reaction of its weaker counterparts. Its bearded face opened its mouth wide, revealing a mouth of blood and thick excess saliva.

The mouth laughed heartily as it drunk in the flames Martin sent hurtling forward like a drunk would down beer.

Bandile's deep laughter as he watched on incensed Martin even further. But he had to ignore it. Had to concentrate.

Spinning his arms in another frantic motion, Martin conjured a violent gust of wind. He lurched his arms forward, forcing a charging Balam to buckle and struggle to keep balance atop his bear.

Resisting Martin's defence, Balam pounded toward him,

trampling him to the ground beneath the bear's heavy, bloody paws.

Martin struggled to climb to his hands, coughing and wheezing.

Each head atop Balam's torso jolted toward Cassy, eyes glowing with instant recognition.

Cassy cowered, stiffening with tepid fear. She turned to run, but heavy gallops resounded behind her and she was lifted in the giant claw of the prince of hell with one swift, effortless swipe.

She screamed, fought against his hands, wept as the sadistic grin of her former tormentor grew.

This was the demon that had kept her captive for more than decade, for what had intended to be an eternity.

This demon had searched her insides with his claws, spending endless nights scorching her in the fiery pits of hell, taking masochistic joy in watching her burn.

The familiar face forced flashbacks to the forefront of her mind, imprinting its wide, joyous face watching as she struggled against his heavy, heaving torso. The foul odour of his breath panting over her as she closed her eyes and tried to ignore his thick thrusts inside of her, followed by thrashing whips and scalding-hot chains smacking against her naked humiliated body.

No, she could not face any of these faces anymore. Her memory clouded her mind in terror.

Balam's smug smile faltered as it dropped her, the result of a tinge of pain. It twisted its human head toward the source, glaring at Martin, who had just conjured something sharp and thrown it into his arm.

Martin breathed heavily, a resolute mind mixed with an exhausted body. His battling had been relentless; first against the heir, now against this creature.

But he would be the one being damned to hell if he let this vile monstrosity harm his angelic friend.

Cassy covered her head, curling into a ball in a mixture of protection and rejection of reality. Maybe if she covered her head, shielded her eyes, she wouldn't have to witness its disgusting characteristics any longer.

Martin attempted to conjure another sharp instrument, another defensive weapon, but was blown onto his back with the roar of Balam's bull head.

The bull swept in a semi-circular motion, colliding harshly with Martin's chest. The punch of this swipe sent Martin sailing yards across the field, landing heavily on his side.

He moaned, turning over, feeling his ribs. He knew instantly something was not right. Something was hurt.

But he couldn't pay attention to it.

Cassy needs me.

He clambered to his feet but fell back to the floor in a moan of agony.

It hurt too much.

But it couldn't.

It couldn't hurt.

He had to battle through.

He lifted himself, forcing his body through the pain, pushing himself to his knees.

After a prolonged struggle, he finally found a way to his feet and limped forward, clutching his side, grabbing his ribs, mentally numbing the ache.

His eyes shot upwards.

It was too late.

Balam had Cassy in its clutches. She thrashed and battled and swore more than an angel should, but it was no good.

It had her.

Again.

It was leaping into the air on the bear's back, sailing out of Martin's reach with Cassy under its arm.

It was flying into the air, and that was one power Martin hadn't harnessed.

He couldn't do this.

The pain in his side…

He collapsed in a heap on the floor.

He couldn't go on.

"Derek… Eddie…"

The floor rumbled.

Balam grinned widely.

It was the last thing Martin saw before he passed out.

CHAPTER FIFTY

*W*ings batted the air with severe ferocity, covering the horizon with its vast scales and sharp spikes. Three heads growled and snarled, eagerly spitting venomous hostility toward Eddie's resolute face. Spikes veered into sharp points down the sides of its torso and onto its serpent tail that continued to thrash, beating the ground, shuddering the stone floor into cracks.

Geryon is a fucker of a demon.

But Eddie was undeterred.

He had fought the devil in hell and escaped with Derek's soul.

This was like breakfast to him.

"Take cover," Eddie instructed to Derek.

It was over now. His imprisonment was over.

This one bastard stood in his way, blocking his escape from hell.

He wasn't about to let it.

Geryon's three heads roared, spraying vile, wet wind in his direction.

Eddie laughed.

"That it?" He shook his head. "You do not know who you're fucking with."

Eddie rose his fist in the air, concentrating hard, and his hand combusted into five fiery fingers.

It had been a while, but Eddie still remembered how to conjure the elements.

Especially in hell.

After all, hell had made him.

It lifted its tail into the air, picking up pace, sailing toward Eddie. Eddie kept his fist of flames raised high, sending this through the tail as it smacked down upon the feeble ground Eddie stood strong upon, causing Geryon to flinch, withdrawing his tail in pain.

Geryon's three heads snarled at Eddie. Within this snarl, Eddie detected a hint of intimidation.

From the demon that guarded the gates of hell?

Maybe being part-devil worked in Eddie's favour.

He leapt into the air, springing toward Geryon with an easy flight, landing upon its centre neck. He curled his legs around its throat and squeezed tightly.

The demon did all it could to throw him off.

It batted its heads against Eddie, swung in ridiculous angles, soaring through the air and smacking Eddie upon the surfaces of stone and lava.

It dove toward the rocky hill Eddie had emerged from and turned over, diving its back toward the ground.

Eddie watched as the ground came imminently closed to his face.

He loosened his grip and dropped off, thudding into the rocky surface with a painful thump – but nowhere near as painful a thump as it would have been had he not let go.

He rolled to his feet, remaining crouched, poised, ready.

Geryon knew it was losing.

Eddie knew it was just a matter of time.

Then Geryon stopped looking at Eddie and turned its twisted grin around.

Derek cowered on the floor.

"No!" Eddie cried.

Geryon took hold of Derek, clutching its sharp claws into his shoulders, and floated into the air.

Eddie sprinted forward, reaching out for his friend, reaching out for the man who had come to save him.

Geryon's wings narrowed and the demon soared downwards, plummeting into a fiery pit Eddie knew would do no harm to him or Geryon, but would burn Derek alive.

Eddie jumped into the air, swiping for them as they sailed past, but missed.

He ran to the cliff edge, where he could do nothing but watch as Geryon plummeted Derek down toward the spewing lava.

Eddie rushed back a few steps, getting ready for a run-up, then backed up even more.

He sprinted forward, gaining momentum from a powerful run-up, and launched himself forward.

Lifting his legs, pushing off on his toes, leaning forward, readying himself to jump.

If Derek died coming to save Eddie...

I couldn't...

It was a thought Eddie couldn't bear to face.

His legs moved quicker, gaining pace. His limbs accelerated, pushing him further and further forward.

As he reached the cliff edge, he placed his final foot on its edge and launched himself into the sooty air.

He spread his arms out, trying to glide, trying to let the humid air carry him, falling quickly toward the beast taking Derek to his demise.

Eddie reached out.

But Geryon had wings. It fluttered back into the air,

hovering as it allowed Eddie to fall, plunging further and further, until Eddie splashed into the fiery pit below. He pulled himself through the lava and onto a rock.

A splash of fiery acid flew over the stony mound, sending a tinge of smoke flying into the air.

Geryon hovered in the air, smirking at Eddie. Holding Derek loosely. Only metres above the surface.

Eddie reached out for Derek, clinging to hope that he could yet do something to save him.

With a final taunt, Geryon grinned as he let go of Derek, sending him pummelling into the fiery pit below.

CHAPTER FIFTY-ONE

*E*ddie peered above him.

Derek pummelled further and further downwards. Closer to the volcanic fluid that would burn him to ash.

He pressed his feet against the large rock.

Bent his knees.

Watched Derek fall.

Waited.

Bided his time.

Then, just as Derek almost fell to his doom, just out of Eddie's arm's reach, Eddie pressed his feet against the side of the rock and sent himself hurtling forward from the air.

He landed in the lava, continuing to sink. But, as he did, he kept his arms rigidly out above the surface, holding them strongly in the air. Ready to catch Derek. Hoping they had enough strength.

Gradually, he ceased sinking.

He had no idea if he'd managed to keep his good friend alive.

But his hands had stayed risen. He had held them in place. If he had caught Derek, Derek would still be alive.

Eddie kicked his feet, pushing himself upwards, forcing his way through the thick amber of the volcanic ocean.

His head reached the surface, lifting, shaking the ash off his face, throwing the thick gunk from his hair.

There, in his hands, was the graceful body of Derek, curling his arms and legs upwards to avoid the lava, to avoid his death.

Eddie kicked against the current, as if he was in a swimming pool back home, pushing himself further back. Once he reached the rock, he placed Derek on it.

Derek flopped, growing limp, feeling his body drain of energy.

Geryon roared. Eddie glanced upwards and saw the demon coming down for another attack.

He jumped onto the rock and raised his arms, watching Geryon open its claws to take him. Eddie ducked the thrashing wings of the demon as it sailed overhead.

Geryon turned and came in for another attempt. As it did, Eddie jumped onto its back, wrapping his arms around its central neck, clinging tightly.

This thing thought it could beat him.

A normal person, yes.

Not Eddie.

Eddie was not a normal person.

He was the heir to the throne of the place Geryon guarded.

He owned this demon.

Geryon pulled its body upwards, soaring into the black sky, Eddie still gripping tightly around the neck of a head that desperately gasped for air.

Eddie squeezed tighter, and tighter, and tighter still.

The eyes of the head bulged out their sockets, the teeth

ground, and Eddie stuck his hand into the weakened neck before ripping the entire head off.

He held it up in the air as Geryon fell back down to the stony surface. Eddie mounted it as it squirmed.

The other two heads looked to Eddie with a mixture of terror and helplessness. Desperate to exact revenge, but terrified of what this man could do.

No one had ever managed to oppose Geryon before – let alone rip one of its heads off.

"Yeah, and what?" Eddie goaded. "That's two more to go."

The two heads shot each other a hesitant glance over the open wound of the absent neck. With a deafening growl, it threw Eddie off, then turned and scarpered away like a scared little child fleeing an angry predator, flying into the distant, dark horizon.

Eddie stood still and proud, gazing over the fiery pits of hell that lashed out at him.

"Derek?" he prompted, searching for Derek, finding the stone Eddie had left Derek safely upon.

Eddie dove downwards, back in the fiery pit, and swam his way through the thick magma to Derek.

"Eddie, you did it!" Derek spoke with astonishment.

"Yeah," Eddie confirmed, turning to Derek with a warm glow as he climbed onto the rock. "Now let's go home."

Eddie grabbed onto Derek, clutching his arms tightly in his hands, gripping to make sure Derek wasn't left alone in hell.

Eddie closed his eyes.

Felt the heir's presence.

Saw the blank unconscious of the heir's state.

He was inside of him.

Every arm, every claw, every sharp, bloody fang.

With a scream, he felt a surge of pain shoot through his body, squeezing through his veins like adrenaline. Wind stabbed at his face, sharp attacks from a sudden rush out of hell.

He felt himself soar through the open gates of hell.

He felt grass beneath his feet.

He lifted his head.

He was inside the heir of hell's body.

He let it go. Let the heir of hell go, sunk out of it, until he was able to look upon the heir, look upon what had been his cage for so long.

He was in a field, Derek on the floor coughing, a few yards away from him.

There was a swing set nearby that Eddie recalled in numerous significant memories, left strewn in pieces.

Martin. The young boy he had watched with pride through the heir's eyes. He lay weakly across the field.

Then Eddie tried to look down. Nothing was there.

He tried to move, but he couldn't.

Eddie was nothing.

Eddie could not help Martin.

He couldn't even talk. Couldn't even budge.

He didn't even have a body, or a face.

He was a ball of energy, small enough to hold in a hand, helplessly dangling in the air.

CHAPTER FIFTY-TWO

*D*erek ran to Martin's side, lifting his head up. Martin's eyes blinked hazily.

"Cassy…" Martin whimpered. "It took Cassy…"

A large growl rumbled through the air.

The heir's eyes shot open as it climbed to its feet.

Eddie was no longer there behind its eyes, preventing it causing any fatalities.

The heir stomped its feet against the ground, flexing its arms to the side, feeling its muscles reinvigorated with energy.

Derek looked to Martin, lying helplessly on the floor, wounded.

Then he looked for Eddie.

A small circle hovered yards across from him, the size of a football. Inside of it multiple colours bashed against each other, mixing with fire, wind, water, and multiple elements that Derek didn't recognise as those of earth.

But that was all it was.

Eddie's soul come to earth.

The heir turned to Derek and snarled.

Derek knew that, if nothing happened, he was moments from an imminent death.

"Martin, release Bandile!" he instructed.

Martin raised a weary hand, forcing Bandile to drop weakly to the floor. Derek grabbed the man by the collar, ignoring his size, ignoring his superiority in terms of muscle and ability to intimidate, and took him forward.

The heir swiped its claw toward Derek.

Derek instinctively lifted his arm, covering his face, as if it would do anything to protect him.

Martin shuffled to his feet, raising his hands, creating a wall of wind to fire forward and shove the heir's claw to the side, causing it to narrowly miss Derek, then collapsed to his knees.

The claw thudded the ground, shaking it, forcing Derek to lose his footing and fall to the heir's feet, inches away from the claw that had so narrowly missed him.

No time to lose.

He dragged Bandile forward and shoved him on the floor in front of the floating circle.

Before Eddie's soul.

This was the only way.

They needed Eddie here and now.

"This is it, Bandile!" Derek shouted above the chaos of the wind Martin continually conjured, fighting against his wounds, forcing the heir's claw to narrowly miss them by inches once more.

The heir grew angry, swiping down its claw and batting it into Martin, sending him flying onto his back.

A brief glance over his shoulder told Derek that Martin was unconscious.

Edward King needed to return now.

They needed Eddie. They needed his powers.

Martin was out of it.

One more swipe and the heir would kill Derek. Would kill Bandile. And it would all be over.

It would all be over.

The heir raised its claw.

Its eyes glared.

Martin wasn't there to save them now.

"Bandile, go!" Derek commanded, pointing at the soul. "Bring Eddie back, do it now!"

Bandile looked at Edward King's soul hovering in the air before him.

Watched its elements bash against each other.

Knowing just a touch of his hand and Eddie would be returned.

Bandile turned over his shoulder to look at Derek. With a sickening grin spreading over his face, his eyes glowing with a sadistic fire, he moved his lips slowly and particularly to pronounce the one word that would banish Derek's hope to hell with the rest of the earth.

"No."

CHAPTER FIFTY-THREE

*D*erek's eyes faltered, his eyelids fluttering. He could feel tears forcing themselves to the corners of his eyes, but he refused to let them out, refused to go out like this.

Hope drained from him like water down a tap.

The rain beating against his face muddied his vision.

He dropped to his knees.

"Wh – what?" he stuttered.

Bandile stood tall, taking a confident stance, clenching his fists tightly beside him. He stood over Derek, beaming callously, enjoying the exchange of power.

"I will not bring Edward King back," Bandile declared. "But I will watch you die."

The next few seconds turned to slow motion.

Derek saw everything flash before his eyes.

Eddie's face. The exorcism. Every piece of hope he had conjured.

He had not foreseen this.

How could he have been so stupid?

The heir's claw swiped through the air. It seemed to

happen to slow, yet Derek couldn't move. Couldn't flinch from the position on his knees.

Bandile had won.

The heir had won.

The antichrist, the devil, and all of hell had won.

Gabrielle was right, he should have left.

They all should have left.

Now Martin was out cold. Cassy had been taken by Balam. Eddie's soul hung helplessly, soon to fade away.

And he was about to die.

The claw bashed into him and he felt himself flying through the air. At first, it reminded him of a rollercoaster ride, a childhood memory of going to a theme park, he hovered in the air for so long, lingering in the abyss of nothing. Remaining in the air, helpless to what would happen to him when he landed.

With a hard thud, he collapsed on the floor. He immediately felt his arm twist and break, the snap echoing against the rumble of thunder.

He tried to make it to his knees but he couldn't. Too much hurt. Too much swelled.

He flopped onto his back.

His shirt became engulfed with blood, dark-red gunk seeping through the fabric, winning its battle against the rain. He had no idea where this was coming from. His whole body ached.

A dark shadow loomed over him and he realised the claw was coming toward him again. Once more, it swept him into the air, firing him across the field.

He landed on his ankle and felt his knee bend backwards, and his bone stick through his thigh.

He screamed and bellowed in agony.

He closed his eyes, feeling the life seep out of him, unable to take the excruciating agony of his broken bones.

"Heir of hell!" he heard a voice boom.

It was Bandile's voice.

That bastard.

That traitor.

"Heir of hell, listen to me!"

Derek groggily opened his eyes, enough to see Bandile strutting arrogantly toward the heir of hell.

"I have saved you!" Bandile announced. "I have refused to turn Edward King into a man, I have led them on false pretences. Give me room in hell!"

It all made sense now.

The pieces fit together and collapsed around him.

Bandile was only ever interested in saving himself.

The king of deception once again.

"Give me my restitution!" Bandile requested once more.

Derek's head dropped, and everything went blank.

CHAPTER FIFTY-FOUR

*B*andile swaggered toward the beast, standing strong before him, standing resolutely.

The heavy face of the antichrist lowered itself to Bandile, scowling at him.

"Heir of hell, I have helped you," Bandile assured the creature. "I have saved you."

The heir's face turned into a menacing frown, scowling at this puny human before him, daring to claim that it helped in the heir's ascension.

"*You* help *me?*" it roared.

"I did!" Bandile begged.

This wasn't what he expected.

He imagined he would be endowed with praise. He would have to remain humble as the heir and the devil told him how indebted they were to him. He would have to choose from a selection of powers, choose which demonic gift he would be endowed with, select his own throne in hell.

He did not expect to have to plead his case.

"Please, my lord," Bandile continued. "I told them I would bring Edward King's soul into human form, but I didn't."

"You said you would bring Edward King back?" the heir's voice reverberated through the surroundings, colliding with the thunder, raising above it with terrifying power.

"No, you don't understand! I made them think I would, then I refused. I did not. I made sure I did not; I did it so you would survive. Please, don't you see?"

The heir screamed out, its rancid breath forcing Bandile onto his back.

"I will kill you for opposing me!" it fired at him.

Shit.

The plan.

It had backfired.

It had all backfired. It had all gone wrong.

The heir raised its claw.

It was going to kill him.

This isn't how it was supposed to go...

"Please, don't you see – this is not what I intended!"

Bandile turned his gaze to the supernatural ball hanging loosely in the air. It was starting to fade. The soul of Edward King was starting to fade.

He turned back to the heir.

Lifting its claw. About to kill him.

He had to bring Eddie back.

It was the only way. The heir was not going to grant him his mercy.

There was no restitution.

No absolution.

No throne in hell. No praise. No godly status.

Only an angry demon hell-bent on tearing him to pieces.

He clambered to his feet, stumbled forward, reaching his arm out for the soul.

The heir's claw sliced through the air toward him.

He reached out toward the ball of energy where Edward King was held.

It was only a few steps away.

I can make it...

The heir's claw brushed against his back.

He leapt forward.

He reached out.

His hands landed upon the ball of energy, and light shone from beneath his fingers.

The ball exploded into particles. Particles that quickly formed the body of Edward King.

The heir froze.

For the first time ever, Bandile saw a flicker of fear in its eyes.

He turned and ran as fast as he could. Away from the heir, away from Edward King, away from Derek, and he did not look back.

CHAPTER FIFTY-FIVE

*E*dward King stretched his arms out. Felt his fingers flex.

No claws. Human fingers.

He looked down at his body. His human body. His skin, his torso.

He wore rags, but he didn't care. They were real rags, over a real body.

He wasn't used to feeling these limbs. His heart beat punching against his ribs, his blood bursting through his veins.

Everything that a human has surging through them.

He was alive.

My God, I'm alive.

He opened his eyes, flinching them against the bombardment of rain drops punching his face and body, relishing the feel of water against his skin.

The heir stood still before him.

He looked to his side, searching out everyone else.Derek lay in a heap on the floor. A bone stuck out of his leg, his arms in a contorted mess. He didn't move.

"Derek…" Eddie whispered.

He rushed to Derek's side, put his hand on the side of his neck.

There was a pulse.

Derek was alive.

Across the field, Martin wearily took to his feet.

Eddie turned to the beast.

The fucker who had done all of this.

It was time to end it.

Eddie sauntered forward with a few confident strides, standing face-to-face with the part of him that had laid dormant throughout his entire life.

Thanks to Derek, his soul had been exorcised and removed from this entity.

Thanks to Bandile, his soul was now a human. In a form he could use to fight.

But it wasn't over.

Eddie stared into his own demonic eyes.

Into the raging eyes of the heir of hell.

This manifestation of his true self, his true nature, expanded into a large, contemptuous creature.

Except the devil didn't count on this. The devil underestimated the soul. The last defence of heaven.

Eddie would hate this thing if he had the time or ability. It was a part of him, a part kept inside of him for so long, a part that led him to do some despicable things.

A series of unfortunate events had led to its full form. Events he could not do anything about.

Ten years old. Cassy died. Taken to hell.

In 1992, Bandile Thato gave Derek a book that told him of the prophecy.

Lamashtu. Attaching itself to Eddie and draining him of life.

Millennium night. When Eddie thought he'd beaten

Balam, but the night had just been used to signal the coming of the heir dwelling within.

Derek's soul being captured and Eddie having to chase him to hell. That was the point at which the devil latched a piece of itself onto Eddie – the devil had successfully lured him down so he could take control of Eddie's darker side.

Jason Aslan's death.

Martin's conception.

Martin's mother being captured before Eddie could realise what it was for.

The Devil's Three. The gathering of Bandile, Jason, and Martin's mother by the devil's messenger to conspire to bring forth the devil's antichrist.

The death of Kelly.

Eddie's hand slicing a knife right through her.

Eddie looking down at the face of the woman he loved as she was betrayed, the final glance of her eyes seeing him murdering her. She was dead before she could understand why.

Jenny. Her meaningless death.

Then this.

An escape from hell. The defeat of Geryon. An exorcism that successfully removed the soul from its attachment to the heir of hell, from its incarceration from the devil.

All of this had led Eddie down a winding path to this moment.

Now it was just Eddie and himself.

Me and the piece of me that hid within me for so long.

Never had Eddie been readier.

Except there was one more thing.

"Martin!" Eddie commanded, circling the demon, both of them scowling at each other as they marked their territory.

Martin refocussed his dizzy mind. He had to get it together.

He still had his part to play.

"Where's Cassy?" Eddie demanded.

"Balam… took her…" Martin muttered.

"We need her," Eddie announced, watching the heir carefully, waiting for it to pounce, waiting for it to make its move. "We need her for what is to come."

"We don't know where she is!"

"Then you need to find out!" Eddie bellowed defiantly. "She is crucial. You need to get her back!"

Martin froze. Where had Cassy been taken?

"Now!" Eddie demanded with one final instruction as he turned his full attention to the heir.

Martin groggily nodded and ran, stumbling to his feet. Eddie felt a pang of worry sending shivers up and down his body, worried for Martin. If they couldn't get Cassy back, this was all over.

"So," Eddie began, scowling at the large, terrifying demon without a piece of fear. "You are the thing that's been hiding within me for my entire life."

The heir growled, frowning, its hefty teeth clenched.

"You don't look that great to me."

"You will die!" declared the heir.

"Yes, except you know what will happen if I do, don't you?"

A speck of perplexity came over the heir's face.

"The body cannot live without the soul," Eddie smugly pointed out.

"You lie!"

"I do not lie. Who do you think I am? You?"

Eddie chuckled at his own joke.

He slowly started twisting his hands in a circular motion. It didn't take long until they were surrounded by flickers of flames, the wind, specks of water, and piercing light.

The heir lurched forward. Eddie flung his arms into the

air, instantly causing an explosion of the elements. A push of fire, wind, and rain accompanied the bang, all aimed at the heir, all firing against him at once.

The heir went flying backwards, landing on its back, causing the ground to tremor.

Eddie jumped high into the air and came landing down upon the heir with a heavy fist.

"Go on," he teased, inches from the heir's face, which was five times the size of his, yet still struggled for breath. "Kill me. See what happens."

The beast snarled, rising to its feet, and throwing Eddie onto his back.

Eddie laughed.

The beast roared.

"That all you got? Just a bunch of roars? I thought you were meant to be powerful!"

Eddie rose to his feet.

Enough.

It was time to end this.

CHAPTER FIFTY-SIX

*C*assy's throat grew sore. She screamed and howled and begged and wept but none of it did a single thing to change what was happening.

If anything, it only fuelled Balam's sick enjoyment.

And she knew she should stop. It was encouraging the bastard, and she knew it. But she couldn't.

Her brow sweated, her arms shook, her heart thudded. She didn't even realise she could feel such things as an angel, but being in Balam's presence once again took her back to those emotions she had buried deep down inside of her. Those mental scars she thought she had covered with thick skin reappeared, penetrating that thick skin like it was wet paper.

Balam lifted her up by the throat, his human head licking its lips, the bull head snorting, and the ram gazing longingly at its prey.

He shoved her against a fence and within seconds the wires of that fence had curled around and turned on Cassy, entwining her in a painfully tight embrace, clinging to her body, wrapping around arms, legs, and torso until she was covered in metal scales digging into her bones.

"It's been a while," grinned Balam, a masochistic, evil smirk wiping its face with destitute pleasure.

"Go to hell!" Cassy screamed out, ignoring the irony of her retort.

Balam dismounted his bear and trod heavily toward her, the weight of his thick legs rising and landing slowly, thudding the ground into trembles. As its human head hovered next to Cassy, soaking up her fear, celebrating her terror, the other two heads breathed over her. His breath was rank, a foul stink through rotted teeth. She was surrounded by the tirade of demonic faces taunting her, enjoying her.

The demon placed its fingers over Cassy's gut.

She cried. She wished she could be more resilient, that she could say fuck you and pretend it wasn't happening, refuse to give in to the sick punishment this demon took pride in giving.

But she couldn't.

It took her back to being eight years old again. A young, innocent mind wrapped up in restraints, over a decade in hell, being opened up for the pleasure of the demon that now returned to its hostile stance before her.

Its fingers grew. She looked down but couldn't see the ends of his claws as they continually enlarged, sinking into her belly, into her guts, through her insides. In heaven, she did not have such feeble human parts – but on earth, she was compelled to take human form.

She wondered if it meant this could kill her. Whether she could die in this form, or whether it meant she would just suffer the pain of a human.

The thought ended abruptly as she howled in agony. She could feel the sharp blades of his elongated fingers wriggling around inside of her, passing through her various entrails, sinking inside her.

Balam quickly withdrew its claws, prompting a spray of blood to squirt over his knee. He laughed triumphantly, enjoying the pleasure of her anguish.

She cried and moaned, even tried to kick out, to escape – but her restraints held her too tightly.

Balam's face remained next to hers, leering with sadistic excitement, enjoying the demented glory of the pain it ignited.

It was at this point she realised that, if she could die, she would be dead.

She wished she was dead.

She wished she had the relief of nonexistence, of passing onto heaven. But her angelic capabilities just meant that this human form was for show. She could feel the pain but bore none of the consequences.

She scowled.

Then thought.

If this body is just an illusion, then so is the pain.

She had to go numb to it. Refuse to let herself feel it. It was all for the show, all for her disguise, all so she could pass as one of them.

All so she could convince them she was not a higher being.

But she was a higher being.

She was denied from heaven now, yes – but she was still an angel. A servant of God.

The pain faded. She smiled cockily at the demon.

"See that?" she spoke cockily. "That's me not feeling a bit of it. Do your worst."

If it was possible, Balam grinned even wider. The ram head lifted back, then dove into Cassy's neck, biting down with its sharp teeth, clinging on without letting go.

It was agony. Cassy screamed out once more.

I must go numb to it.

But she couldn't. It was too painful.

She knew she could, but at that moment in time, she did not have the sound mind to do so. All she could think or feel was the pain. The continuous grip it had on her neck.

Once the head retracted, she concentrated, focussed on ignoring the heaving, bloody mess trickling down her neck, a huge chunk of her flesh missing.

It went. It took a while, but the pain went.

"You can't hurt me," she spluttered, her resolve faltering.

Balam shook its head.

It knew what it could do to hurt her.

He could give her more invisible scars than she could endure.

Just like he had done night after night after night after endless night.

It pressed its claw against the inside of her thigh, raising her elegant white dress that was now stained and splattered with red.

She scrunched her face up. Closed her eyes.

She remembered how it felt.

The thick thrusts, the pain, the bleeding.

She did not want to go through it again.

She subsided. Gave in.

It *could* hurt her.

She struggled frantically against her restraints, pulling and fighting manically, with more and more ferocity. But with every attempt to release herself the wires only gripped tighter and she grew more claustrophobic.

There was nothing she could do.

She was going to have to take it. Close her eyes, think of something else and take it.

Like she used to.

Think of a happy family, the life she could have had. Occupy her thoughts with such positivity that she went completely numb to it.

It's what she did before.

It hadn't worked well back then.

But she was stronger now.

She had to be.

She closed her eyes, shutting them tightly, tensing her body, clenching her fists.

She waited.

And waited.

Nothing happened.

After a few seconds, she reopened her eyes, expecting Balam to be heaving over her, waiting for her to watch him. To witness what he was doing.

But he wasn't.

He was laid on the floor, legs kicking and flailing, thrashing out helplessly.

Martin stood over it.

CHAPTER FIFTY-SEVEN

*G*abrielle stood awkwardly alone, staring at the lavish golden gates. Her hands fidgeted uncomfortably. She sighed, knowing she should step back through them, but knowing what that would mean.

"Are you coming?" came a confident voice.

She glanced over her shoulder at the route back to earth. Once she stepped through those gates, she would not be able to open them again until it was over. The rapture had ended, and hell's attack on earth had begun.

It was time for those gates to be locked.

She bowed her head. Took a small step toward the gates, then turned her head back once more.

How could she do this?

"What is your worry?"

"Nothing, my Lord. It's just..." Gabrielle's voice faded away.

"Tell me."

A sickening feeling grew inside of her. It made her shake, made her feel nervous. For the first time in her long existence, she was unsure about whether she was doing the right thing.

"It's Cassy. Balam has her. She has been taken once again."

"It is done. She has made her choice. Please, Gabrielle, enter our sanctuary so we can shut the doors to earth."

She took a few wary steps forward, then halted. Standing directly before the gates, just one single stride to go, she looked upwards.

Her head shook.

"I can't."

"Gabrielle, this is not the time."

"Do you know what they say about you on earth? What Derek Lansdale has said?"

"Derek Lansdale is a great man, but he too has made his choice. Please hurry."

Gabrielle turned around, facing the route to Cassy and Eddie, gazing at the path to an earth that would now be full of malevolent violence. So much death. So much suffering.

"Derek has fought in your name for so long," Gabrielle continued. Her voice was soft and wary, but also had an air of firm hesitance in it; confidence in her evident worry. "They think you don't care."

"I gave them a child conceived by heaven. I listened to their prayers and aided in exorcising their demons. I have done enough!"

"But have you, my Lord?" Her whole body shook. She knew she shouldn't dare oppose him, but somehow found herself doing so. "I mean, look at all they are doing. All they want is a helping hand."

"It is not up to me to justify my actions to you, nor for you to question them. If you wish to join them, do so. But make your hasty decision quickly."

Gabrielle smiled.

She couldn't enter heaven. Not now. Not with this burden of guilt spreading through her like acid.

"I'm going back," she decided. "And I need your help."

An echoing silence was her response.

"Please, Lord. If they succeed in defeating the heir, there is one more action required to prevent this happening again. I know you know this."

"Yes, I do."

"And they will need our help. It won't even require you to go to earth!"

Gabrielle turned back to the gate and moved to one knee. She pressed her hands together in a praying position, bowing her head.

"Dear Lord, I have followed you for millennia after millennia, and never asked for anything in return. Please, answer me this one prayer."

She waited.

Then she got her answer.

"What is your wish, my child?"

Gabrielle smiled as she delicately fluttered her lips in a heavenly whisper, explaining what she needed him to do.

CHAPTER FIFTY-EIGHT

The heir could growl all it wanted. It could roar, threaten defiance, thrash its arms about.

It did nothing to Eddie.

The heir *was* Eddie. It could do no harm to itself.

Neither could survive without the other.

That was why Eddie needed an angel to help him. He needed Cassy to return quickly. She was going to be essential.

He lifted his arms and, as the heir charged at him, he flung his arms to his side, causing an impulsive explosion that sent the heir flailing onto its front. The earth shuddered as it landed but Eddie didn't care. It was time to end this.

The heir returned to its feet, but Eddie would not let it regather its strength. He waved his arm, sending the heir back to the floor with a deafening thud.

The heir rose once again, but Eddie waved his arms, pinning it down.

"Stay down!" Eddie demanded.

The heir obeyed.

Derek's eyes slowly opened as he watched on. To his surprise, the heir followed Eddie's instructions exactly.

Eddie stood beside the heir's giant head, watching it with gritted teeth. Its size did not deter him. Its appearance did not cause any trembling or terror in Eddie.

The heir's eyes widened as Eddie stuck his arm into the heir's throat.

With a final roar, the heir twisted and contorted, struggling against the agony, but managed to muster only a feeble resistance. It tried raising its arm to brush Eddie away, but he simply waved the efforts down and continued digging his arm deeper and deeper into his opponent's throat.

Eddie felt the heir's oesophagus in his hand. He gripped it, tightened, pulled and pulled, ripping the throat further and further.

The heir thrashed out its arms, but Eddie simply froze it with a raise of his, refuting any attempt to halt the proceedings.

With a large, agonising pull, Eddie ripped along the edge of the heir's neck., and tore out a chunk of its wind-pipe.

The heir cried out aggressively and Eddie dug his hands back into its throat, sinking them in, gripping the underside of its head.

He shouted under the strain of his muscles, his voice echoing through the night, watching the heir's eyes grow with alarm then freeze as he tore its entire head off.

Buckets of blood splashed over the field, followed by fragments of coarse skin and gory entrails.

He picked the head up and threw it across the field.

The heir's eyes widened one final time. The mouth opened to roar but whimpered, crumbling into submission, lips shaking as the life seeped out of it.

The eyes grew still. The mouth became static.

Eddie was grateful for what he had done, but knew it meant nothing. He had only killed himself.

And now he was bound for hell if his sister did not return.

Eddie fell to his knees. Suddenly growing weaker. Suddenly unable to stand.

Eddie coughed up a mouthful of blood, falling onto his front, his eyelids shaking.

"No..." he wept. "Not yet..."

Eddie weakly collapsed, his body seizing. He tried to lift his hands but his touch felt weak, a soft absence draining from him.

"Cassy... I need Cassy..."

Eddie closed his eyes, attempting to gather strength. He felt the life leak out of him. His legs went first, paralysed into heavy weights he couldn't so much as twitch.

He turned to Derek, lying unconscious across the field from him.

"Derek..." he tried. "Please..."

Derek didn't respond.

"Derek... As my soul dies, it's going to travel to heaven or hell. I need Cassy."

Derek's eyes fluttered, then closed once more.

"Cassy is the only one who can access that journey... she needs to be here when I die to make sure my soul goes on to heaven..."

Eddie closed his eyes solemnly, wishing Martin would reappear.

"The devil will try and take me, Derek. She can't let it. The devil will try and claim my soul as I pass through; he will try and take it to hell."

Derek didn't respond.

Eddie's eyes closed.

"Then all this would be for nothing."

He listened out for Martin.

Listening out for his sister's voice that never came.

"He would just take me to hell and make another heir…"

He felt himself slipping away.

Cassy and Martin were nowhere in sight.

CHAPTER FIFTY-NINE

*M*artin staggered to the floor, tripping over his own feet. He fell flat out on his chest, his breath heaving, choking on oxygen.

Balam's laughter boomed.

"This is it?" Balam mocked. "This is the saviour?"

Martin struggled to his feet, balancing himself precariously on two weak, shaking arms.

"This is what heaven conceives?" Balam continued. Even the bull head snorted laughter and the ram head seemed to chuckle.

Martin did all he could to muster his strength, trying to climb to his feet, to create some kind of opposition to the prince of hell.

He could feel Cassy's worried gaze. Her tears of knowledge that not only was she about to be tortured for eternity, but that she was going to watch heaven's greatest weapon die in the process.

"We get Edward King, the great heir of hell – and this is what you were given? This is heaven's warrior?" Balam dropped his head with a snort of laughter. "Pathetic."

"Edward King is not your heir any longer!" Cassy shouted a cry that was met with an aggressive growl as Balam turned its heads toward her.

It looked over its shoulder and saw its bear beating down the track. It obediently dove across the air, landing its teeth into Cassy's leg.

She howled in agony. Her face tried to stay resolute, her arms tried not to shake, and her tears tried not to pour – she had to convince herself or it wouldn't work.

Martin watched as she writhed in pain, attempting to lift himself to his feet once more. He fell once again.

Balam took a few menacing strides toward Martin, encapsulating the young man in its shadow. It loomed over him, its ram head snapping its jaw forward, and its bull head salivating, dripping in messy puddles on the floor.

Martin rolled onto his back, groaning, peering up at the villainous wretch readying its eager claws to slash Martin's throat. He could see the demon enjoying this. Savouring the moment that it destroyed the greatest weapon forged by its enemy.

"This is a glorious moment," Balam spoke, surveying the scene with hungry eyes. "The moment when you die and take the world with it."

"My brother has come back! He will destroy you!" Cassy persisted, the bear consequently biting into her thigh even harder.

"Is that so? I have fought him before, and I would love to fight him again…"

Balam lifted his hand, leering at his own claw as it elongated into a curved, spiked, lethal weapon.

Martin stared wide-eyed at the impending spike about to sever his throat.

"I am the prince of hell!" Balam declared.

Martin clenched his fists, grabbing pieces of grass, urging adrenaline to surge through his body.

"I am the devil's right hand, even if the heir is not ready to take such a place!"

Martin closed his eyes. Felt the wet blades against his palm. Listened to the distant thunderous rumble. Felt the specks of rain dripping on his head.

"I am the king of deception!"

Balam swung its claw downwards, sailing toward Martin's throat. Cassy's voice cried out in a terrified gasp.

Martin stuck his hands together, catching the blade of the claw between his palms.

"I dunno," he mused. "I think I'm pretty good at deceiving too."

He leapt to his feet, full of spritely energy, dropping the weakened façade as Balam's eyes widened into humiliated dread.

Martin twisted the sharp claw he had clutched between his hands upwards, curving it toward Balam's human throat, pushing and pushing. Balam tried to resist but could only watch helplessly as his own claw sliced into his human head's throat.

After holding the claw in place, Martin avoided the ram's snapping jaw and quickly withdrew the claw, allowing various shades of dark red to spray over the wet surface below, covering it in a river of blood.

The bull did not fight back, but instead, withdrew in fear. Martin swung his final strike into the bull's throat and dove to the side as Balam's destitute remains thudded to the floor in a glorious quake.

Martin ran up to the bear, conjuring a line of flames and setting it on fire. It ran off, shrieking wildly.

Martin frantically peeled away the barbed spikes constraining Cassy. It took all the energy he had to try to peel them back, but still they would not budge. He waved his hands until he created a solid thin line of fire, using it to pierce through the metallic wires like a welder.

She dropped to the floor and Martin caught her in his arms. She moaned weakly, but Martin knew that time was of the essence.

"Cassy, we need to go," he urged her.

"Why?"

"Eddie needs you, he says it's crucial."

Martin helped her wearily to her feet but she lay back down again.

He grabbed her around the waist, pulling her into a fireman's lift, and ran for his life.

CHAPTER SIXTY

*E*ddie's mouth filled with blood, dripping down his cheek and onto his collar. His vision grew blurry, unfocused, and nearby voices sounded muffled, like they were being shouted through a wall.

He could feel himself being shaken, his body moving somewhere way off in the distance. His head drooped heavily, feeling like a dead weight under the pressure of gravity.

"Eddie!" A vague, muffled shout became temporarily clearer. "Eddie!"

Eddie turned to his side and saw a bloody mess next to him. Derek had somehow dragged himself across the field, laying in a heap next to him, constantly moaning from the pain, his hazy face staring at Eddie beneath his heavy eyelids.

"Derek! I'm dying..."

"Me too..." Derek whispered.

Eddie tried to lift his hand but couldn't. He grew confused, his head muddled with unrecognisable thoughts, unable to understand why he couldn't lift his arm.

"My body is paralysed, Derek. I can't die. I can't die before Cassy gets here."

Eddie's eyelids drooped.

"Come on, Eddie... Stay with me..."

Eddie's eyes opened narrowly. The sky above was grey. Black clouds hovered. It was a dismal scene.

"Keep talking to me, Derek..." Eddie feebly requested. "Keep me awake..."

That's what he needed. Constant interaction. Constant keeping him conscious, keeping him stimulated, ensuring he did not drop off.

"Erm... I missed you," Derek admitted.

Eddie felt a smile appear on his face and disappear under its weight almost as quickly.

"I missed you too, man."

"Where were you? I mean, how could you not find us?"

"I don't know..."

Eddie fell away for a moment, then suddenly became alert once again.

"Jenny. She, erm... she died believing in you."

"Jenny...?"

In his messy state, Eddie suddenly thought she was nearby, then realised she was not.

"She died trying to get through to you. She never stopped believing, even when I did. She kept going, kept trying to get through to you. She wouldn't back down."

"Jenny..."

"I'm sorry, Eddie. I'm sorry I didn't believe in you like she did. If I did, then..."

Eddie tried to shake his head, unsure whether he had or not.

"You had to... you had to do what... you could..."

"I was just stuck, trying to figure out what to do with you gone. I spent so much time teaching you, I never realised, you were the one teaching me."

Heavy steps grew louder, and for a fleeting moment, Eddie thought that the heir was back.

"It's Cassy and Martin," Derek declared. "They are here, they are back."

Eddie tried to lift his head.

"Rest," came a woman's voice. "It's okay. I'm here."

He didn't understand whose voice it could be.

Then it hit him.

Cassy. He had never heard her adult voice. Her angelic voice. He owed her so much.

"Cassy…" he tried. "Thank you…"

"What do we do now, Eddie?" came a shaky, younger voice echoing in his ears.

"Martin…"

"I'm here."

"You have one more thing to do."

"What is it?"

Eddie turned his head toward him, allowing it to slump on its side, unable to hold its weight.

"You have to kill me."

"What?"

Martin's eyes filled with terror. "How am I meant to kill Edward King?"

"One more thing you need to do," Eddie told Martin. "Then you are free. Free to live your life."

"But why me?"

"Then Cassy…" Eddie feebly mustered.

"I'm here."

"Grab onto me. Take me to heaven."

"What?"

"The devil will do all he can. He'll be ready. He and his legions of hell will be ready. You need to grab onto me and don't let go."

"But, Eddie… I've been banished from heaven. And you killed Kelly… We both have…"

"But then the devil w–"

His head flopped. His eyes closed.

A familiar set of soft hands clutched onto his arms.

He could see nothing. Sounds grew fainter.

It felt like a while, but eventually, he felt it.

A sudden stab in the centre of his chest.

"Where is our God now…" the disappointed, solemn voice of Cassy whispered from afar.

Then he heard nothing more.

CHAPTER SIXTY-ONE

*M*artin collapsed into the chair beside Derek's bed. The life machine beeped a rhythmic pulse. Derek's leg was held up in plaster, as was his arm, and various tubes went in and out of his body.

The doctors had said Derek was lucky to be alive. That the pain of his broken arm and broken leg was not only intense enough to render him unconscious, his head had shown severe signs of concussion and his body had taken such a beating they were hesitant to let him off the machines any time soon.

What's more, Martin knew sooner or later he was going to have to answer questions.

But the Church would arrive soon, if they hadn't already. Clear up this mess. Sort out the answers.

For now, he was happy Derek was alive.

Martin leant his head back, feeling content, calm, happy it was all over.

His mind relaxed. His eyelids grew heavy.

His mind drifted to heavy dreams.

He was back on the field. Staring at Eddie's broken corpse

beside him. The blood from Eddie's torso pouring through his hands.

He was breathing heavily, sweating profusely. He clutched a knife, staring at it, in adamant disbelief of what he had just done.

He turned to the face laid beside him. It didn't move. Eddie's eyes stared straight ahead, fixed in a rigid position with nothing behind them.

A thin slit in his heart where Martin had just withdrawn the knife still gushed blood. It poured down his sides like spilt wine, sinking into the grass beneath him.

Martin's first thought was – *how is he still bleeding so much when he's dead?*

Then his head dropped.

Oh, dear God. I killed Edward King. I killed him.

He looked down at his hands, eyes wide, face full of terror. His arms shook, his legs shook, his entire body seized.

He bolted upright and his eyes flung open. He was beside Derek's bed, peering around himself, perspiring heavily, his head a complete daze.

"You were talking," came a reassuring voice.

Martin threw his head up, elated to be staring at the open eyes of Derek.

"Derek!"

After his initial excitement left him, a growing concern at Derek's feeble state filled him with alarm. The man could barely lift his arms. Yet he was still staring happily in Martin's direction, a weary smile spread from cheek to cheek.

"I'm okay," Derek reassured him. "The question is, are you?"

Martin shook his head.

"I killed Eddie, man," he answered, his voice drifting into a whimper. "I killed Eddie…"

"Martin, listen to me," Derek spoke once more, reaching out, finding that his arm would not stretch more than half an inch. "It's okay," Derek kept repeating. "It's okay, it's okay."

Martin vigorously shook his head.

"But... aren't I going to hell?"

"Martin, look at me," Derek commanded. "Look at me."

Martin finally gave in, looking Derek in the eyes.

"You did well," Derek spoke sincerely, making strong eye contact, assuring Martin knew that he did the right thing. "You did well, you did what he asked. You didn't kill a human, you sent a soul back to heaven – you just restored the natural order. It's over."

Martin froze.

Those last words rang in Martin's ears again and again and again.

It's over.

It's over.

It's over.

"Is it?" he asked.

"What?" Derek replied.

"Over? Is it really over?"

Derek smiled and nodded. His smile grew, and Martin joined him in a happy grin.

"For our part, it is," Derek answered. "It's up to Eddie and Cassy now. Our part is done."

Martin nodded, dropping his hand to his side. Within seconds he had become an emotional mess, tears rolling down his cheeks, looking through the window at the black clouds which were now parting, revealing a pleasant image of a clear, starry sky.

When he looked back to Derek, he was asleep again.

"Good luck, Cassy," he spoke, wondering if they could hear him.

CHAPTER SIXTY-TWO

Cassy's right hand gripped Eddie's ankle as tightly as she possibly could. Her white dress, stained with splatters of blood, fluttered manically in the surge of the wind as they travelled at what seemed like a million miles an hour.

The only thing that was stopping her from falling into the aerodynamic resistance was her grip on Eddie that was feeling less and less secure.

They were in a narrow passageway, soaring ahead, speeding along a cylinder casing that would lead to either heaven or hell.

Vague colours and blurs streaked past their eyes, super-natural elements surging against them too quickly to make out. She struggled to lift her other hand against the resistance of the speeding wind beating against her. She persisted, scrunching up her face, battling the elements until she finally managed to grip both hands around his ankle.

She peered toward Eddie's face to find that his eyes were closed. This was the passageway to the afterlife – no one is ever conscious for this, and she knew his eyes would not open again until they reached their ultimate destination.

He would not know whether she was successful until he landed in either a saintly garden or a malicious pit of hell.

It was her job to get him to heaven, and she had to do it on her own, praying against the odds that they would even be let in.

Numbing herself against the rapid ferocity of their tumultuous speed, she clung on, wrapping her hands firmly around him.

All the fighting would mean nothing if she let hell take him now.

Using his leg to climb, she pulled herself up his body, gripping, squeezing, until she reached his chest and could wrap both arms around him.

It was okay.

She had him.

They were on their way to heaven and she had him.

Just as a sense of security settled in, she felt a painful hit pound into her side and spin them in manic circles.

She grew dizzy against the rotations, doing all she could to remain around him, to make sure it did not derail her.

As the spinning slowed she looked to her side, gasping.

A grinning, malevolent, red face glared back at her. She had never seen the face before, but recognised what it was instantly, understood what was happening.

Hell was mounting its attack.

She was staring into the eyes of Satan.

The devil himself had come to claim Eddie's soul.

His dark-red hand gripped its blackened claws around Eddie's leg, seemingly holding on with far more ease than Cassy had been afforded.

The devil reached a scarred fist backwards, then launched it forward into Cassy's face.

A bolt of pain and burst of shock shook her, sending a painful surge through her nose.

She loosened her grip on Eddie for a brief moment, but managed to clutch back onto him, ignoring the flickers of blood soaring past her, determined to keep hold of him.

Not just for humanity's sake, but for her loving brother's soul.

He'd fought for hers on millennium night, now it was her turn to save him from an eternity of damnation.

The devil cackled, lifted its arm and shot a line of ongoing fire in Cassy's direction. She ducked her head and withstood the fire, feeling the heat burning her skin, scorching her, forcing her to endure agonising pain.

Her hands slipped, and she ended up back at Eddie's ankle, grasping on for dear life.

She had to endure it.

It didn't matter whether she survived, she just had to see Eddie's safe passage to God.

My life means nothing now.

Whatever the devil threw at her, she had to take it. Had to suffer the agony.

Still, the devil's continuous burst of fire hounded her skin, berating it with a temperature she couldn't withstand. She felt her insides singe, her body burn with severe torment.

The stream of flames paused, allowing her to look down at herself, recoiling at the sight of her blackened skin. Her entire body was scarred and covered with smoky residue, throbbing with the torture of a thousand burns, her white dress now black.

Ash floated out of her hair and she had to blink it out of her eyes.

Her hands throbbed with burns, causing her continuous pain as she forced her muscles to cling on. She had to resist the temptation to loosen her grip and relieve the pain.

Must withstand... Must keep hold of Eddie...

More cackles, roars, and growls echoed within the hollow cylinder, sadistically cackling voices accompanied by faces.

More and more demons announced themselves, leering at her, following her as she sped through, filling her gut with dread.

She gulped.

She was vastly outnumbered and outpowered. She didn't know how she was going to do this.

Can't.

Let.

Go.

Must.

Keep.

Going.

Another rapid burst of flames fired toward her and she felt what it was truly like to be burnt alive. It went through her skin, penetrated every cell, pounded her head, filled her body with piercing heat.

I'm not going to be able to do this...

The burst of flames ceased and she noticed tinges of black ash flying off her body.

She wished Eddie could help her.

But he was dead. His soul was sailing, but he would not know. He would not know who was winning this battle.

I'm going to end up letting go, I can feel it...

She tried manoeuvring herself around Eddie's body so that she was shielded from the fire, but simply found herself surrounded by further masses of flying demons chasing after her with their arms surging an onslaught of flames in her direction.

She was not about to be afforded mercy.

What should I do?

She had no powers. Heaven had its naivety in assuming the truce with hell would hold. Being an angel granted immortality, but nothing else.

It all seemed so silly now.

A truce with hell.

A truce with creatures made of nothing but evil.

Fools.

She closed her eyes, scrunched her face, and tensed her body. Readied herself for further attack.

She had to withstand it.

Had to be resilient.

Be strong. Like her brother.

Like Derek, like Martin, like Jenny.

This was her part in the war.

This was the final part in the war.

She had to see it through.

A sudden roar of fire exploded against her ear drums and she felt it hit her from all directions. It travelled inside her, mixing with her bones, killing her muscles, filling her with dread and agony.

She looked up at Eddie's resting face.

The fire scorched her knuckles.

It was too much.

"No!"

Her hands slipped.

She let go.

When the fires stopped she opened her eyes.

She searched her empty hands.

She was no longer travelling or flying. She was static. Hovering helplessly in the middle of nowhere. Eddie was gone.

She was entirely alone.

She tried to travel forward, tried to chase after them, but

it only made her realise she did not have the powers that demons did.

She was completely stationary.

They had Eddie.

And Cassy was left floating in the abyss.

CHAPTER SIXTY-THREE

"No!" cried out Cassy defiantly. "No!"

But it did nothing.

Eddie was gone. She had let go. It was done.

All that they had endured was for nothing.

She looked down at her blackened skin. Her burnt, destroyed body.

Her skin flaking off into ashes.

She sobbed. She thought of Derek, thought of his face covered in disappointment. Thought of Martin, his face sympathetic, most likely understanding – and that, she decided, would be even more devastating.

She thought of Jenny. What she would do. How she would not give up, and she would continue fighting for Eddie until the very end.

She had failed.

She had disappointed everyone.

Eddie.

Her brother.

The one who lived whilst she died.

The best older brother she could have asked for. He took

care of her, raised her, never once getting annoyed by the irritating little sister who followed him around.

Eddie had battled hell for her.

Eddie had defeated Balam for her.

Now he was taken. Aimed back to hell, for this all to start again. For the heir to rise once more. Only this time, the devil would know how the heir could be defeated. That would give him the advantage. He would take extra precautions, kill more people, do anything to ensure the heir of hell would rise.

Humanity would not succeed in a second war.

She closed her eyes.

Allowed herself to hover weightlessly in the never-ending tube, the path to purgatory, heaven, or hell.

Eddie would awaken later. He would awaken with the knowledge that Cassy had failed him. That he would be returning to hell to live out the rest of his life as a demon hell-bent on death and destruction.

She allowed herself to remain still, lifting her arms out, keeping her eyes shut.

Her body relaxed.

Her mind overwhelmed with thoughts of inconsolable sorrow bashing against her skull.

Something tucked around her waist.

Was it a demon?

Something come to finish her off?

No...

It was something else.

Something soft. Reassuring. Two sensitive arms wrapping securely around her.

Without warning or expectation, she found herself flying forward again.

Soaring through the tunnel, travelling faster through the beyond than she ever had before.

She opened her eyes.

How am I doing this?

Something had a hold of her. Something gripped her shoulders.

She grew alarmed.

Are the demons taking me, too?

She looked up.

It was no demon.

"Gabrielle!" she acknowledged. "You came back!"

"Cassy," Gabrielle smiled. "We never left."

"We?" Cassy exclaimed.

Gabrielle nodded.

As they travelled faster and faster, Eddie and the mass of demons came into view. They all had their claws dug into Eddie's body, ensuring they had him on a secure passage. Flames followed them, echoing in their wake.

Gabrielle and Cassy soon caught up.

Then, in a sudden bright, shining-white light, the fire ceased.

An overpowering light pushed into everything. Cassy shielded her eyes, watching the bodies fall past her.

Demons fell. All of them. Plunging downwards, masses after masses of them, soaring back to the pits of fire, flying away from Edward King.

Cassy couldn't understand.

Who had created that bright light?

Who could possibly have the power to push so many demons away at once?

The only thing left clinging onto Eddie was the devil. The defiant devil, snarling downwards at them, roaring adamantly. His hand grabbing hold of Eddie's leg.

He would not let go.

Defiant to the end.

As Gabrielle took Cassy next to Eddie, Cassy wrapped

her arms around his chest, holding him in a secure and loving embrace.

"Hold on tight," Gabrielle whispered in her ear, not letting go of her.

Cassy squeezed, wrapping her legs around Eddie's waist for extra security.

The blinding white light grew bigger.

A dawn of realisation hit.

Cassy finally understood who it was.

This was Cassy's answer.

Her answer to her resolute question of, *"Where is our God now?"*

He had finally answered them.

The devil cowered. His face flickered with fear as his grasp loosened. With a final, reverberating, insolent snarl, it let go and went floating downwards into the beyond.

Gabrielle let go of Cassy as she and her brother continued to fly upwards on their own accord.

Cassy smiled.

He had come to help. He had actually come to help!

The devil flew in the wind, eyes widening, aware that he would not be able to pass this Light.

He disappeared into the nothingness, knowing that he had lost.

The white light grew bigger and bigger until it surrounded them, encapsulating the entire surroundings.

Cassy looked down.

The devil had reappeared. He hovered, as if waiting to see what was going to happen.

Cassy held on tight, refusing to let go.

Gabrielle disappeared into the bright light. Back into heaven.

Cassy closed her eyes.

Her body pounded against a solid surface, and she stopped floating.

Her head throbbed, as if she had just hit a large piece of glass.

She opened her eyes.

Gabrielle had gone into the bright-white light.

Cassy's body had hit against it. She couldn't get through

Now her and Eddie's unconscious bodies lingered solemnly in the abyss, immobile, unable to gain entry.

She could not enter heaven. She had killed Bandile's followers, and was denied entry.

As was Eddie.

The devil floated back up toward them, spreading its fearful frown to a knowing smile.

The devil's hands wrapped around Eddie's ankle.

His grin grew wider.

There was nothing Cassy could do. She could fight him, but she wouldn't last long.

The devil had hold of Eddie.

Now all that was left was for the devil to take him back to hell, and make this entire war mean nothing.

CHAPTER SIXTY-FOUR

"*E*ddie..." Cassy urged. "If you were going to wake up, now would be the time..."

But she knew it was pointless.

He was on his journey to the afterlife. No one was awake for this.

"Cassy..." the devil hissed. "You lose..."

His hands clenched around Eddie's body, his elongating claws entwining him like roots of a tree, wrapping around him until he had him secure for the descent to hell.

"No!" Cassy screamed.

She kept her arms around Eddie's neck, clinging on for dear life, doing all she could to muster the last, pointless fight for Eddie's soon-to-be-damned soul.

Cassy lifted her head upwards toward the bright-white void, the entry point to heaven where she was so pertinently denied.

"*Gabrielle!*" she bellowed. "*Gabrielle!*"

They had to let her in.

It was the only way.

They had to.

But she had killed. Two men had perished by her hand. She had done it to save Martin's and Derek's souls, and in turn had cursed her own.

God didn't budge on his commandments.

Even if it meant giving hell their greatest weapon...

Was He really going to do this?

"Come on!" Cassy insisted. "After all I've done! And you still won't let us in!"

The devil yanked Eddie teasingly, enjoying watching him being ripped away from his sister and her eternal, undying love.

She clung onto Eddie helplessly, wrapping her arms even tighter around his neck.

"No, you will not take him!" she resisted.

The devil grinned, exuding a slow chuckle.

"I'm taking him," the devil announced. "Time to say goodbye."

The devil yanked Eddie out of her arms and out of her reach.

Her arms dangled, helplessly grasping for him.

The devil paused mid-air, smiling a final taunt at Cassy.

"Come on, Gabrielle..." she whispered. "Please... After all I've done..."

"You did all that..." the devil cackled. "And still they won't have you."

The devil turned to take Eddie away, to soar into the blackness that consumed the beyond.

In a sudden burst of light, Gabrielle soared out of the passageway to heaven, firing toward the devil and wrapping her body around Eddie.

"Gabrielle?" Cassy asked hopefully.

Gabrielle lifted her head up.

"We still need your help!" she cried out, staring past Cassy at an emerging face.

Cassy turned over her shoulder.

The light parted, allowing a figure to appear. At first it was a magnificent silhouette. As it entered the light it turned into something far greater, something not of the human world.

Something transient.

Something powerful.

Something Godly.

The devil looked up, eyes full of fear.

The raise of an arm from their Godly apparition was enough to send the devil pummelling back into the pits below.

Gabrielle took hold of Eddie and swam through the air, placing him at the feet of the mysterious figure.

The figure knelt, placing a hand on Eddie's face.

"You are forgiven," He whispered.

It turned its holy face to Cassy.

"As are you."

He took hold of Eddie and sank back into the light, disappearing.

Gabrielle turned back to Cassy, holding out her hand.

"Are you coming?" she asked.

Cassy smiled, took Gabrielle's hand, and followed.

"For I know the plans I have for you. Plans to prosper you and not to harm you, plans to give you hope and a future."

Jeremiah 29:11

CHAPTER SIXTY-FIVE

*E*ddie's eyes opened.

His hand swung to his heart, clutching manically.

It was fine.

There was no wound.

In fact, there wasn't even a heartbeat.

He sat up, looking over himself, astonished at his weight-lessness. He held his hands out in front of him. They were clean and unblemished.

He looked up, surveying the magnificent surroundings, marvelling in amazement.

A bright sun beamed proudly down upon him, scorching him with its rays, yet causing not an ounce of sunburn. He sat in a budding field, lively trees and magnificent plant life surrounding him, springing out of the ground, and twisting into the air with grace. There was a clear, blue sky above, and trees full of life and colour fluttering in a perfect breeze.

He stood.

He was so light. He felt nothing inside.

He even tried pinching himself.

No pain. Nothing.

"You okay?" came a woman's voice.

Eddie turned to his side.

Cassy.

She stood proudly beside him with a smile spread wide across her face. Her skin was smooth, her hair long and neat, her dress glowing with the white of an angel.

The stains of blood were gone. She appeared as a transient being, a magnificent figure of holy ascension.

He threw his arms around her. Her arms pressed back around his. They squeezed tightly, full of joy, full of hope, feeling nothing but love and happiness.

His tears fell like rain. But there was no rain. Just sunshine. An overwhelming sense of pure, unaltered happiness.

A feeling of resolution casting itself through his body.

A feeling of this being his glorious end.

"Cassy..." he sobbed.

"I know."

Finally reunited.

After nearly twenty years. After saving her from a torturous demon. After battling and fighting and killing and dying and hating.

Finally.

He pulled back, looking her solidly in the eyes, full of adoration, full of relief, delight.

"Cassy, is this...?" he trailed off, unable to say the words.

He didn't need to.

She nodded. Smiling tearfully, elated to be able to confirm.

They were there.

I've made it...

He hugged her once more, clutching on for dear life,

never wanting to let her go. Years of suffering poured out into relief, into an eternity of love.

It was over.

It's all over.

"Are you ready?" Cassy asked.

"Ready for what?" Eddie replied, turning his head inquisitively, unable to stop himself from beaming triumphantly.

"To see them."

"See who?"

Cassy smiled.

"Kelly and Jenny. They are waiting for you."

Eddie's eyes widened. He practically glowed, his jaw dropping in amazement.

"You mean, they are…"

"Yes." Cassy grinned. She couldn't help it.

Eddie's mouth stumbled in disbelief. Tears of ecstasy filled his eyes.

Finally.

Finally, I can be at peace…

"Yes! Yes, I am! Right away!"

Cassy turned, holding her hand out to him.

He took it, savouring the relationship robbed of him so long ago.

He could finally be a brother again.

And a friend.

And a boyfriend.

They were waiting for him, and he could not wait to see them.

"This way," she spoke softly, leading him through into the garden and past the gates.

CHAPTER SIXTY-SIX

*A*ugust 3, 2003

FOUR MONTHS later

DEREK GAZED LONGINGLY at the picture set atop his desk. Him and Eddie, both looking so young. Not the aged man he was now.

He bowed his head, giving a faint smile and a solemn prayer, then packed the picture in his box.

He fetched the box out of his office and into the lecture theatre. He took a moment. Gazed upon the place where he had educated so many students.

Yet none of them would ever know the truth.

No one ever would.

The Church was good at covering its own back, and it did so efficiently. The mess was gone within hours, like it had never been. Bodies disposed of, blood washed away, cracks smoothed over, and buildings brought back to life.

It was strange, saying goodbye to this place.

But it wasn't enough anymore.

He couldn't do it. He couldn't teach these people anymore. He couldn't knowingly bring innocent people into this, knowing what the stakes were.

That's why he intended to seek out the other people involved. Those with newly endowed powers. A new challenge lay ahead, and he was ready to leave this one behind.

Gabrielle had visited him. Told him heaven's plans. Told him what they had done. Now his only task was to let Martin know of their mission.

Although, I think we could do with a holiday first...

He turned off the lights and walked leisurely down the corridor and into the car park, smiling at Martin, who leant casually against Derek's car.

"Getting emotional?" Martin teased.

"Shut up," Derek joked, smiling widely. He opened the boot and placed the box inside.

He turned and looked at the university. Despite Martin's teasing, he couldn't help but feel a sting of sadness. It had been so long since he had chosen this path.

Once, he had chosen to give up a fiancée for this life. At the time, he thought that was going to be his biggest sacrifice.

How little he knew.

"So, what did Gabrielle say?" Martin asked.

Derek raised his eyebrows.

"You knew I was going to ask," Martin sighed.

"Yes. I did."

Derek hesitated.

He remembered a time he was stood next to this car with Eddie, giving him guidance, not so long ago.

He was hesitant to do the same with Martin. His previous student had ended with…

But that's when he told himself that he needed to have faith in Martin, just like he'd had to with Eddie.

"Heaven has made preparations in case of another attack."

"How?"

"I'm afraid you're no longer the only special one."

"What do you mean?"

Derek sighed and leant against the car next to Martin.

"A number of years ago, when heaven learnt of what was inside Eddie, they created a backup plan. Knowing what was to come, they conceived many children in response to hell's actions. Same way you were, but now… Well, now if hell was to try something, they would have a whole army of people with your powers."

"Is that good?"

Derek shrugged.

"Maybe. Maybe not."

"So, what do we do?"

Derek straightened up his tie. Tucked his shirt in. Neatened his collar.

"We help them. Teach them about their gifts. Teach them about their sensitivity to the paranormal."

"Sensitivity? Is that what we're calling them? The Sensitives?"

Derek nodded, chuckling at the suggestion.

"I guess so."

"So what are we doing first?" Martin asked. "Where's the first sensitive? I want to meet these people who are stealing my thunder."

Derek laughed, a response that was cut short by a wave of hesitance casting itself over Martin's face.

Martin turned solemn, and Derek's smile dropped as he returned the gaze.

They had been through so much. It felt strange to be laughing and joking about it.

"Do you think we'll ever see them again?" Martin asked.

"What do you mean?"

"Eddie. Cassy. Do you think we'll ever see them again?"

Derek grinned, joining Martin in gazing happily upwards at the clear sunny sky. It was a beautiful day, no doubt about it.

"No," he answered. "I don't think we will."

WOULD YOU LIKE TWO
FREE BOOKS?

Get the prequel to The Edward King Series FREE and EXCLUSIVE at **www.rickwoodwriter.com/sign-up**

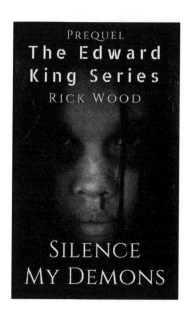

OUT NOW

Set ten years after The Edward King Series...

Download

23305655R00317

Printed in Great Britain
by Amazon